DARCY
AND
FITZWILLIAM

a tale of a gentleman and an officer

KAREN V. WASYLOWSKI

Published by Sourcebooks Landmark, an imprint of Sourcebooks, Inc.
P.O. Box 4410, Naperville, Illinois 60567-4410
(630) 961-3900
FAX: (630) 961-2168
www.sourcebooks.com

Library of Congress Cataloging-in-Publication Data

Wasylowski, Karen V.
Darcy and Fitzwilliam : a tale of a gentleman and an officer / by Karen V. Wasylowski.
p. cm.
ISBN 978-1-4022-4594-7 (alk. paper)
1. Darcy, Fitzwilliam (Fictitious character)--Fiction. 2. Male friendship--Fiction. 3. England--Social life and customs--19th century--Fiction. I. Austen, Jane, 1775-1817. Pride and prejudice. II. Title.
PS3623.A8683D37 2011
813'.6--dc22

2010047161

Printed and bound in Canada
WC 10 9 8 7 6 5 4 3 2 1

This book is dedicated to
the love of my life,
my best friend and fiercest champion,
my better half,
my Richie

"I assure you, I feel it exceedingly," said Lady Catherine; "I believe nobody feels the loss of friends so much as I do. But I am particularly attached to these young men; and know them to be so much attached to me!—They were excessively sorry to go! But so they always are. The dear Colonel rallied his spirits tolerably till just at last; but Darcy seemed to feel it most acutely, more I think than last year. His attachment to Rosings, certainly increases."

Lady Catherine de Bourgh
Pride and Prejudice
Volume II
Chapter XIV
1813

Prologue

1813

THE TWO MEN STARED off in different directions, making their awkward final good-byes to each other. They were, in appearance and comportment, as dissimilar as two men could be.

Though both were exceedingly tall, Fitzwilliam Darcy, the younger by nearly two years and a gentleman, was dark and handsome, elegantly dressed in the finest coat and neck cloth, breeches, and boots. His air was one of a man of elegance and breeding, his demeanor of a man three times his age: heavy, solemn, serious, and levelheaded. He was also shy to the point of seemingly rude indifference. The owner of one of the largest and wealthiest estates in England, inherited by him at the grand old age of twenty-one and then doubled, he had achieved his great success at the expense of his youth.

The elder of the two men, Colonel Richard Fitzwilliam, was bulkier, barrel-chested, and slightly rougher looking, dressed in his unkempt colonel's uniform. An uninhibited joy of life exuded from him. He was like a large, gangly puppy, a happy, wild spirit trapped within a respectable soldier's body. What he lacked in physical beauty he more than made up for in character, the magnetic center of anywhere he went and of everyone he knew. A second son, he had bought his commission into the army near the beginnings of the crusade to rid Europe of Napoleon. The past nine years of that devastating war had made him snatch life and laughter wildly, wherever and whenever he could.

Where the younger cousin was cautious to the point of being a recluse, the elder cousin was exuberant to the point of indiscretion. Each had adapted to his circumstances, impelled by an unconscious and very human bid for survival.

"Darcy, I cannot tell you how badly I feel about this business with Miss Bennet. If you had but told me of the depth of your feeling for her, I would have backed off. I would not have flirted half so much, and I wouldn't have wagged my tongue so carelessly." Feeling a bit guilty now for his actions Fitzwilliam leaned against the bureau in his cousin's room watching as that man packed the remainder of his clothes. It was evident that his dearest friend and cousin was devastated over Miss Elizabeth Bennet's refusal of his marriage proposal. Worse yet for the colonel's conscience, her refusal had been in part based on his own gossipy revelations regarding the destruction of her beloved sister's romance through Darcy's intervention.

Darcy looked out through his bedroom window, across his aunt Catherine's immense estate, Rosings Park, his intense gaze cast in the direction of the vicarage where Miss Bennet was visiting; reluctantly he returned his attention to his packing. Her emotional reaction haunted his thoughts. In her judgment, his very character was wanting to such a degree that she could never marry him, and worse, he was no gentleman. Her words stung his pride and his honor; her rejection caused him to question values he had regarded as inviolate.

"It's done and over, Fitz." The solemn young man sighed as he snapped his valise shut and then dragged it from the bed. "I'm sure I shall survive." But his eyes were hooded and hollow, his shoulders drooping a little too low for the light weight of his bag. "This was a bleak Easter visit, though, I must confess."

"Let me go over there one more time and speak with her; she may have returned by now. I can't help but think that if you were willing to confide in her about Georgiana and Wickham, she must mean a great deal to you."

"Leave it, Richard. It just wasn't meant to be." Darcy placed his bag on the floor and checked his pocket watch. "Besides, I think you have more important worries than my love life at the moment." He looked at his cousin, his hands clasped behind him, his weight casually resting on his back leg.

The two were like brothers, closer really, and had been each other's best friend and arch rival their entire lives. One was returning to his solitary existence in the country, the other to war.

"You're going straight to it, then?" Darcy searched his cousin's eyes, frightened for him, amazed at the man's calm. Nine years of campaigns, and he was still alive with all his limbs, a monumental accomplishment in this never-ending battle with France.

"Yes, I go immediately to join my regiment in Spain, but I believe the decider will be farther north. I'll see Wellington upon my return, and then I'll know better what's to come." He smiled brightly at his cousin, but the cloud of an unknown future for both men had already begun to overshadow their eyes.

"How do you get through it, Fitz?" Darcy asked as he stepped forward to take Fitzwilliam's hand to shake.

"Prodigious amounts of liquor, brat." Fitzwilliam pulled his cousin to him and, ignoring any reticence he might encounter, proceeded to give him a great manly hug, and although Darcy was not normally a demonstrative man, he returned the hug unashamedly, steeling himself once again to the possibility that his cousin might not return from this fight.

Pushing away, suddenly somewhat embarrassed by his emotions, he grinned. "Oh, that reminds me. Aunt Catherine told me to discreetly remonstrate with you on exactly that point. Seems she feels you drink far too much, and I'm to explain the evils of overindulgence to you."

Fitzwilliam let out a loud hoot of laughter. "Poor old soul would faint if she knew the half of what I do in excess."

"Well, consider yourself told." Darcy smiled warmly at him. "But for my part, whatever gets you through this safely and in one piece, I say go ahead."

The servants came for their luggage as the two men headed down the staircase, waiting a moment as they watched the odious clergyman, Mr. Collins, run from the house, his face contorted in a silent scream, his daily interview with their aunt Catherine evidently over.

"Actually, Darcy, I have a good feeling about you and Miss Bennet. I think she and you will eventually suit perfectly." Fitzwilliam chuckled at his cousin's groan.

"You just will not let this lie, will you?" Darcy said, his voice showing his exasperation.

"Well, no. Not now that I have the satisfaction of knowing it will annoy you so much." Fitzwilliam grinned mischievously. "Surely after all we've been through together, you know me by now."

Darcy's shoulder was leaning on the closed door, his hand grasping the doorknob to their aunt's sitting room, as they hesitated for a moment to rally their courage for one last bout with the Grande Dame of their family before they left.

"In that case, I'm afraid I will have to tell Catherine about your sudden and sad addiction to opium."

"Why, you lying bastard. You know I'd never touch that horrid stuff; she'll attack me like a mad ferret!"

Darcy smiled wickedly as he opened the door, calling out, "Aunt Catherine, I have shocking news for you!"

Fitzwilliam slapped the back of his little cousin's head as he entered the room behind him.

Volume One

FITZWILLIAM DARCY
A GENTLEMAN
1815

His years are young, but his experience old;
His head unmellow'd, but his judgment ripe;
And in a word (for far behind his worth)
Come all the praise that I now bestow,
He is complete in feature and mind,
With all good grace to grace
A gentleman.

—William Shakespeare

Chapter 1

It was now a full two months after their wedding, and a sunny, crisp winter morning to boot. The newly wedded Elizabeth Darcy, née Bennet, was making a concerted effort to look out the window at the beautiful winter expanse below and not turn her gaze immediately upon waking to her magnificent husband as he slept, admiring his strong jaw line and his long eyelashes. He was, to her eyes, simply put, beautiful.

She would stare at him all day if he had not whispered to her during a performance of "The Magic Flute" that her gazes were unsettling to him and that she really must stop. But then, of course, his own eyes had been dark with longing as he squeezed her hand and kissed it during his reprimand, so how serious could he really be?

She decided to compromise and just gaze at him when he couldn't possibly be aware, like in the morning, when she always awoke before him, or perhaps when she watched him ride his horse from the stables, or maybe at breakfast as he read the daily reports from his estate manager.

All right, I think I've been very good and deserve my reward. I can allow myself another quarter hour to watch him again. She rolled over to lie on her stomach facing him. *My heavens, he's so handsome. What a wondrous gift you have given me, dear Lord. Whatever could I have done to deserve this much happiness?*

"Elizabeth?" He said her name softly, his eyes still closed.

She pulled up the sheets to just beneath her eyes, which were sparkling with anticipation.

"Elizabeth," he repeated, "are you watching me again?"

They were both lying on their stomachs, each facing the other, both bathed by the same streaming sunlight. She knew if she kept very still and didn't answer him, he would open those beautiful eyes. She just had to be patient. Just wait a moment longer… just a moment… aaahhh!

And suddenly, his one visible eye popped opened, and she giggled, still hiding her face up to her lashes. "Good morning, husband," she whispered, closing her eyes tightly, giddy with the knowledge that she would soon receive the first of her morning kisses. She puckered her lips.

After what seemed like an eternity she felt a soft kiss on her forehead and then on her nose and finally on her lips. "Good morning, beautiful one," he said dreamily. His morning beard stubble tickled her, and she rubbed her face quickly. He raised himself up on his elbow and pushed her hair back from her forehead. "Did you sleep well, little angel?"

"Yes, very well. And you?"

"Like an earl." He laid his head back down very near her face, their noses almost touching.

"Is that good or bad?" she whispered.

"I don't really know. I am too tired this morning to care, and too happy." He reached for her and pulled her close. "You were very enthusiastic last night, Lizzy."

She blushed and buried her head in his neck. "William! Please have a care! You'll embarrass me!"

"Why? How could I? It's just us here. No one listening, no one to hear our enthusiasms." He softly kissed her mouth and stared into her sweet face. She was all sweetness and delicate femininity, with beautiful eyes, rosebud pink lips, and a quick mind that kept him always on his toes.

He reached down and began to tickle her sides. "And besides," he whispered, "young lady, if you would be a little quieter, you wouldn't have to be so embarrassed." His tickling intensified as they tussled, both laughing, tears streaming down her cheeks. He held her fast around her waist and pulled her closer to prevent her tumbling from the bed.

She squealed, giggled, and squirmed, and as he laughed at her excitement, he found himself becoming excited in a wonderfully different way. Unfortunately, however, in their gyrations, her hand had mistakenly grabbed the bellpull.

She broke from his grasp and raised herself up, turning toward him with her pillow high above her head ready to strike, naked as the day she was born. Almost too late, she heard the doorknob turn, signaling the imminent arrival of her husband's valet. She lunged for the floor.

"You rang for me, Mr. Darcy?" Raising one eyebrow was the only outward evidence that Darcy's valet Bradford was aware of the bloodcurdling shriek that had greeted his entrance. Well, there was that and the flutter of the bed cover and a thud that was heard on the side of the bed not within his view.

Darcy, lying alone in the middle of the massive antique

structure, smiled broadly. "The devil you say. No, Bradford, I didn't ring for you." He rested his clasped hands casually behind his head, looking very smug and quite cheerful, closing his eyes and grinning when a disembodied and very heartfelt "ouch!" was heard from the floor beside him.

"Well, this is quite the quandary, is it not? Perhaps Mrs. Darcy rang for you. She was here only a moment ago." Bradford discreetly turned his gaze away and toward the ceiling. Darcy lifted up the sheets to peer within. "Hello?" he called to his legs and feet. There were muffled pleas and giggles as the covers began to slowly be pulled off the edge of the bed.

Darcy waited for a while and then grabbed them back with a jerk, tucking them neatly around himself. Phantom murmured threats and muffled indignation could be heard, along with stifled laughter. A pillow sailed up from the floor, which he easily deflected. "No, no I don't see her anywhere. Perhaps she's out riding." He leaned his body over the mattress, off the far side of the bed, and looked down toward the floor. "Why, Mrs. Darcy, wherever have you been? By any chance did *you* ring for Bradford?"

Lizzy reached up and pinched his nose very hard, causing Darcy to yelp and laugh. "No, no, I don't believe she needs you either," he offered rather nasally, rubbing the injured protuberance as if to put it back into place. "You may go, Bradford; sorry to have bothered you."

"Very good, sir." Bradford bowed and closed the door. As he walked back down the hall, he allowed his mouth the smile that had more and more invaded his very professional demeanor. Shaking his head, he laughed softly. *Was I ever that young or that in love?*

Life had certainly changed at stately old Pemberley since the newlyweds had taken up residence. He thought fondly back to when he had begun working for Mr. Fitzwilliam Darcy, and the lad's transformation from callow young Corinthian to somber estate owner and now to besotted bridegroom.

⁂

Mr. George Darcy had passed away after a brief illness, in the early evening hours of 17 April, 1806. His son, Fitzwilliam, was named his heir, inheriting at barely twenty-one years of age the single largest privately held estate in all of Derbyshire, as well as being named co-guardian to Georgiana, his nine-year-old sister. Overnight, young Darcy seemed to age, to mature, to toughen; he soon became obsessed with responsibility, with achievement and success.

A natural leader, he astounded men twice his age, and this when he was still little more than an adolescent. Now he moved among a new circle of acquaintances bringing about new interests—viewpoints more conservative than the young. Darcy gradually abandoned the ideas and pursuits of youth as well as the follies and mistakes that would have been his by right to make, and became more appreciative of class and privilege. He rarely relaxed and was seldom carefree, still naïve enough to believe a serious demeanor more befitting his station in life than frivolous laughter. Time and responsibility were sedating his youth.

It was an unfortunate incident involving his beloved sister, Georgiana, that pushed him that final meter into premature dotage. He and his co-guardian to Georgiana, his cousin Colonel Richard Fitzwilliam, had relaxed their vigilance, assuring themselves that

Georgiana was a sensible, well-bred young woman, but little more than a child, still with childish interests. They both adored her but took no real notice of her maturing; after all, the colonel was far away in Portugal, chasing Napoleon, and Darcy was drowning in drainage concerns at Pemberley.

At fifteen years of age, she ran away with a hireling, a thoroughly unsuitable young man whom she had known her whole life, had loved and trusted. Darcy discovered them before her ruination, but destroyed was any measure of folly that remained lurking within him. Darcy aged from twenty-six to sixty-six within two days. Georgiana was devastated with guilt.

Fitzwilliam, the closest thing to a true brother Darcy possessed, acknowledged that gone forever was his coconspirator in disasters, his fiercest competitor, his staunchest defender, his best friend. In his place was the reincarnation of his stolid and sensible old Uncle George, only without the powdered wig.

But, no matter how proud, how aloof, how miserable he became, it was inevitable that a wealthy, handsome, single young man would inspire great matrimonial interest. Feverish competition exploded among the masses of aristocratic women vying for his hand, with the fiercest, the most vocal, and the most relentless of these being two particularly ambitious women.

In the country, his aunt, Lady Catherine de Bourgh, insisted to all who would listen that he would marry her sickly daughter, Anne. In the city, his best friend Charles Bingley's amoral sister Caroline informed all in her circle of friends that he would choose her.

Neither was correct.

Speculations and prophesies ended with Fitzwilliam Darcy's surprise marriage to a little country mouse named Elizabeth

Bennet. All who thought they were "in the know" were stunned when Darcy fell in love with the sparkling Elizabeth, a poor but gently bred young lady of infinite humor and intelligence, and although Miss Eliza Bennet never once chased Mr. Fitzwilliam Darcy, he was run to ground like a fox, and happily so.

He was alive again, a bit older perhaps, but a healthy young man rescued nonetheless, besotted and hopelessly in love.

Chapter 2

"Oooh, you are an evil, wicked, vile man." A mortified Lizzy emerged from the floor as soon as Bradford left, closing the door to their bedroom behind him. Covering her burning cheeks with her hands, she squeaked with laughter. At first faking his remorse, and badly at that, Darcy swiftly grabbed her and tickled her back into the bed, beginning again his inventory of kisses. First her forehead, then her eyes, then her nose…

"No! No, you don't. Not this morning, oh please, William! You have made us late for breakfast every morning since our return. It is past embarrassing. The whole staff knows we're up here." She then tilted her head to the side and pointed to a spot just beneath her ear, thereby ensuring a continuation of his barrage of kisses to the underside of her throat. "…Ooh, here, you've missed a spot, aaahhh lovely… and they know what is going on; they are not stupid! Please, dear, let us just get dressed and go down to breakfast before they stop bothering with it altogether."

"Maybe tomorrow," he growled, and truth be told, she capitulated happily.

❧

It was very late in the morning when the smiling bride and groom finally emerged hand in hand from their suites. Nearing the middle of the grand staircase, they encountered Mrs. Reynolds.

"Good morning, Mrs. Reynolds."

"Good morning, Mr. Darcy, Mrs. Darcy." The aged housekeeper smiled warmly up at her beloved boy, silently thanking the Lord for his obvious happiness.

"Mr. Darcy, Colonel Fitzwilliam has arrived and is waiting for you in the library." Mrs. Reynolds beamed with the joyful news. She knew how deeply her master had mourned when they thought his cousin dead, and how hard he had fought back tears when the news had arrived of his safety.

"Why that old degenerate; we didn't expect him for at least another two weeks! Has he been waiting long?" Darcy's pace down the stairs quickened. Lagging behind but still holding her husband's hand, Elizabeth began to feel flutters of embarrassment and turned her head away, wondering how she could perhaps better blend into the wallpaper.

"Well, about three hours, I should say," continued Mrs. Reynolds. "He arrived very early, as always, and has settled into the library with 'Fanny Hill.' Oh, he's not lost his appetite, I can tell you. He's already had several servings of breakfast and even went downstairs into the kitchen to hug the cook—greeted everyone below stairs. Why, he had us all laughing like fools, he did. He specifically requested that we not wake you, insisted that the 'newlyweds' not be disturbed."

A low moan escaped Elizabeth as she blushed crimson from her forehead to her toes.

Darcy tried not to laugh and patted Lizzy's hand. "It could be worse, believe me," he whispered. "Knowing my cousin, we're lucky he didn't barge right in on us with his morning tea." He continued down, Elizabeth dragging in tow. "Mrs. Reynolds, Could you send a tray into the library with some breakfast for Mrs. Darcy and me?"

Elizabeth suddenly stopped. "Oh no, William, I don't... I mean, I'm really not that hungry. I think I'll take a walk in the garden... my afternoon walk... I mean morning walk... if you don't mind."

Her face was flushed, and she chewed viciously on her lower lip, all the while trying to appear perfectly reasonable. How in the world was she expected to face Darcy's cousin now? He had just sat there in a room directly beneath theirs while they were so busily enthusiastic upstairs. No, thank you, she would just as soon take a brisk walk.

"But it's too cold for a walk this morning, isn't it?" He successfully kept the smile from his face. She was still so easily embarrassed by so many things, and he loved her all the more for it.

"No, it's fine, really. I'll merely walk faster." Her face brightened up a bit. "You know how I adore a good trudge in the mud. Excuse me, I'll just run up and get my wrap." Elizabeth turned, retreating quickly up the stairs, muttering bitterly all the way. "This is so humiliating! How am I supposed to behave rationally with dozens of people around knowing what's happening? Even when we haven't done anything, I feel obliged to blush just for decorum's sake."

It had been much easier in Scotland and Wales where they

had honeymooned. For eight wonderful weeks they were alone and in love, traveling and seeing new wonders daily, a romantic dream come true every night.

Their first time had been thoroughly embarrassing, romantic, and very funny—all at the same time. *How could a country girl have been so ignorant?* She was blushing again at the remembrance and smiling to herself. *However, one day he'll have to tell me how he knew so much himself.* He *certainly wasn't ignorant.*

Still grinning, she grabbed her wrap from her dressing room and headed down the stairs, spying the back of Fitzwilliam's head as he stood to greet Darcy, just before the door to the library was shut. *They will probably be in there for hours. I'll go in when I return and say a quick hello. That should suffice for the moment.*

✧

When Fitzwilliam saw Darcy enter the library, he immediately stood and extended his hand in greeting, a huge grin spreading across his tanned face. The colonel had not been back to Pemberley since the great victory at Waterloo, when after being wounded on the battlefield, he had been listed as missing and mourned as dead for several days. The sensationalized reports of his valor, his injury, and his extraordinary recovery had all made him a darling of the *ton* and a favorite of the newspapers, one amidst a handful of the surviving heroes of the long Peninsular War.

And, worse yet, it had made him a national celebrity.

Darcy grabbed his hand and struggled to suppress misting eyes. "I am afraid that just won't do this time, you old bastard." He spoke huskily, pulling his cousin into an uncharacteristically emotional embrace. Moved by Darcy's sentiment, Fitzwilliam fought back his own tears as they both began to pound each other's backs in manly fashion. He was nonplussed. This was not the normal greeting received from the reserved and achingly proper Darcy, at least not the morose Darcy that Fitzwilliam had left eleven months earlier. This was more like the mischievous companion of his youth.

Slightly amazed, Fitzwilliam pulled himself back to stare intently into Darcy's eyes. "I'm sorry that I missed your wedding, brat, but good Lord, if you haven't all the markings of a lovesick puppy!" Richard shoved at the side of Darcy's head, just a tap really. "God's indeed in his heaven, and you look like a grinning idiot!"

Darcy laughed happily and chucked his cousin's arm, a mere glancing blow. "And you look like shit itself." They hugged each other's shoulders once again briefly, moving a little farther into the room as he ripped a dangling button from Fitzwilliam's ancient uniform then grimaced at some crusted food on the sleeve. "No, really. My Lord, a sorrier sight I have never seen. Look at you, Fitz, you're a disgrace! Did your batman commit suicide when he learned you were still alive?"

The pushing and taunting back and forth increased until they suddenly began to wrestle in earnest, knocking over the odd table and chair, and then, just as suddenly, they began to laugh uproariously.

"You're weak… as an… an old woman, Darcy." Fitzwilliam gasped for breath.

"This is no time to discuss your sorry love life… Besides, *I… held back* because you're getting old… and fat." Darcy wheezed and waved away all further comments with his hand. "But who gives a shit about you—tell me about Waterloo! I heard it went badly at first." Darcy knew his cousin hated to speak about the battles in which he had fought during the past ten years, but good heavens, this had been Waterloo! Their energy spent for the moment, they both leaned back upon the huge library desk.

"Badly?!" Fitzwilliam made a rude noise with his lips. "That's an unfortunately inadequate description. It was a fiasco! It was bungled almost from the start." He stopped speaking for a while to shove tangles of errant dark blond hair from his forehead as Darcy set the tables and chairs to right. "I tell you there were times during that battle when I would have happily sacrificed my brother Regis for just a few dozen medieval English archers."

Darcy let out a bark of laughter. "Not impressed, Fitz—not by half. Over the years, you have volunteered to forego your brother for many lesser things. A hot cup of coffee, better seats at the opera; once it was a desire to obtain quicker mail delivery in Portugal."

"You are a small and vindictive man, Darcy. I don't have to stand for this type of character assassination." With that, Fitzwilliam dragged over a chair and sat, reaching into his pocket for his ever-present pipe and tobacco pouch.

"So, how is newly wedded bliss?" His gaze narrowed on his cousin for a moment. "As if I need to ask, you smug-looking little ass. I am sorry now I insisted they not announce me upon my arrival." He studied his tobacco pouch intently, dipping his pipe bowl within it and then packing down the brownish flakes. "I was beginning to fear that the two of you would never come up for air! My, my, I had no idea you had such staying power, brat." He leaned back and lit the pipe. He puffed once or twice to get it going. "I am quite impressed. But you know, Darcy, even the Huns pulled out occasionally." He leaned his head back to study the ceiling and then began to chuckle when he heard his cousin's groans.

Scowling, Darcy sat down heavily on the chair behind his desk. "You see, this is what I feared. All right, let's get this thing settled up front. I would appreciate it if you would watch your tongue in front of Elizabeth; she's still very shy about all this. I don't want you making crude remarks like that in front of her."

"Please, Cousin, I am desolate. You wound me until I bleed upon your fine carpet. Do you think me completely devoid of feeling or sensitivity?" Fitzwilliam did attempt to appear upset. "I am highly offended. If I thought you had at least one friend to serve as your second, I would call you out."

Darcy threw him a sardonic look and poured himself a cup of coffee. "I have plenty of friends, dozens in fact."

"Name six."

"Well…Bingley, for one. He's a tremendously fine fellow and likes me very much."

"Bingley doesn't count. He is notoriously indiscriminate, likes everyone, even me."

"A lot you know."

"Oh, very funny. Now, let us come back to all the lurid details, such as whether or not you were you able to perform all night." Darcy threw a pen at Fitzwilliam's head. "Terribly sorry, momentary relapse." He puffed once or twice on his pipe and blinked innocently at his cousin. "So just where is this new missus of yours? Still gagged and tied to the bedposts? Drugged, perhaps?"

Darcy stared fixedly at Fitzwilliam. "If you must know, she is as far away from you as I could send her." Darcy lifted the cup to his lips and sipped. "Is it any wonder that decent families hide their daughters from you?"

"I resent that, Darcy. I truly do."

"Do you deny it?"

"No, of course not, but I truly, truly resent it—cuts dreadfully into my social life."

"In actuality, she's taking a walk."

"In this weather?! Bah! You see, she has no sense. It is no wonder she was willing to marry you."

"I told you she is very shy, and she'll sort it out herself if you will but refrain from teasing her."

"Say no more, say no more, my good man. Please, Darcy..." He shook his head. "I am the soul of discretion with the ladies—a gentleman always, as you well know." The knock on the door brought in the requested breakfast tray.

"Capital. Very wise. Keeping up his stamina. Excellent."

"Fitzwilliam!"

His cousin scrubbed his face with his hand, grinning continuously. "Sorry, I don't know what gets into me around you. You're just so damn easy to fluster."

Shaking his head, Darcy abandoned any attempts to hide his own laughter and eagerly began his breakfast. Fitzwilliam reached over and swiftly grabbed a piece of ham and toast, his hand just missing being slapped away.

"May I offer you some breakfast?" Darcy asked sarcastically, his mouth full.

"Oh, Lord, no. Your exemplary Mrs. Reynolds was most obliging and provided me with no less than three breakfasts as I cooled my heels down here, plus coffee and cakes until I almost burst. I couldn't eat another thing." He reached over and grabbed a scone. "By the way, brat, I've just been visiting the Grande Dame herself, and she's still spewing poison about the two of you. How long is this feud between you going to continue? She requires some guidance with that great old horror house of hers and was almost desperate enough to turn to me." He leveled a gaze at his cousin, his eyebrows raised high into his forehead, an eloquent expression conveying how totally futile that would be. "I loath to admit this, but I am a complete imbecile when it comes to grand-manor types of things."

"Don't sell yourself so short, Fitz." He shook an admonishing finger at his cousin. "Believe me, you're a complete imbecile about a *great* many more things than that."

"Very humorous, brat. Very droll. Seriously, is this war going to continue for a long time? You *will* be back in the immense bosom of our aunt by Easter, won't you?" He lowered his voice to its sincerest depth. "Please, Darcy, have a heart. Stop thinking only of yourself...think of me." He looked pathetic. "You know how I so hate having my own pleasures curtailed, and I would miss our annual pilgrimage of penance." He grabbed for another piece of food, a fork just missing his hand.

"This war, as you aptly call it, was begun by Aunt Catherine, and it will need to be rectified by Aunt Catherine. As neither she nor my beloved mother saw fit to consider my feelings regarding marriage with Cousin Anne, I feel no remorse at disregarding her opinion about whom I *did* marry." Darcy poured himself another cup of coffee, splashing it all over with his angry, jerky hand movements.

Fitzwilliam darted a glance at his irate cousin, all the while trying to get his own cup beneath the moving spout. "...Yes, well, as long as you keep a happy thought..." he mumbled.

Darcy slammed down the coffee pot. "No, I won't let her abuse Elizabeth ever again. She doesn't deserve that kind of treatment." A smile softly crept into Darcy's eyes, his lips twitching at their corners. "She is the kindest, sweetest, most delicate creature God ever created." Darcy's face had a faraway, glazed, and grinning expression, very similar to an empty-headed jack-o-lantern. It became too much for his cousin.

"Hold that thought for a moment, if you would, Darcy. Please. Could you pass that trash pail. No, not that one—the other—yes, the larger one. Yes, thank you. Why? Because I feel I'm going to throw up at any moment!"

Darcy tried not to laugh but had little success. "If I remember correctly, you were besotted with her once yourself." He leaned back in his chair, smirking broadly.

"Incorrect yet again. An unbroken streak, I might add. Now, I may have been bemused by her and bewitched by her, even beguiled, but I was never besotted. That, my friend, I left entirely to you." While Fitzwilliam sipped his coffee, he regarded his cousin with warm affection. "I will, however, admit to a bit of envy for your happiness, would even consider marriage for myself one day... if I could meet a woman of character, integrity, compassion, intelligence, gentleness..."

Darcy regarded Fitzwilliam as if he had just grown another head. "Who are you, and what have you done with my cousin?"

"...with a face like a goddess and a body meant solely for sin..."

"Ah! And the world returns to its revolutions; all is right again with the universe."

"Getting back to Catherine," Fitzwilliam continued, never missing a beat, "I have thought a great deal about this—now don't go giving me that haughty Uncle George expression. I firmly believe that Elizabeth is the one person in this pathetic little family circle of ours not needing protection from Aunt

Catherine. I seem to remember your teeny wife having the backbone of a Viking. I have every faith that she is more than able to hold her own with the Marble Countess."

When Darcy began to protest, Fitzwilliam put up his hand to stop him. "No, Darcy, I think it was your own pride that was offended by Catherine's highhanded behavior more than anything she may have said to Elizabeth. Come, Cousin!" he whined pathetically. "To hell with Aunt Catherine—have pity on *me*! You will have to let this thing go eventually. Remember, 'Family is Everything.'" Fitzwilliam raised his hand in salute to their aunt's favorite quote.

"You're probably right. I can't judge myself anymore, it seems. I only know that she said some very mean things to Lizzy about her family—yes, I realize I'd said the same things she did, but I recognized my deplorable behavior and apologized for it. Now Aunt Catherine will have to do the same. Let's not discuss this anymore, please."

"Do you have any idea how similar you two are? How similar you are to the Queen of Hubris? Arrogant and stubborn, the both of you. I myself am the most good-natured of men, and yet I remain ruggedly handsome and charismatic. I truly believe it impossible that I could be related to either one of you. I must have been dropped at the door by some Scottish circus group."

Chapter 3

Elizabeth walked briskly around the house, clasping her cape tightly at her neck and her hood close around her face. She reflected on what she considered her Embarrassing Predicament. Or was it? First and foremost, she was a realist and a sensible country girl. *All right*, she began to shiver with the cold. *Just of what am I ashamed? I'm no different than any other young woman, am I?*

No, Elizabeth, you are not.

We are married; we want children, do we not?

Yes, most emphatically you are and you do! Honestly, this is ridiculous. Eventually the embarrassment of marital relations will fade, if only through the sheer bliss of repetition. Finding herself vigorously nodding in agreement, she could not help a bit of giggle and blush. She then forced herself to regain her composure. *And, the embarrassment may very well fade quicker if you do not make such a childish spectacle of yourself, bringing more attention to it than you already have.* She felt her backbone stiffen with her resolve—*or perhaps it is just freezing into place*, she mused as she gazed longingly up at the massive back of the main estate house with the windows steaming from the heat within, smoke billowing from its many chimneys.

She began to walk rapidly. *Besides, it is bloody cold out here, and that is surely curing me of my "flutters and spasms!"* She laughed out loud with that common quote of her mother's, causing the vaporous air of amusement to flutter about her. *In fact it is curing me much quicker than delicate female modesty would care to admit.* The rapid walk soon became a run. She entered the house through the closest door available, her eyes slowly adjusting to the dim light, and realized she was in the servants' hallway.

Surprised maids and footmen jumped back as she passed, giving her quick bows and curtseys, grabbing for their coats, straightening skirts, spitting out half-smoked cheroots and hiding them beneath their boots. Pushing her hood farther back on her head, she smiled and nodded hello, all the time humiliated by the reality that she had no idea where she was or how to get out.

Finally someone thought to alert Mrs. Reynolds, who hurried toward her. "Mrs. Darcy, is there something with which I can help you?"

Lizzy shook her head and smiled sheepishly. "I am so sorry to disturb you all, but I seem to have entered a strange door, and now fear I am lost."

"I understand perfectly." Mrs. Reynolds gave a ready nod. "Please allow me to show you the way upstairs." Thankful for her rescue, Lizzy followed the housekeeper through the winding corridors of underground kitchens and bedrooms, linen rooms, pantries, and servants' parlors and sitting room.

"It's much like a little city down here," Lizzy marveled as

they walked past dozens of servants and room after windowed room where she could observe the work being done. She saw women washing and ironing, polishing this, repairing that. "I had no idea there were this many servants at Pemberley!" She felt like an intruder in their domain.

"We really have a much smaller regular staff than most of the great estates. Many of these young people are actually from our tenant families. They train here for future work in other great houses. The added money they earn here helps the families, and a recommendation from Pemberley, as you can imagine, is a tremendous asset. I don't think we've ever had anyone trained here who did not go on to a very respectable position."

Humbled by the realization that so many depended on her husband for their very existence, Elizabeth felt the pride and love she already had for him swell. He had taken command of all this from such a young age, increasing his holdings and wealth to become one of the most successful landowners in the country. He was amazing and wonderful, and she decided she would kiss him senseless as soon as she was able. *He has all this to worry about, and I make a ninny of myself, blushing at anyone who cares to look at me, causing him more problems. Enough, Elizabeth, it is time to grow up.*

In the meantime, Mrs. Reynolds had been very proud to finally exhibit the servants' hall to the new mistress, stopping at the doorway to look back at the hustle and bustle that hummed along underneath the main house. Elizabeth took the woman's hand in hers and gave it an appreciative squeeze. "I am all amazement at this." Mrs. Reynolds, a woman who prided herself on seldom betraying her feelings to Mr. Darcy, blushed with happiness.

As they emerged into the light of the first-floor landing, she could see that they were right outside the grand library. "I believe Colonel Fitzwilliam is still in with the master. Would you like me to show you in to them?"

"Yes, please, and thank you, Mrs. Reynolds. I hope I have not inconvenienced the household too much with my wanderings."

"Not at all, madam, it was an honor. Besides, this is a huge house, one of the largest in the country. It takes a long while to get accustomed."

They walked toward the library, and Mrs. Reynolds, knocking softly, opened it for her. Darcy beamed when he saw her and stood. "Elizabeth, I'm so glad you decided to join us!"

Fitzwilliam also stood as Lizzy rushed into the room, watching as she melted into the arms of her loving husband. He regarded them both fondly, seeing the obviously deep affection between them the very moment the other was within view. *You would think they had been apart for a month and not twenty minutes. Well,* he reflected a bit wistfully, *I might not envy you Pemberley, my dear cousin, but this type of joy I do envy you.*

Laughing, she gazed up into Darcy's face. "Did you have time to miss me at all?"

"And you are...? Of course, little goose. I counted each second." He smiled as he wrapped her within his arms. "Elizabeth, we have a trespasser."

She turned her head and looked over at Fitzwilliam.

"You look lovely, Cousin," he said sincerely.

Her eyes were beginning to moisten. "It's so nice to hear you call me Cousin." She walked quickly to him, her hands extended in greeting. Waggling his eyebrows, he ignored her hands to give her one of his great hugs.

"May I be the first non-spousal family member to kiss the bride?"

Darcy nodded, and Elizabeth beamed up at Fitzwilliam once again, offering her cheek for the kissing.

"Well, the married state certainly does agree with you, Elizabeth! You are positively glowing." It was an emphatic statement of truth from Fitzwilliam. She did look lovelier, more alive than he remembered. "You look gorgeous and nearly as smug as your husband." Darcy winced, thinking Lizzy would be mortified at the allusion. He was surprised and greatly relieved to see her in good spirits at her new cousin's words.

"I highly recommend marriage, Colonel." She took her place in the chair next to his, still holding tightly to his hand. "In fact, I have two unmarried sisters ready and eager for the altar." She lowered her voice dramatically. "Beware."

Their discussion was very animated, like two dear old friends meeting again after a long separation. Darcy sat back contentedly to watch, remembering the first time the two had met, several years before. Lizzy was visiting her friend Charlotte and Charlotte's new husband, the Reverend Collins, vicar on the estate of the formidable Lady Catherine, while Darcy and Fitzwilliam were spending their annual Easter visit with their aunt.

At that visit to Rosings, when Lizzy and Richard would talk and laugh with each other, he remained aloof from them, envying as always his cousin's easy charm, his way with words and strangers. He had felt unwanted and alone, his only consolation being the certainty that if Richard considered marriage at all, it would need to be an heiress, and Lizzy had been far from that. Fitzwilliam could not and would not encourage any serious *tendre* within himself for Elizabeth, even though it was obvious he was utterly charmed by her.

Now, assured of the love of his wife, Darcy could watch two of the people he treasured most in the world enjoy each other's company and not feel excluded from their joy.

❧

"Scotland and Wales were absolutely wonderful." Lizzy's face was animated. "I had never been beyond my own little garden before, except when lost in a book. What a revelation!"

"I have always thought so, but it's much more exciting to see it fresh through the eyes of another." He began reciting a list of his favorite haunts, some having been visited by the Darcys and others not, the surprise and slight disappointment of which showing clearly on her face.

"William, how stupid I am. How could we have missed Hadrian's Wall?!" she gasped. Darcy winced at the name she had called him.

"William?" Fitzwilliam's eyebrows rose slowly as he looked at Darcy. Ah, but this was going to be a great source of sport.

Darcy shot an irritated glance off to the side before answering. He could sense his cousin's internal laughter. "Elizabeth, we did see Hadrian's Wall, and you were annoyed at the obstruction to your daily walk. If you remember, the evening before we had indulged a little too much in champagne, and we were both suffering the effects of it."

"William?" Fitzwilliam repeated, nasally this time, nearly licking his lips in delight.

"Yes, Fitz, now let's get beyond it... Apparently Elizabeth felt having two Fitzwilliams in the family was too confusing."

Richard beamed with pride at causing any sort of discomfort for his cousin. "Well, as it turns out, you are in grand company, Elizabeth. It also confuses Aunt Catherine, especially when she's in her cups." He laughed at Lizzy's shocked hoot of surprise.

"Fitzwilliam is such a very formal sort of Christian name, isn't it? It is much easier for me to just say William. Actually, I also was hoping to avoid the confusion I have when you both begin yelling 'Fitz' at each other." Lizzy tried to school her face into a serious expression, but her mouth twitched at the sides.

"I could not agree more, dear Cousin." Fitzwilliam attempted his own serious demeanor as he puffed on his pipe. "I've always felt Fitzwilliam an excellent surname but rather pompous for a first name. However, it could have been worse—much worse." Fitzwilliam was rewarded with the expected groan from Darcy.

"You see, the gossip in the family is that his father could have married Lady Diana de Carsie. Apparently, at one time, the toddler Uncle George and the infant Lady Diana were quite an item within the nursery set." He took another puff on his pipe. "And then, of course, our boy here would have been the one and only DeCarsie Darcy."

Lizzy gave way to her laughter, and even Darcy was finding it difficult to retain his somber, disapproving countenance. He shook his head at his wife. "You only encourage him, Elizabeth, and it takes precious little to do that."

At dinner, Fitzwilliam caught them up to date on all the gossip within the family, and with stories of the tenants at his father's estate in Somerton, many of them childhood friends now grown men with families of their own, having taken over the family farms. He had been on extended leave from the military after Waterloo, traveling the months that followed, visiting his father, aunt, and uncles. Curiosity pecked at Elizabeth until she brought up the subject of Aunt Catherine, anxious to know if she was still as upset with them as she had been before the wedding.

"Aunt Catherine is in no better humor now, I'm afraid. No. Quite the contrary, as it happens. I was telling Darcy earlier that both your names evoke a tirade of abuse and the most fanciful accusations. Evidently, in her twisted mind, it was your use of feminine wiles, Elizabeth, that caused mankind's expulsion from the Garden of Eden, and then, of course, Darcy's arrogance initiated the Flood."

Darcy's hand suddenly rammed angrily into a bowl of fruit and grasped an innocent, unsuspecting orange. "Enough. The woman is demented. Our marriage is simply something to which she must become adjusted. She insulted Elizabeth and her family, and in so doing, she insulted me." With an expression as black as pitch, Darcy commenced to vivisecting the orange. By the time he finished with said orange, it was completely dead, thoroughly dead, with no semblance remaining of its prior orange existence.

"That's all well and good for you to say, *old man*, but now she's so desperate that she has turned to me for management advice and help. I mean, really! She would have a better chance shooting an arrow into the ocean and impaling a carp than my comprehending all that gibberish." As he spoke, he snatched the knife from Darcy's clenched fist. "Come, Cousin, you know she loves you best. You were always her *golden child*, the second coming, her *beau bebe garçon*."

Elizabeth sadly watched her husband as months of emotional breakthroughs and insights shattered like so much glass. He became more withdrawn, more aloof by the second, his face a cold mask of sobriety.

Suddenly, Darcy threw his napkin upon the table and stood. "Shall we go into the family salon for some brandy and cakes? I believe those chairs will be much more comfortable for Elizabeth than these hard ones."

"I am in no discomfort here, William." Elizabeth's voice was very soft as she and Darcy shared a tense glance.

"Come on, Cousin, can't you thaw a little? Seriously, Catherine is having real concerns with those tenants in the..." The look in Darcy's eyes told him he needn't finish.

"Richard, this is the last time I wish to talk about Lady Catherine. She has chosen her course, and I have chosen mine. Now let us go into the parlor and have no more discussion about it." Darcy quickly left the room.

Elizabeth looked at Fitzwilliam in amazement. "I had hoped that the proud Mr. Darcy I met at Netherfield Hall had mellowed a bit. It appears, however, that we have regressed."

"Damnation—excuse me, Elizabeth—you know, for both their sakes, I hope they find common ground soon," he said gently. "This is hurting them."

Fitzwilliam rose as the footman pulled back Elizabeth's chair. "You know as well as I how stubborn he can be," Elizabeth said. "It would appear that any attempt at reconciliation may well have to generate from Lady Catherine herself."

"And from whom do you think he learned this damnable Fitzwilliam pride and stubbornness?" Richard smiled sadly and gave Elizabeth his arm as they followed Darcy into the parlor.

Chapter 4

The end of the year came quickly, with private balls, public assemblies, house parties, and concerts. Elizabeth's sister Jane and her husband, Charles Bingley, one of Darcy's closest friends, arrived at Pemberley a month before Christmas, followed two weeks later by Mr. and Mrs. Bennet and Kitty and Mary, the remainder of Elizabeth's family. It was the first real opportunity for Darcy to socialize with Mr. Bennet, a gentleman for whom he discovered he had a great deal of empathy, especially after experiencing the constant attentions and fawning of Mrs. Bennet.

As rude and insulting as she had been to Darcy before his marriage to her daughter, she was now the complete reverse, hanging on his every word. (Reason and Mrs. Bennet never resided in the same location for very long.) She followed him constantly, all worshipful eyes and servile admiration. She murmured, she whispered, she gasped.

"See how he stands? A spine like a pitchfork, straight and true. He's like a Roman statue, I'm sure: a true aristocrat!"

"Look how he butters his toast. Watch and learn!" she would remonstrate in all seriousness. "Watch and learn!"

Of course everyone had their particular favorite of her observations. Jane's was, "You can always tell a gentleman's character by how he eats his chicken."

Charles's was, "See how large his feet are? You know what that indicates, do you not?" Charles nearly choked at the dinner table the night *that* remark was made and glanced toward a red-faced Darcy.

When Lizzy's mother nodded to one and all and explained, "The mark of a great mind," they both exhaled loudly with relief.

When he sat to read, she would sit as near him as possible, somewhere behind, always in the great man's shadow, near enough to worship, not near enough to intrude. If he looked up, she was at his side in a moment, inquiring if he needed anything—tea, wine, pillow, quill, ink—and she very shrilly castigated Elizabeth if she did not exhibit the same zeal in anticipating his wants.

He remembered how odd he had found Mr. Bennet's behavior the first time he had sought him out at Longbourn when asking for Lizzy's hand. The man could evaporate into thin air, would disappear into his library, sometimes walking off in the very midst of a conversation. Darcy now thoroughly shared his father-in-law's literary fixation. That his own Pemberley library would be his only escape was obvious, and that had been within the first few minutes.

In fact, Mr. Darcy and Mr. Bennet were embarrassed to find they had both scrambled to the library independently of each other the second night. They competed fiercely for first hand on the knob then slipped inside, waiting in the dark for several moments before lighting the candles. Charles Bingley, as always trying to be kindhearted, charming, and obliging, attempted to step up as host in Darcy's absence, only to end up with the other men a mere half hour later.

It was still, though, a very pleasant family time, a precious and happy holiday marred only by the two or three angry chair-throwing free-for-alls most families experience during this holiest of seasons. On Boxing Day, Jane and Charles announced their expectancy to squeals and flutters and spasms. Sisterly confidences were exchanged and unlooked-for motherly advice loudly dispensed. Darcy and Bingley rode to freedom almost daily, and Mr. Bennet napped whenever possible. Days began to drag into weeks that felt like months, and finally, with a sigh of relief, the Darcys waved good-bye to her sisters and parents and settled into what would become a fateful new year.

It was the beginning of the year of our Lord, 1817. Winter had come to Pemberley.

At Easter, Fitzwilliam returned home from Spain to find the whole county stricken with some sort of fever, both his father and his aunt among them, Catherine attended by no less than three physicians who attempted in vain to keep her quiet and secluded. A tenuous truce between Richard and his older brother, Regis, held only for the length of time it took for their father to be on the mend.

He missed teasing Catherine and even missed her constant nonsensical lectures, the hours and hours of bizarre and unlooked-for advice on health and happiness that she felt obliged to provide as matriarch of the family.

Fitzwilliam stayed longer than his usual visit, sending word to the War Office, extending his leave, and left only when assured the two old lions were improving. By early May, he arrived at Pemberley for a shortened visit, happy to spend his last two weeks with the Darcys before returning to his regiment.

The cousins quickly fell into their old routine of competition and teasing, racing their horses and hunting, and in the evening, would sit with Lizzy and Georgiana, talking and laughing into the early hours.

By the second week, after another delicious dinner with conversation consisting mainly of family gossip, laughter, political opinions, and reminiscing, it was a visibly satiated Fitzwilliam who finished his meal and gave sincere compliments to the cook, which Elizabeth accepted with all formality and promised to pass on.

"By the way, how was Easter, Richard?" Elizabeth knew that his father had been ill. Her mother, too, had been fighting off the same malady.

"I didn't know if I should mention anything." His eyes darted uncertainly toward Darcy. "Truthfully, it was far less enjoyable than in prior years, without the brat here in attendance." Fitzwilliam's demeanor turned somber. Placing his elbows on the table, he hesitated then looked directly across the table at Darcy, seeming to choose his words very carefully. "You know, as well as my father, Aunt Catherine has been very ill. I don't know if anyone has shared this with you as yet."

Elizabeth saw Darcy's body shift suddenly, spilling wine on his hand and the tablecloth. He swore slightly under his breath but didn't take his eyes from Fitzwilliam.

"What is her complaint?" Elizabeth asked gently, sensing the question Darcy most wanted to ask but could not. He raised his glass slowly to his lips and held his breath, watching his cousin over the rim.

"Oh, it was the same as my father—cough and lung inflammation, high fever. In fact, Aunt Catherine was so ill that Cousin Anne began nursing *her*, if you can believe that. Truth be told, I think I have never seen Catherine worse or Anne happier."

Darcy sipped his wine, returning the glass to the table. "Elizabeth's mother has had a similar complaint. I'm sure it will pass with the warmer weather. What do her physicians say?"

"Well, that is exactly what they are hoping, and in fact, both Father and Catherine are much improved already. If you wish, I can have Father apprise you of her condition, should it change."

Darcy hesitated. "Perhaps..."

Elizabeth saw the reluctance in his eyes and reached over to cover his hand with hers. "Yes, and thank you, Richard. We would very much appreciate your father keeping us informed."

Darcy's eyes shifted to hers and then stared sadly across her shoulder to the darkness outside.

The following morning, Elizabeth was reading in her favorite flower garden and enjoying the budding warmth and the moist smell of spring that had infused the air. She had recently confirmed with her doctor that she was also with child, and only she and William knew of it. It was still early in her pregnancy, a sacred time for them to enjoy privately as a couple, as well as a time that was making her sick to her stomach most mornings. This morning was no exception, and her nausea had awakened her very early.

Fitzwilliam appeared, a determined look upon his face.

"Well, I'm off tomorrow, I fear. I have just received a communiqué from Wellington. He's fed up with my lazy bones and won't allow me to put him off any longer. It appears I am needed for meetings with the allies in the coming months, and it may be a while before I am able to get leave again."

"We'll be unhappy to see you depart, Richard." She placed her hand gently on his arm. "William has so enjoyed having you here, as have Georgiana and I." Richard smiled and kissed her hand, then kept hold of it as he settled in next to her.

"Elizabeth, please see if you can persuade Darcy to end this strife with Aunt Catherine." She seemed surprised at the intensity of his request.

"Truthfully, Richard"—Lizzy's free hand gripped her shawl a bit closer and she looked down—"I am ashamed to admit how hesitant I am to reinstate their relationship, even if I could. I care little what she thinks of me, but she deeply hurt my husband, and that I find very hard to understand, let alone forgive." She squeezed Fitzwilliam's hand and smiled kindly. "However, I am truly very sorry that she was so ill."

Fitzwilliam turned to look unseeing at the far horizon, at a loss as to how much he should confide, not knowing how many of the family secrets Darcy had as yet revealed to her. He leaned closer, touching his shoulder to hers, bending his head to speak in confidence. "I know she hurt you both, but perhaps you don't know their history together, hers and Darcy's."

Elizabeth slowly put her book aside and turned toward him. "No, he has never told me anything, but I know his feelings run deeply for her."

Sighing, Fitzwilliam rubbed hard at the back of his neck. "Well, where to begin? Were you at all aware that Catherine and George Darcy were very near to becoming betrothed? I thought not. It's quite true, though. They were seriously in love from what I have been told. This is all wild family gossip, you understand, unsubstantiated and strictly confidential."

Stunned beyond belief, Elizabeth could not speak for a moment. "I had no idea! What caused him to ask for her sister Anne's hand instead?"

"Lord Louis de Bourgh was the cause, and Aunt Catherine's pursuit of a title. At any event, that is what my father always believed. It was Catherine who put pin to their betrothal—she ran off with Lord Louis, figuratively speaking, and married him. Darcy's father was devastated, brooded for several years. However, he was also very young, very handsome, and very healthy. Eventually he noticed Anne Fitzwilliam, Catherine's baby sister, a child he had teased and laughed at for years. Well, the child had grown into an even more beautiful woman than Catherine. It was a happy day for them both when he turned to her for comfort. In any event, they soon developed a true love match and married.

"However, my father always believed Uncle George never fully forgave Aunt Catherine, though to his credit, he did not attempt to keep the two sisters apart. The women were famously close, supported each other through joys and sorrows; both had suffered several miscarriages before their firstborns. My father swore Darcy's feet never touched the ground for his first four years, between Anne and Catherine. After his mother's death when he was twelve, he was very often with Aunt Catherine—much more than I ever was."

Elizabeth was speechless.

"Whatever Darcy may say to you now, it was Catherine who consoled him, took him into her home and comforted him when his mother died—after all, she shared his tremendous grief at Aunt Anne's passing. Darcy remained at Rosings for several months while his father dealt with his overwhelming grief and his new baby daughter. Poor Darcy refused to be in the same room with Georgiana at first. It was Catherine who reassured him and told him that his mother had given her life for the babe, making Georgiana the most precious thing in the world. Obviously, Darcy, being the excellent man he is, soon cast himself as his sister's protector and loved her unquestioningly, above everything else."

Elizabeth rose to pace the garden. "My goodness, Fitzwilliam, she could have been his mother if she hadn't chosen title over love"

Fitzwilliam nodded. "Please don't let Darcy know that I have told you all this; however, I wanted you to be aware that there is a special history between the two of them, and both are hurting. If something should happen to Aunt Catherine, it will dearly affect Darcy."

It was later, alone with her thoughts, that Elizabeth realized the full impact of what she had learned. *No wonder William had been so unnerved by the news of Lady Catherine's illness.* She immediately felt she should do something or say something to him, but Fitzwilliam had sworn her to secrecy. She vowed to herself that she *would* think of something, some opportunity of repairing the rift between the two.

Chapter 6

It was soon after Fitzwilliam's departure, only a few days, while preparing for bed that Elizabeth mused again about Catherine—one of the few people who had ever taken a great dislike to her. It was human nature to want to be thought well of, and the notion that someone harbored such a disgust of her was unsettling. She could not think of another soul who had turned against her in that way, looking upon her with jealousy and hatred in their heart.

But wait. She was seated before her mirror, hairbrush in use. *Wasn't there was another person who had taken an instant aversion to me, and on as grand a scale as Catherine?* The name itself sent shivers of resentment down Elizabeth's spine.

Caroline Bingley.

Her hairbrush paused for just a moment. *I haven't thought of that harridan in months.* She smiled to herself, embarrassed by the sheer depth of her own dislike. Caroline Bingley had been vicious and cruel when they first met, deliberately hurting not only Elizabeth but also inadvertently hurting the sweet

Georgiana. Since her sister Jane's marriage to Caroline's brother, Charles, an uncertain truce had been called.

Jane had written her of Caroline's newest *affaire de coeur*, a titled gentleman once again, a viscount and friend of both Charles's and their sister, Mrs. Hurst. It was hoped by all that this time, Caroline had finally found happiness. *Caroline Bingley and Lady Catherine.* Two women she had known in her life who absolutely detested her. She absentmindedly braided her hair as she pondered.

Why? What could I have possibly done to either that they hate me so? The only common thread Elizabeth could imagine was Darcy. Yes, it had to be Darcy. Unthinkingly, she undid her braid once again, ran her fingers through the long tresses to unwind them, and began to brush. What was the main reason that caused women to hate other women?

Jealousy.

Elizabeth stopped her hairbrush in midstroke. *They both loved Darcy. In different ways, of course, but the intensity of their love for Darcy had turned them both against the one person whom they perceived had taken him from them. Jealousy.*

Caroline was in love with Darcy. Oh! Good heavens, Elizabeth. Only took you a year and a half to figure this one out—so much for your quick mind. I must ask him about this. I wonder if he knew how much Caroline may have loved him. Lizzy wrinkled up her nose in revulsion while a surprisingly belligerent-looking female stared back at her from the mirror. One eyebrow arched. *Upon further reflection, perhaps it would be unwise to remind him. If he did know, it would only bring back those memories. If he did not know, it could cause him to think of what might have been. No, no, no, that's ridiculous. I'm surely more secure than that.*

She entered their bedroom to see her husband at the windows, staring pensively out over one of Pemberley's beautiful small lakes, brooding thoughts apparently taking him a dozen miles away. There was a troubled look on his face that cleared immediately upon seeing her. "There you are, little one. Did you know I was watching you brush your hair for quite a while? You were so lost in your thoughts you braided and unbraided your hair twice." Wearily, he rubbed his hand across his eyes as he walked toward her. "Have a care, Lizzy, you'll be bald within the year, brushing with that much ferocity."

He came to a stop before her, a contented smile on his face as his eyes swept lovingly over her. It was a pleasant surprise to him how her young woman's body was already changing subtly with her expectancy—her delicate breasts beginning to swell, her slim hips becoming rounder. "How are we feeling? Has the child moved yet?" He pulled her into his arms, wrapping them protectively about her as he hugged her close.

She nuzzled into his chest. "Heavens no, we're not even two months into this. I shouldn't even have begun to show yet—or have I?" Like a purring cat, she rubbed her cheek against the exposed part of his open shirt and kissed his skin, the smell and warmth of it always arousing. "Do I look heavier?" Although she was laughing, she appeared nervous, vulnerable.

"No, of course not. You look beautiful, incandescent. You are Mother Earth." He gave her bottom an affectionate pat as they walked toward the bed. Lizzy's side had already been turned down, the counterpane folded neatly across the foot. She climbed in, and he tenderly covered her, then he blew out the candle on her nightstand.

"William..." she began as she held up his side of the comforter, smiling sweetly at him as he climbed in.

"Yeeessss, Mrs. Darcy..." He drew her body to him, kissing her soft, white neck, his hand moving sensuously down her side and around to cup that darling little bottom he loved so. Deeply inhaling the sweet powder scent at the swell of her breasts, he tugged the tiny bow of her nightgown open with his teeth.

"I have a rather delicate question to put to you."

He groaned and chuckled. "Can't it wait, Lizzy?" he murmured into her cleavage and then licked her there delicately. "I am otherwise occupied at the moment. Just getting to the good part, if you catch what I mean."

He felt her body stiffen in his arms. "No, William, it cannot wait. Not if you want my full participation." He stopped at once. It was very quiet as he lifted his head up to rest on his hand.

"Well, this sounds a trifle ominous. Very good, Mrs. Darcy, I am at your service. Ask away."

In the darkness he felt more than saw Lizzy lean back onto her pillow, uncharacteristically hesitant and unsure of herself. It had been difficult for him to put brakes to his lust, but he sensed that something was bothering her this evening. Suddenly he became fearful about the pregnancy and braced himself up onto his elbow, trying to make out the look in her eyes. His hand brushed hair from her face then covered her stomach. "What is it, dearest? Is it the babe?"

"Did you ever have the feeling that Caroline Bingley was in love with you?" She blurted the question out before she could think twice.

He was startled, but initial relief quickly rushed through

him, an amused grin teasing the corners of his mouth. "From where, in heaven's name, is this question coming?"

She let out the breath she had been holding. "Nowhere, really. My mind just wandered as I brushed, grown weary, I suppose, of being concerned with nursemaids and new clothes for after the confinement. I believe it is a fairly straightforward question, however. Was she in love with you?"

"Caroline Bingley was involved with several men, Elizabeth."

A premonition, only a slight quiver, touched at Lizzy's heart.

"So I have heard repeatedly; however, that is not what I asked, is it?"

He remained very still for several moments, the room in quiet shadow. "Something must have motivated this line of thought. What has made you ask such a thing, Elizabeth?"

"Well, I was making a sort of mental comparison between Lady Catherine and Caroline."

With that, Darcy gave a short laugh and quickly apologized. "Go on, dear, you were saying?"

"I believe that Lady Catherine took such a dislike of me because she loves you deeply and felt that I was taking you from her and her plans for your future. Caroline is the only other person I have ever known to take me into such disgust."

They stayed without speaking for several moments. *Either he has fallen asleep, or he's upset with me*. She fidgeted with the blanket edge, frustrated at not being able to clearly see his expression in the dark. Her heart was pounding.

"Elizabeth, I don't wish to lie to you, and I really don't think there would be any advantage to either of us if we continued with this conversation."

Elizabeth stopped breathing before the sentence's end. It

was a while before she found her voice again. "It is a simple question, Mr. Darcy." Raising herself onto her elbow, she turned toward him, steadying her voice as best as she could. "It requires a simple yes or no answer. I will not think badly of you if you realized that she was in love with you, and I will not think badly of you if that was something of which you were ignorant." *And I hope that's all there is to this.*

Abruptly, Darcy lay back down and turned his back to her. "I don't believe it is in our best interest to converse about this any further. End of discussion, I'm afraid. Good night, Elizabeth."

She had been dismissed.

It became deadly quiet in the surrounding universe, not a breeze nor a whisper nor a breath could be heard. Even the cicadas and frogs were stunned. Only the snores of the two mastiffs lying before the foot of their bed interrupted the quiet night. Elizabeth waited, terribly alone it seemed, for several minutes.

"William, are you angry with me?" she whispered but received no answer from his side of the bed.

Elizabeth was becoming extremely alarmed. Darcy was never cruel, always a gentleman. Oh, he could still be aloof at times, but never with her. She sat up in their bed to try for a better look at his countenance. The faint outline of her husband's back in the dark revealed him to be facing the opposite wall of their bedroom.

"William?" she said softly. No answer.

"Fitzwilliam?" Still he did not answer.

Suddenly, a flash of perception, the unerring intuition of the female brain, illuminated her mind. She gasped.

"Mr. Darcy, did you have a love affair with Caroline Bingley?"

His silence was deafening. Elizabeth's heart pounded as she

repeated the question, a little louder and much more strident. She roughly shoved his shoulder.

"Mr. Darcy, did you have sexual congress with Caroline Bingley?!"

His continued silence was all the answer she really required by that point. She scrambled from the bed, refusing to allow any part of her body to be contaminated by him, and stared down at that dark and now-evil form. It was as if Satan himself had crawled into bed between them. Eventually, he rolled onto his back then ran his fingers roughly through his hair. Next, he sighed. He then said the words all women dread to hear.

"Elizabeth, it was such a long time ago."

The following morning brought a surprise to Darcy's majordomo. When he entered the couple's bedchamber, the fire in the grate was completely cold, and the bed was empty. He looked in mild apprehension around an apparently deserted room. He knew instantly that something was dreadfully wrong as he scanned the broken vases and overturned books. The two dogs, Buck and Milo, looked up. They had been calmly ripping apart several bed pillows between them, feathers laying everywhere. Happy woofs were their greeting to Bradford, anticipation of their imminent run outside and breakfast sent tails loudly thumping. There was, however, no sign of human life anywhere.

It was clear that the bed had been entered at some point, but the covers were still in an almost pristine condition, not wrestled about, half off the bed and half on, as on most mornings. A movement on the settee in the adjoining sitting room, a figure covered by a great quilt, caught his eye.

The form groaned and turned toward the light streaming in

through the windows where Bradford had just pulled back the curtains to reveal the extent of destruction. The form was Mr. Darcy!

He shielded his eyes quickly from the brightness, and once he had made out who the intruder was, put up his hand in greeting. "Bradford, good morning. Terribly sorry for this mess." He waved his arm vaguely to encompass the bedroom and then the rest of London. He let his head crash back down on the sofa.

He looked hideous—well, as hideous as the handsome Mr. Darcy could look. Bradford slowly entered farther into the room, now seeing broken picture frames and torn clothing, overturned chairs and one or two mirrors balanced precariously on their sides in the corners.

"Is everything all right, sir?" It was an absurd question. Clearly evident were the remains of the couple's first out-and-out brawl. It was also painfully evident to him that Darcy and Elizabeth, for the first time in their young marriage, had not slept in the same bed.

Darcy moaned and turned his face into the sofa again. "Mrs. Darcy and I have had a bit of a *contretemps*." He then slowly pulled the cover up over his head.

In another first in their relatively short months of wedded bliss, there was no evidence of the mistress of the house at breakfast, her most favored meal, or again at lunch, her other most favored meal. Several of the staff began to speculate about dinner and if the bottom of the lake should be investigated. The gossip in the servants' hall would stop whenever Bradford came through but revived the moment his door closed.

Darcy paced back and forth, alternately angry and contrite, unsure of what to do or how to say it. How could he explain something that had happened so long ago, at a time when he was incredibly naïve?

He had been introduced to the lovely Caroline Bingley by his older and hopelessly randy cousin, Richard Fitzwilliam, during a fashionable dinner party at Carlton House. A favorite with the high flyers, Caroline had been much younger when she initiated her ultimately unsuccessful campaign to barter morals for an advantageous match. Alas, when push came to shove, she was only a tradesman's daughter, and always would remain one.

She had pursued the incredibly handsome newcomer, Darcy, until he succumbed after a night of heavy drinking and unsuccessful gaming. It had been a satisfying three hours, vaguely remembered, but three hours that he never cared to repeat. It had meant little to him then and was conveniently forgotten with time.

Standing before his wife's sitting-room door, he was prepared to knock but hesitant. How could they discuss this problem in an adult, rational manner when they appeared to be one rational adult short? The Elizabeth he had seen last evening was a stranger to him, a spoiled child with her screeching and outrage. The behavior she exhibited had confused him; her lack of emotional control baffled him. He stared at the closed door and sighed. What could he do? God alone knew how much he missed his beloved angel and closest friend, and that after only one night apart. Why, he missed her so much that he wanted to strangle her. This was ridiculous; he *was* head of his household, after all. He would simply demand she listen to him.

Darcy abandoned that idea when the first flowerpot hit the wall.

"Elizabeth!" He was shocked, his indignity magnified as he spun around clumsily to avoid being crowned by a water pitcher that sailed just to the left of his head and hit the doorframe. "This is insupportable! This is outrageous! You cannot throw water pots!"

"You are right yet again, Mr. Darcy. It would not usually be my first choice. I personally believe it's because their center of gravity is so low. If you will but allow me another opportunity, I will switch to statuettes! My ability with those has grown leaps and bounds!" He quickly closed the door before it was smashed, fittingly, by a small replica of Cupid, and leaned his back against the frame, his hands fisted at his waist. *Well, it's obvious that she has lost her mind.* Darcy prided himself as always on his calm, his reasoning capabilities. *I am married to a madwoman.* How much more ridiculous could this argument become? A fit caused by an affair that had happened so long before her, not even an affair really—more a frisky moment. Did she believe he had lived like a monk all those years?

"Elizabeth!" he called through the closed door, "will you please allow me to enter so that we can discuss this rationally, like adults?" He heard nothing from within. "Oh cut line, Lizzy, please give me a chance to explain."

"There is nothing in the world you could say to me at this moment, sir. We are through. I never want to set eyes upon you again. Would you be so good as to help me pack my things and drive me to my father's house?"

"Elizabeth, you are being incredibly foolish. Any association I had with Caroline Bingley happened ages ago, before my friendship with Charles."

Darcy never imagined that his sweet, beloved, elfin wife could be capable of such rage. Of course, he had never before been subjected to the delicate sentiments of a pregnant woman. It was ghastly. He grew truly concerned when he heard her sobs begin, and then her labored breathing coming in gasps. "Sweetheart, think of the child and calm down."

After several moments, the door slowly opened. "Speak," she commanded as she turned to walk back into the room. She then sat in regal silence, her eyes red-rimmed and her hair sticking out Medusa-like from her head.

Darcy took a few steps in and closed the door behind him. "Now you are being sensible. Good thing you let me in; I believe the servants were beginning to suspect something was amiss."

She lifted her hairbrush threateningly.

"All right, all right." Raising both his hands in a plea for truce, he took a seat directly opposite her. *Where to begin? How to begin?* "It happened years ago, a short time before I first met Bingley, when Fitzwilliam and I returned from our grand tour. We were both just out of university."

An unblinking Elizabeth gazed straight past him, her hairbrush still poised to attack at any moment.

"It is all Fitzwilliam's fault, you know. He introduced me to Caroline. They had met through a mutual acquaintance, an officer friend of both, and I have to admit I thought she was very, very pretty." With that, Elizabeth turned cold, dead eyes to Darcy. They narrowed on him dangerously. "Well, she is, or was, anyway. Maybe one 'very' would have been sufficient, eh?" When Elizabeth didn't respond to his jest, he continued with the narrative.

He rubbed his hands nervously across his thighs. "As I was saying," he began, "it was after a gathering we had all attended, one of many that had been, well, more than a bit wild and bawdy, and we, uh, all had a great deal too much to drink, and... and..."

"You are a drunkard and a debaucher. Thank you. I feel ever so much better." She was not letting him off the hook so very easily.

"Well, I was not her first, Elizabeth, if that's what you're implying. I was no seducer of an innocent."

Elizabeth allowed an exaggerated eyebrow to rise. "Oh, really?" Suddenly her mood became ferocious. "How many times were you with her?" she barked out. The Spanish Inquisition had been more gregarious.

"Once. Well, twice actually, but both on the same night. The first time, I believe I fell asleep on her. Well, not exactly *on* her..." The lethal hairbrush was quickly on the rise again.

"Does Bingley know?" she snapped.

"Good Lord, I hope not. No one knows except you... and Fitzwilliam. She had several men before me, Lizzy, and after me, too. She had become quite legendary. Just ask him."

Lizzy's eyeballs opened wide. "Really? He also...?" she asked, more interested now in acquiring the *ton* gossip than her own problems. Darcy didn't really know for sure, but Fitzwilliam *had* introduced them and *had* been mildly attracted to her, as well, *had* spent some time with her, and knowing Caroline, it was very possible. "Don't be naïve, Lizzy." *What the hell.* "Yes, of course Fitzwilliam, too. He's no saint, you know."

She lowered the hairbrush. "Well… once I could somewhat imagine, when you were exceedingly drunk. Blind and deaf as it were. But twice tells me you regretted missing out on the first and waited around to have a try at her again." Her lower lip quivered in a small pout, and her arms crossed in front of her.

"I was very young, and she was making herself extremely available. Men are different than women."

Elizabeth rolled her eyes and harrumphed. All at once she looked exhausted and defeated. "That, Mr. Darcy, is one of the sorriest excuses ever used by men for their abysmal behavior. And believe me, sir, I have never found the comparison used in a good light." She placed the hairbrush down onto her dresser. "Is there anyone else I need worry about from your wild and reckless youth?"

"No, of course not, Elizabeth. Not unless we happen to meet Elinor Prescott-Pickard at a *ton* function," he muttered and tried to think of the odds that they would come in contact with Jennie Dewar or her twin sister, Lady Cathie, more Carlton House lovelies. Elizabeth grunted and massaged her sleepy eyes.

"Will you come back to our bed tonight?" he asked softly, and she nodded after making him wait just a few minutes longer.

"Will you forgive me for not telling you sooner?"

Again she nodded, and he could see that the storm had passed. "William?"

"Yes, Lizzy?"

Her eyes began to twinkle. "Can we get some food sent up, please? I am famished. See if Cook can make up some spinach-and-cheese puffs. And some ham. Maybe those tarts we had last week—the cherry ones. Oooh, and honey. I have a craving for honey with pickles..."

Darcy walked over and quite energetically pulled her into his arms.

"One more thing"—she looked deeply in his eyes—"I do not want to be in the same room ever again with Caroline Bingley, is that understood?" Darcy nodded in agreement. He was so relieved, he would have agreed to most anything. This was an easy promise.

"I will have to explain something to Jane. I don't know what I would do if I ever saw that husband-stealing, wretched, common tart person again!"

Chapter 8

Not many of life's wishes and dreams can come true, and certainly Lizzy's hopes to avoid Caroline were thwarted almost immediately. A short while after Lizzy's porcelain-throwing demonstration, and much to everyone's surprise, Lizzy's mother passed away quietly in her sleep. She had been a relatively young woman, merely in her late forties, and so, although the poor woman had been ailing for quite some time, complaining for years, in fact, the first impression in the little town of Meryton was that the doctor must be exaggerating the seriousness of her condition, might want to examine her again. After all, she was known far and wide as a sound sleeper.

When her demise was confirmed, the second impression was that it was such a pity—she had so counted on her husband dying first.

Jane and Lizzy both agreed that their mother must be absolutely furious, wherever she was. There was a cruel injustice in this, of her being denied time to reap the rewards of having her two eldest daughters so wealthy and well situated, and then there was her youngest married to a handsome, if disreputable, commissioned officer. Three of five daughters married within a year. It was almost biblical. Why, she was a female Moses having led her two remaining unmarried daughters to the very edges of the Promised Land and then not being allowed to enter.

For his part, Mr. Bennet was certainly as put out as his wife, possibly more so, horrified at finding himself suddenly alone at the forefront of his family, a man who had paid little if any attention to their needs before. He had no idea of what to do, so he did what had worked so well for him in the past. He went into his library and remained there, never to come out, at least not until he was absolutely certain that the body had been examined by her physician and carted away, and positively not a moment before he had handed the unpleasant responsibility of funeral arrangements to his son-in-law, Darcy. A situation which seemed completely natural to all concerned.

❧

The funeral day had the appropriate grey cast along with a slight drizzle of rain when the little group of mourners gathered around the open grave site. Mr. Bennet stood with Kitty and Mary on either side. Darcy had a protective arm around Lizzy, while Charles was doing the same with Jane. The only one of the sisters not there was Lydia, who was due to deliver her third child at any moment and could not make the journey south.

Charlotte and Mr. Collins, Charlotte's parents, and one or two representatives of the Meryton community were also there. It was not a large group, but a group that sincerely mourned the passing of a member from their small circle.

If anyone had asked her opinion, however, Elizabeth would

have suggested that there was one too many mourners for her liking at the funeral. A very uninterested Caroline Bingley was spied yawning in the background, shivering and rolling her eyes at the Reverend Collins's heavenly words. Jane had been delivered safely of a baby girl a few weeks prior to her mother's passing, so Caroline and her sister and brother-in-law, Mr. and Mrs. Hurst, were already residing at Netherfield Hall, Charles and Jane's leased manor house situated a few miles from Mr. and Mrs. Bennet's home.

"We'll return to your father's house and have a short rest." Darcy cupped his wife's elbow, steering her in the direction of Longbourn and to their room after the early morning burial with its damp air. "I'll have them get a nice warm fire going for you. We've plenty of time before the luncheon at Netherfield." They were staying in her old bedroom, the one she had at one time happily shared with her older sister. It was a charming reflection of both Jane's and Lizzy's distinct personalities—flowery wallpaper, chair flounces and pink bows alongside books, a writing desk, walking boots and stick. The drizzle of rain had thankfully stopped, leaving behind only the clouds and gloom. Lizzy nodded to her husband, and so the couple made their excuses and returned for a nap before venturing to Jane and Charles's home.

Relieved of her gown and ankle-length pantalets, Elizabeth scooted onto the bed and snuggled into the pillows feeling warm and cozy, her stomach finally settling down from its daily pilgrimage upward. It was such a relief knowing that she could now relax, but not so her wonderful husband. Her exhaustion, her health, her pregnancy, all were his now constant concern, often causing him sleepless nights.

As she sipped her hot chocolate, she prattled on to him about the morning service and how kind everyone had been and about the pretty flowers. However, her speech became quieter and her words stilled completely the moment he began undressing for bed. He possessed a magnificent figure, the viewing of which she never tired, and his regimented routine always fascinated her. It rarely varied.

He first loosened his neck scarf and waistcoat, then sat erectly upon a chair to remove his boots. Next he stood and unbuttoned his shirt and cuffs, careful as always to place any jewelry on the nightstand beside the bed. His waistcoat, scarf, and shirt were next removed in that order, folded and draped with the utmost care across the back of his chair. After unbuttoning his breeches, he sat at the edge of the bed and yanked them off, folded them, and laid them neatly across her old dresser.

"Oh, bravo." She clapped, grinning impishly.

He turned and arched his eyebrow at her.

"You zany scamp—you have unhinged me with your recklessness."

His eyebrow went somehow higher.

"You unbuttoned your pants *before* you sat on the edge of the bed, and not *after*, as is your usual order. Such extreme behavior—whatever possessed you to such flights of abandon?"

"Are you quite finished?" His lips twitched with humor as he lowered himself back onto the bed and let out a heartfelt sigh. "Now please be quiet. You are exhausted and need your sleep. All I ask is one uninterrupted hour, Elizabeth."

"Did you see who was at the grave site?"

He groaned.

She was snuggling farther down into the covers while motioning toward her aching back, so he slipped his hand down within her chemise and kneaded and rubbed until her tense muscles began to relax, the warmth and firmness of the back rub quickly beginning to loosen all the anxiety of the sad morning. Giving her shoulder a quick kiss when he finished, he pulled his wife's backside against him, and they then easily fell into their normal spooning position from home, fingers intertwined together, arms laced, and hugs secured.

"Did you hear what I asked you?"

"Yessss." He sighed, no immediate sleep in sight. "I imagine you are speaking of Lady Catherine and Fitzwilliam. I saw them only briefly, and they were gone before I could approach." In truth, he felt very guilty that he had not contacted her directly during her illness, only receiving reports from Fitzwilliam and her doctors. The sight of her there today shamed him and brought to the forefront of his mind the folly of holding this grudge. Life was short, he was learning, and never to be taken for granted.

"She looked very pale and fragile, did she not?"

"Yes, she did." She could feel him shift uneasily. "I'm not that surprised that she was there, really," he said quietly. "In some fuzzy area of her brain she has accepted that you are part of her family, and family obligations are paramount to her."

They were silent for a moment. He pulled another cover over them.

"Did you remove your stockings?"

"Elizabeth, I beg of you to be quiet."

She was, for a moment.

"If you don't remove them, your feet will become very warm, and then you shall have nightmares. And your boots will smell."

His teeth ground for an instant, but he contained himself. "I never have nightmares—largely due to the fact that I seldom sleep anymore. And my boots do *not* smell."

They were silent. He suddenly sat up and removed his stockings, again placing them with the utmost precision atop her dresser.

He'd make a fine valet, she thought briefly. *Best not to voice that opinion out loud.*

They were silent.

"Did you see Caroline Bingley?"

Darcy fought back an unpleasant curse. He was learning that infinite patience needed to walk hand in hand with marriage. "Yes, dear, I did. Will you be all right with Caroline there today?" he whispered.

"Yes, of course." It was so quiet in their little room. "The real question is, will you?"

Gently he turned her chin, tilting her head back toward him.

"Elizabeth, let sleeping dogs lie."

She smiled and nodded, kissing his mouth tenderly, but her heart and her newfound insecurities were fighting a silent battle with logic. She gave out a noncommittal "mm-hmm."

Darcy sighed. *This is going to be a long week.*

The prior evening, Fitzwilliam had dreaded another lecture from Aunt Catherine. For two hours, she had vacillated between arguments for going to the funeral to pay her respects, or for not going and continuing the family conflict. In the end, as he knew it would, family duty won out over personal pride, and her carriage took them the long thirty miles to Meryton for the funeral, returning them back to Rosings almost immediately afterward.

Upon their arrival back to Rosings Park, Fitzwilliam barricaded himself within the business office with orders to all who would listen that he was not to be disturbed, unwilling to admit the fact that he was thoroughly mystified by his own accounting methods of a previous visit. He pulled at his hair and muttered vile obscenities, searching through what seemed like hundreds of receipts and reports and tenant requests. Everything looked the same, and nothing added up or made any sense.

Lady Catherine's daughter, Anne, was in her bedroom suite, fearful that somehow a remnant of the illness that had felled Mrs. Bennet would return doggedly attached to her mother or cousin. She breathed into a boiling pot of clove-and-basil ointment, clutching a towel around her head, allowing only her paid companion to accompany her.

So it was that Lady Catherine sat alone that evening, her memories agitated, her ire poking the embers of her thoughts into flames as if bringing a dimming hearth fire to life on a winter morning.

It is insupportable…that he should look so well, never missed me at all, the ingrate! Where is the loyalty among the young these days? He's even gained a little weight! Dread flooded her confused brain. *Or, perhaps that is water retention. Oh no, the poor dear is retaining water. Oh, dear God, he probably has developed serious heart ailments of which he is not even aware!*

Fitzwilliam burst into the room. "Do we grow peas?!"

She was startled, her thoughts still agitated. Already mourning the passing of her beloved Darcy, she stared at him several moments before she could respond. "What… yes, I believe we have lentils, peas, and barley on some farms to the north." She gulped back the sense of foreboding that always arose when Fitzwilliam attempted anything agricultural. "Why do you ask?"

"Nothing… nothing…" He began to close the door then stopped, staring intently back at her, nearly obscured within the deep shadows of the doorframe. "By the by, have you ever heard of gray mold?" She could see he was clutching a written report her estate manager had prepared shortly before the accident that had incapacitated him for nearly eight months. She let out a whimper.

Chapter 9

The day following the funeral an exceedingly kind note was delivered from Elizabeth to Rosings Park. Among many pleasantries and concerns expressed for her health, Elizabeth thanked Lady Catherine for attending the funeral and expressed her sincere hope that they would see her again soon.

Very courteous, very proper, Lady Catherine thought to herself, so pleased was she that her heart began to thump again, the cavernous labyrinth of her rather bizarre mind beginning to expand and contract with plans and machinations.

"It is as I have always said," she spoke aloud to her daughter, Anne, as the young woman sat testing her vision by placing one hand alternately over each of her eyes. "Breeding is inbred, Anne, remember this. It cannot be crushed by paucity of means. A gentleman is a gentleman to his bones, and his offspring cannot help but absorb this."

Anne gave an involuntary shudder and checked the pulse on her left wrist. She compared this to her right. They differed. She was doomed.

"Perhaps I *was* too harsh on the girl, even though she rudely spurned all my attempts to help her. The poor thing must be in want of a mother's direction now. It really never was her fault that she was so impertinent or ill mannered; after all, she never had the advantages that should have been hers, had she had a more civilized upbringing." Catherine glanced toward her daughter for verification, a daughter who now held two fingers against her neck to verify her previous pulse readings. "Anne, you have such exquisite posture, and you know you look absolutely glowing in that shade of lavender."

Anne wheezed.

As excited as Catherine was becoming, she was hard put to retain any sort of dignified expression. "Imagine that mother attempting to raise five daughters without a governess! My goodness, how can a young girl possibly be expected to acquire any polish in that havey-cavey sort of atmosphere? I always felt that was odd, didn't you? Her mother alone was obviously not up to such a task. Yes. Well, I can understand now how dear Elizabeth could have resented my kind offers of assistance."

Catherine turned sharply toward her butler, the man innocently bringing in her afternoon tea and cakes. "It was never her fault, after all. I hope you realize that now!" she snapped.

Jamison automatically inclined his head for forgiveness.

"The poor dear had no training. None whatsoever! Think on that, Jamison, and try to show a little compassion in the future!"

"I am desolate, your ladyship." The penitent Jamison bowed and backed out of the room.

"Fitzwilliam, are you in there? Fitzwilliam!" she called out as the footman forced the business-office doors open. "Why has this door been bolted?" When she looked closer at her nephew, she saw that he looked like death itself, his hair standing on end, a half-empty bottle of whiskey at his side. "Whatever is the matter?" She saw nothing but disaster in his bloodshot eyes.

"Evidently we took care of that gray mold, but now—brace yourself, woman—now we may have leaf yellowing. Damnation for this cursed bad luck of ours!" He took a giant pull straight from the bottle. "By the way, what the hell is leaf yellowing?"

"Do not tell me that you spent two hours last Easter boring me to tears with your explanation of Linnaean taxonomy and you cannot figure out what leaf yellowing is. They are leaves that turn yellow, and we eliminated them last month."

He growled, slamming his hand down on the desk in exasperation.

Crossing to his side Catherine began to rummage wildly through a disordered pile of receipts from the desk. "Are you still trying to do those books?" she demanded incredulously.

"I am not altogether convinced that your estate manager had an accident." He snatched the receipts back. "He was more than likely taking the easy out and attempting suicide."

"Don't be ridiculous! I would never allow him to commit suicide before he finished the books! You must be mad." She promptly walked around to the front of the desk.

"We are going to visit Longbourn tomorrow morning. Please arrange for the carriage to be ready at nine."

Fitzwilliam grimaced and rubbed his hand raggedly over his face, slouching farther into the chair. She had a scrawny old neck that he could break like a twig. Tossing his pen onto the desk, he cast a malevolent look at her.

"Gracious, toughen up, will you? Why, when I was your age, I was a wife and a mother and the most brilliant hostess in all of London. I could throw a party for three hundred, go without sleep for days on end, and yet be ready at a moment's notice for Lord Louis's political meetings. I will have you know, young man, that in those long ago days, my opinion was greatly regarded in the highest circles of government."

"Excellent," he said as he handed her the ledger and walked from the room. "Then *you* finish up—I'm going to bed."

Late the following morning, Elizabeth and Jane were resting in their mother's room, looking through some of her keepsakes. To Elizabeth's amusement, there was little to be found among them of her childhood or, for that matter, the childhood of any of her sisters, but Jane's life was on display from birth until her marriage. Locks of hair, notes on her progress, dance cards from assemblies.

"I seem to have been somehow misplaced in here"—she smiled and indicated the albums—"along with my poor sisters, save but one."

Jane was humming a lullaby as she sat in her rocker, nursing her baby. "I was the first born, Lizzy. Firstborns are always fussed over more."

"I am not offended, Jane. I only wish I could have had the kind of closeness with my mother that you enjoyed."

"I truly think she would have wanted that, too, but then you were always much closer to Father, weren't you? You and Father were both cleverer than the rest of us. I imagine it probably intimidated her."

Lizzy leaned over to stroke the head of the baby as it nursed, then touched her own stomach absently. Darcy and she had decided that no one would be told of her pregnancy until they were reasonably certain that it would be successful.

They sat in silence for several minutes, Lizzy poring over old letters and Jane staring contentedly out the window.

"Lizzy?"

"Yes, dearest?"

"I noticed at luncheon yesterday that you avoided Caroline but spoke with Mr. and Mrs. Hurst. Do you still feel a strained relationship with Charles's sister?"

Lizzy broiled inside at the very thought of that wanton but schooled her appearance to appear complacent. It was neither the time nor place to have her talk with Jane about Caroline.

"I am sorry if in any way I offended you or Charles. It was not my intention. I was only lost in my own thoughts."

"I don't think anyone noticed." Jane placed her baby across her shoulder to rub its back. A small burp, one of a mother's greatest rewards, quickly followed. She settled the child at her other breast. "Darcy was attentive to her, kind and thoughtful as always, so I don't think she noticed anything untoward."

Lizzy froze. "Was Darcy speaking with her? I hadn't realized." She spoke evenly as she refolded the letters. At that moment, a terrified-looking serving girl knocked on the door. With a pale face and a trembling voice, she whispered that there were visitors downstairs.

Chapter 10

Since purchasing his commission in the spring of 1806, Colonel Richard Fitzwilliam had been involved in the worst battles of the Peninsular War, from the Battle of Vimeiro in 1808 through Coruna, Porto, Talevera, counter attacks at Fuentes de Onoro, Ciudad Rodrigo, pushing eastward to Salamanca, Vitoria, Maya, and into France. He had suffered through unthinkable deprivations, unbearable heat and mind-numbing cold, sloshed through mud and ice storms, fought savagely amid the slaughter and brutality of men driven insane with hatred and revenge.

And yet… all these seemed preferable to sitting across from his aunt Catherine for the two-and-one-half-hour carriage ride from Rosings Park to Lizzy's family home, Longbourn. If she poked his knee one more time with that bony finger of hers, she would be retracting a bloody stump.

"Cut line, Catherine!" he finally hissed.

"I beg your pardon! I realize I am old, Fitzwilliam, and feeble…" He snorted his opinion of that. "…*and feeble*," she yelled, indicating with a circle of her finger her heart area, "but I do believe that as matriarch of this family I have a right, nay, a certain obligation to point out the error of your excesses. Never mind that you are involved in illicit relationships with opera dancers and shop girls. Never mind that you cuckold titled members of the aristocracy..." Suddenly she halted midscreech, looking confused.

"Well, please don't stop there, Aunt. That cannot be the end of your tirade, surely. We have another hour yet to go sealed within this tomb of horrors, and you have not even begun to mention my excessive drinking, my indifference to my heritage, or my disloyalty to Somerfield House."

"Yes!! Oh, thank you, Richard, thank you. I knew there was something I had forgotten!" She laughed. "La, my mind sometimes..."

Fitzwilliam moaned.

The demon reentered her body. "You do realize that idiot brother of yours has yet to marry and produce an heir. Of course, I have tried to reason with him, but he's nonsensical, prancing about with those artist friends of his. You have obligations, young man, to your family, and yes, to your heritage. Heaven knows what you see in these loose women..." She flung up her hand. "Do not even dare to speak of it to me. I can interpret an eyebrow waggle when I see one! Only destruction and misfortune can come from this behavior. There is no future with harlots, as well you know. You are behaving like the very worst rakehell of Carlton House."

"Forgive me, but is there a very best type of rakehell?"

"This amuses you? If your sainted mother were alive today, this would kill her. Your health is failing you, Richard. Your career will be affected. I demand that you settle down and marry immediately. Why can you not select from the daughters of the many excellent families that are within our circle? My goodness, Pamela Tyson Briggs must be nearly twenty years old and has the hips of a good breeder."

"She has the hips of a good rhinoceros," he mumbled.

And the discussion began its inevitable spiral downward after that.

The carriage arrived at Longbourn at nearly half past noon. It was a vastly improved Longbourn from when Lady Catherine had last visited, that horrible day when she confronted Elizabeth, shouting out her views on the unsuitability of any sort of relationship between the poor country girl and Darcy.

Both Darcy and Bingley had together refurbished and beautified the old household of their in-laws. The garden was once again fine-looking, the house itself painted, the roof repaired, the drainage problem that had flooded the front yard and back was easily solved by Darcy, and the inside saw new wallpaper, sofas, tables, and draperies courtesy of Bingley.

It was an elegant little manor house that now stood before Catherine as Fitzwilliam handed her down from the carriage and they began to walk up the drive.

"Well, it seems quite an unexceptional home," she offered kindly. "Much better than I remembered." Perhaps the girl was not as much beneath her nephew as she had believed. Guiding her by the elbow, Fitzwilliam proceeded to lead her down a lovely little walkway through the front flower garden, a path that was lined by a beautiful low box hedge. It was a lovely day, the quiet interrupted only by the chirping of the blackbirds, the robins, the Tits—Blue, Great and Coal.

When they reached the first of four stepping stones that led to the main front veranda, a strange sort of keening noise began, faintly at first, growing louder and nearer in proximity. They stopped, quizzically looking first at each other and then about them. The sound grew more strident.

It was then that a medium-sized porker appeared from around the back of the house, streaking across their path and squealing at an ear-deafening pitch, followed closely by a barefoot, unkempt serving boy wielding a butcher knife and swearing like a drunken sailor. Catherine gripped Fitzwilliam's arm and tightly closed her eyes.

They stood frozen for several moments. "Steady on, old girl." Fitzwilliam struggled valiantly against the urge to laugh.

Catherine stared straight before her and swallowed. "Richard, really… you know how… Richard, I dislike… cant terms… such as 'old girl'… *Was that a pig?!*" she finally spit out.

His chin hit his chest as he bit his upper lip. It was a while before he could speak. "Actually, I believe that was dinner."

She winced and paled.

"Remember, dearest, in warfare it is always best to choose your battles." He squeezed her elbow gently. "Shall we proceed?"

She shut her eyes again and nodded.

❧

Compassion replaced the apprehension that had nearly paralyzed Lizzy after sending the serving girl to find Darcy. There was true anxiety in the face and mannerisms of the proud woman who stood before her, and Lizzy curtseyed respectfully to her new aunt. "Lady Catherine, I cannot tell you how happy we are that you are here."

Catherine nodded, nervously shifting her feet. "I am very sorry for your loss, Elizabeth. Please accept my condolences to you and to your family." Her voice wavered only once, and she cleared her throat, pulling fretfully at her gloves before continuing. "It was never your mother's fault, nor her wish, I am sure, that her garden is so small." Fitzwilliam turned his head to the side, coughing once to cover his bark of laughter.

"That is very kind of you to say, Lady Catherine." Lizzy motioned for them to be seated. "Your condolences are dearly appreciated."

"It's Aunt Catherine, now, Elizabeth." Catherine bestowed upon her a brief, strained smile that quickly faded. She stared at the ceiling, perhaps hoping to discover written there some mutually enjoyable topic of conversation. Finding nothing, she sighed.

"It's good to see you also, Richard, dear friend. How are you able to be away from Paris at this time?"

"I am on the diplomatic circuit, Elizabeth. I have been shuttling between London and Paris for several weeks now."

At that moment, Darcy entered the room. "Your ladyship," he said quietly as he walked toward his aunt and bowed, taking both her hands to kiss. Her eyes were on Darcy and him alone now. She fought back a warm smile that would have betrayed her joy, but her eyes grew moist with emotion.

"You look very well, Darcy, indecently so. Marriage certainly agrees with you. How is your heart?" She poked her finger into his hand to see if an indentation remained which would expose his water retention. There was none. She nodded in relief and smiled.

"My heart is quite well, Aunt Catherine. Thank you." He took a step toward Fitzwilliam, and they both shrugged at each other before pulling up their chairs.

⁂

The four sat down and made small talk for a while, Elizabeth surprised that her reaction to Lady Catherine was so different from their initial meeting. *Perhaps living with Darcy has made me more compassionate.* A strong feeling of love for this new family of hers welled up within her.

Like Darcy, Catherine was accustomed to a world where people jumped when she spoke, where people never entertained the thought of voicing an opinion contrary to hers. The Darcys and the de Bourghs and, for that matter, the Fitzwilliams, all took for granted their world of privilege, would know no reaction to their existence other than acquiescence to whatever they wished.

Experiencing a surge of empathy for Catherine, Lizzy noted the way the older woman looked at Darcy, all the love of a mother toward her own son. In the end, it turned out they had something very important in common after all—they both loved him dearly. Absently, Lizzy placed a hand on her stomach. She must have had a smile on her face, because she noticed Catherine was looking straight at her.

"Elizabeth?" Catherine looked deeply into Elizabeth's eyes. "You are with child, aren't you?" Elizabeth's and Darcy's heads shot up with a start, and Fitzwilliam let out a hoot.

"Are you, Elizabeth?" he asked with delight.

Darcy knew not what to say, but Elizabeth answered happily, "Yes, Aunt Catherine, I am."

"All right, Catherine, I realize you know all and see all, but how on earth did you divine that?" His aunt amazed Fitzwilliam with her ability to wheedle information from people that they had previously been able to keep secret from the rest of humanity.

"Well, Fitzwilliam, if you did something more than ride horses all over the Continent, drink inferior brandy, and chase loose women, you would be able to spend some time studying human nature. Elizabeth has placed a gentle hand on her stomach each time I have asked about her health, and then she has looked contentedly at her husband." Catherine smiled proudly.

"You are a wonder, Aunt!" he proclaimed.

"Yes, of course I am." She was mildly surprised that the fact even needed to be voiced.

When Catherine and Fitzwilliam stood to leave, Lizzy reached out and took her new aunt's hand in both of hers, sincerely regretting the shortness of their visit. "I am so sorry my father was not here to greet you. I know he would have been greatly honored by your visit, Aunt Catherine."

"Well, of course he would have been, my dear. Indeed, who would not?" Catherine patted Lizzy's hand in return.

Darcy walked up to her and kissed her cheek, "Thank you, Aunt, for coming today. It has meant a great deal to both Elizabeth and me." Tears welled up in his aunt's eyes as she placed a gentle hand on his cheek. "You have shown yourself to be the better person, and as always, you have my sincere admiration and love."

"Stuff and nonsense. This is family, and family is the most important thing in the world. Didn't I always teach you that, Darcy? Both you and Richard?"

Fitzwilliam tucked her hand under his elbow. "Indeed you did, Aunt Catherine. You taught us well."

"You must all come to Rosings soon, perhaps next month," she announced grandly as the door to her carriage was closed. Her mood was ecstatic, a new burst of enthusiasm for living putting bloom to her cheeks, and she looked lovingly through her carriage window at the smiling couple.

"Your father and sisters, also, Elizabeth. It will do them all good to get away from this horrid little house anyway." She settled back into her carriage then suddenly came forward, poking her head out of the window again. "Your sisters will benefit greatly from my experience. Mark me on this. I will have them drawing in two weeks. And I have heard your sister Mary is a great proficient on the pianoforte. She shall be able to use the one in the children's wing, as long as she's in no one's way and does not play too loudly." With that, she nodded to Fitzwilliam, and he signaled the driver to be off.

Darcy and Elizabeth spent the next few weeks with her father, ensuring that the new housekeeper was well established before they returned to Pemberley and Georgiana.

Try as she might, Elizabeth could think of little else but what Jane had told her about Caroline and Darcy, although she did not dare bring up the subject again, considering the last episode, what with her unfortunate destruction of furniture and all. However, a seed of doubt had been placed in her mind.

If she had only asked Darcy what had really transpired between Caroline and her husband at Netherfield, she would have eased her fears.

Darcy had been avoiding Caroline as much as possible the afternoon of the funeral luncheon; however, after seeing Bingley walk away from a conversation with him, the siren struck.

"Caroline, I didn't see you there, excuse me."

She had brought him a cup of tea. "I believe I prepared this as you like, cream and no sugar." Her eyes skimmed over his shoulders and chest and boldly wandered down farther before returning lazily to his eyes.

"Thank you, Caroline. That was thoughtful of you. I am sorry I have not had the opportunity of visiting with you."

"I understand your dilemma quite well, Mr. Darcy. However, I do admit to a fear that you have been attempting to avoid me this whole week. I hope that our friendship has not been strained because of your change in marital status?"

Caroline was generally all smiles and fluttering eyelashes at the sight of any man. Resenting her loss of Darcy, especially to Elizabeth, she exaggerated this affectation with him, thinking it made her more alluring and feminine. It did not.

"Not at all, Caroline. It is just that my time has been quite taken up elsewhere these past days. I am sure you can appreciate that the loss of Mrs. Bennet has been felt deeply by her family."

"Yes, this *is* the essence of a family in mourning, I have noticed." She gave a wicked little laugh as she motioned to Mr. Bennet, sitting alone in a corner with his back to the room and examining an old manuscript, Kitty and Mary arguing over who would take the last seedcake, and the Reverend Mr. Collins quoting Philippians to any poor soul who would listen. "The only thing wanting are jugglers and the elegant Lydia dragging along her dutiful husband, Wickham, picking at his teeth."

She had a hard, cruel mouth when she spoke, and Darcy wondered how he had ever thought her attractive. It infuriated him that she believed she could insult his wife and her family even as they mourned. "Please excuse me," he said coldly and turned to leave. Caroline clutched his arm and leaned in to kiss his cheek. "You are the most noble and long-suffering of men. I don't know of another who would take on this ridiculous family with such grace and dignity."

Darcy gently pried away her fingers. "You are gravely mistaken, Caroline. I am neither noble nor long-suffering. I merely love my wife with all my heart. Now, if you will excuse me, I need to speak with Mr. Bennet."

Caroline watched angrily as he approached his father-in-law, who stood to shake his hand and embrace him in thanks for all that Darcy had done. It was obvious he was gifting Darcy with some bookish treasure they both admired.

Caroline was furious. She was still only a tradesman's daughter, regardless how wealthy her father had become or how many peers she had bedded. The idea that the poor little country innocent, Eliza Bennet, was now among the elite of the land was galling in the extreme. Caroline decided it was time for her to either finally win him or trade in on their nasty little secret.

Chapter 11

In was not until late September that Mr. and Mrs. Fitzwilliam Darcy, Mr. Horace Bennet, Miss Georgiana Darcy, and Colonel Richard Fitzwilliam descended upon Rosings Park for a short two-week visit with Lady Catherine and her daughter, Anne. Aunt Catherine was overjoyed to have her two darling nephews back in her home and was determined to make this visit unforgettable, removing forever the strain that had tested them over a year before.

Nothing of the prior rancor would intrude on this visit, and she made certain that all were afforded the best of servants and rooms. As they began arriving in the late afternoon, Catherine greeted each personally and suggested they retire to their suites to rest and refresh themselves. Dinner would be served at eight that evening.

Lizzy was amazed at the difference in her reception by Lady Catherine, let alone the attention being lavished upon them all. Her father had his own suite of rooms across from theirs, both breathtaking in their splendor. The view from the balcony was beyond beautiful, the very best in the manor, overlooking the park and the lake beyond. Flowers, candies, and fruit had been placed everywhere, and a bath would be drawn, for both husband and wife in their respective dressing rooms, whenever they desired.

"This is unbelievable." With awestruck reverence, she wandered through room after room then out onto the massive stone balcony. The view of the park really was overwhelming.

"You needn't whisper, Elizabeth. Rosings Park is not holy ground, no matter what my aunt thinks."

"To imagine this is where you were sleeping while I was stuffed into Charlotte Collins's tiny little cottage, listening to her husband's ruminations on St. Paul and the place of women in the home."

"You are very much mistaken, madam." Darcy walked up behind her, wrapping his arms around her fast-expanding waist. "I've never stayed in these rooms before. These rooms are usually reserved for visiting royalty. No, my pathetic room was down another hall and much smaller. I think she's attempting to make amends," he whispered in her ear.

"Well...I must admit to it working—I feel a bit less animosity with every door I open. Why, look at this sitting room, William. I have never seen so much silk and gold in my life! Look at these murals! And even the ceilings are magnificent!!"

"The real telling point will be the bed. My old bed here is an abomination." They walked back into the bedroom toward a massive canopied four-poster surrounded with heavy brocade draperies. Beautiful antique tapestries lined the walls of a room crowded with elegantly carved furniture, crystal, and marble anywhere there wasn't gold. Darcy immediately jumped atop the bed.

"Good heavens! She really must be feeling guilty. This is certainly a great improvement on my old bed. I should have married you long ago, Miss Bennet—my back would have been spared years of agony."

Elizabeth turned to the huge double doors of their balcony, opening them wide to better enjoy the gardens that were just beginning to explode with autumn beauty and fall flowers. "The fragrance from these gardens is overpowering. It makes me feel quite wanton."

"Well, in that case, come over here, ducks."

Elizabeth turned toward the bed but barely saw her husband now lost amidst the curtains, pillows, bolsters, and feather covers. He raised up his hand. "I'm in here. Wait there, and I'll come over and fling you up top."

She ran giggling to the side and tried to leap up, but her legs were too short and her stomach grown too big. She bounced backward. Darcy was at her side immediately, and together, they laughingly hoisted themselves onto the mattress and then collapsed into laughter.

"Do you realize that King George himself, as well as many from the royal court of Vienna, princes from Spain, even the Dauphin have all slept in this very bed?" Darcy was struggling to pull them over toward the center.

"They may very well still be here..."

Georgiana was already speaking with Lady Catherine and looked up as her brother and Lizzy entered the room. "Good evening, Brother," she said as she ran to greet them.

"Ah, there you all are at last. Georgiana, Anne and I have

had a wonderful visit while you all were napping. I hope your rooms are to your liking and you are warm enough."

"Warm enough?" Fitzwilliam scowled. "Are you mad, Catherine? It must be nearly eighty-five degrees up there, at least as hot as Spain in July. It's late September, you know, not early January."

"Well, you may be accustomed to sleeping on the ground, exposed to heaven knows what with cloven-hoofed animals and ensigns milling about, Hottentots running naked here and there. But gently bred ladies, especially those who are breeding, need warmth and comfort."

Fitzwilliam bowed. "And, evidently, parboiling."

Lady Catherine's foot began tapping in aggravation. "Richard..."

"Very well, I stand corrected, once again, dear Aunt Catherine. If Elizabeth, Anne, and Georgiana are comfortable, the Hottentots and I can just open a window."

"Well, no need to drag foreigners through the house." Nodding majestically to her guests, Catherine turned toward Lizzy's father. "Mr. Bennet?" She smiled warmly, and her eyes twinkled. *My goodness, but he is quite a handsome man.* "Would you be so kind as to escort me in to dinner?" *Quite handsome.*

"I would be most honored, your ladyship." Catherine placed her hand upon Mr. Bennet's arm while Fitzwilliam escorted Anne and Darcy escorted his wife and sister into dinner.

All at once, the doors to the dining room were flung open to reveal a magnificently decorated table in the finest-looking room Lizzy had ever seen. There were huge murals painted on the walls and ceiling, and tapestries that rivaled any museum's. Vases of immense floral bouquets graced the halls and table.

Larger-than-life statues in cut stone stood in a huge circle that surrounded the dining area. Massive crystal chandeliers glittered above, being magnified by huge gilt-edged mirrors. It was breathtaking.

❧

"Darcy, you won't believe who's still in service here. Old Margaret MacLeod. Can you believe it? I've had my eye on that bit of fluff since she was a vixen of seventy-two." Each heavily ornate chair had its own footman who hurried forward to assist with seating.

Everyone laughed, except for Lady Catherine, whose eyes narrowed at him. "Richard! I really cannot condone this manner of discourse. Old Margaret has been with me practically from my conception, even before, if my memory serves. Please show her some respect." Lady Catherine took her place at the head of the table, motioning to the others to be seated.

"We often speak of you, you know," Catherine continued, nodding for the wine to be poured. "Yes. When I assure her you will probably one day be hanged, well, it just seems to cheer her so."

It was a pleasant surprise to Mr. Bennet, the atmosphere in the dining room so informal and lighthearted, everyone laughing and talking at once. It wasn't at all what he had expected. A rather unusual family, this, not the stuffy aristocracy he had vaguely remembered from his youth and had been dreading. Not in the least.

He looked first at Fitzwilliam, whose head had shot back with laughter at his aunt's remark. Mr. Bennet liked Fitzwilliam immensely, admiring his disarmingly easy manner and gentle wit.

He cast his gaze at his son-in-law, who had become a constant source of friendship and strength to him. It was evident now that the proud, arrogant man Mr. Bennet had feared would dominate his beloved daughter had never really existed at all. In reality, Darcy was a well-read, educated gentleman, and more importantly, someone who adored Lizzy, providing her with a happy, secure home.

He looked across at Darcy's sister, Georgiana, normally shy and modest away from her brother's side. She was relaxed and laughing heartily here, a reclusive beauty emerging in their midst.

Finally, he looked to his side at his beloved Lizzy, happier than he had ever seen her. *What a shame her mother could not be here with us, to see that our daughter is so blessed.* He felt suddenly overcome with the grief of his recent loss.

"Mr. Bennet," called Aunt Catherine. "No introspection is allowed at table this visit. There will be no serious thought tonight in deference to the youngsters with whom we find ourselves. We would not want to call attention to their intellectual inferiority in any way. We are family and will enjoy the time we have together, for too quickly it can be taken from us." Aunt Catherine looked meaningfully at him. She understood the devastation in losing a spouse, no matter how tenuous or difficult the relationship. It was half of your life that would never return.

"My very thoughts, Lady Catherine," replied Mr. Bennet after a moment's pause.

"Tell me, Mr. Bennet, how can we amuse you during your visit? Do you hunt?" Lady Catherine was spooning her turtle soup, blowing delicately to cool it.

"No, Lady Catherine, I am afraid I do not," Mr. Bennet replied, also sampling his soup. "I am certain an animal would sooner die of laughter than gunshot wound if I even made the attempt."

"Excellent, excellent. I abhor blood sports of any kind, animals being far superior to many people of my acquaintance." She selected a small roll and broke it, dipping it deftly into her soup.

"Charades? Do you enjoy charades, Mr. Bennet?" Motioning to a footman, she signaled him to clean up the crumbs that had mysteriously appeared around her plate after she broke open the roll.

"Unfortunately, I detest them, your ladyship." Mr. Bennet nodded when asked if he would like more soup, and his wineglass was again filled. "More often than not, I shout out the answer so that I can return to my seat and then feign embarrassment at my faux pas. With my advanced years, younger people usually assume me to be lack-witted and forgive me."

"Wonderful. Very clever." She was beginning to warm tremendously to her guest. "Anne thinks they are absolutely ludicrous, and I am in complete agreement with her. Even though she would be an excellent player, if her health would permit it."

They all glanced over at Anne, who blushed at the attention being shown her and then spit something she could not chew into her napkin.

"Cards, Mr. Bennet? Do you play cards?" Lady Catherine was pointing energetically to him with the leg of a small capon. "Answer this correctly, Mr. Bennet, and we have the promise of an exceptionally enjoyable two weeks ahead of us."

"I am afraid, your ladyship, that I tend to drift off while playing cards. At least I make a concerted effort to, and then I deliberately snore very loudly in the hopes that I will be thought enfeebled and asked to retire early."

Lady Catherine was overjoyed. "Thank heavens. Ladies and gentlemen, I believe we have the perfect houseguest in our midst, and I was afraid this was going to be a taxing two weeks of nonsense. Now we can just relax and do whatever we want. I, for one, plan to read, eat, and sleep, hopefully not all at once."

Mr. Bennet relaxed visibly. "I believe I know now why Lizzy loves this family so well."

Darcy had little prepared Lizzy and Mr. Bennet for the quality of service and the quantity of food served. There was at least one attendant for each person at table, and a stream of servers coming and going with all variety of removes—exotic meats and strange vegetables, out-of-season fruits, and generous libations. There was even a string quartet in attendance, playing at the far end of the room.

Mr. Bennet watched amazed at the carefully orchestrated ballet of service. If they were not so professional, he could easily have expected flying trays and dropped puddings, he mused.

"Darcy, I see you two have the imperial apartments up there in the golden tower. Quite an improvement, or so I was informed by your valet." Fitzwilliam had finished up his meal and was leaning back in his chair. "While you are dreaming happily in the suite usually reserved for royalty, try to keep in mind that I am located over the poultry house. It is just as you remember, I am sure—thumbscrews, the rack, chains on the walls. You both must come and visit me there once the ice lining the hallway thaws. Bring a physician."

Lady Catherine was unsympathetic. "When you finally marry—and you *will* marry, Richard, even if I have to drug you—you also will have the use of one of the larger suites. Until then, you will have to make do with the rooms you have always occupied." She leaned over to feed pâté to several of the whimpering dogs who had gathered at her feet. "I'm not made of money, you know."

"Well, I was thinking, dearest Aunt, that since I am now a famous and decorated war hero, you would feel obligated to accommodate me with one of the grander suites, a suite befitting my new stature and popularity." Fitzwilliam grinned devilishly at his aunt, who was summoning her faithful retainer, Jamison, to her side. She handed the man three of the dogs, one at a time.

"Well, I am surprised, Fitzwilliam. I am truly surprised." Catherine motioned for the fruits and sweet desserts to be brought in by the waiting footmen.

"What surprises you—that I would attempt to capitalize on my newfound fame in order to upgrade my rooms?"

"No, my dear, merely that you were thinking."

Amidst the groans and the laughter, Catherine raised her hand to protest. "No, I am quite serious, Richard. One hears such shameful reports about the conduct of our army, and you and your little flock of associates in particular were most scandalous."

"Yes, Cousin," beamed a mischievous Georgiana. "There were some very outrageous incidents hinted at in the papers. One in particular I always wondered about—did your officers really smuggle in ten opera dancers disguised as French prisoners?"

The shocked and discomfited look on Fitzwilliam's face made Darcy light up with amusement. He had heard the story two years before over an entire night of drinking when Fitzwilliam was home on leave. "Yes, old man, please tell us the story of the ten opera dancers."

Fitzwilliam shot him a daggered look. "It was not ten!" he declared, incensed. As they all waited in silent suspense for his further explanation, he exhaled a disgruntled breath. "All right, all right. There were only eight of them, and it was not as unseemly as you imply, brat!" He squirmed at the laughter now incapacitating them all and looked away, fighting his own laughter. In point of fact, it had been worse than unseemly, it had been downright debauched. The women actually were common Portuguese whores disguised as French prisoners, had been paid by a pool of money collected in a hat passed by him and his fellow drunken officers (eager to take advantage of the women's generous holiday rates) and then, to the accompaniment of their giggles, the women had been used as dinner plates. He vaguely remembered a drunken moment in which he was eating fried eggs and kippers right from within a naked woman's...

"He's blushing!" Elizabeth was delighted. "Oh my goodness, Richard, please enlighten us!"

Knowing what had happened, Darcy was in heaven. "Oh yes, Richard," he mimicked Elizabeth's high-voiced excitement. "Please enlighten us."

"This is not now, nor ever could be, dinner conversation!" He began to bluster with his embarrassment. "You are making me out to be some sort of deviant, and that could not be further from the truth! We lived in ungodly conditions and suffered horrible deprivations..."

"That must have been those times when the Duchess of Hanover was not renting a nearby villa in some quaint Spanish town. I heard you saw quite a bit of her..." Catherine's eyes were like slits. "...and still do."

Georgiana wrinkled her nose. "Ugh. She's such a peahen."

Darcy was laughing, his eyes dancing with delight. "Lord save me, I had not heard of this. And where was the duke during these encounters?"

Elizabeth nearly felt sorry for her cousin-in-law, but not nearly enough. She turned to Georgiana instead for the gossip. "Is she the one with the really large"—she hesitated, raising her hands briefly before her chest—"inheritance?"

Mr. Bennet stared in wonder. They may have been the bluest of the blue bloods, among the most aristocratic of aristocratic families, but a true family they were, with all the fights, teasing, suspicion, and retribution inherent in the word. It was definitely a family that was insane, *but whose family was not*?!

Georgiana, joining in the raucous laughter surrounding her, suddenly became uneasy when she realized her aunt was intently watching her. Catherine's concerns often shifted quickly and without warning.

"Georgiana!"

"Yes, Aunt Catherine." Georgiana jumped to attention, turning toward her imposing aunt.

"Should you not have made your presentation by now?"

"Yes, Aunt Catherine, however..."

"You must be nearly thirty-seven, I should think. Never tell me you have not been brought out yet."

Darcy came to her rescue. "Aunt Catherine, Georgiana is but nineteen. We decided to wait an extra year because of Elizabeth's mother's passing and the baby being due."

"Also, I *am* a bit shy and truly didn't feel really ready before this year." She gulped and stared nervously at her aunt. "I am not overly fond of crowds, you see." Huge understatement, that.

Darcy and Georgiana's eyes met. They had discussed this moment, but her knees still wobbled. He smiled his encouragement and nodded. The time had finally come, and there was no avoiding the unavoidable. "Aunt Catherine." Her voice crackled a little, and she began to blush. She inhaled deeply and closed her eyes before proceeding in her sweetest voice. "Dearest Aunt Catherine, would you be so kind as to sponsor me?" Georgiana, having finally blurted out her request, glanced momentarily to Darcy for reassurance. The barn door had officially been thrown open.

Catherine looked up, stunned that it was even a question. "Why, yes, yes. Of course." She blustered and rocked back and forth in her chair. "Who else in this room could possibly qualify as your sponsor?" Although she tried to look nonchalant, a small tear ran down her cheek.

Catherine had only two unfulfilled dreams in her life. One was to plan the grandest society wedding ever for her daughter and nephew at St. George's Cathedral. The likelihood that her daughter, Anne, would marry, now that Darcy was taken, was remote at best. She had swallowed that bitter pill and learned to live with it.

Her other dream was to present her daughter at court and preside over her coming-out. Anne had been too sickly all her life for either. Over the years, Catherine watched as her friends, one by one, had presented their daughters and then their granddaughters.

Finally, one of her dreams would be coming true.

Georgiana jumped up and ran to her, threw her arms around Catherine's neck and hugged her. "This will be a most wonderful year. I just have a feeling about it," she declared to everyone at the table as tears moistened her aunt's eyes. "There will be a new baby in the family, my presentation at court, finally, and..." Georgiana looked devilishly at Fitzwilliam. "Perhaps if we are very lucky, a bride for my cousin!"

Everyone toasted this proclamation—everyone except Fitzwilliam, who very dramatically turned over his glass to the cheers of the men and the indignant squeals of the women.

After dinner, when the ladies left the men to their cigars and port, Lady Catherine turned her attention to answering any questions concerning pregnancy and childbirth she believed Elizabeth must be anxious to ask her. As she was opening her mouth to speak, they heard a raucous burst of laughter coming from the male threesome remaining in the dining room.

She stood for a moment and stared curiously at the door. "It is so very odd. That always happens when Fitzwilliam and Richard entertain the men after dinner. I hope I have enough port set aside; it is something that they certainly seem to enjoy so." She sat back down and removed several pages of script from her ample bosom. "Now, Elizabeth, I have written down my beliefs concerning this time of your pregnancy, all of which I will give you to take home. I have knocked about this world much longer than you have, and since, thankfully, your mama is no longer around, I want you to feel free to inquire of me anything that may be concerning you at the present time."

Lizzy stared blankly at the woman, her mind a tumble of terror.

"Go ahead. Ask away. Speak freely. Never be shy." Catherine's smile quickly began to go grim. They stared at each other for several moments. "Elizabeth, are you deaf or merely dumb?"

"Thank you, Aunt Catherine, for your concern. You are very kind, but I assure you I have no questions." She bent her head over her ever-present book, praying that the inevitable discussion to come would be brief and somehow not humiliating. Or that a comet would fall from the sky and come through the roof.

Lady Catherine scowled. Lizzy was nearly five months pregnant, already quite large, and without a mother's guidance, even a mother as odious as the late Mrs. Bennet. "No need for such courteous regard for my sensibilities, dear. I give you my wisdom freely." Taking Elizabeth's hand, she proceeded to launch into a long list of mother-to-be dos and don'ts, making especially clear all her thoughts and opinions on fresh air and exercise while with child (she was totally against them both, the reason being that the child's limbs and lungs were much too small and thereby would too easily tire), on eating large amounts of fresh fruit and vegetables while with child (again, another problem in that they produced poisonous gas within the system, infecting the unsuspecting unborn), and on getting plenty of sleep while with child (positively the worst thing one could do, as that it placed the child in awkward positions for long periods of time that could cause facial disfigurement).

Also strictly forbidden were excessive laughter and spicy foods and any sort of physical expression of emotions, especially marital obligations.

"I suspect that it must frighten the baby, you know, all that bouncing and moaning and such. And then there is the problem of that protuberance repeatedly going in and coming out, going in and coming out, going in and coming out..." She rolled her eyes, all the while ensuring that Georgiana and Anne were not listening. After one or two seconds, she motioned Lizzy forward again, whispering very gravely into her ear, "At least that's what the earl and I decided when I carried Anne. In retrospect, however, it may very well have frightened the earl more than the babe."

Lizzy stared at her for several seconds, her lips twitching. "Thank you, ma'am," was all she could finally squeak out.

Chapter 12

It was turning into a horror of a night. There were room-rattling booms of thunder and frightening light flashes, both competing with the rain that slashed across her windows. Catherine heard and saw none of it, her mind occupied solely with events of the past. Though not quite an old lady yet, she was well on her way, or at least that was how she felt on nights such as these, the nights she sat alone with her memories.

She had more memories now in her life for company than realities, so she often would revisit her youth and what she considered her "useful" days. Just now she was thinking back to the summers and springs and autumns when families thought nothing of caravaning halfway across England and Scotland to visit, loaded with gifts and servants and dogs and children.

She smiled, remembering all those children, especially her two boys, so different from each other and yet boon companions, mischievous, competitive, and loyal as brothers. She laughed softly. Had there ever been a time they were together that was not disastrous for her?

She loved those boys fiercely, especially Darcy, as if he was her own, and perhaps he would have been if she hadn't chosen the path of prestige over love. She rarely admitted to regretting anything in her life, but that decision, in retrospect, had possibly been a mistake.

There was a soft knock on her door. "Come in," she called, dabbing away any trace of her melancholy.

"I wanted to say good night," Darcy said as he entered, closing the door behind him. It had been his lifelong nightly ritual when in residence to visit her before he retired. He looked sleepy but happy. Even with his hair tousled, without his jacket or cravat, he looked magnificent.

"Is everything all right? Is Elizabeth settled?" She reached out her hands to him.

"Yes, everything is perfect. She's rather overwhelmed by your kindness to her and to her father. I am, also, by the way. Thank you, Aunt Catherine." Darcy took her hands and, after kissing them both, he sat next to her on her settee. He tucked his aunt's arm through his own.

"Well, I behaved rather badly before. I do freely admit it, but only to you. I will deny this to anyone else. I was so very disappointed, you see. I had really come to believe that you and Anne would marry one day."

"I always told you we would not, though. Neither Anne nor I wished it. Why did it come as such a surprise?"

"This may come as quite a shock to you, Darcy, but I can be a very stubborn, opinionated person." She immediately raised her hand between them in order to deflect any protests to which he would certainly give voice. He remained aggravatingly silent.

"No, please don't contradict me." She lifted one eyebrow

at his firmly sealed lips. "I know my faults, few as they may be." When Darcy dared look, he saw she was grinning back at him, and he laughed softly.

"Tell me truthfully, how did Richard fare in overseeing?"

He groaned then laughed, rubbing his hand across his forehead. "Well, we just went over a few items; it will take awhile to review everything, but all in all, it is rather a mess. He cannot add, you know, nor spell, and his record-keeping is abysmal. He paid several merchants more than once, and we'll need to contact your tenants to see who actually forwarded their rents. I'll tell you one thing, however—he has a real love for the land. He kept excellent accounts of crop and timber proceedings. He'd make a good tenant farmer, maybe even an adequate squire one day."

"I tried to sit with him, but we're like oil and water so much of the time. He has no experience in running an estate this size, no training to speak of, being a second son, and yet he was the only one who stepped forward with assistance."

"I am sorry this all came about. I had no idea you were that ill, or we would have been here. As it was, he informed us about it later, when you were already on the mend." Darcy shook his head "Regardless, I should have contacted you; it was unforgivably childish of me to sulk so long, and he never told me about your steward or your secretary! Both incapacitated at the same time—imagine that. Quite a bit of bad luck, that."

"Don't give me that smug look!" She glanced sideways at him and smiled. "Yes, Darcy, I know they are old—just as I am, but, heavens, I cannot just push them out if they don't wish to leave! I owe them so much, and they are part of my family. They are just as much a part of Rosings as I am and I will keep them all around me for as long as I can!"

They sat together for more than an hour and talked about old times and memories long forgotten. They laughed a little and cried a little until Darcy let out a great yawn and stretched his arms.

"Well, I must get to bed, and so should you, Catherine." He helped her to her feet, and she suddenly appeared very tiny and frail to him. Gone was her immense wig, and in its place, a graying braid rested over her shoulder, most of her hair hidden under her favorite nightcap. Her feet were in slippers instead of the higher-heeled shoes she wore to give herself a needed inch or two, and the wrinkles around her eyes and face were more exposed now that she was unadorned with powder or lip rouge or the mysteriously moving patch that Richard and he used to laugh about.

"I don't sleep as much as I used to, Darcy," she said. "As you get older, it becomes harder to turn off memories, and believe me, they devil you to distraction at night. You get off to bed, though. The storm is still wailing outside, and you have a lovely young wife awaiting you who will want comforting during all the thunder. You need not give this old woman any more of your time."

Darcy hugged her tightly and kissed her forehead before saying good night. Then she was alone again. She thought that perhaps she would go to Anne's room and check on her, a mother's habit that would never die.

Picking up her candle, she went out into a hall dimly lit with wall sconces, smiling when she saw Darcy close the door to his suite of rooms. That was good—another of her babies would soon be safely in bed.

She padded her way down to Anne's suites to look in at her sleeping daughter, walking over quickly to close the windows that were allowing in some of the pouring rain. Clucking and grumbling, she brought a towel from the linen drawer and placed it over the rain-soaked carpet. *Will these children never learn to listen to me?* She harrumphed.

With relaxation still eluding her, she decided to check on the other rooms, to make certain servants were everywhere if needed. Jamison had done a good job, she noted to herself, as there appeared to be a footman every ten feet, the lightning outside illuminating the old mansion every few moments. She turned down the far hallway toward Fitzwilliam's rooms, laughing to herself at his earlier comments. He truly was rather far from the main part of the house. He and Darcy had always had the west wing of rooms to themselves whenever they visited. She felt bachelors should have their privacy, especially from a nosy old aunt.

She saw a faint light below his door. *Is Fitzwilliam still awake? It must be nearing 3:00 a.m.* The two footmen assigned there bowed at her approach, which she amiably acknowledged, and then on her signal, one knocked softly on the door. After a few moments, she heard her nephew's gruff bark. "Who is it?"

"Eleanor of Aquitaine. May I enter?"

She heard him chuckle. "Enter at your own peril. The Lionheart is in residence."

When the door opened, he arose slowly from his seat before the fire. Her eyes immediately focused on the balcony doors as she approached him. They were flung wide, allowing in the cooling air.

"Good heavens, Richard, it's raining outside, you fool." She marched over to the doors to close them, barely refraining herself from closing the windows also. "It is freezing in here."

"Aunt Catherine, the rain is not coming in this direction, and the room is only now beginning to cool down. God in heaven, woman, how can you think it freezing? Are you completely devoid of blood?" His eyes were scowling even as his lips fought off a smile.

"What a ridiculous thing to say! Of course I have blood, extremely blue blood, as you well know, and don't call me 'woman' in that tone, as if I'm a tavern wench or camp follower or French." He turned away to hide his grin as she sat in the chair next to his.

"What on earth are you doing up at this late hour?" She leaned toward him as he sat, stared at him with concern, noting the dark circles beneath his eyes. An empty glass and nearly empty whiskey bottle were on the table next to him.

"I couldn't sleep." His voice sounded a bit rough. "It happens to me now and then, especially during thunderstorms. That's why I like the doors and windows open. I dislike being locked in when it rains."

"You're a young healthy man; of course you can sleep. Don't be ridiculous! Apply yourself."

As he settled his back into the chair, he studied her face from lowered eyes. Much of the weight she had lost during her illness had not returned, and he noticed that her skin looked paper-thin, that her graying hair looked wiry where it was not confined within her braid. She looked brittle almost, fragile as glass.

"God, but I feel old tonight, Richard." She removed her cap to vigorously scratch the back of her head, yawning loudly. Gradually her eyes became accustomed to the dim light, and she saw a room in disaster—clothes and shoes thrown about, dishes resting upon the floor. His valise was opened but unpacked and rested on a bench beneath his window.

Her eyes grew huge. "Good heavens!" She was certainly wide awake now. "Richard Fitzwilliam! Did I not send up a footman to act as your valet this visit?" As any mother would instinctively do, she arose from her seat and began picking up shirts and pants, straightening chairs and stacking the amazing array of dirty plates, all the time grunting and clucking her tongue with every dirty stocking and wrinkled neck scarf.

This was the last thing he needed this evening. His eyes rolled in irritation. "Yes, you did… I sent him away."

She turned to him. "Whatever for?"

"He didn't like me."

"Well, of course he didn't like you—*he's a servant*!" After placing the folded clothes upon his dresser and the plates on the sideboard, she sat back down again. "To paraphrase our dear Lord, 'No prophet is without honor except with his own valet.'"

For a moment she engaged in a struggle to return her nightcap properly to her head, finally assuring herself that it was situated correctly. Exhausted from her ordeal, she sighed loudly. "Not all servants are as loyal as your batboy, O'Malley. Where is he, by the way?"

Fitzwilliam rubbed his eyes. "That's my batman, not batboy, and for some unexplained reason, he wished to remain in London and spend some private time alone with his wife before we return to Paris."

His aunt's only response was an uninterested, "How fascinating."

He regarded her with a mischievous grin on his face. "And what on earth are *you* doing up at this late hour, stalking the hallways like the demented Lady Macbeth?"

"Well, as people age, they don't need quite as much sleep as the young."

"In that case, I wonder that you bother coming up to your room at all," he mumbled then grinned when he saw her glare.

"I heard that. You are becoming much too cheeky, young man. I was talking with Darcy, if you must know." She smiled. "It was good to speak of old times again with him. But he went off to bed, and so should you!" Her gaze slid once again over the bottle on the table then to the empty glass. Their eyes met.

"You seem to be drinking quite a bit, Richard." Her voice had grown serious and quiet. "Much more than I ever remember, and I am growing more and more concerned about you, do you know that?" Her brow arched in inquiry as she watched him, waiting for his response. She was never one to be subtle.

"Awww... please do not start in on me again, Aunt," he groaned. His shoulders hunched forward, and he rested his elbows on his knees, rubbing his neck with his hand. "I am not up to battle form tonight."

"This is not to be borne, Richard, it really isn't. You have such a... a heaviness about you at times that it breaks my heart. If there is something bothering you, you should speak to someone. Speak to Darcy. Do you feel ill? Or do you still feel the effects of the battles? Your injuries? Waterloo? Talk to a doctor, perhaps, but find out what troubles you so."

He stared into the fire for a long time. Although the nightmares and flashbacks had, thankfully, begun to lessen, lightning and thunder always seemed to trigger his memories once again. How could he tell anyone of what he had been through, what he had done, what brutality he had seen these past ten years, battle after battle, mankind's atrocities to the weaker and more vulnerable? War was nothing but legalized butchery. It was condoned insanity.

The ghosts of the past would sometimes flood back with the dark, so he kept the candles burning. Still, he was haunted with the sounds of men and animals screaming, the smell of blood and gore in his hair and on his hands, the smell of urine and shit and fear, the screams of maniacs in the heat of battle, the soldiers who viciously raped and tortured. His eyes squeezed shut at the memories. The storm outside raged on.

"What are those?" she asked, pointing to a stack of letters strewn across his desk.

"Believe it or not, those are words of sympathy I am still writing to the families of fallen soldiers, telling each and every one how their sons and husbands died valiantly in battle in the service of their country." His voice sounded lifeless, and his eyes were red-rimmed. "That is finally the last of them, for now."

"Is there any truth to what you write?" she asked quietly.

He shrugged. "I've written hundreds of these letters, thousands perhaps. There is no way to know how even a fraction of them met their ends, but no one wants to think of a loved one dying without honor or dying alone. I just hope it helps someone, somehow." How could he describe to her the mutilated corpses, stripped naked and robbed, buried in mass graves with no hint of their identities? God, he felt so old tonight.

He was tempted to pour himself another drink but stopped, ashamed for her to see him. She looked different without the wigs and jewels, paint and elegant clothes, older than her fifty-odd years, rather grandmotherly and touchingly concerned. He would pour himself the drink once she left, and then maybe he could get a few hours sleep yet.

He reached over and grabbed her hand. "Thank you, dear Aunt, for your concern, but I shall be fine." He squeezed her hand and released it, fighting off the depression that could sometimes devastate him. He sensed that she watched him but would not allow himself to look into her eyes.

"Richard," she said softly. "Richard, look at me, Son." His eyes finally came up to hers. "Whatever is causing this melancholy, *do not* try to drown it in drink. It does not work." Tears began to well in her eyes and blur her vision. "I know that it does not work because I have already tried." By the end, her voice was a mere whisper.

They stared long and hard at each other. He broke the gaze first, and she could sense that he was closing his feelings, drifting from her once again. Soon his familiar emotional barricades would be up, and he would be joking and teasing to fend off his demons.

She stood, her heart saddened, not knowing what else to do or say. It had become increasingly apparent to Catherine that Richard had lost his place in the world during the wars, weighed down by all the years away, years of sacrifice made for his country, memories and regrets for what he had seen and all the years of normal living he had missed. He could not give up hope for a future now that the wars were over. Well, she simply would not let him. It was time for him to rejoin the living.

"You *must* somehow find your way home to us, Richard, in both body *and* soul." Her voice was gentle but firm, and she looked lovingly down at his bowed head.

"Remember, Son, *true character is revealed in the dark*." Her hand softly cradled his cheek. "And I have every confidence in yours. You are a fine man." She kissed his forehead. "Choose life, dearest." When she began to straighten, his hand brought her cheek back to his for a moment. She could feel the moisture of his tears.

"Good night, Aunt Catherine." He spoke so brusquely and low that it was barely audible. "And thank you." Reaching the door, she turned to say something but saw he was again lost in thought.

After the door was shut, Fitzwilliam studied the bottle he had automatically reached for… and stopped.

He replaced the cork.

"To bed," he whispered as he pushed back his chair.

Unknowingly, Catherine had won.

He chose life.

Chapter 13

Lady Catherine and Mr. Bennet spent the first day of their visit discussing common ailments and aches and commiserating with each other over the loss of a spouse. She personally took him on a tour of the house and grounds, and was very impressed with his knowledge of horticulture. He was particularly interested in her many greenhouses, where flowers, fresh vegetables, and exotic fruit were grown year round. He lingered in the greenhouse that specialized in experimental farming and talked at length with the head gardener.

"Mr. Bennet, I have saved the best for you, I think, for last." They came back into the house and headed up the long marble staircase to the second floor. The staircase ended directly before an impressively large set of double doors at the middle of the first landing.

"Whatever can you show me to exceed the wonders I have already seen, your ladyship?" he asked and then stepped back in awe when she opened the doors to the Rosings library.

"I believe we have the most extensive private library in

the country. My husband was an avid reader and collector of rarities." She arched her eyebrow. "I think if he could have, he would have moved his bed into this room. I want you to feel at home here."

Mr. Bennet walked hesitantly into the two-story wonderland and spun around slowly. He had never seen so many books, so many rarities housed in glassed cabinets, so many manuscripts and globes. A huge mullioned window with beautiful roses and twining vines dominated the back wall from top to bottom. There were four circular stairways leading to the balcony surrounding a second level of books and glass cabinets, and a series of sliding ladders against two of the main walls. It was magnificent.

"I am overwhelmed," he whispered as if in church. "Thank you, dear lady, for this."

"Not at all," she replied kindly. "You deserve some time to indulge yourself. You need only ring for anything you want." She pointed to a bell pull near the massive fireplace. "We shall see you later for dinner?" she asked. Still in shock, he waved her vaguely away and wandered into his holy of holies.

Elizabeth awoke later that evening to Darcy crouched on his heels before her, his hand resting gently on her stomach. She had fallen asleep after dinner as the others talked quietly around her, and now they were the last to retire. "Elizabeth, do you know that when I called your name I could see a ripple move across you here!" His eyes were filled with awe, and she smiled up at him.

"I noticed earlier that whenever you speak, I am able to feel him move slightly." This was the first time they allowed themselves to speak openly about their child. "It started earlier today, thank goodness. I confess I was beginning to worry a bit."

"You said 'him.' Do you have inclinations in that direction?" he asked, helping her to her feet.

"Right now I feel only happiness and relief that there is movement. Whatever it is will be fine with me. What of you, William?" He nodded and kissed her lips tenderly. They then held each other for a long time before turning to make their tedious, slow ascent up the staircase again. Even though she looked happy, Elizabeth's eyes were rimmed and dark, her body moving unsteadily behind the stomach that appeared suddenly larger each day. Darcy worried at the spurt of growth within her, anxious that perhaps there were twins coming, and she was so very petite.

"Your aunt seems very happy now about our marriage."

"Yes, she does, but her attention shifts are legendary. We will have to wait to see which way the winds blow."

As they entered her dressing room, Darcy called for her maid. "Oh, Lizzy, your legs are swelling up badly. You will not be walking tomorrow."

"No, please, William. I so love my morning walks. You know that."

"You will be better served by staying in bed resting with your feet up."

She tried to protest, but he put up his hand to stop her. It was then that he noticed a letter had arrived for Elizabeth from her sister Jane but had been left unopened.

"What does your sister write?" he asked, trying to divert her attention. He crouched before her to help remove her shoes.

"I've no idea. I haven't opened the letter yet, as you can well see." Lizzy was disappointed at the thought of not being able to get outside in the morning air, and her mood had shifted to definite crankiness. "Why do you care if I read the letter from Jane?" Yes, she definitely was in a bad mood.

He looked up at her patiently. "I care because she is your sister, and you love her. That is all. If you do not wish to read it, it is your concern alone."

Immediately regretful, she caressed her husband's cheek in mute apology then turned her back for him to rub. "I think your son has landed on my spine," she said softly. "Forgive my testiness, but I hate that you feel distress about me so much."

He leaned down and kissed her neck. "I myself may be a bit at fault and will try to restrain myself in the future, I promise. Just let me know whenever you need anything...or whenever you do anything...or whenever you want anything, so I can be there with you."

Elizabeth privately rolled her eyes then turned to smile sweetly up at him, pointing once more toward her back. Almost as soon as he began to massage her, the maid entered. The bashful young girl waited patiently for him to finish. "Please help your mistress get ready for bed," he said and dropped a kiss on his wife's shoulder. "I'll be back in a few moments." He walked into their bedroom and then into his own dressing room and closed the door. The letter marked urgent, which he had received from Bingley, sat on a tray. He picked it up and read it again.

Dear friend,

Would it be possible for you to come to Netherfield Hall as soon as possible? Please tell Elizabeth nothing. This is of a somewhat private nature, a very personal problem. Forgive the secrecy, but something has come up that may be important.

Yours,

Charles

He was impatient to learn if Elizabeth had received some further explanation in the note from Jane, and concerned that whatever its contents were, they would bring stress to his wife. But in the end, he decided to wait and not press her. The last thing he wanted now was to cause Lizzy any anxiety or concern. Her pregnancy was taxing them both to the limits, and they still had four months left. *Four months, kill me now, God.* He sighed and shook his head. If there was a problem, which must have been the case, else Bingley would not have even suggested keeping something from Elizabeth, he would quickly find a solution. But it *would* be best if he could evaluate it first.

For Darcy, not to be in full possession of the facts was pure hell. The knowledge that those facts could in any way distress his beloved wife was unacceptable in the extreme. *I hope I can help with what's to be done, whatever Bingley's problem may be,* he reasoned. *But I will protect Elizabeth and our child before anything.*

Chapter 14

Lizzy awoke the next day to a bright and beautiful morning, her husband already up and dressed, sitting at the desk in their room, writing a note. "Oh good, you're awake." He sat on the edge of the bed and kissed her tenderly. "How are you feeling this morning, Mrs. Darcy?" he asked, thinking to himself that she looked very drained.

"I feel a bit tired." She squinted back at him through sleepy eyes.

"I was just leaving you a note. Fitzwilliam and I are off for the morning to check on some timber problems. I have arranged for you to have your breakfast brought up here, and I would like you to spend this entire morning, at the very least, in bed and resting. Is that understood?"

Groggily nodding, she scratched her ear then lifted herself up on her elbow, foggy about what she had just agreed to and even where they were. She pushed her hair back to look blankly about the room and shrugged. "Yes, your lordship." She plopped her head back down on the pillow. A loud, indelicate yawn caused her husband to laugh.

"That's my girl," he said, kissed her, and was off.

Within an hour of his departure, Lizzy was up, dressed, and downstairs, ready for breakfast. "Lizzy, I had heard you would be staying abed today." Her father was surprised to see her in her walking shoes. He and Lady Catherine were sitting alone at the breakfast table.

"I cannot imagine why you would think that, Father, especially on a beautiful day such as this. Good morning, Aunt Catherine." Lady Catherine smiled broadly at Lizzy. "I believe William *was* somewhat concerned about my swollen feet, but as it happens, they are quite acceptable today, so I am going out."

"Well done, Elizabeth. I don't approve of lying about, nor would I allow unnecessary swelling in any part of my body, especially feet—very bad for the posture. There is no profit in assigning physical limitations upon oneself or in behaving as if one were an invalid. My own daughter, Anne, would have been a great exercise enthusiast if it were not for her own large feet. Quite threw off her balance."

"Elizabeth, where are you off to?" Lizzy's father began to rise, seized by a growing panic at being left behind.

Lizzy thanked the footman who set her breakfast dish before her and then grabbed several pieces of toast. "I thought I would cross the park and visit Charlotte Collins to see her new little one. Won't you join me, Father? I am sure our cousin, Mr. Collins, will be there, and it must be 'interesting' to hear his ideas on child rearing." Lizzy smiled at the apparent relief on the face of her father.

"Of course, I have provided Mr. Collins with all of his

ideas, including those on child rearing. It is best not to leave that sort of business to new parents. Anne and I will join you."

Mr. Bennet's eyes crossed. Although Catherine de Bourgh had proved a much more enjoyable companion than expected, the thought of both her and Mr. Collins within the same room was more than anyone could be expected to endure.

"Are you not awaiting Fitzwilliam and Darcy to return with their observations from this morning's inspection? And then, of course, Darcy still has to finish his notes from the other night."

"You are absolutely correct, Elizabeth. My, your vigilance toward Rosings is most admirable. Yes, I am sure that Fitzwilliam and Darcy will both want to get my input into whatever their observations are. I am afraid, Horace, that you will have to proceed without me."

A visibly relieved Mr. Bennet quickly regained his composure. "What a great disappointment this will be to Mr. Collins and his good wife."

"Of course it will be, the poor dears. However, they will join us tomorrow for dinner. Make sure they know this. I so hate disappointing those beneath me, you know."

Mr. Bennet deeply regretted not remaining at home with Lady Catherine. He felt miserable and trapped and duped by the fates. In his arms lay Charlotte's wriggly baby, Everett, a happy, rambunctious infant who was at the moment enthralled with Mr. Bennet's nose, attempting to force his little fingers inside. In fact, they were all feeling miserable and trapped, obligatory listeners as they were to the Reverend Mr. Collins's rapturous description of darling Everett's latest bowel movement.

Everett was an incredibly beautiful child, much to everyone's surprise, except for his adoring parents, of course. "He is my life and my joy, Lizzy," Charlotte whispered. "He has made everything worthwhile." With that said, she glanced meaningfully at her husband and then back at her boy. "How are you feeling, Lizzy? You look exceptionally tired today; are you getting enough rest? You know this childbearing is not as easily accomplished as we thought as young girls." Charlotte and Elizabeth were snatching snippets of conversation the moment the reverend turned his back. At this time, he was reaching for a shelf behind him, searching for his Bible.

Lizzy grinned and hastily whispered back when Mr. Collins turned his head to sneeze several times from his allergies, "I am feeling fine, Charlotte. However, I do find I am often in possession of not only titanic feet but also a baby suddenly leaping about whenever he hears his father's voice." Charlotte and Lizzy giggled toward the floor.

After a few more minutes of Mr. Collins's monotonous monologue, he suddenly closed his eyes and raised his hands in deep supplication to the Lord. Lizzy leaned toward Charlotte. "I also have had some very troubling dreams that have caused me to wake in the middle of the night. That tires me more than anything." Charlotte stared deeply into her friend's eyes, sensing a troubled spirit.

"Mr. Collins, could you and Mr. Bennet please excuse us? Forgive me, dear, but I must have a private moment with Elizabeth." Mr. Collins looked reprovingly at his wife, unhappy with this interruption of his personal address with God, while Mr. Bennet gamely attempted to rouse himself from a trancelike stupor.

Charlotte took her baby from Lizzy, patting and kissing the

child's head as it nestled happily into her shoulder. At her husband's continued silent reproof, she pronounced the sentence that no man on earth can withstand. "I am truly sorry, dear," she whispered, "but it is regarding *female trouble*." Mr. Collins's face drained of all color. "Female trouble," she mouthed once again, nodding.

With that, both Mr. Collins and Mr. Bennet quickly waved them off, avoiding at all costs any possibility of eye contact.

Alone outside in the sunshine and peace of her garden, Charlotte laughed softly. "I tell you, Lizzy, that is the most useful phrase I have learned as a married woman. No man seems to want to know about female trouble."

Laughing, Lizzy made her way slowly to a secluded bench.

"Now, what is this about bad dreams? I find that most interesting. I know I had many dreadful nights when I was carrying Everett."

Lizzy hesitated at first but then confided to her friend about her concerns with Caroline Bingley and Darcy, hinting broadly at their relationship years ago. She said she sometimes found herself dreaming of them together, or of her strangling and disemboweling the meddlesome redheaded witch, slicing open her throat or gouging out her eyes. Charlotte's eyes opened wider and wider with each description of mayhem.

"Well, that is rather serious, I suppose. Oh, but, Lizzy, you cannot really believe that Darcy would betray you. He is so much in love with you that he would never consider hurting you, and it is not in his character to deceive."

Lizzy smiled as she leaned her head back, letting the sunshine wash over her for a moment. "Oh, be honest, Charlotte. Don't you think it is within everyone's character at some point to deceive? Whether it be for good intentions or bad is the telling point, but I do agree that he would never deliberately hurt me or disgrace his family."

Charlotte sensed, however, that the idea of Caroline and Darcy still bothered Lizzy. "Didn't Jane say that Caroline was involved with someone? I had the impression she was almost engaged."

Lizzy snorted. "'Almost' is never as good as 'is' in my estimation. Also, 'engaged' is not nearly so fine as 'married.'" Elizabeth became more and more animated as she continued. "And 'married and settled on another continent' is best of all. Besides, Caroline's been 'almost' engaged more times than any other woman I know."

❧

By midafternoon, Darcy and Fitzwilliam were already waiting in the reception room for Lizzy and her father to return.

"Compose yourself, brat. Did you really believe you could just command her to stay home and she would?"

Darcy looked bewildered, affronted. "Yes, of course I did."

"Good God." Fitzwilliam shook his head. "Well, it's your head, Darcy. It was splendid knowing you." Hearing Elizabeth and her father in the hallway, he left quickly.

"Hello, dearest. Was that Richard rushing off? How odd. Oh, we had *such* a wonderful visit with Charlotte, and her baby, Everett, is glorious. Such a beautiful child emerging through the services of such a father—who could have imagined…?" Lizzy's voice trailed off when she saw the look in Darcy's eyes.

"Could you excuse us, please, Mr. Bennet? I wish to speak privately with *my wife*." Sensing trouble, his father-in-law was already making a hasty retreat.

Lizzy's eyes were huge as saucers and innocent as a newborn. "Whatever is the matter, William?"

"You know perfectly well what the matter is, *Mrs*. Darcy."

The certainty of this remark slowed her in her short waddle over to a seat. "No, I definitely do *not*, *Mr*. Darcy, else I would not have asked." Now riled by his rudeness, she plopped down primly, raised her chin to stare boldly up at her pacing husband, and impolitely kicked one after the other of her shoes to the side.

For a moment he just glared at her then stooped to pick each up. "I believe I told you, madam, to stay in bed and rest." He pointed directly at her with one of her shoes. "Your legs were very swollen and sore last evening. Am I mistaken in this?"

"Evidently, you are unaware that my legs and feet are much better this morning." Pulling up her skirt, she stuck her feet straight out for his perusal. Lizzy congratulated herself on the graciousness of her reply.

"And what of the staircase, Mrs. Darcy, that gloriously lethal block of greased suicide? Perhaps now you will tell me you had a footman assist you down the staircase, as I instructed you to do?" He loomed over her, his hands fisted at his waist, her shoes now badly mangled. "And do not bother to lie to me, Elizabeth. I have already asked."

She blinked her eyes rapidly, caught in his trap like a rat. "I walked very slowly and carefully, and held onto the banister." She hated him when he was right.

"Elizabeth, I confess I do not understand your flippancy. If you did not truly desire children, you should have told me outright!" Darcy knew the moment the words were said that he had jumped far over the line.

"Mr. Darcy!" She was up in a shot. "That is a terrible and unfeeling thing to say." Tears immediately welled within her eyes, and Darcy at once regretted his outburst.

"Dammit, woman. Forgive me, but I am very concerned. You have had so many problems with this pregnancy—the nausea, the swelling, the exhaustion. I want you in a controlled environment where I can ensure your safety and the child's health."

"Mr. Darcy," she choked out in anger, "I was at Charlotte Collins's home, not insanely rolling around in a field somewhere. We were with my father and Mr. Collins, two gentlemen who are capable of summoning help on the off chance that I would become seriously ill. And I *was* careful on the stairs! I was! If you think me so thoughtless and heartless that I would endanger our baby on a whim, then you should have entrusted this task to another and not have married me." With that, she hurriedly padded past him and headed toward the grand staircase, stumbling awkwardly in her haste, slipping once in her stocking feet on the slick surfaces. She clutched at the railing for support.

"Elizabeth! Slow down, and be careful!!" Darcy was at her side in a flash, grabbing at her arm. However, there was no way in the world that Elizabeth wanted to be touched by her husband at that particular moment, so she roughly pulled her arm away and used both hands to steady herself as she climbed the stairs. Darcy had no recourse but to walk behind her, angrily grumbling, all the way to the top.

Mr. and Mrs. Darcy were not seen at dinner that evening, but they were, unfortunately, heard.

At dawn on the following morning, a contrite Darcy pulled his wife's back against him in bed and kissed the nape of her neck. "Cut line, Lizzy," he whispered, his hands tenderly cupping her breasts. "You cannot still be angry with me." He could hear the chuckle as she rolled onto her back and looked up into those beautiful eyes she loved so dearly.

"Never tell me! I thought you were still mad at me."

"Well, yes, but you look so beautiful when you sleep, especially with your mouth shut, that I can't hold onto anything but absolute adoration."

"Does that insulting line generally work with all your wives, Mr. Darcy?"

"We'll soon see," he whispered back.

Lizzy and Darcy were very late for breakfast that morning, everyone else finished and discussing the day's activities. When they entered the dining room, they were both smiling like lunatics. Elizabeth avoided Aunt Catherine's eyes, realizing that she had just enthusiastically participated in activities that would certainly 'frighten the baby,' while Darcy looked around the room in a smugly contented manner.

"God, but everything smells wonderful in the morning, especially food..." He patted his stomach as they made their way to the sideboard.

"Yes, and especially when you haven't eaten the night before," muttered Lizzy.

"Well, thank heavens you are both up; it's nearly time to change into afternoon caps. I was afraid you would be ill all day." Lady Catherine eyed them warily then turned to order the replenishment of the breakfast buffet. "You *were* ill earlier, were you not?" Lizzy and Darcy nodded once and then avoided all further eye contact. "Oh, Darcy, you've had another letter delivered here. It's on the salver."

Darcy walked over to pick up the letter as Elizabeth passed behind her father, distracting him with a kiss atop his head while stealing leftover toast from his plate. She bent down to kiss Georgiana on her cheek.

At that moment, Fitzwilliam came sauntering into the room. "Good Lord," he groaned loudly when he caught sight of Darcy's preposterous grin. "Taking to sleeping in, I see." He walked over and took a plate from the footman stationed at the buffet. "*Very* reminiscent of Pemberley, I must say. And there is joy once again in paradise. Thank heaven."

"Fitzwilliam, is this not now your third breakfast? How in heaven's name can the empire afford to keep you fed?" Catherine studied her nephew's plate in awe.

"Well, dearest, actually, I have been known to shoot new recruits for their rations." He sat down happily and buttered his bread. "And besides, I much prefer to think of this as my first lunch."

Darcy read the note from Bingley with alarm.

Dear Darcy,

I am in dire straits, old friend. I need you at Netherfield as soon as possible. Please hurry, and again, please do not say a word to Elizabeth. Hurry.

Charles

"Is something wrong, William?" Elizabeth stood at the breakfast buffet watching her husband's brow darken.

"No, dear, nothing much really. However, some business does seem to have arisen that I will need to attend to as quickly as possible."

"No trouble at Pemberley, I hope." Georgiana quickly looked up from her tea.

"No, no, Georgiana." Darcy folded the letter and put it into his pocket. "But it is something I must see to as soon as possible. Elizabeth and Georgiana, I am afraid I shall have to leave for a while. I will notify you as soon as I can ascertain the length of my departure. Aunt Catherine, is that all right with you? I should only be a few days at most."

Catherine looked insulted.

"Whatever do you mean, 'Is that all right?' Why of course it's all right! They are both welcome in my home for as long as they like." Catherine picked up her teacup, muttering crossly to herself before her focus was derailed by several of her dozen or so dogs, now fighting over the scraps of ham and bacon and cheese she had thrown to them on the floor. "Spartacus! Ulysses! That is beyond enough! You are worse than spoiled children." Two King Charles spaniels stopped for a moment and then assailed each other once again. "Whatever gets into those two?!"

"A few days?!" Elizabeth stopped halfway into her chair. "William, what is the issue?"

"Nothing, dear. Boring stuff really. It is the... drainage. Yes. A new drainage system is being tested by Charles at Netherfield Hall, and I promised him I would help out if he ran into any difficulty." He leaned toward her to kiss her head. "Evidently, there's a glitch, and Bingley is in need of some consultation. You know I am widely regarded as the local expert on drainage."

Fitzwilliam mumbled into his coffee, "Evidently, water really does find its own level."

"I will go and speak with him," Darcy continued after glowering at his cousin, "and if I am unable to quickly remedy the situation, I will put him in touch with whatever professional is needed and return immediately."

"Go take care of that business. I can watch over our Lizzy for as long as you need, Darcy." Mr. Bennet, as usual, displayed no desire to know what problems there may be concerning physical operations of the estates. He immediately forgot about Darcy and hurriedly set upon finishing his breakfast so that he could return to "his" magnificent library.

"Thank you, sir. I will return as quickly as possible."

Elizabeth was worried, despite his assurances. She knew his every mood and nuance; he was plainly concerned about more than drainage. She smiled sweetly at Darcy when he touched her hand and kissed her cheek.

The following morning, Lizzy watched from their bedroom window as his horse rode away. *He sits so well on his horse, and he's so handsome and kind and brave and noble and sweet and bold and heroic.* Placing a protective hand over her stomach, she decided to have a word with their child.

"I must speak with you (we will settle on a name soon, I promise). Papa will be gone for a little while, helping out your uncle Charles. You will come to realize, when you are older (say one day old or two) that this is often the case with your father, since he is the most clever and decent of men. The happiness of many people, as well as our own, rests on his magnificent shoulders."

She walked slowly to the bed. Still morning sleepy and already lonely for her husband, she lay down, tenderly holding her stomach. She yawned and smiled.

"Your mama is very clever also, you know." Lying on her side she brought her knees up and cuddled her stomach in her arms. "I put a trinket in his coat pocket to surprise him, a locket within which is a lock of your mama's baby hair. Hopefully this will make him feel so hideously guilty and wretched that he will return to us sooner than he had thought."

This was, incredibly enough, Elizabeth's first brazen attempt at wifely maneuvering, and she was quite proud. She was also extremely tired, gently patting her tummy and pulling the cover up to her shoulder, relieved that the little sprite within her had finally stopped booting her spine.

~

"Mrs. Darcy, Mrs. Darcy." Her maid was trying to wake her by gently shaking her shoulder.

"William?" she garbled and looked around, blinking at the semidarkness of the room.

"No, ma'am, sorry, it's just me, Cara. A message was delivered to you from Mrs. Bingley. Lady Catherine thought it might have something to do with Mr. Darcy's errand. She said I should bring it right up to you."

Elizabeth tried to shake the sleep from her thoughts, surprised to look around and see a darkening room. "What time is it?"

"Nearly supper time, ma'am." Cara curtseyed and left the room.

Jane wrote a letter? Wait! I had another letter on the windowsill in my dressing room. Oh my, that was two or three days ago. Lizzy tore open the new message, dismayed with herself for not having read the earlier one.

Lizzy,

We have arrived safely and are having the most wonderful time. I feel very guilty about enjoying myself so much and Mama gone so recently, but after all that sadness, it is good to be alone with Charles and the baby, and just relax. Charles says we are to spend a second month here, so please do not worry.

Were you as surprised as I at Caroline's generosity? She has, unfortunately, broken off another engagement, evidently. It happened before mama's passing but is something of which we have only now learned. She arranged this trip for us shortly after that. You see, there is good in everyone, even Caroline Bingley. Give my love to Papa and William.

Lizzy got up from the bed and went to her dresser, searching for the original letter from Jane, and found it in the back of a drawer.

Dear Lizzy,

I wanted to let you know that Charles and I will be away for at least one month. We are going to Bath for a small vacation as a gift from, of all people, his sister, Caroline. It seems she has been planning this for a few weeks.

Perhaps that is what she and Darcy were discussing at Mama's funeral luncheon. They seemed to be very secretive; remember, I mentioned it to you? This does seem more something you or Darcy would think of, rather than Caroline. But I am being very ungracious, as this is a most generous gift.

I will write to you upon our arrival there. Have a wonderful time with Father. Give him and Darcy both our love.

Chapter 16

"CAROLINE?! I DIDN'T EXPECT to see you here. Where is Charles?" Darcy had handed the butler his coat and hat, and was immediately shown into the formal drawing room at Netherfield Hall. He looked hastily around the very familiar room, immediately feeling the vague apprehension he always experienced when alone with "the Viper," as he and his cousin sometimes called her. All of these emotions were evident on his face as Caroline beckoned to him, her hands outstretched in welcome.

"Mr. Darcy! How wonderful to see you, handsome as ever I must say! Charles told me to expect your arrival and that I should make you as comfortable as possible. You have only just missed our sister, Louisa, and Mr. Hurst. I believe Charles said he had some urgent matter and then suddenly galloped off. He asked me to have you wait for him, said he would return as soon as possible."

After giving her a chaste peck on her perfectly rouged cheek, Darcy took a seat across from her. She looked charming in a simple, pale country frock, the neckline of which, though low, was demurely trimmed with delicate ecru lace. Her fiery red hair was loosely tied back with ribbons. It was a puzzle to Darcy how she could continue in looks as she grew older, while her character seemed to diminish.

"Where is Jane?" he asked, nodding at her butler's offer of tea.

Caroline waved off the butler, announcing she would pour, and then stared blankly at him for a second. "Oh, yes! Jane. Jane has gone to London with the baby. She is seeing her doctors there."

"I hope they are in good health. That isn't the problem about which Charles means to talk, I hope?" Why ever would Jane be in London, seeing doctors, without Charles? Apprehension brought Darcy forward on his seat. If anything were to happen to her beloved sister Jane, Elizabeth would be devastated.

"Oh heavens, not in the least. She and the child are visiting her aunt and uncle Gardiner. Please calm yourself. Charles will join her there shortly. She is doing splendidly, and so is the little one."

Relieved, Darcy rested back again in the chair, fumbling for his pocket watch and instead finding the locket Lizzy had slipped inside. The feel and look of it was familiar and an immediate comfort to him, bringing a quick grin to his face. Lizzy knew him so well. The locket had been given to her when she was a small child by her mother, and it meant the world to her. It contained some of Lizzy's first baby locks. What a conniver she had become! *Well, maybe I can find out what's wrong and have my solicitor take over the problem. I can send off a message to Hastings & Griggs tomorrow and then leave early Friday morning, back home by the afternoon. Thirty miles is not a great distance.* That thought brought back a vivid remembrance of one of his and Lizzy's early battles, that long year before they wed, and in particular, his opinion that the thirty miles between Rosings Park and her parent's home, Longbourn, were not nearly enough. He winced with the memory. God but he had been insufferably arrogant with her in those days.

"Do you know what Charles was contacting me about?" Darcy asked finally, replacing the locket in his pocket.

"I haven't a clue. He doesn't share his personal information with me, and I don't share my private, personal life with him."

The hairs on the back of his neck stood in alarm, and his eyes glanced up quickly as Caroline advanced toward him with his tea. He tried in vain to deflect his vision from the exposed mass of white flesh bouncing toward him. Her low-cut gown, though perfectly in fashion, left nothing to the imagination. Nothing about Caroline was left to the imagination.

Suddenly, the immense parlor seemed too small to contain them both. In panic, Darcy began to rise, but she pressed his shoulder, encouraging him to sit back and relax. Her breast just slightly skimmed his ear as she leaned across him to pour cream into his cup. "Let me service you, sir," she whispered. "It's not often I have the opportunity to please a man as handsome as yourself." Deep cleavage loomed before him.

Elizabeth will rip my head off. His thoughts were calm, his castration inescapable.

"You *will* stay for dinner, won't you?" Caroline continued as she settled back into her chair. Darcy was squirming in her presence, and his reaction thrilled her. It was, after all, a reaction she was completely expecting. She could afford to go slowly now; they had all night. "Hopefully, Charles will be home by then. He must be mortified to have had to leave like this; he's such a kind soul and would be devastated if he thought he had offended you in any way. Pray, do not become angry with him over this and storm off."

"No, of course not, Caroline. Charles is the finest of friends. I don't mind in the least." His hand clutched Lizzy's locket.

"What do you hide in your pocket, by the way? I am intrigued by what little I have seen as you keep returning to it over and over. Is it some extravagant watch fob you've purchased? A diamond stickpin, perhaps, or a pearl? I do adore pearls."

"Far from it, Caroline." He held the locket loosely in his hand, the chain dangling. "As you can see, it is a very simple, inexpensive locket." She reached out her hand, and he reluctantly placed it there. "It is my wife's," he said meaningfully.

"A child's heart locket, with a cutting of hair. How quaint." Her lip curled as she swiftly assessed what little monetary value it held. Smiling politely, she turned the locket over and over in her hand and then returned it to him.

It was seven o'clock in the evening, and Charles had still not returned, so Caroline called for the dinner to be served. They ate a delicious meal and talked of old friends and common acquaintances. Caroline could be a very warm and charming companion when it served her purpose, and she had many humorous stories of Carlton House escapades. A gracious hostess, she frequently signaled for the wineglasses to be refilled.

"Caroline, this has been a very pleasant evening, but I am growing concerned about Charles. I hope nothing's happened to him on the road."

"More than likely his meetings went over time. Perhaps he has taken refuge for the night. You know very well that my brother, Charles, can easily become muddled. Business affairs go quite over his head. He doesn't possess your natural brilliance and experience. Frankly, I am of the belief that his attentions have been so taken with his marriage and new family that a problem arose of which he was unaware until it grew too late. He is most fortunate to have a friend like you to whom he may turn."

Darcy had never been someone who appreciated or sought out flattery and was becoming more and more guarded with Caroline's adulation. In possession of an accurate and honest opinion of himself, knowing most of his own strengths and admitting to more than a few weaknesses, he rarely courted others' approval. He eyed Caroline narrowly. Her brother had left the house and never returned, and she appeared unconcerned by it all? Something was not right about all this. The Caroline he knew was many things: self centered, amoral, cruel, calculating, and diabolical. However, she *was* a good sister. She loved her brother.

He was also keenly aware that they were alone, late at night, in this big house deep in the country, thirty miles away from his wife, a wife who would slaughter him if she ever found out. Good God. He had a mental image of three cackling Lizzies standing before a caldron, stirring and stirring what appeared to be his head grinning from the pot, his eyebrow raised in slight alarm. He chuckled and looked toward the fireplace.

"It's so good to see you smile and relax, Mr. Darcy. You are devastatingly handsome at rest but even more so when you smile. I daresay that your responsibilities have more than doubled now with your new family. I'm sure that you often wish to have some time away from all those obligations and give yourself… relief?" Above her wineglass, she smiled wickedly at him, the last word of that sentence a taunting question. Darcy's heart started to quicken as her tongue licked the rim of her glass. She had a long, soft tongue—he remembered that.

"It is too late now for you to return to your aunt's estate. More's the pity, the roads are treacherous after all this rain we've had. Charles would insist that you stay here in your old rooms this night. He will return soon, I am quite certain, possibly even later this evening. Let us retire into the drawing room and have our brandy."

❧

As they sat and talked before the warm fire, the effects of the wine and the brandy began to percolate, and Darcy had to remind himself not to have too much of a pleasant evening. But, God in heaven, it *was* a relief to be away from the stress of the baby and the estate problems of his aunt's, his sister's fears about the upcoming presentation, his cousin's guilt from the war—even if for just a few hours. Yes, it was like old times to sit here with Caroline and flirt and laugh and gossip about old friends. And drink. How long since he had felt the effects of a tad too much alcohol? In fact, he was already good and foxed. He closed his eyes as the room spun around him, resting his head on the back of the chair while he loosened his neck cloth. He shook his head vigorously and squeezed his eyes. Nothing was helping.

"Are you tired, Darcy? It is getting very late. Perhaps we should go upstairs to bed?" He was startled awake by Caroline's husky tone.

"No, no, 'm fine, Caroline. 'M a bit sleepy, though. Oh, thank you. And just what is this brandy called?" He reached out his glass to the footman who had opened a new bottle. "It's actually very good. Very smoooooth. Barely feel a thing."

"Well, that settles it. You will be staying tonight, seeing as you, my friend, are well into your cups. I'm certain Charles will be along by the morning."

Doubt and suspicion struggled for a coherent foothold in Darcy's well-oiled brain. His eyes narrowed at her, making Caroline begin to giggle. "Upon my word, of what are you afraid, Darcy? I am but a small, frail woman, and our history is long over, is it not?"

"Actually, Caroline, m' dear, 'm afraid we really have no history." Ha! Surprised her with that one. Darcy tried to keep his voice steady and friendly and his mind alert. She was still *somewhere* in that room. Had to be alert with Caroline, he remembered that.

"Well, then, you have no reason to refuse my hospitality. We are both of us adults, Darcy, and old intimate friends. If Charles has not returned by tomorrow, we can send a note around to see why he has been detained."

It all sounded so very reasonable to him, the words she spoke ones of hospitality and kindness, so why did he feel so guilty? Ach! He was just so bloody tired. Darcy shook his head to clear the fog that had settled in, and rubbed his eyes, and pinched the bridge of his nose.

"Is something wrong?" Caroline asked innocently.

"No, no, nothin' really, Caroline. Jus' wonder why Charles would ask me t' come here and then leave. Are you certain Jane's all right? Why would he leave Jane 'n city and come back here t'see me?"

"Well, I believe his problem is of a very personal nature, one that he felt more inclined to discuss here at Netherfield. Shall we retire?" Nothing was making sense to him, but Caroline never did make sense. He remembered that.

Chapter 17

Darcy had stayed in this house many times and had always had the use of this particular bedroom, so he relaxed and finally allowed himself to feel at ease. His first time here had been those long weeks when he met and fell in love with Elizabeth Bennet. During those early days, she had also stayed at Netherfield to nurse her sister Jane, who had become ill during a visit—*that* had been hard having her so near to him and then falling head over heels for her. Of course, there also had been the small problem of her hating the very sight of him. He had ached for her until returning the following spring, finally courageous enough to ask for her hand a second time after her initial rejection. Yes, this house had many powerful memories for him, but being alone in the place with Caroline should not be one of them and would be impossible to share with his wife.

He shuddered to think of her learning about this. The picture of three Lizzies boiling his head was replaced with one of her leveling a blunderbuss at his groin. Even though the images had changed, she was still cackling. If it was not so late, he would tie himself across his horse and escape to her father's home. But Mr. Bennet was not home either; he was at Rosings, too. He was, wasn't he? Darcy groaned and hiccoughed. His thoughts were tumbling around, rarely connecting or making sense.

Without thinking, he took another draw from the brandy bottle. Then another. *I am worrying needlessly. 'Course I am. Caroline and I have both matured and gone our separate ways. She's been 'gaged 'bout five times since we were together, at least five times, certainly enough times t' have forgotten me. And she's m' dear friend's sister, after all. Good ol' Bingley.* He convinced himself that perhaps he had misjudged her, and even if not, there was a lock on the hallway door that he had fastened and a chair secured beneath the knob. Ha! He chuckled to himself. She was crafty. He remembered that.

He sat heavily on the bed and unbuttoned his breeches. *This is so unlike good ol' Bingley*, he reflected as he tugged off one boot, the momentum of the movement rolling him over on his side. "Oooops."

He lay there, his cheek pressed into the sheets. They felt nice and cool against his skin. *Don't like mysteries. Like concrete things. Mr. Concrete. Mr. Drainage. I hope he and Jane aren't having difficulties.* (Hiccough) *I would hate to be in the middle of that one. Ha! I have my own marriage to contend with, without trying to figure out another's.* He righted himself slowly, shaking his head to settle all the confusion. He tugged off his second boot, reverse momentum continuing him over, facedown onto the bed in the other direction.

"Oooops." He began to laugh, softly at first and then loudly snorting as he pushed himself up onto his elbows. "Don't snort,

Darcy. Ha!" He nearly tumbled forward as he placed the second boot down very carefully next to the first, which had apparently moved, then stood to remove his shirt, pants, and smallclothes, staggering a bit. Respectfully holding the locket containing Lizzy's hair, he tried several times unsuccessfully to kiss it, finally placing it reverently on the nightstand next to the bed. "Good night, m'little angel," he whispered to his phantom wife.

He waved bye-bye just before he passed out.

He was dreaming of horses. Beautiful Arabians and Andalusians. It was a painting he had seen as a child come to life. They were charging toward him, but he was thrilled, not frightened. Suddenly there was his father's beloved mount, Jezebel, another distant memory from his childhood. Jezebel had been a magnificent beast. She and the grand old stallion, Caesar, were both responsible for many of the current stock in the Pemberley stables, and they were both running to him, as if they were young again and alive. All at once he was atop Jezebel, enjoying the wind blowing through his hair. She galloped faster and faster, her sinuous strong legs moving beneath him, changing again into a huge bird that flapped her wings, and off she was flying, over Pemberley and over Netherfield and over Rosings.

I should return home, he tossed about fitfully once or twice, fighting the joy of shirked duty, but he felt so free. No worries about babies or stress or complications, only the soft, sweet breeze on his face, now the tender erotic sensation of moisture tingling his neck and back, the sensuous feeling of arms and legs wrapping around him, full breasts pressed against his bare back. Oh my, but he really and truly loved women's breasts, was always guilty about his unseemly and unwavering obsession with them. It was indecorous and common. If only he could stop smiling. He grinned happily now at how warm and soft they were, like spongy pillows, firm and big. He imagined his Lizzy before him, slim once again as she was prior to the pregnancy, her breasts not the tiny delicate buds she possessed before but engorged with milk as they were now. He loved looking at them and touching them. *Hell*, he reasoned, *this is my dream. I can think whatever I want.* He hoped she would breast-feed the baby for a very long time, possibly twenty years or so.

His chuckle turned into a moan as he found himself becoming more and more aroused, and he began to force himself awake, forgetting completely that he was not at home.

"Lizzy?" he gasped in pleasure, a soft tongue moving inside his ear and then delicate nibbles on his neck, a small, warm hand reaching around from behind, taking him and stroking him harder and harder. "Oh God, Lizzy?!" He was waking quickly now. She was never this bold with him, not usually, anyway, and his hand moved instinctively backward to grab at her. But… something was terribly wrong. Something felt different. Rounder. Sitting suddenly upright, he turned to face Caroline. Lying behind him, she was wearing the sheerest of nightgowns and smiling the brightest of smiles.

And she was still intimately holding him in her hand.

"Surprise!" She laughed softly, her eyes sparkling in the moonlight.

Darcy swatted away her hand and jumped from the bed, then grabbed at the sheet to hide his nakedness, still staggering a bit. "What in bloody hell are you doing, Caroline? How did you get in here?" He stared stupidly at the adjoining door to the sitting room that now stood wide open, while the hall door still remained solidly barricaded.

"Why, I'm seducing you, Mr. Darcy." She grabbed at the sheet he had wrapped about him so tightly and, hand over fist, began pulling him back into the bed. "At least I am making an attempt at it! You could help me, you know."

"The hell you are." Darcy yanked furiously back on the sheet and stood fuming, his fists clutching the material. "The hell I will!"

"Oh, come back to bed. Don't be such a child." Her gaze drifted up and down his body as she stretched out her legs and pulled her nightgown hem up to her knees. Reclining seductively on her side, she patted his half of the bed.

"Mr. Darcy, you are aging uncommonly well, I must say. Your shoulders are much larger than I remember. In fact, *everything* is larger than I remember." Grinning, she arranged her hair over the pillow then rested her arms above her head, which lifted her breasts seductively.

"Honestly, Caroline, you must be insane… or a congenital idiot." She pouted and began again to reach for his sheet. "Oh, for heaven's sake, stop this at once!" Glaring at her, he angrily flung the sheet in her face then stomped over to the chair, roughly beginning to dress, throwing on his smallclothes, pants, and shirt. He was staggering still and somewhat drunk, his head pounding wickedly. He wanted to vomit. "You must be mad, woman! Have you no sense of decency left within you?" He sat down with an "oomph" to pull on his boots. "Sneaking in on a man… taking liberties… got me drunk…" He slammed down his foot to settle his boot firmer. "God damn it, Caroline! God damn it to hell! I feel violated! Of all the imbecilic, asinine stunts you have pulled, this is by far the worst." He slammed down his second boot to settle it. "How dare you do this to me! I gather that Charles and Jane are miles from here, and that I have been a dimwitted ass."

She rolled her eyes at him. "Well, you are never an ass, Darcy."

He shook his head in disgust.

"I did say, 'Surprise.' And I am not insane, as you say, or an idiot. I know what I want and shall not be denied."

"Bah! If you are not insane or an idiot, I recommend you not breed. Madness could be hereditary!"

"Darcy, do grow up!" She slapped the bed, sounding exasperated. "We are both adults, and there is no one who would know. Surely you must remember that the regent's court is quite sophisticated. No one thinks twice about this sort of thing." She pouted at his wrath. "Oh, you used to be much more fun."

"I am married, you idiot! Your brother is one of my dearest friends! His wife is my sister-in-law! Gad, I cannot believe even you would do this, Caroline," he huffed, trying to clear his head but feeling nearly as drunk as when he had retired. "Besides, our one brief moment together was over ten years ago, and I have moved on with my life, matured. What in the world would make you think I was even remotely interested in you? I really wasn't much interested back then, and believe me, madam, I am even less interested now."

She pursed her lips, vastly annoyed at his comments. "If you would only but notice I am in even better looks than I was when we were younger. Don't tell me you have lost all interest in sex since you married that country frump?" She sat upright in the bed, leaning back on her hands, thrusting her body into a seductive pose. "Or has she completely turned you away from the sport?"

She finally really looked at him, noticed his stance, his facial expression. Everything revealed his sincere disgust of her, and she began a slow rage.

"You're like a bitch in heat, Caroline, and I don't mean that in a Carlton House good way either. Truthfully, the only thing I do see from here, *Miss Bingley*, is that you are not a natural redhead. Good evening, madam," Grabbing his coat, he stormed out the door, slamming it on a tirade of curses and crockery from within. He was down the stairs in a moment, somehow saddled and mounted his horse, and was gone within fifteen.

It was still the middle of the night, however, dark and starless, and he was still drunk. He made his way as far as the Longbourn barns, where he collapsed into a mound of hay, falling fast asleep, his preferred companion to a scheming redhead being the old mama cat who curled herself up at his back. He slept as an innocent, deeply and gratefully, having escaped "the Viper's" clutches once again.

Unfortunately, however, he had not remembered to retrieve Lizzy's locket from his nightstand.

Chapter 18

Darcy's return to Rosings late the following afternoon was greeted with much excitement by his wife, relieved that the visit had been so much shorter than expected. She explained that the baby had missed him and that she was no longer comfortable sleeping alone, especially in that large, cold bed. They retired to their rooms soon afterward, and she watched as he removed his dusty riding clothes, curiously encrusted with hay, and as he handed his baggage to his valet to unpack. While he loosened his neck cloth, a hot bath was being prepared for him, and he slumped back on the settee, his arm snug around her waist.

"Did you see Bingley?" she asked.

"No, he wasn't there at all," he replied truthfully, omitting the fact that Caroline had been.

"I didn't think he would be. You know that letter from Jane I failed to open? It appears they are vacationing for the month. Why ever did he ask you to meet him at Netherfield, then?"

He mumbled something and then kissed her forehead, telling

her that his errand had been for nothing. "Just a miscommunication," he muttered into her ear. She quickly forgot it, happy he was safely home with her again.

"The big discussion at the moment," Lizzy informed him, "is Lady Catherine's sponsoring of Georgiana for her presentation at court! We have been up all night, talking." Her enthusiasm was infectious, and Darcy was soon laughing and marveling at her energy.

"We have even been pressing Fitzwilliam into rehearsing his services as escort, practicing the delicate art of train maneuvering."

"Is he any good?" Darcy shook his head in laughter.

"He nearly decapitated her, insists he cannot possibly be expected to work with tablecloth. We might need the real thing on which he can practice. Something in silk may be easier for him to handle."

"I wish I could share your excitement about this, but I am dreading her entrance into society. I won't have my baby sister anymore."

Lizzy smiled her understanding. He was such a very good man, and he looked so boyish with that wistful, half smile on his face. "She will always be your little sister, my love; you both will always be there for each other. But it is time she was allowed to spread her wings. We cannot delay this any longer."

Just then Georgiana knocked softly on their door. "Might I enter?" The quality of her voice seemed suddenly very grand and sophisticated to her brother's ears.

"You see"—Darcy's eyes looked cheerless—"she's already speaking as if she's a forty-year-old duchess."

Lizzy giggled and patted his cheek lovingly. "Enter, Your Grace," she called out.

The door was flung open to reveal Georgiana with her nose high in the air. She was wearing her childish flannel nightgown, the bosom of which was heavily padded beneath the material, giving her an overweight, matronly appearance. A tiara of dead flowers sat upon her head, and a tablecloth was tied around her neck, resembling a long white train. Epaulets from one of Fitzwilliam's old uniforms dangled from her ears. Lastly, her feet were encased in old socks, and she held Darcy's walking stick in her hand as if it were a scepter. She glided regally into the room, ruining the effect completely by bumping into a chair and rubbing her knee for a moment before standing up straight.

"You will now address me as the Grand High Exalted and Honorable Lady Georgiana Catherine Darcy, spinster, if you so please." She raised a quizzing glass of their late uncle Louis's to her eye to observe Darcy and Elizabeth. They all burst into laughter.

"Well, perhaps I have nothing to worry about just yet."

⁂

The following week, Darcy left with Mr. Bennet early in the morning, returning his father-in-law to Longbourn. Although Mr. Bennet had been horrified at the prospect of meeting Lady Catherine, going so far as to publicly bemoan his fate at being away from his books and projects for so long a time, it was with some degree of sadness that he left her company and Rosings Park. He shivered a bit at the thought of his empty house.

Darcy turned a concerned glace at him across the carriage. "Are you chilled, sir? We can stop for more hot bricks at the next station."

"No, William, I am quite warm. I was only thinking of Lady Catherine."

Darcy's momentary surprise turned to amusement. He nodded at his father-in-law. "She has had the same effect on many a younger and heartier person than yourself, sir."

Mr. Bennet smiled. "She certainly is a force to be reckoned with, is she not?" He turned his gaze out the carriage window, his mind drifting back in time for a moment. "You know that she was generally regarded to be *the* great beauty of the county in her day, do you not? I myself was quite enamored of her—from afar, of course. Many a young buck was."

Darcy smiled at the thought of Lady Catherine as a flirtatious young girl or as a beauty driving youthful Corinthians to distraction. "I am afraid that I can only think of her as my beloved aunt or as a well-coifed battering ram, depending upon her mood."

"I understand completely. Thinking of a parent figure as once enjoying youthful urges is a repellent and unpleasant undertaking for the young." Mr. Bennet suddenly laughed and turned to Darcy. "Shall I tell you something you may find even more disturbing?"

Darcy smiled back at him and nodded. "Feel free to do so, sir." Knowing Mr. Bennet's humor to be so similar to Lizzy's, he had learned to appreciate their talks more and more.

"I find her *still* damned beautiful."

Chapter 19

ELIZABETH HAD BEEN SPENDING more and more of her visit in her room, her swollen feet once again worrying her and her back throbbing. She received word of Caroline Bingley's visit as she sat drinking chocolate and resting. "Downstairs?!" she gasped. "Here?! To see me?!" She could scarcely believe her maid as the young girl ran off to search for a pair of slippers that would fit.

Elizabeth was frozen with fear. Dear God. Here, in the same home, were the two people that she feared most in the world. What if Lady Catherine turned on her now? She was in no physical shape to take them both on at once. Her first instinct was to take the coward's way out and faint. *I should really remain in my room, bolt the door, and send down my regrets. It is what William would want me to do. It is definitely unhealthy for me to venture anywhere, being as I am so unsteady and wobbly.* Then suddenly, she noticed that the swelling in her feet had receded. "Traitors," Elizabeth hissed.

Her trust in Catherine was tenuous, her confidence in

herself as solid as jam preserves. *This will not go well for me, I fear.* She struggled to her feet. *Why is William never here when I need him? Where is Fitzwilliam? Perhaps he can come down with me.* She sent her maid off to find him as a footman arrived to help her slowly make her way down into the parlor.

Well, here was a scene from hell, she thought to herself, a nightmare revisited. She found Lady Catherine sitting across from Caroline, both turning their dead, doll-like eyes toward her as she entered. Anne was also on the settee, along with her ever-present companion.

"Ah, Elizabeth. *Finally* you have come down and joined us! You have a visitor."

Elizabeth waddled into the room with as much grace as possible, horrified at the note of censure in Lady Catherine's greeting. "Yes, I see that, Lady Catherine. I am all amazement at this rare honor." Lizzy crossed the room and sat alone in a high-backed chair positioned between the two opposing sofas.

"We have had quite a revealing chat while waiting for you to arrive."

To Elizabeth's disgust, Caroline looked beautiful in a fawn green batiste gown that complimented her red hair and pale skin. She looked stunning. Lizzy hated her. She felt like a dead, bloated cow left out in the sun to explode.

"Although Miss Bennet and I are but recent acquaintances, your ladyship, I have friendship of long standing with your wonderful nephew, Mr. Darcy."

Elizabeth eyed the redhead from under lowered lashes. Suddenly she looked a little too redheaded, if Lizzy was any judge. *If I were only a little lighter on my feet, I could poke that beady little eye from her perfect little face.* "Evidently your memory is failing you, Miss Bingley. I am Mrs. Darcy now, and our acquaintance is of several years' duration, not moments."

Caroline grinned slyly, knowing she had made a direct hit.

"Elizabeth, must I remind you to please be more gracious to your guest?" Lady Catherine's voice was cold and cutting, and she glanced disapprovingly at Lizzy. *I knew she would turn on me at her first chance.* Lizzy sighed deeply. *I am done for, a bleeding corpse for when he returns. It serves him right.*

What Lizzy had not noticed, however, were Aunt Catherine's eyes narrowing as they looked back to Caroline. "You must forgive my niece, madam." She turned her attention once more to Lizzy. "We must strive to be more Christian, my dear. It is never good form to speak unkindly to tradespeople. We must always be unexceptional and condescending in our manner with those who are in service... and therefore beneath us."

Elizabeth, who had been blindly staring down at her folded hands, feeling miserable, froze. A glimmer of something—hope, maybe? Shock, certainly!—made her head snap up and her eyes dart quickly to her new aunt.

"I beg your pardon, your ladyship." Caroline, refusing to acknowledge an offence, seemed amused with the older woman's apparent confusion. A smile twitched at the corners of her mouth. *Older people are so dear.* She patted the edges of her mouth delicately with her napkin. *If only they did not hang onto life so tenaciously. Like this old goat.* She delicately sipped her tea, placed the cup lightly back onto the table then smoothed a hand over her very French, very fashionable, very expensive gown. She began to speak, but Catherine raised her hand.

"No matter, young woman. But please be kind enough to commence with your presentation. As you can see, my niece is with child and cannot be bothered for too long a period of time. And I do hope you've had enough presence of mind to bring chemisette samples." She nodded to Elizabeth and then to Anne. "And a goodly variety of fichu caps in sensible shades of white. I am hopeless when it comes to imagining these colors from their names. Don't you agree, Anne?" Anne nodded morosely, cleared her left nostril, and then gagged up some phlegm into her handkerchief.

Other than that, it was dreadfully quiet in the room. The clock on the mantel, a clock that had once graced the boudoir of Marie Antoinette, ticked on and on. Caroline stared uncomprehendingly at Lady Catherine, affronted by the Countess's error. "Your ladyship has been greatly misinformed, most likely by *Miss Bennet* here." Caroline looked angrily at Lizzy. "I am no *tradesperson.*" Her nostrils twitched at the mere scent of that word. She pulled herself up into a most majestic seated posture.

The condescension apparent in Lady Catherine's voice of before turned cold and hard. So did her eyes. "You must forgive *me*, madam. I was unaware before this that you are ill." Her eyes did not move; in fact, she momentarily did not look human. "Evidently you are experiencing the unfortunate effects of continuous brain seizures."

Caroline's natural color completely deserted her, leaving only the painted surface.

Lizzy stopped in midsip, her gaze darting back and forth over her cup, between the women.

Anne sneezed.

"Sorry...? What...?" Caroline sat rigidly on her chair. Her eyes were blinking wildly.

"My niece has already twice informed you of her name; however, as yet you seem incapable of retaining that small parcel of information." Caroline's eyes moved from Lady Catherine to Lizzy and then to Anne. Caroline returned her gaze back to Lady Catherine.

"But, *if* indeed you are not someone who has, unfortunately, become mentally impaired through disease or accident, then, I must say you have adopted a most impertinent attitude for a seamstress." A small, thin smile broke the gravity of Catherine's face, and her eyes became oddly merry again. "And, I would modify your prior comment to state that, although you are, indeed, a tradesperson, you are apparently not a very good one. You will never be a great success with this offensive sort of attitude."

"I-I-I don't understand what you are saying, your ladyship."

"Are you not Miss Bagley, the seamstress my dear friend Lady Jersey recommended?" Aunt Catherine raised her quizzing glass.

"No, madam, I most certainly am not!" A brilliant flush of color rushed to Caroline's face and was spreading from her cheeks into her bodice. In her indignation, she began to rock forward and back on the chair.

"Just who are you, then? Who are your people?" Catherine snapped open her fan and worked it vigorously. "By what counterfeit means have you gained entrance into my home?" Her eyes flashed with indignation. Quietly, Jamison and two footmen entered the room.

"My name is Bingley, Lady Catherine. Caroline Bingley."

"Bingley? Bingley? I have never heard of such an odd name. Are you quite sure?"

Unaware how to answer that question, Caroline opened

and then closed her mouth. "Of course I am quite sure! It is my name, madam! How would I confuse it?"

"*Bingley?!* No, no, no, that's too absurd. Are you having fun with me, missy? 'Bamming me,' as the young and uncouth would say? I must caution you, it is well known that I do not approve of merriment in any manner, very bad for the humors. Merciful heavens, Bingley indeed! How you can sit there and presume... I believe that is a variety of produce, anyway. No, no, no, you must be mistaken." With that final proclamation, Catherine proceeded to flatten out the pleats on her skirt and closed her fan.

Caroline was as bright red in her face as in her hair. "I assure you, Lady Catherine, my name is Bingley! Bingley!" If steam could truly be produced by the human body, it would by this time be escaping through Caroline's ears.

Lady Catherine turned toward Elizabeth. "Is this person actually known to you, or is she merely aspiring to an association with her betters?"

Elizabeth could hardly speak. She cleared her throat. "Yes, actually, I do know her, Aunt Catherine." Not wishing to expose her enjoyment, Elizabeth tried to enunciate from behind her teacup. "My sister Jane Bingley is married to her brother, Charles. Charles *Bingley*." Adding the name Bingley again so often had not been necessary, but it had been fun, so Elizabeth couldn't resist throwing it out there once again. "They have just had a daughter, Marianne Louise Bingley."

"Good Lord, *more* Bingleys?!" Aunt Catherine's eyes were ablaze. "Madam, I must tell you that I have a total of ten greenhouses on this estate alone and have no need of your fruits and vegetables. You will fail miserably in this business if you are as sloppy with your research as this indicates."

"Your ladyship!" Caroline screamed. "We are not fruit vendors! Or street merchants! And we are also not common snipes like your niece here and her ragamuffin family!"

The quiet that followed was dreadful. Truly dreadful. Lady Catherine arose slowly, all color absent from her face. She loudly slammed the business end of her walking stick onto the floor.

"My good woman, you are speaking of my niece! A member of *my* family. Married to *my* nephew. Her father is a gentleman, who has just left this house having been *my* guest for two weeks."

Caroline sat back and stared at Lady Catherine in mute shock.

"I believe I can speak for myself and for both Mrs. Darcy and my daughter, that we are no longer interested in your produce, or whatever it is you have come to sell. Take your samples and good day to you, madam! I say good day to you, and I mean it most heartily!"

Turning aside, she motioned to her butler. "Jamison, please show Mrs. Bagley out. Through the service door, Jamison! Not the front!"

Jamison had taken Caroline's elbow and was leading her, when Lady Catherine clarified her orders. He quickly switched directions, toward the service entrance, and Caroline was gone.

It was very quiet for several seconds, when suddenly Anne blew her nose and sniffled. Lady Catherine patted down some stray hairs on the side of her coiffure as she turned to Lizzy. "Well, that was rather enjoyable, wasn't it?"

Elizabeth's jaw dropped.

Catherine began to rise from her seat. "You know, dear, I don't believe we should wait dinner for Darcy. It looks like the rain may be delaying his return from your father's. I do believe he would be very vexed with me if you postponed your dinner too long."

Just then Fitzwilliam came running into the room.

"I came as quickly as I could. Is everything all right?" He stole a worried glance at Elizabeth.

She looked like the cat that had gotten into the cream. "Oh, yes, everything is quite splendid, thank you." Elizabeth reached for his proffered hand. With the proper momentum and one or two false starts, she was even able to rise from her chair. "I am famished!"

Darcy had indeed delayed leaving Mr. Bennet's house to return to Rosings after a light drizzle had churned the roads and slowed their journey. Mr. Bennet found he was not looking forward to an evening alone and begged Darcy to stay for early dinner, a favor which Darcy could hardly refuse. Kitty and Mary had been in London with their aunt and uncle Gardiner and were due to return later that week.

Although eager to return to Elizabeth, he was glad that the last two weeks had given him the opportunity of becoming better acquainted with her father, and wanted to continue in the man's good graces. They had surprisingly much in common—a love of books, an interest in horticulture, and a mutual devotion and respect for a certain young lady.

When the light dinner was served in his library and a fire made to warm the room, Mr. Bennet began to show his son-in-law some of his most favored manuscripts and drawings. Dusty books were dragged out from under piles of writings, and original sketches from a variety of well-known artists were thrown in stacks next to new plantings being readied for his experimental garden.

"Sir, you have a treasure trove here. Have you ever catalogued these items?" Darcy lounged in Mr. Bennet's desk chair, looking over a very rare handwritten Bible, whose pages were beginning to crumble from exposure.

"There is never enough time, William, never the right occasion. And I confess that I am not very well organized. Lizzy helped me often, but I've let it all go bad again."

"Well, I would be glad to send someone over to help you. Let me see about procuring a librarian for you, initially, every day for as long as it takes, and eventually, perhaps once or twice a month for upkeep. These are much too rare and valuable not to be protected."

Mr. Bennet was overcome with gratitude. Lizzy's husband was indeed a very excellent fellow.

Chapter 20

It was late when Darcy reentered his coach and was off again for Rosings. He was exhausted and aggravated with himself for delaying his departure for so long. *It will be well after midnight by the time we return now.* He parted the carriage curtains to look out. *I pray she won't be too worried.* He urged his driver to go as quickly as the wet roads would allow and then settled back for the long ride home.

Lately, his concern for Lizzy had become obsessive, all encompassing. She loved him deeply, and her emotions were so erratic that he feared causing her stress of any kind. *Hopefully, she will have reasoned that I stayed a while due to the rain and to comfort her father.* He watched anxiously as the terrain flew by the window. "Please try to go a little faster, Henry. Thank you," he called up to the driver.

They finally pulled into the great stone-encased portico of Rosings at just after midnight. Darcy thanked his driver, tipping him extravagantly for the speed and care he had taken, and then entered into one of the side halls. It was eerily quiet. Few lamps were lit in the foyer, and it seemed that only the night butler was awake in the great house. Walking quickly through the downstairs, he handed over his greatcoat then stood at the foot of the grand staircase.

He was always taken aback at the oppressive quiet that could chill a manor house this size. It was positively tomblike with the endless marble floors and soaring ceilings. Huge statues cast ominous shadows in the diffused light. The smallest sounds were magnified tenfold, and his footfalls had been echoing loudly in the halls as he walked. He cursed himself for a fool, he should not have stayed so very long at Mr. Bennet's. Hopefully, Lizzy was asleep upstairs and not in a frenzy of worry.

He heard a faint sound in the distance, up in the higher reaches of the house, somewhere in the dark. He waited.

It was Lizzy's voice far off in the stillness, coming from upstairs, possibly from the small sitting room in their bedroom suite. He could discern nothing of what she said, but he began quickly to climb the staircase, making it his heart's destination. After a moment, he recognized the deeper timbre of his cousin Fitzwilliam's voice.

Their voices grew in strength and distinction. He had just approached his sitting-room doorway when Lizzy burst into giggles at something Fitzwilliam had said, and then they both began laughing. It was in that attitude which he found them, vastly amused with each other, laughing so heartily, in fact, that they never heard the door open or Darcy walk slowly in behind them.

The room was stiflingly warm, the candles softly illuminating the two merrymakers as they sat side by side, their backs to the door. Both of their chairs were pulled up companionably before the fireplace, both sets of feet up on footstools, shoes off, coffee cups and biscuit remains on the small table between them. What struck Darcy was how tightly they held each other's hands across this brief expanse, their fingers interlaced. Fitzwilliam brought her hand up to his lips to kiss as they laughed once again.

It was really quite a cozy, heartwarming domestic scene—that is, if it hadn't been *his* wife and *his* cousin.

⁂

He stood there a moment before he was captured in Lizzy's side vision. "William!" she cried as she jumped up from the chair and ran around to him.

"It's about time you returned, brat. We feared highwaymen had snatched you." Fitzwilliam smiled broadly and began to stand. "We didn't even hear you enter."

"Evidently," Darcy said, his tone as ice cold as his eyes. Lizzy was just reaching her arms up to him when he stepped back and walked over to the decanter of port on the desk behind him.

"I was very concerned that you would be grievously worried about me, Elizabeth; however, plainly I had no reason for distress. It's good to see you in such agreeable company, alone here with my cousin. Such good company, in fact, that he was able to relieve your darkest qualms." He poured a glass for himself, downing it in one gulp, then he slammed the decanter down on the desk.

Fitzwilliam gave a grunt. "Aw, now...don't start to pout, Darcy. It doesn't become you. You'll get wrinkles on that elegant brow of yours." Chuckling, he sat back down in his chair to finish off his coffee, tossing back the few remaining biscuits. He was annoyingly amused, making Darcy all the angrier.

Lizzy stood motionless, confused, staring up at her husband. "Well, of course I was concerned. Richard has stayed with me for company and was a most welcome support. I would think you would be glad of that." She was both surprised and hurt at his reaction, her voice barely audible.

"Oh, I know he always has your best interests at heart, don't you, Fitz? In fact, ever since he first set eyes on you, Elizabeth, your best interests have been uppermost in his thoughts, amongst your other many lovely attributes." Lizzy gave a little gasp.

Fitzwilliam put down his cup and burped, excusing himself. He used his napkin to brush the crumbs that littered his pants and jacket, then began to wipe his hands. "A word of caution, if I may, Cousin." He turned to stare steadily into Darcy's eyes. His voice was very quiet. "Do not say anything now that you will later regret."

Darcy leaned back on the desk with his arms crossed over his chest, his eyes flaming daggers. The two cousins stared, unspeaking, for several tense moments.

The colonel sighed and shook his head. "Very well, I will leave you both. Good night, Elizabeth." He bent down to kiss the top of her head. "Don't fret, dearest—Darcy and I have had bigger rows than this, much bigger, and have survived." He tossed his napkin to Darcy as he passed. "Good night, brat." With that, Fitzwilliam left the room.

Lizzy turned and stared at her husband in disbelief. "William! How could you?!"

Darcy struggled to loosen his collar, a dark and hateful look on his face. "You know, that's another thing, my name is Fitzwilliam—Fitzwilliam Darcy. Not Fitz, not William, but

Fitzwilliam. I am awfully sorry if it gets you muddled, but there's nothing I can do about that."

He sat down heavily into the desk chair and immediately turned his back on his wife. *God, I am so tired, so very tired of waiting for this child.* Closing his eyes, he rubbed them with his fingertips, feeling guilty and petty and stupid. He knew perfectly well that there were no illicit feelings between his cousin and Elizabeth, knew he had made a muck of things this night when he should have been trying to keep stress from her, knew he should have told her of his disastrous encounter weeks prior with Caroline.

Lizzy struggled to pick up her shoes, waddling out of the room with tears beginning to sting her eyes. *I am supposed to trust him without question, and he does this.* She was fighting emotions from anger, to hurt, back to anger again. *How humiliating! How will I ever face Richard again? Ugh! My feet are killing me.* She wanted to go pound on Fitzwilliam's door so she could complain about her husband, but she realized that was not the best nor most logical plan at the moment.

Am I to have no friends at all? Is he allowed jealousy with no basis in reason, while I am allowed none, when he's already admitted to a relationship with that woman? She walked slowly to their room, angrily swiping away her tears with the back of her hand. *He looks very tired though. He looks tired and concerned.* She stopped by her dressing room and pressed a hand to her heart. *We'll be home soon in London, and then we can relax and wait for the baby.*

All will be fine as it once was.

It has to be.

For the first time in his life, he looked a mess. When he walked into her dressing room, he was barefoot, his hair wild, his eyes red-rimmed from exhaustion, his coat off, and his shirt pulled out from his pants, the tails hanging down from his waist. Their eyes met.

"May I?" he asked quietly. She had been standing before the immense French doors overlooking the garden, staring unseeing across the moonlit expanse, a brush in her hand. She turned to look at him, tears streaming down her cheeks, and she nodded, offering him the brush.

"Thank you," she whispered. "I find it hard to hit upon a comfortable position when I sit on that antique vanity chair, and I am so very tired tonight." He tenderly took the brush from her hand and began to glide it through her soft, shiny hair, then set down the brush to loosely braid it for her. Quiet surrounded them.

"Shall I rub your back?" His hands lay warm and gentle at her waist.

She nodded, and when she looked up, she saw him watching her in the dark reflection of the window. *He looks so sad and tired*, and her heart broke for him. She placed her hands upon his.

"Forgive me, Lizzy," was all he could manage to say as he pressed his forehead atop her head. She turned quickly and reached up, struggling onto her tiptoes to wrap her arms around his neck. They stood like that for a time, holding each other, then softly kissed.

He led her over to the bed, helping her up the two steps and onto her side to rest. Sitting next to her, he began to massage her back and hip through her night robe, a sad, embarrassed look upon his face.

Finally, he spoke. "I'll apologize to Fitzwilliam in the

morning. I don't know what came over me; I think I may be losing my mind. I saw the two of you holding hands and…"

She turned on her back and placed a finger to his lips. "Hush! It is all right, William. I was crying, and Richard heard me, so he asked if he could enter. He was almost equally concerned, you see. I welcomed his company because it was frightening waiting alone for you with that storm blowing."

Darcy lay down beside her and gathered her into his arms, pulling a coverlet over them. "I don't think he sleeps well. Catherine is concerned and wants me to speak with him; it seems that some nights he just roams through the halls. I imagine he was lonely as well."

"He is such a kind man, William. Truthfully, if you had come home an hour before, you would have seen a hysterical banshee instead of a wife."

He took her palm from his face and kissed her soft hand.

"You're tired, William, and you worry much too much. Let's go to sleep. This will all be over in a few months."

He grunted loudly. "I'll collapse well before then," he murmured in her ear.

The following morning, he found Fitzwilliam at breakfast early, as he knew he would. Fitzwilliam had to be off and on the roads to make London late the following day.

"Morning, Cousin. And how are we feeling today?" Fitzwilliam called out when he saw Darcy approach the breakfast room.

"*We* feel like a complete ass, thank you very much, and how do *you* feel, Cousin?" Grabbing a cup of coffee, he sat down across from Fitzwilliam, stretching his long legs before him.

"Very well, actually. Finally slept like a baby." He was eating three eggs, ham, and bacon. He also had a huge slice of buttered, freshly baked bread, which he was carefully stuffing into his mouth. "God, you are so predictable." He let out a hoot of laughter. "I knew you'd feel absolutely miserable this morning. Made the whole thing completely worthwhile."

"You truly are a black-hearted bastard." Darcy roughly rubbed his sleepy eyes and then destroyed the achingly perfect coif his valet had given him by rubbing his hands through it. Resting his cheek on a fist, he gazed in amazement at the quantity of food his cousin could consume.

Fitzwilliam stopped in midbite. "What?" he groused defensively then swallowed. "An army moves on its stomach."

"Well, it better not be going far. You're going to be puking before the first road station." He motioned with his hands for Fitzwilliam to pass food to him.

Fitzwilliam handed him an empty plate, sliding an egg onto it and a huge slice of ham. He then reached for the scones for both of them.

"I'm going to try to get an extended leave the month Lizzy's due to deliver. Let me know if you need me for anything before then." Fitzwilliam leaned back in his chair and stretched, finishing up his morning coffee.

Darcy nodded. "Thank you, by the way, for staying with her last night. At least *you* kept her calm. I, however, managed nearly to give her apoplexy." He grabbed several pieces of toast.

"I know you, brat, and I know what is eating at you. There is no evidence for it. Many women never miscarry; some miscarry and then go on to have a perfectly normal delivery. Your mother had a history of troubled pregnancies. Her death was unfortunate but not something that will happen to Lizzy. You are worrying unnecessarily and driving everyone insane."

"Then why are you taking leave at the time she's due? Hmm?" It appeared that Darcy's appetite was returning with a vengeance as he reached for Fitzwilliam's nearly empty plate to bring it across and add any remnants onto his own. He grabbed for more toast and pastries.

"That's entirely different," Richard said. "That's me. I am a military genius, or hadn't you heard? Battle-ready whenever needed."

"You're an idiot, and you want to be there to torture me when the child is born," replied Darcy, finishing up the ham and scones.

"That's true, too." Fitzwilliam nodded deeply and in complete agreement. "Where do you go from here?" Fitzwilliam had poured himself one more helping of coffee and was ready to push away from the table.

"We go directly to London; I want Elizabeth to be as near to the best medical minds as possible. I have left nothing to chance, believe me. Her physician is world renowned and has assured me he will be in residence, near Pemberley House, the entire final month. Furthermore, he guarantees that the midwife he has secured is the very best. Also, I have contracted with no less than three other physicians and apprised them of the situation. They have all agreed, for a not-so-slight remuneration, to remain in town that last month of her pregnancy. It is all costing a small fortune, but the peace of mind is priceless." He stared unseeing out the window, not bothering to hide his distress from his cousin.

"Something else is bothering you—out with it."

"What if there are twins in there?" Darcy shook his head.

"She's so big, much larger than I had imagined she would be at this point. But mayhap it is because she's such a tiny thing. I don't know anymore. The proportions appear all off to me. And her delivery is not until sometime at the end of January." He sighed heavily. "At any rate, do not forget about Georgiana's debut and presentation. That will require Elizabeth and me to reside in London from before Christmas and then throughout the entire social season."

"I *have* been trying to forget. Georgiana cannot be ready yet for this. I'm not ready yet for this."

"She can, and she is. She and her maid have already arrived in London, and she's commenced shopping. From what I have heard, she and Elizabeth are planning a major campaign. To them, we go to London for the dressmaker, not for childbirth. It's a good thing I'll be there to keep Elizabeth in check, or she'll be wielding that immense body of hers around every shop in town. As Georgiana's other guardian, you will be expected to be on hand for the presentation at court and the presentation balls and Almack's, so save some leave time for then, also. One must never forget Almack's."

Fitzwilliam threw down his napkin and pushed back his chair. "Well, evidently I'll be using a lot more time this year than I had anticipated. I do have it coming, unfortunately, so that should not be a problem. Surely, though, you will want to present her at court yourself alone?" He looked hopefully at Darcy. "You are, after all, her closest male relative."

"Forget it, Richard. We will jointly have that pleasure. As her co-guardian, I would not think of depriving you of this bliss."

Fitzwilliam smiled evilly.

"I've just had a delightful thought. Do you realize, Cousin, that if our baby girl is not successful in her first season, if she does not snag a prospective suitor, if she is not married by next year, you will have to go through the whole season again, Almack's and everything, and without me. I'll be in Paris with the returning army of occupation."

"Black-hearted bastard," Darcy mumbled to his cousin's retreating back and finished off the last of the coffee.

Leaving Rosings had been harder on Lizzy than she could ever have imagined three weeks before, let alone two years ago.

Once Darcy and Lizzy had entered the carriage, Darcy called up to his driver, "Henry, take your time going home. I'm bound that we're going to enjoy this solitude." He settled himself back into the seat and pulled Lizzy to him, resting her back on his chest for support then, finally beginning to relax, he stretched long legs out to the seat across from them, and they took off toward home.

They rode for a long time in silence, his cheek resting on top of her head, his arms encircling her and holding her close. "This could go on forever, and I wouldn't mind," she whispered sleepily.

Her back didn't hurt for once, and her feet weren't too swollen. She was in heaven. He kissed the top of her head and rested his cheek there again. Both of them closed their eyes to the rest of the world.

"Oh, William, in all the excitement last night, I forgot to tell you something." He groaned a little in reply, preferring his drift into unconsciousness to conversation.

"You will never guess who came to see us the day you

escorted Father home." He barely heard her voice. The carriage was rocking like a cradle, and he was half asleep and half awake. "Caroline Bingley."

The name slowly made its way into his brain but elicited no impression for several seconds. Suddenly, his eyes popped open.

"Who did you say?" He attempted to sound casual.

"Caroline. Caroline Bingley." Lizzy giggled at the memory of the beast's meeting with Lady Catherine. "I imagine she actually wanted to see you but had to settle for Aunt Catherine, Anne, and me." Darcy's heart began pounding, his voice trying to remain steady.

"What did she have to say for herself?" he asked.

"Nothing too much. At first I was horrified having both Caroline and Aunt Catherine alone in a room with me, but believe me, it wasn't long before Caroline was being eviscerated by Aunt Catherine." Lizzy gave a delighted chuckle, any attempt at pretending indifference being long forgotten.

"I'm sorry to be so gleeful about it, but it was truly a sight to behold, watching someone else being attacked by your aunt. I have the distinct impression either Aunt Catherine is completely dotty or she is the slyest fox in the henhouse."

"More than likely it's a combination of both." Darcy closed his eyes, trying not to panic. It didn't sound as if Caroline had said anything to her. He should have just told Lizzy the truth about Netherfield, saving himself from another lie. *I can tell her everything later*, he reasoned, *after the baby is here*.

"She didn't give any explanation for a visit though?" he asked.

"No. I truly think that Aunt Catherine had her so confused that she completely forgot what she was about." Darcy smiled, relieved that Caroline's deception and his visit to her were still unknown to Lizzy.

"That's the first time I heard you call her Aunt Catherine instead of Lady Catherine." He kissed her head again and rested his chin on it. "I think we are making real progress."

"I'm feeling more part of the family every day. After ten or twenty years, I shall be right at home in all this luxury."

"Get some sleep, will you? I need the rest." He pushed his hat down over his eyes and closed them, letting his thoughts ruminate. *Why in the world had Caroline come all that way? What could she have up her sleeve?* He began drifting deeper and deeper into unconsciousness.

"By the way"—Lizzy's voice sounded groggy—"where is my mother's locket? I should like to be wearing it when I have the baby."

His eyes opened with a shock. The locket! Oh, dear merciful God in heaven, he didn't have the locket. He had left it at Netherfield and never returned.

"William? Are you sleeping?" He didn't answer her and remained very still. "I'll pester you tomorrow," she murmured and was soon snoring softly. Darcy, however, was not going to sleep any time soon.

Volume Two

COLONEL RICHARD FITZWILLIAM AN OFFICER

1817

Here's forty shillings on the drum,
For those that volunteer to come,
With shirts, and clothes, and present pay,
Then o'er the hills and far away.

O'er the hills and o'er the main,
Through Flanders, Portugal, and Spain,
King George commands and we obey,
Over the hills and far away.

Hark! Now the drums beat up again,
For all true soldier gentlemen,
Then let us 'list and march I say,
Over the hills and far away.

—Traditional soldiers' song,
Peninsular Wars

Chapter 1

Fighting a brutal and sudden gust of frigid November wind, Colonel Richard Fitzwilliam was making slow headway in his march across Mayfair, advancing doggedly toward the townhouse of his cousin, Fitzwilliam Darcy. Onlookers not distracted by their freezing extremities saw a tall, broad, and very familiar soldier passing by them. Hunched shoulders beneath a nearly floor-length, battered military greatcoat, muscular legs resembling tree trunks encased in scruffy military knee boots, gloved hands grappling at the cloak's broken neck closure. This pathetic excuse for an ensemble was topped off by a large, dark bicorn hat that had been pulled low and was plain and battered, absent of fancy feathers or brass.

Bent against the cold and sleet, he was presently lost in thought, having just left his general's home. It was November 11, 1817, and Colonel Fitzwilliam was returning from a disturbing morning meeting with Arthur Wellesley, the Duke of Wellington—his mentor, commanding officer, and dear friend.

"Halloo, Colonel!" someone yelled from a passing coach,

a stranger to whom Fitzwilliam automatically raised his arm in response, smiling pleasantly and nodding. Two gentlemen passing by noticed this and boldly approached him, insisting on introducing themselves when they realized who he was. They pressed their cards into his hands and, winking broadly, hinted that they would do right by him if he would merely endorse one of their enterprises, lend his name to one of their products, or if he would allow them to use his likeness in any way. He smiled politely, as he always did, saying he would certainly consider their requests, and then excused himself to move on, pulling his collar up higher and his hat lower, ostensibly against the cold.

It had been like this for the two years since Wellington's Anglo-allied army's magnificent victory at Waterloo, and still the city of London was mad with patriotic fervor, and Richard's valor having long since elevated him to the lofty status of celebrity. For several years now, the military's every battle, their wounds, and even in some instances their deaths, had been liberally seasoned with florid prose then served up by the daily news sheets as entertainment. Animated discussions on every corner encouraged opinions to flow as freely as wine, thereby enriching the dreariness of the baker's and the blacksmith's lives, alleviating the tedium of the shopkeeper or the farmer.

It was the Battle of Waterloo that propelled him into this truly legendary status. Stories in the daily papers immediately after his return had revealed his wounding and heroic struggle to survive amidst the onslaught of barbaric French soldiers swooping in for the kill of this high-ranking British officer. That the story, as it now was told—told and retold and told again some eighteen months after the fact—bore little resemblance to the reality of the event... well, that seemed irrelevant to the editors.

Devotees called out to him from windows, from passing horses and carriages, or as he lounged within the gentlemen's clubs. It made no sense to him at all. He was the same man who had spent ten years living like an animal in Portuguese and Spanish mud, often grudgingly caught in the reflected glory of being one of Wellesley's favored officers. Then, shortly after Waterloo and his highly publicized heroics, he returned home to a frenzied reception.

He squinted through the sleet to check for carriages prior to his crossing, wondering if the adoring masses would be as impressed were it known that a moment of abysmally poor judgment had him fighting alongside his men that fateful day, that a military blunder on his own part had caused his beloved horse to be shot out from under him. Stupidly caught by a sudden French cavalry charge, he was a very high-ranking officer trapped in the wrong place at the wrong time, then tossed into the bloodlust of battle. It was the reason officers stayed remote, far back from the fighting, a dictum he had failed to follow. "Kill the head and the body will die," common knowledge in warfare. It was his misjudgment to have lingered so long near the front, and his lovely Domina was brought down, pinning him beneath her and crushing his leg.

"Hold square! Hold square!" He roared the command to his men as he lay injured on the open field before them. His officers defied that order, a first for them, and had run out to drag him back within their square to safety, completely ignoring his threats of courts martial. He never did follow through on those threats, musing that they had all fought to save each other that day, not for patriotism. Over and over he fired the rifle that had been unceremoniously thrust into his hand, a rifle grabbed from a dead soldier, eventually ending up slashing and butchering blindly with its bayonet. The French soldiers kept coming for him, and too many of his men, his band of brothers, thieves, and drunks as they were, had been injured or killed trying to defend him. *If I told the masses that I had to piss into the barrel of the rifle in order to clean it, would they still be so enthralled with the story? Oh yes, Fitzwilliam, you're a regular Lord Nelson.*

He waved in his good-natured manner to another well-wisher then hurriedly turned a corner, momentarily relaxing his shoulders a bit, protected from the storm by a large building. Now that there was relative peace in Europe and a new world order on the horizon, he would need to decide what to do with the rest of his life—whether to stay in the army or resign his commission, work for Wellington at the Board of Ordnance. It was a hard decision either way.

Staying with the status quo would mean continuing in a peacetime army and a lifestyle within which he no longer felt comfortable, a lifestyle of loose women, drinking and carousing, and avoiding the responsibilities of adult life. He paused in his steps for a moment, forgetting just why any of that was so bad, and then continued on, laughing softly.

Then again... he could follow his mentor, work on the Board... well, that would necessitate embroiling himself in political infighting and backstabbing. Rather like battling the Frogs but with better meals and no honor. And he knew Wellington. Wellington was ambitious, ruthless really, and would not stop until he was made prime minister. The man was obsessively victory driven. It was the main thing he admired in his friend and a character trait they shared in common.

Then again… he could return home and fight twenty-four hours a day with his wretched older brother, Regis.

Any of the choices before him made him want to gag or get good and drunk.

❧

Another shout out came from a group of young Corinthians racing by in their phaetons. "Whoo! Hoo! Well done, Colonel!" "Capital fellow!" "Come have a drink with us!!" He smiled vaguely then winced as one phaeton slid sideways on the ice, almost toppling itself and nearly injuring the precious horses. *Goddamn stupid idiots*, he thought as he smiled and waved. They righted themselves soon enough and laughed uproariously at their own daring.

The wind was kicking up more now, and it was biting cold. *Bloody hell, did Darcy move his goddamn house? I don't remember it being this far of a walk.* He should not have told his batman to go home and get warm so that he could continue alone and think. *Thinking is highly overrated* he decided as he stomped his feet while awaiting traffic. *I'm going to freeze my fucking balls off if I don't…* "Ladies…" Smiling warmly, he bowed and tipped his hat, flirting outrageously with the three giggling lovelies who slowed their pace as they walked by, whispering and staring back at him as they did. His spirits rose considerably when they spun around to follow him.

There definitely was an upside to fame.

The sad truth was that the one thing he really would have wanted to do with his life was the one thing that he could not. In his heart of hearts, Fitzwilliam wanted nothing more than to be a simple country squire. He wanted to work the soil, chop trees, and visit his tenants. He wanted to read and actually understand cattle and crop reports, or bicker over terms with tradesmen. He wanted a quiet, neat little home and the chance to doze off in a chair in his own garden, after he'd had a good pipe and glass of port. He wanted to smell the daisies handed to him by an adorable little moppet daughter, and to teach a son to ride a pony and how to fish. He wanted an innocent, demure, quiet, and biddable heiress wife, a shy lady who would be a model of English propriety by day and a whore for him in his bedroom by night. He sighed and grunted at his own foolishness.

After all, he had no money of his own.

He was a well-bred English second son.

⁂

He also was thirty-two years old and had spent the first blush of his young manhood sitting in mud and worried about getting enough food for his troops. Enough food and enough blankets, bullets, boots, horses, etc. Scavenging and stealing had occupied much of any time not spent in battle or being blind drunk, and the years had just slipped away. To his mind, he was too old now to start afresh, had no home of his own and no income. Of course, he could ask his father for any amount of money his heart desired, but he could not and would not take advantage of a man he so respected. He was back to wondering what to do with the remainder of his life. Most second and third sons could be assured of benevolence from the firstborn who inherited all; however, once his father was gone, he was certain Regis would cut him off without a farthing. They hated the sight of each other.

He truly should plan for the future, but not today.

Well, I have finally struck bottom, he suddenly realized. *I am wandering the streets, destitute, lost and homeless, and waxing maudlin. I'll be sobbing on some poor bastard's neck soon, drunk as a lord. If I am very lucky, perhaps Darcy will adopt me.*

A gentleman slapped him on the shoulder. "Good show! Good show!" the man exclaimed then planted himself squarely in Fitzwilliam's path. "I say, Colonel, may I call you Dick? Excellent! My, you're a tall one, aren't you? How's the weather up there, what? Ha! Ha! Dick, did you happen to know my cousin? Major Billy Hench? Average height, light hair. Oh, surely you knew him. He was at Waterloo, also, and made quite a show for himself there."

Fitzwilliam stared down at the diminutive man, expecting a little more information, and when it wasn't forthcoming, he decided he would speed things up a bit.

"Excuse me, sir. Was your cousin also with the Coldstream Guards?"

"No, he was with the 72nd. To tell the truth, he did not actually see much action in the battle, per se, but he did attend the Duke of Richmond's rout the night before. Surely you were there yourself! No? Are you certain? But my dear Dick, you must be mistaken. It was *the* place to be, I am told! It's quite a humorous story, actually; he became frightfully drunk and nearly missed the whole fracas. Got in the game rather late in the day, I'm afraid. Oh, I am certain you must have met him—he wore a red uniform jacket with black boots."

Oh my God, some people should just be drowned at birth. Fitzwilliam smiled down politely at the eager gentleman. "I don't recall meeting him, sir, but I am certain I heard about his bravery. If you will excuse me, I must be going. I am late for an important meeting. Good afternoon." *Thank God this bloody war is behind me.*

~

Truth be told, though, the war years were not completely behind Fitzwilliam, whether he acknowledged it or not. Unknown to his friends and even to some of his family, Fitzwilliam had been experiencing the aftermaths of war—battle fatigue and its accompanying nightmares, flashbacks, and panic seizures.

The more these symptoms plagued him, the deeper he fell into his old cycle from the years before—drinking, women, and gambling—until he himself was becoming aware of the adverse effect it was having on his physical, as well as mental, health.

The tide turned upon one comment from his beloved aunt Catherine. "*Character is revealed in the dark, Richard.*"

Damn old bat.

The remark had struck home. He knew his dark had become more and more appalling, possessing moments he would be loath to have exposed to the world, behavior of which he had become deeply ashamed.

One day he would open up to Darcy. He knew that a day would come eventually, probably during a drunken weekend and after several bottles of whiskey, and maybe then he could begin to confront the demons that tormented him.

He wanted so to have better life.

He wanted so to be a better man.

Chapter 2

THE COLD WIND BIT viciously at the little slice of his face still exposed to the elements. He held his hat down and averted his eyes from the sting of the icy crystals that were blowing everywhere. One more blasted block to Darcy's, and he was already muttering scandalous oaths into his scarf. He heard the horses' whinny at the last minute, just in time to avoid crashing into the back of the private carriage sitting alone in the square.

His initial aggravation was soon replaced with concern for the coach's livestock. *I dearly hope this groom is sensible enough to bring his horses out of the blasted cold,* he worried. A cavalry man by trade and a country gentleman in his fondest dreams, he rated horses on the same level with few people he knew, and on a higher level than most others. He approached the man, speaking loudly to be heard over the wind.

"Excuse me, John Coachman."

The man turned a jaundiced eye toward him, only to have his demeanor dissolve into the excited wonder to which Fitzwilliam was now accustomed. "Well, bloody 'ell! I say, I say.

You're 'The Waterloo Colonel,' ain't you, sir?! Let me shake your 'and, sir. Let me shake your 'and. Well, cor, what a honor this is, to be sure! Bloody 'ell!"

Nodding, Fitzwilliam firmly clasped the man's hand in both of his, saying loudly over the wind, "I don't think it wise to keep your cattle still like this for much longer. Perhaps you should walk them around for a bit."

"Imagine you takin' a interest in these poor, dumb beasts, but ain't you the finest there is. That's wot everyone says, and so it is, so it is. Don't worry yerself, Colonel, sir. 'Er ladyship will be off just as soon as the young 'un brings 'er blanket. She works the poor tib somethin' fearful. 'Ere she come now."

The older woman, a very disagreeable old tabby he recognized as being of his late mother's slight acquaintance, had snapped down the carriage window and was leaning forward, her two hands clasped on the edge. "Amanda! Attend me, you ignorant girl! Did you remember to bring my woolen shawl also? I do need my woolen shawl," she screeched. "And my fan—be quick about it, do you hear? We haven't all day!" The window on the carriage snapped upward again. Fitzwilliam turned, amused and curious now as to whom she would call so rudely, when his breath caught in his throat. The whole square suddenly hushed.

He recognized her instantly. Over the years he had always been eager to smile in greeting and tip his hat in the hopes they could meet; she had been his dreamlike ideal of beauty, always mysteriously vanishing before he could reach her… and now here she was in the solid form of a plain, simple, dark grey cloak and gown.

She was blindly running up behind a young girl who looked to be around Georgiana's age, a child dressed in the top stare of fashion and waiting to be handed into the coach by a distracted footman. The young woman had squeezed her eyes shut against the sleet and misjudged the distance to the young girl, colliding into her and causing them both to start a fit of giggles. The old tabby launched into yet another heated tirade.

He was unaware of how intensely he stared or how long this little scene lasted, struck senseless as he was by this elusive beauty now so close before him. She had dropped her reticule and was spinning, searching the ground, clutching at the old woman's shawl that swirled about her legs. Long, dark blonde tendrils escaped from a bonnet threatening to be blown off, and her eyes blinked against the flying, stinging ice crystals. He bent to pick up the bag lying unnoticed in the wild wind and, stepping up behind her, rested his hand gently upon her arm. Electric.

She gasped and spun around, looking first at his chest, which was eye level, and then turning her face up higher, her eyes wide with surprise. She smiled her recognition instantly. His heart stopped. When he spoke, he raised his voice over the wail of the wind. "I believe you dropped this, madam." He then warmly smiled back at her. Those huge eyes were a breathtaking almond shape, the deepest, darkest brown imaginable and innocent as a baby doe's, fringed with long, thick black lashes. Delicate dark blonde brows arched above them like willowy, graceful caterpillars. Her skin was smooth as porcelain, creamy and flushed, the rosy red tint of the freezing wind accentuating broad, high cheekbones. Her nose was not the tiny button of an English miss but strong-looking and slightly wide. He stared at her lip's full, soft moist form and nearly began to salivate, actually forgot to breathe. The whole effect was exotic, exhilarating.

Taking the bag, she nodded in thanks and was just opening her mouth to speak when a muffled threat barked from within startled her, commanding her to enter the carriage. The footman quickly approached and took her hand, forcing her to step up onto the coach steps while the driver leaned toward Fitzwilliam to apologize. "Sorry, Colonel, sir," John Coachman yelled into his ear. "'Er Royal 'ighness 'ere is in rare temper today. Let me shake your 'and again, though, sir. 'Tis a honor, sir, a honor, and one that I shall lord over me mates tonight!"

The old tabby angrily pulled the carriage door closed once the beauty was barely within and then bellowed for them to be off immediately, furious that they were scandalously late for somewhere already. John Coachman tested and secured the door, touched his hat respectfully toward the colonel, and jumped up into his seat.

Fitzwilliam stepped back as the carriage jerked forward and started moving, making a turn at the end of the square and then once again slowly crossing his path. He watched it closely, his eyes searching within, his heart pounding against his ribs when he saw she was looking directly back at him, clasping the bag to her bosom and smiling in thanks. It was her eyes that seared him, melted into him, creating an emotion that sent intense waves of heat rushing throughout his body. When the carriage moved quickly away, only the back of her bonnet showed in the window.

"Look at me, love," he whispered, willing her to turn around so he could see her again… and then she did. He had never been so affected by a woman before in his life, nor had he seen a face so beautiful and so unique and so riveting. She watched through the back window and continued staring at him until the carriage was out of sight.

It seemed then that the world around him had been sitting in a sort of muted shock, as if a new day gradually was dawning in his conscious mind. He continued his watch long after the coach passed from view. When his heart started beating again, he harrumphed and pulled his collar up to hold tightly around his neck, blowing out the breath he was suddenly aware he had been holding.

What in bloody hell was that? He tried to shake off the emotional bond that seemed to have sparked to life between them. *This is ridiculous*, he snorted. *Too much cheap claret at lunch.* He laughed to himself, willing his nerves to somehow stop trembling. It wasn't until another carriage passed by and someone he knew called out a greeting to him that he roused himself and continued on to Darcy's.

Chapter 3

"And where's our Little Behemoth? I hope she's not lodged herself within some doorway again." Fitzwilliam stood gratefully before the roaring fire and rubbed his raw, cold hands briskly together. Elizabeth had become very, very pregnant of late. They teased her mercilessly. She was immense.

Without raising his eyes, Darcy motioned upward with his pen, in the general direction of Lizzy's private sitting rooms. He was ensconced at his desk, surveying the reports spread upon it, reports brought to him that morning by the estate manager of his massive holding, Pemberley, in Derbyshire.

"Unfortunately, we had a bit of a disagreement at breakfast. Apparently LB is questioning the fairness of this whole pregnancy situation and at present is hosting a lively protest in her room. She and Georgiana have finished off two boxes of chocolates, a dozen scones, and are now into the peach tarts."

Fitzwilliam laughed while he turned the chair across from Darcy around and straddled it, happily accepting the coffee handed him by the butler. "Thank you very much, Winters. You are a prince among men. It is bloody freezing out there." He turned his attention back to his cousin as he sipped the hot drink. "Well, I don't mind lending my support for her escape as long as the peach tarts hold out." He tilted his chair forward to clutch an uneaten sandwich from Darcy's plate. "Perhaps you can provide us with some type of hoist."

Darcy abruptly looked up from his paperwork. "You are excessively tardy, as if that surprises me. Never tell me you've been at Wellington's all day? I thought it was only to be a breakfast meeting."

"Yes, well, it started out that way, but as usual, the breakfast meeting stretched into a chatty luncheon visit. We wasted an awful lot of time as he shaved this morning. I think the man is part ape; in fact, I'd swear to it. I could see his beard growing while I ate my Jerusalem artichokes. Put me off my feed for a while, I can tell you."

Darcy's snort served as his opinion regarding that possibility when he belatedly pulled his now empty plate back from within his cousin's reach.

"And how is his good wife?"

"An idiot. Say, Darcy..."

"I hate to admit that was my impression, also, poor dear. Still, she has some basis for her arrogance, you know, comes from very good stock, wonderful bloodlines. If she was a horse, I'd *admire* her fetlocks and the astoundingly broad fullness between her eyes. By the way, has he finished remodeling his new townhouse? I'd say he bit off a bit too much with that one. Good location, though, excellent for resale."

"Who cares? I say, Darcy..."

"Bingley heard that he's resigning his commission. Is that true? Smart move if he is. Mark my word, he'll be prime minister one day.

"Gad! Can we forget about Wellington for one moment, please? Good Lord, he puts his little breeches on one leg at a time, just like you and I. Now, try to pay attention. I wanted to ask you about that woman who lives across St. James square. You know who I mean—the old beastie with the hairy mole on her chin—lives in that house across from Aunt Catherine."

Darcy shivered in recollection. A ruder, more snobbish, social-climbing harridan did not exist in all of London. "Yes, she's lived there for years—name is Pennwalt or Pensky or Petterson. She's an absolute horror. What on earth would you want with that old woman?"

"Didn't she have a son that died a few years back? On the Hamilton yacht wasn't he... when it sank... or some such accident?" He settled his chin on his folded arms, surreptitiously eying leftover biscuits.

"Yes, I believe she did have a son who drowned, but not on the Hamilton boat." Darcy didn't bother to look up from his writing. "Sit up straight—you're going to break the legs on that chair, lurching back and forth like that! It's like having an elephant bouncing on a twig." He slapped at his cousin's hands. "And stop grabbing at my food, you thieving bastard."

Fitzwilliam grunted. "You're sounding more and more like Aunt Catherine, the older you get, did you know that? Even beginning to look a bit like her. What else do you know about the matter? I mean the hag's son."

Darcy returned to his figures. "I believe he was a baronet. He was on his way to confront a wayward wife who had left him and run off to America. His ship went down during a storm or at a blockade. I can't remember which."

"Well, I wonder who I saw, then. The woman I have seen coming and going in the square was certainly not a baronet's wife. Dresses rather plainly, and now she accompanies a young girl. Mayhap she is a governess or teacher," Fitzwilliam was muttering.

"What *are* you going on about?"

"The old tabby wouldn't have perhaps produced a beautiful daughter somehow of which you are unaware."

"She couldn't produce a beautiful anything, if I'm thinking of the same person." This interruption was causing Darcy to lose focus. Rubbing his forehead, he stared intently at his cousin. "I don't suppose you would be interested in helping me with these accounts, seeing as you are just sitting there doing nothing but annoying me?"

"Help you with accounts?" Fitzwilliam let out a hoot of laughter. "That is rich, Darcy! Really, you have the most wonderful sense of humor!" Fitzwilliam chuckled casually as he shook his head.

After a moment, Fitzwilliam pressed on, once again disturbing the silence. "Do you know if she has any visitors at the present? The beast, I mean."

With a resigned sigh, Darcy removed his spectacles, pinching his nose at the bridge. "Richard, I have no idea what goes on in this neighborhood. I can't even direct my own household." After replacing his glasses, he picked his pen back up and set to work again. "Ask Aunt Catherine if you require the latest *on-dit*."

Fitzwilliam shivered and sipped his coffee. He was very quiet, unnaturally so for him. After a few moments, an anxious

Darcy looked up. "What has you asking these questions, please?" Fitzwilliam was on an extended city stay as plans were implemented for the allied armies to begin leaving Paris the following year. The prior two weeks with his brother had done little to relax him. He was ripe for trouble.

"Well, since you bring it up, I just saw that beast in her carriage, and a young woman walked over and got into it with her." Fitzwilliam smiled wistfully. "Absolutely lovely. The young woman, I mean. I have seen her before upon occasion, from afar, but never met her, never even knew where she lived. She gives one the impression of being very ethereal, very otherworldly, very foreign."

He grabbed absently at some papers on the desk, reshuffling them, replacing them gently when he realized he had ruined their order. "Sorry." He returned his hands to his knees. "She may be accompanying a young girl Georgiana's age, perhaps an acquaintance?"

A grinning Darcy leaned back in his chair, studying his cousin closely. "Shall I describe this lovely lady of yours? A dimwitted little pocket Venus—a redheaded slow top." Chuckling at his cousin's glower, he picked up his quill again.

"You are not, in any way, shape, or form, amusing, Darcy."

Darcy rolled his eyes. "Yes, well, the only trouble is that you always get bored with these silly creatures within a week, sometimes less, and then you have the problem of where to dump the bodies. And if she *is* a servant or governess or even a paid companion, that never ends up well, does it?"

Fitzwilliam opened his mouth to argue but realized that Darcy was pretty much on target. He grunted and went back to sipping his coffee. "Are you going to finish that pie?" he asked and reached for the apple tart on the side of the desk.

Darcy quickly snatched back the plate, never taking his eyes from his books. "Yes, I am going to finish that pie. Don't you have a barracks or something that provides you with food? I'm not made of money, you know."

"Are you insinuating that I take advantage of your good-natured hospitality?"

"Who's insinuating?" Darcy abruptly looked up from his paper and stared hard at his cousin. "A man your age, really, Fitz! You should have a home of your own by now. You should be over this constant need for conquests, unless you truly don't want to marry and have a family."

Fitzwilliam shifted in his seat and studiously avoided eye contact. "Well, certainly I do, Darcy. One day. Perhaps in the future. The distant future. When I am old and defenseless. Stop staring at me like that! There is no immediate rush, is there? There are so many lovely ladies I have yet to meet in the time God has allotted to me. Besides, I have little income, no home, and no immediate prospects. So, unless I can impregnate a ninety-year-old virgin heiress with a dickey heart, I am not inclined to rush the event." He put down his coffee cup on the edge of the desk and brushed off the crumbs that had been collecting throughout the morning.

Darcy rolled the quill between his fingers and looked with benign pity upon his cousin. "You should, you know. It's a wonderful feeling to be the head of your home, with a wife who adores you and whom you adore in return."

Fitzwilliam whipped out his pocket watch. "Oh, look at that. I have to run."

Ignoring him, Darcy turned his face to the fire, a besotted look in his eyes and a smile on his lips. "It's a good feeling to care for your family and their well-being. It makes you finally grow up, I can tell you." He sighed deeply and began attacking his figures once more, his mind filled with unlimited love and joy, thinking on his upcoming paternal responsibilities. "I myself find women to be unbelievably wonderful creations."

"I suppose you will continue with this treacle even as I beg you to stop."

"Well, think about it..." Darcy continued, looking up from his work.

Fitzwilliam groaned.

"They give back to you double and triple whatever little you hand them."

"I think I'm going to be ill, Darcy. Please stop."

"You hand them disparate items of food, and they give you back a wonderful meal. You provide them with four walls and a floor, and they give you back a loving home. You give them your seed," Darcy's eyes misted, his voice choked with emotion. "You give them your seed, and they give you back the most precious thing of all—a child..." They sat in silence together.

"And God help you if you give them shit." Fitzwilliam was calmly packing tobacco into his pipe, and his eyes met Darcy's for a moment. Understanding flashed between them.

"Amen to that, Cousin." Darcy crashed down to earth, quickly resuming his work.

Not to be dissuaded for long, Fitzwilliam continued. "She had a lost look to her. Perhaps she's a widow, a French war widow. She looked foreign somehow."

Struggling to suppress his grin, Darcy returned his attention to his papers. "You are incorrigible," he muttered.

"Well, I can dream, can't I? A lovely, willing young widow

of a certain station is better than going off to Mrs. Cleary's house to buy a woman's affections. Don't look at me so affronted, I saw you there once. I was there myself."

"I was never there! I deny it. Anyway, I went merely for the gaming."

"Tell it to Bingley, brat; perhaps he'll believe you. I saw you myself, upstairs, entering a room with a very busty brunette, not more than six years ago. I was briefly in on leave and not about to go yelling your name down the hallway."

The wind taken from his sails and shamefully red-faced, Darcy shrugged in annoyance.

"Well, it is true that a man does have certain needs." Darcy glanced up briefly.

Fitzwilliam sat back, restless and eager to be doing something. "Besides, widows are so damn grateful…"

Darcy let out an aggravated yowl, "You have no conscience to speak of, do you?"

"Well, what should I do? I will more than likely never marry. I'm not about to go ruin some eighteen-year-old debutante. Then the older they are, the more desperate their ploys. You could be trapped with someone you wouldn't want to spend five minutes with, let alone your entire life."

Fitzwilliam raked his hands through his hair several times, leaving its appearance wildly on end. It was thick and unruly and tended to go its own merry way once its morning duty was over. "You know, I am rather disappointed at your attitude toward me, as well as offended," he huffed. "You do owe me some gratitude, brat. I was, after all, your example in polite society, your role model, as it were, especially with the ladies."

Darcy stared at him in disbelief, the fighting anger just as strong at that moment as it had been when they were ten and eight years old.

"*Role model?!* You farted on my head."

"You peed in my face!"

They glowered at each other for several seconds.

"Apparently we have a stalemate here, relative to degrees of bad behavior. In the interest of family harmony, however, I will concede the peeing was worse than the farting."

"Thank you, Darcy. Damn big of you."

Fitzwilliam again picked up his coffee cup. "Getting back to our subject," the professor continued, "married women are, of course, also quite acceptable..."

Darcy slammed his hand down on the desk and gave Fitzwilliam another warning look.

"Well, they are! But they tend to have angry, pistol-holding husbands, and that can sometimes be very tricky. Now on the other hand," Fitzwilliam continued with a gleam in his eye, his brows waggling, "widows have experience, and if they have attained a certain station in life, they rarely wish to remarry. They are generally well-bred and can converse with a man, and by thankful, I mean thankful for the attention, not the other, you lout."

Darcy was still shaking his head in disbelief.

"All right, maybe they are grateful for the other. The ones I've entertained certainly have been ecstatic." Fitzwilliam beamed, wallowing in his memories.

"I would ban you from my house if I thought for a moment you would pay any attention. Get your coffee cup off my desk, you are making a mark." Darcy picked up his pen to write again, noticing the tart was missing. "And quit eating my food!"

After a few minutes of silence Darcy finished his work and began to blot the ink. "So, you are hoping for an introduction to this pretty-faced, eager, young cork brain—is that the gist of what you're saying?" Darcy looked up to see a surprised expression on Fitzwilliam's face.

"No, actually, and I would appreciate it if you would not speak of her that way." Fitzwilliam suddenly felt protective of the exotic-looking woman with the fawnlike eyes.

Darcy watched his cousin to see if he was being serious.

"I am dead serious," Fitzwilliam said, reading his mind. After addressing several letters, Darcy folded up his papers and placed them all into a packet for his secretary, while Fitzwilliam poured them both more coffee.

"I am sure I shall regret this, but the Winter Ball is this Wednesday at Lady Jersey's mansion." Darcy picked up his newspaper to read, flicking it once or twice before surgically folding it in half, then reached over to his plate to search for his half-eaten cucumber sandwich, now long gone. He looked taken aback that the plate was empty. "I was going to ignore the invitation since Elizabeth will be unable to attend and Georgiana is still fearful of being in large crowds without her. However, perhaps with the two of us...?" His eyes darted in vain for any remaining food. His stomach was growling. "If there is a young woman of presentation age visiting, I am positive the old goat will have finagled an invitation. She is said to be a most avaricious social climber. Perhaps your lovely lady will also attend."

"Absolutely perfect." Fitzwilliam smiled broadly at Darcy.

Darcy's mouth twitched a little at the side. "Are you sure you are brave enough?"

Fitzwilliam leveled a steely glance at his cousin. "I laugh at fear. I sneer at danger. I..."

"Aunt Catherine is co-hostess."

"Oh bloody hell." Fitzwilliam's tossed a wadded-up piece of paper into the fireplace.

Chapter 4

The Winter Ball, an eagerly anticipated annual event, was considered very important socially, due to its exclusivity, the herald of the coming Season, and the initial exposure for debutantes about to be presented at court. It was a small *fête* by *ton* standards, only the upper half of the socially acceptable being invited, marriageable daughters, nieces, and sisters firmly in hand. The middle-aged women present were on the whole a rather plain-faced bunch. They attempted with diamonds, paint, and feathers to achieve what nature could no longer—a countenance worthy to compete with their youthful charges.

The men fared little better. In general, they were middle-aged and balding, wearing gaudy-colored waistcoats as well as high-point starched collars that sliced into their cheeks. Frighteningly large jowls were created this way, framing ridiculous cravat creations.

And, as always, there were officers everywhere—the current darlings of society.

Fitzwilliam elbowed and pinched his way past the doorway idlers, coughed in the face of celebrity gawkers, forced a pathway through the chattering, teeming gentry. A terrified Georgiana could do nothing but keep her head low as he dragged her behind him through the crowd, an apologetic and mortified Darcy following in their wake.

It was when they approached the footman who would announce them that he saw her, her simple presence outstanding amidst a multitude of inbred and odd-looking individuals gushing and fawning over each other. Wearing an outmoded, drab gown meant for someone much larger and much, much older, she was tenderly patting stray locks of a young girl's hair, adjusting the bow on the back of the girl's dress, in short, fussing about the girl like a mother hen with her lone chick. He was thunderstruck. Even without the feathers, paint, lace, and jewelry, she far outshone the posturing aristocratic ladies surrounding her, who competed in vain for attention.

At this distance, the youth she tended to appeared to Fitzwilliam as little more than an infant—small, frightened, and frail. However, it was not the anxious-looking girl who was causing him concern, drawing his offense. It was the activity surrounding the two that began to fuel his indignation, the admiration of the many men milling about ogling *his* Beauty, commenting upon her shimmering blonde hair. Fellow soldiers gaping and drooling over *his* Beauty's eyes as they sparkled with amusement within a perfect, heart-shaped face, long, dark lashes lowered now to her task and shadowing *his* Beauty's cheeks.

It was a testament to her good looks that those who circled overlooked the other grander, more-opulently gowned women, to be drawn instead by a loveliness that appeared both alien and delicate at once.

The young girl nervously whispered something, and the Brown-Eyed Beauty laughed gently, her face softening as it tilted to the side, lighting up with open joy, her eyes twinkling in devilish delight. Deadly dimples suddenly appeared.

Instead of being charmed, Fitzwilliam was furious.

"Why do you look as if you've just gotten your foot caught in your stirrups?" As he followed Richard's rapt gaze, looking across the ballroom in the same general direction, Darcy discovered the object of his interest. "Ah. Well, well, well..." he muttered.

"What?" Fitzwilliam turned momentarily toward his cousin.

"I take it that is the woman about whom all your fuss has been?"

After one or two tense moments, Richard responded. "Yes, Darcy," he bit back icily. "That is the woman about whom, as you so haughtily say, all my fuss has been. What of it?!"

"Nothing. Nothing at all." Still he hesitated, staring.

Seeing Darcy's reaction, Fitzwilliam bristled. "You wish to make some sort of observation, brat? Yes, that is the woman, and please do not stare at her like some sort of bedlamite."

"Well, pardon me, Your Worship. She's just not what I had expected."

"What do you mean by that?" Fitzwilliam glared. "She is the most beautiful woman in this room, if not the whole city."

"Jesu, calm yourself, Richard. I didn't say she wasn't. It's just that she's so... so..."

"So... what?"

"Well..." Darcy's eyes made a quick appraisal of the woman in the distance. "Well, for one thing, she is rather plainly dressed for such a grand assembly, and she does appear rather foreign-looking with those cheekbones. Here's an aside. Whatever happened to your dream of a deathly pale, full-bodied, and terminally ill English Rose due to inherit an estate the size of Kent? Hmm? In case you had not noticed, this young woman is very healthy and quite slender and apparently poor. At the very least, you must admit that she doesn't have the usual voluptuousness of which you are known to be so fond." Without even looking at his cousin, he could feel his eyes boring into him. He sighed.

"She is not that slender," Fitzwilliam said coolly. "And you are still staring at her. I don't like it, I tell you."

Darcy rolled his eyes in exasperation. "Please try and behave as an adult. I'm sure you've seen them about—emulate." The air crackled between them. "All I am saying is that she has a leaner frame than the average woman you prefer. She is tall and slim and, well, frankly, she appears small-busted." Darcy eyed her critically and then turned to look at a furious Fitzwilliam. "Maybe it is just that the dress is so huge. Stop scowling at me!"

He sipped calmly from a glass of wine he had just been handed by a footman. "Merciful heaven, aren't you suddenly the sensitive one! I have nothing against the woman at all. She is quite as lovely as you say, perhaps more so." Fitzwilliam's green-eyed rage was turning boiling red from his struggle for control. "And she is definitely not your type."

Fitzwilliam stiffened. "Aside from your previous gibberish, what is it about her, exactly, that you do not consider *my type*?"

Darcy hesitated for a few tension-filled moments before proceeding at his peril. "Truthfully? All right. Well, she's not at all fussy or overly made-up. She's naïve-looking, soft, elegant, and pleasant. None of those are your usual requirements—in fact, quite the opposite." Darcy and Fitzwilliam stood glaring at each other before Darcy finally broke rank and turned back. He then gestured toward the woman under discussion. "I mean, she really is quite beautiful, to be sure. Oh, and my goodness, what an exquisite smile she has, such luscious, full lips. And dimples, too? Good God!" He chuckled and shook his head. "No, she's definitely not your type at all."

"All right, that does it. I should call you out."

"Well, think about it. You could actually grow to love this woman, then where would you be?"

"Never mind about all that. I don't care for the way you are looking at her, brat, with your insolent eyes. And how dare you comment upon her lips, goddamn it. You're almost drooling."

Darcy turned to coolly assess his cousin. "You should be medicated."

"You were leering at her."

"I was not leering, you apelike menace! I was asked my opinion."

"Aha! Well...you are the demented one—you were never asked for your opinion, and I, above all people, know a leer when I see one, and I certainly don't need your approval. I was merely pointing her out to you."

"What's going on, gentlemen?" Georgiana returned to their side after freshening herself. The carriage ride had been long and blustery, a frigid winter storm approaching with snow and sleet threatening to descend upon London at any moment.

"Oh, Fitzwilliam has finally lost what little was left of his mind. He is annoyed with me for glancing at his newest obsession," Darcy whispered loudly. "He is also exceedingly upset because I have been pointing out to him the many ways in which she would not suit him at all."

"Really? What fun! May I take a stab? Where is she?" Darcy indicated the far corner where the beauty was standing.

Fitzwilliam threw up his hands and turned his back on them. "I am leaving you both. I know neither of you. Good-bye."

"Oh, how charming she is and how different are her features! Truly a paragon!" Georgiana gushed. A slightly mollified Fitzwilliam waited. "And not your type at all, Richard. Definitely not!" Georgiana's clear assessing gaze darted from the beauty to Fitzwilliam and then back to the beauty. He turned slowly around and faced her.

"Et tu, Judas?" He crossed his arms over his chest.

"Heavens, Richard, just look at the color in your face! Are you feeling all right?" She regarded him with great concern.

"That is not my type of woman... exactly how, may I ask?"

"Well, no offense, dear one, but..." Fitzwilliam simmered as Georgiana wrinkled up her nose, hesitating for just a moment before she continued. "Well... frankly... I oftentimes feel a need to bathe after meeting one of your lady friends. Some of them have looked positively feral. For heaven's sake, some have not even appeared human, ha, ha, ha... Excuse me, that *was* unkind."

Darcy stepped away briefly to disguise his laughter as Fitzwilliam's fists balled up to his sides. It was then Georgiana took a better look at his face and stepped backward.

"Thank you so much, Darcy and Georgiana, for your candor. If, by any chance we should meet again, say either of you lie bleeding on the street or twisted beneath a carriage, please do not be offended if I cross the road to the other side. My, what a little nest of vipers are my family."

Georgiana gulped and whispered to her brother, "Heavens, what have I said now?"

Fitzwilliam glared down at her for several seconds. "Here's the thing, Georgiana. I require you to get me introduced to that woman—it is the only reason I'm attending this blasted nonsense. I don't know how you will do it. Fact is, my dear, I don't really give a damn."

Georgiana blanched at the horde surrounding them, her fear of crowds once again rising. She had so hoped to continue hiding between her two male family members, but Fitzwilliam was not to be put off. "And, if you do not, I will tell your brother here about a certain young acquaintance of which I have heard rumors."

Darcy's eyebrow arched neatly into his hairline. "Georgiana?!"

"Sorry, Brother, I have a mission to accomplish." With her eyes averted, she had just turned to scamper off when she was stopped by an elegantly gloved hand clasped onto her wrist.

"There you are." The familiar and grating voice pierced their bubble of gaiety. Fitzwilliam cringed as Darcy turned to greet their aunt.

"Aunt Catherine"—he bowed to kiss her cheek—"what a delight to see you." He lied on behalf of them all. "We feared we would have difficulties finding you in this crush."

"Crush? I've taken baths with more servants in attendance. By the way, why on earth are you arriving at this hour? You were both taught better manners than this!" Darcy noted that her shiny eyes were having some difficulty focusing, possibly from too many glasses of sherry.

"Catherine," Darcy said calmly, trying to be patient, "it's only half-past nine."

"Exactly! Well, it can't be helped now. I must take you all to greet Lady Jersey. Where is Georgiana? Where is my little one?"

The two men parted to expose the trembling debutante.

Catherine's hands flew up to her cheeks, tears welling in her tiny and slightly dazed eyes. "Georgiana, you look so like your dear mother. She was my sister, did you know that? Well, you look absolutely exquisite, no other word to describe. Who designed your gown, dearest? It is lovely. Who is her dressmaker? Who...?" She looked questioningly at her nephews' blank stares and immediately gave up. "Oh, never mind. It's like talking to cheese."

"Madame Collette," Georgiana supplied, smiling.

Catherine nodded her approval then evaluated Darcy's appearance and glowed with pride. He was, as always, dressed in the height of elegance. She flinched visibly when she turned her attention to Fitzwilliam, cocking one eyebrow as she scanned his boots with her quizzing glass.

"I fell under my horse at Waterloo. Haven't had a chance to get them buffed up as yet."

Losing interest quickly in her nephew's boots, Catherine returned her attention to Georgiana and smiled kindly. "Do you have a lady's maid?"

"Aunt Catherine." Darcy was not amused. "I can assure you Georgiana has several lady's maids *and* a companion. She also has a number of homes at her disposal whenever and wherever she desires, all bursting with staff, horses, sixteen dogs, and five cats."

"I do so like your hair, Georgiana. I cannot abide a maid who is unable to properly attend to hair. Yours looks exceedingly well. Who did it? The cook? The laundress? The groundskeeper?"

"My maid, Aunt Catherine."

Darcy's foot began to tap furiously, but Catherine's infamous pendulum-like attention had now swung back to Fitzwilliam.

"Why on earth are you turning around every five seconds?! Have you a palsy or some other like condition?"

"Yes, Lady Catherine, and I appeal to you to excuse me. I feel the need to lie down and rest for a while."

Catherine huffed. "Oh, you have a condition, I'll warrant, but it isn't palsy. I am beginning to question your eyesight. You keep looking across the room at those old dowagers." She squinted harder and then turned back to him, aghast. "At least I am sincerely hoping it is the dowagers. Never tell me you are casting those longing looks toward the atrocious lavender dress. She is not suitable, Fitzwilliam. Don't repeat this to a soul, but I believe she is wearing wool."

He stared down at her in fuming silence.

"She is a servant, Richard! That is obvious by the meanness of her attire! You cannot be serious!"

Fitzwilliam's voice grew ominously quiet. "I am not in the habit of judging people merely by their garments, *Aunt*. Besides, how can you of all people consider her a servant? She is still young enough to walk without assistance."

"Don't you get so high and mighty with me, young man! No woman of quality would be seen out in the evening without jewels, with no gloves, no hair adornments—in *wool*! Where is her fan, I ask? Ugh! Merciful heavens, this is not to be borne!"

Darcy cleared his throat. "Aunt Catherine, we had considered that possibly the young woman in question may be a foreigner, perhaps in mourning attire. That would explain the rather drab clothing as well as her lack of embellishment."

"Oh, the poor dear, a war widow, do you think?" Catherine's hand went to her heart in devastated compassion, completely forgetting her previous outburst.

It swiftly passed.

"Very well, come along, everyone," she chirped. "Fitzwilliam, it appears that you will be having a bit of competition for your widow—oh la, that sounded rather ominous, didn't it?" Catherine had been motioning toward an officer circling Brown Eyes when she realized what she had said. She took Fitzwilliam's arm and pulled him behind her. "Well, never you mind, sirrah. At the present, you will have to settle with charming your viperous hostess."

It was nearly a half hour later before Fitzwilliam and Darcy made their escape from the high-pitched, squealing voice of their hostess, Lady Sally Jersey, in addition to the whining Lady Castlereigh, the barely audible Lady Cowper, and the baritone Lady Sefton, all audibly thrilled to have such distinguished gentlemen in their midst.

"Kill me if I ever agree to do this for another female relative," Fitzwilliam spoke pleasantly to anyone within hearing.

"Aunt Catherine wants me to dance with Princess Esterhazy's daughter..."

"Oh, you poor sod." Fitzwilliam's attention was distracted suddenly.

"Can I leave you alone for fifteen minutes without your causing a scene? Richard? Richard?"

Richard had already stomped away.

Merde.

Chapter 5

Amanda Sayles Penrod sat among the dowagers, widows, and poor-relation chaperones that occupy the draftiest, farthest, and darkest corners of any ballroom or assembly, and happy she was for even this little diversion. It had been months since she had seen been at a public gathering, years since she had attended a society ball with music and dancing. If only her dearest Anthony had accompanied her this night, she would have felt safer and more relaxed, less alone.

She was momentarily drawn from her daydreams to be introduced, along with her late husband's cousin, Emily, to a beautiful young woman, a member of one of the grandest families in England, the Darcys. A gracious and sweet young lady, Georgiana Darcy was much less intimidating than the other debutantes in attendance this night, and Amanda could sense Emily's immediate ease. She wistfully waved the two off, both girls emboldened now by the presence of a kindred spirit, as they began meeting other young people.

Amanda sighed. One day perhaps she, too, would again know

the joy of beautiful clothes and dancing and love and romance. Her heart quickened as always at the thought of a certain oddly attractive and very tall colonel who, if not classically handsome, was very masculine and self-assured and commanding. She had noticed him over the years, followed his brilliant career, had smiled shyly at him from across the square, but had never come face-to-face with the man until he retrieved her reticule from under the carriage. Still and all though, they hadn't really met properly and probably never would. Well, it did no harm to fantasize. Fantasy was all she would ever allow herself. She could never meet anyone now, not when her little boy so needed her.

Of a sudden, she was aware of movement around her. Officers had approached and were attempting to converse with her. Pretending ignorance, Amanda shrugged her shoulders and shook her head, an impressive dumb show of confusion if she did say so herself. She lowered her eyes to hands folded demurely on her lap and just prayed to heaven that the men would forget her and leave.

Instead, the two old women who had been seated beside her and in front clucked their tongues and walked away, uninterested in assisting a young woman who looked so poor and acted so servile. A third old tabby dozed fitfully, her head lolling back and then jerking forward whenever her snores awakened her.

At first, the men seemed to be enjoying what they interpreted as shyness, quickly becoming emboldened by her apparent lack of understanding and protection. The discourse between the drunken officers spiraled into the colorfully ribald. "Could she be a delectable little soiled dove in disguise as a housemaid?"

One inebriated officer laughed hysterically as he attempted to see the color of her eyes. As she kept lowering her head to avoid him, he kept bending over until, at one point, he nearly lost his balance.

"Neddie, at the very least tell me if she rouges her nipples, please."

The color was rapidly draining from Ned's cheeks with his head bent down so far. He hiccoughed and nearly lost his footing again. "With this ghastly dress, it's hard to tell if she even has bubbies." He stumbled a bit and then plopped down on the floor before her. "I can't even be assured she has lips. But, by God, I believe there is a true beauty hiding in these dowdy duds, if only she would raise up her eyes! Bunty, poke her shoulder. Make her look up."

"I should indeed love to poke her, Ned—but in the shoulder is a bit perverse, even for me."

The raucous laughter brought another soldier up, a major. "You two are making complete clodpoles of yourselves!" The major shook his head, and standing behind her boldly placed his hand upon her shoulder to keep her seated. "You are both far too into your cups to be of any service to this sweet young thing. Bugger off and leave her to me!"

Chapter 6

Moments passed that felt like years while the whimpering in her head continued unabated and her heart pounded. Afraid to raise her eyes, she was flushed with embarrassment, only gradually realizing that the bawdy comments had ceased and the area around her was now silent. She held her breath, though, knowing that she was still not alone. Someone stood before her, a form leaning over her and large enough that it blocked out much of the light provided from the wall sconces behind.

She slowly looked up, first at his dusty and beaten-looking riding boots (*My stars, what big feet*), and then at the muscled legs encased in white trousers (*Must be a lifelong horseman)*. She blushed, realizing that she should not be gazing quite so intently at those. Next came the impressive barrel chest, the fine masculine shoulders made broader by epaulettes wide enough to serve dinner upon, a scarlet military jacket with its sash, golden buttons, braids, and medals...lots of medals (*Oh no, another soldier!*) His gloved hand rested on the hilt of a beautiful dress sword.

When her eyes finally reached his face, she saw the kindest bluest eyes she had ever beheld, a prominent jaw with a crooked, easy smile, tousled muddy-colored blond hair... With a gasp, she realized that it was the celebrated colonel, the man she continually fantasized over, her hero from the street. She sat bolt upright.

Huh.

In stunned silence, she glanced around to see that the other men had fled, and she sat alone, staring up at that tender face. It was unbelievable, her shock and his sudden presence crushing her ability to speak.

Huh.

He spoke to her at length in French, appearing surprised when she blinked back in wonder. He laughed a little and straightened up, looked around the room, and then stroked his chin. He then began speaking in Spanish, and after that a language she had never heard before.

After running off the drunken soldiers with unsubstantiated threats and one menacing eyebrow, Fitzwilliam turned to the beauty before him and bowed. If he imagined she was lovely through a blinding sleet storm or from the frosted window of a carriage or from across a ballroom, she was breathtaking up close, staring at him like a fairy-tale princess awaking from a trance. A gradually awakening Sleeping Beauty, perhaps, her eyelashes slowly fluttering open.

Then, her full, red, luscious lips opened to pronounce what sounded like a muted "Duh?"

He winced. Oh, shit. A horrible fear gripped his gut that

Darcy would be right again and she might be yet another brainless twit. He would never live this down. Never. His heart sank further as she revisited her first observation with an even louder "Duh?"

He spoke to her eloquently in French, apologizing for his boldness in approaching and for the inebriated officers, all the time admiring her beauty if not her conversation. She was beginning to blink more rapidly, at least, her squint appearing more intelligent, or was that just wishful thinking on his part? She certainly did not look Spanish, but he tried that, too. Her eyes opened wider. He finally tried Danish. She shrugged her shoulders. Perhaps the poor darling was truly mentally impaired.

"Well, I have run out of languages, beautiful one. Now what shall I do?" He turned around and searched the crowded ballroom. "Where the hell has Georgiana gotten to?"

Her hand immediately reached out and briefly touched his sleeve. She was terribly alarmed; desperate that he was about to leave. "Pardon me for being so forward, Colonel, but she should return here in a moment. I heard her mention that she needed to find her brother and cousin."

Fitzwilliam spun around in shock. "You speak English!"

"No. I'm sorry, sir, I do not. I'm an American."

Georgiana, along with her new dearest friend Emily, reached the laughing couple several moments later. "Cousin?" she whispered kindly and tapped his shoulder, but he was lost to the world, staring into the loveliest eyes he had ever seen, so that he felt nothing and heard little else.

"Cousin?" she repeated more loudly and with a bit more force, then flicked his ear sharply with a hard snap of her fingers.

His wits quickly returned, and he turned to his left, stunned to see people surrounding them.

"Georgiana! How nice to see you. Whatever are you doing here?" Fitzwilliam looked genuinely surprised by the crush surrounding him, suddenly being encircled as he was by eight giggling, squealing little females. It was appalling. He then recollected sending Georgiana around for his introduction.

"What do you mean, 'Nice to see you; whatever are you doing here?'" She looked curiously at him. The girls all squealed and giggled, batting their eyelashes and whispering to her their wishes for introduction. "You just sent me on a breakneck tour around this room, which was no walk in Hyde Park, I might add, in order to get you an introduction, and you end up storming across the ballroom like a man possessed!" Georgiana had an annoying tendency toward honesty, a habit of saying exactly what she was thinking the moment she thought it. Fitzwilliam briefly considered gagging her mouth.

"Well, I am sure I have no knowledge of what you are speaking," he murmured then raised his brows in what he hoped would be some sort of silent communication to her to keep her unholy trap shut. "I happened to see this lovely lady being accosted by some anonymous soldiers and came to offer her my assistance."

"You mean Ned Jeffries? And Bachman? I swear I saw Bachman sidle over here. I thought you knew them. Ooh! You did, didn't you? Yes, of course, you were all on the same cricket team for several years, and didn't Bunty play football with you and Brother at Harrow?"

Not wanting to eavesdrop on the two cousins' whispered conversation, Amanda had been watching the excited debutantes with great amusement. They were bouncing up and down, awaiting their moment to impress the famous "Colonel of Waterloo," edging Amanda and Emily farther into the background. When Georgiana finally began the introductions, the girls squealed anew, gushing and jockeying for closer positions. They preened and flirted, fanning themselves ragged, competing so outrageously that a scuffle began between them, and just when the whole situation threatened to get downright ugly, it was announced that Daddy Hill and Sir Frederick Maitland had just arrived. The herd stampeded in their direction.

"Fame is fleeting," marveled Fitzwilliam and turned again to his Beauty.

Amanda laughed. "Thank you so much, Colonel, for coming to my assistance. I apologize if I have caused you any alarm."

"Not at all, madam." He took her hand and held it gently. "It is I who should apologize to you for the behavior of the younger officers. Often at these little parties, there is too much wine and not enough common sense."

She was introduced to him then by Georgiana as the widow of the deceased baronet Augustus Penrod, and the young girl as the late baronet's young cousin, after which Georgiana tugged on his sleeve. "Excuse me, dearest of Cousins," a clearly perplexed Georgiana said with a sigh, "but I am still somewhat confused. About those soldiers who were bothering Lady Penrod—did you not rent a villa in Capri with Major Bachman just two years ago?"

"And her mouth continues unchecked..." Fitzwilliam returned his gaze to Amanda. "Ignore her, madam," he said. "We all do," he concluded under his breath.

"I hope that the officers were not too forward with you, Lady Penrod. I will be happy to have a word with them and make certain they apologize to you directly. I can assure you that I will enforce strict disciplinary measures on them all."

"Oh, no, please don't bother yourself. I am just so thrilled and honored that you, of all people, came to my rescue."

Fitzwilliam felt like a strutting peacock.

Chapter 7

For the next two hours, the glittering favored of London society stood up for their dances or sat for their gossip, changed partners with elegant nonchalance, chatted and visited and basked in the intoxicating glow of too much money coupled with too many choices and much too much time. Everyone wanted to be seen and heard, and no one cared much about listening. It was all a performance, honed and perfected over centuries, a familiar presentation that allowed for no surprise conclusions as it continued unchecked through the night. Indeed, to the teeming multitude, it secretly felt as if the orchestra had been playing eternally.

The couple sat alone on the fringes of the assembly, he a high-ranking British officer condescending to speak with a forgotten widow of low status, an unfortunate meeting of complete opposites. They could have nothing in common, coming as they did from different classes, embracing different mores.

However, of all the glittering attendees at this party, it was these two people who felt a spark ignite between them. From the beginning, they set into teasing each other, laughing outrageously at anything the other said, even finishing each other's sentences. They thought similarly about nearly everything, she with an ease of manner and simplicity that he found delightful, as if they had known each other for years and not moments, he with his lack of pomp or proper attitude. He was easily self-assured without being arrogant. She was warm and friendly without fawning.

Although the woman's beauty fed the embers of this pursuit, it was the purity of character that fanned the flames into fire. There was humility in her self-deprecating laughter, and joy of life at her core. She made him feel alive and happy to be a man.

For Amanda, she felt her prior attraction to him only intensify. She no longer saw only the famous celebrity whose attentions had flattered and excited her. His masculinity, his strength, made her heart tremble. His self-confidence mesmerized her. He made her feel desired and secure.

"I believe that there will be a waltz played next, Lady Penrod. I would be honored if you would dance it with me."

Amanda was initially thrilled, over the moon with joy at the prospect of dancing, of again being young and carefree. Her innate common sense, however, soon overcame her. To be seen with this famous man would be courting her former mother-in-law's ire, to hold him in her arms emotional suicide. He was too attractive, too appealing, her interest too passionate. "I appreciate the honor you do me in asking, Colonel Fitzwilliam; however, I do not dance this evening." She sighed and repeated the excuse she had prepared earlier, "Out of respect for my late husband."

He was undeterred. "Your late husband is lucky indeed to have a wife faithful to him so long after he has passed."

Watching her eye the assembly, he sensed the undercurrent of fear for the first time, and his heart ached for whatever was troubling her. "Perhaps if we were to go to a less-conspicuous area, away from quite so many revelers, it would be less objectionable to you. I see that the conservatory is available for dancing." He motioned toward a series of large glass doors that opened onto a lush greenhouse. "It is a lovely setting and visible enough for respectability, but at the rear of the ballroom, away from being on display, as it were."

Amanda's mind began to spin. *If I am to be allowed only one night with this man, I must surely seize the moment*. Besides, she had not danced in so very long. Looking into his intense gaze, she knew instinctively that she would be protected by him.

"P-p-perhaps... Perhaps that would be acceptable." Blushing crimson at her stuttering response, she cleared her throat and beamed.

From the first notes of the waltz, Amanda was swept up into what seemed like the twirling flight of angels. The conservatory was very large, large enough for exotic, flower-laden trees to tower easily above them. The beautiful ferns, the fragrant blossoms, and marble statues were wasted on the entranced couple, however, so new and exciting was their attachment. It was perfect and private and safe from the public scrutiny she so feared. She closed her eyes and enjoyed the totally female thrill of being protected and cherished, held in the arms of a man for whom she felt the first stirrings of love. It was heaven.

When the dance was over and while still in each other's arms, they looked intently at each other as couples politely clapped and angled by, trying to escape from the narrow and rather humid confines. Fitzwilliam watched her eyes, understood and shared all her unspoken emotions. He was a mere moment away from enclosing her in his arms and smothering her mouth with his.

Someone nearby cleared his throat. Startled, Fitzwilliam looked to his side to see the three errant officers from before and introduced them to her after a few tense seconds of hesitancy. The major bowed politely. "It is an honor to meet you, madam. I am afraid that we behaved abominably to you earlier and have come to beg your forgiveness. Had we known you were a lady acquainted with Colonel Fitzwilliam, we would never have behaved so ungentlemanly, nor said such things to you. Again, please accept our apologies."

"No apologies are needed, gentlemen, but they are accepted." Amanda was touched by the sincerity of the apology. "In truth, I did not understand much of what you said."

Too late, she saw the effects of her speech, not because of her words but because of her American accent. One of the captains swore crudely, and the other glared. The major, seeing Fitzwilliam's livid reaction, immediately stepped in front of his friends. "You have been most gracious, madam, and again, it was an honor to meet you. Make certain that the colonel brings you to the refreshment room. Good evening, madam, sir." With that, he turned and roughly shoved the two soldiers on their way.

There remained an edgy silence that hung in the air between them. Fitzwilliam was furious, with himself as much as the men. He knew them and how they had changed over the years, become more calloused and bitter from warfare, from the deaths and maiming of their friends in battles both on the Continent and in America. He had been distancing himself from many of these former colleagues, uneasy as he was with their hatred and talk of vengeance.

"I thank you most kindly for the wonderful waltz, Colonel. Please do not feel any obligation to bring me refreshments. I will return to my seat." Her eyes looked sadly into his. "Believe me when I say how beholden I am to you for making this a joyous evening for me." She bowed and began to turn, when he took her elbow.

"You won't escape me that easily, madam." His voice sounded gruff as he placed her hand upon his arm. "Never again."

Chapter 8

Darcy was grinning, still delighting in the memory of his cousin's irritated reaction to the elegant bow and gracious compliments he bestowed upon Lady Penrod at their introduction. In fact, he was purposely continuing those attentions as he now joined the couple at their table for refreshments.

"Don't let us keep you, Darcy." Fitzwilliam grunted as Darcy ignored him to pull up a chair and turn to address Amanda. Within seconds, Georgiana and Emily also arrived. "I'm certain you all have somewhere else to be... anywhere else..." He was growing very tired of trying to be subtle. Soon he would be flinging them all out the door.

"Nonsense, Cousin, we don't mind." Georgiana was sipping happily on her lemonade, relieved to be away from the crush. "It is just so good to have some quiet privacy, is it not? It is impossible to visit intimately with all those people surrounding you. Well, you two seem to be hitting it off quite splendidly."

"Yes. I am afraid I have monopolized too much of the colonel's time this evening, and he has been very kind."

"I have enjoyed every moment." His eyes devoured the young woman then turned to Darcy and silently commanded him to leave. Darcy gleefully ignored him.

"Georgiana has told me of the officers who were bothering you earlier this evening. Apparently the colonel rescued you from some scoundrels." Darcy had to avert his eyes from his cousin's obvious irritation.

"Oh yes, he was quite magnificent." The besotted couple stared at each other, lost to the world. Amanda forced herself to turn away. "Truth be told, I did not understand much of what they said. There are so many colorful terms."

"Give us an example, madam, and we shall do our best to enlighten. The cant vernacular can be confusing even to a native."

Amanda began to share with them some of the slang words that had been used by the officers. They were able to explain one or two to her, amid growing laughter. Phrases like "plant him a facer" and "watering pot" were easily explained.

"'Lobsterback?'" Amanda chuckled.

"'British soldier,'" supplied Georgiana.

"Really? What about 'soiled dove'?"

"'A lady of the evening,'" muttered Fitzwilliam, "and I'm going to kill them."

Amanda patted his hand tenderly. "I am not offended. Please do not cause a fuss; besides, this is such fun. There was one officer who fancied himself a 'rum cove.'"

Fitzwilliam explained that was a word for a 'clever rogue,' his voice rising to be heard over the raucous chatter of a particular group walking by them.

"Oh, then perhaps that was what the other word meant, the word that was said back to him."

"What word was that, madam?" Darcy strained to hear as he retrieved champagne from a passing waiter.

"'*Bollocks*,'" she called out loudly at the very moment the chattering stopped.

Georgiana, Darcy, and Fitzwilliam were waiting alongside the fringes of the ballroom. "Do you think… she'll ever return?" Darcy spoke aloud to no one in particular. With his hands clasped behind his back, he stood casually, biting his lip, his eyes cast toward the ceiling. Fitzwilliam did not respond, just leaned his shoulder against the wall and thrust his hands deep into his pockets. He lowered his head in a vain attempt to disguise his grin.

Georgiana was angry. "You are both no better than twelve-year-olds." She shook her head while her brother rubbed his face rather vigorously.

"If only she had not spoken so loudly." After a moment, the two cousins turned their heads away from each other as they choked back laughter.

"I see I do a disservice to twelve-year-olds."

"Georgiana is right." Fitzwilliam attempted a more serious look. "I only hope we haven't upset her too much with our teasing." It took only a second for the men to begin laughing again.

"I am going to find her. Richard, I think you should come along, and, Brother, you go see to our aunt, who is again turning this way." Georgiana stared at the two men, daring them to refuse.

"I'll go intercept Aunt Catherine." A still laughing Darcy went off, dramatically sighing at his martyrdom.

They saw Emily standing in the hallway, patiently answering the questions of two extremely elderly society matrons scrutinizing the consequence of her ancestry. She excused herself and approached Fitzwilliam and Georgiana.

"Is Amanda all right?" Georgiana asked.

"She's fine, only a little upset."

Fitzwilliam's heart sank with regret. "I am so sorry if we hurt her in any way."

"No, no, Colonel. No, she was vastly amused, actually. As a matter of fact, we laughed all the way here." Emily gently placed her hand on his arm. "She was asked to leave the ladies' retiring room. It was all quite humiliating. It seems several of the ladies mistook her for a servant and were incensed at her entering." Emily shook her head sadly. "When she began to explain, they laughed at her, called her a backwoods colonial."

Georgiana's tears threatened to fall at any moment. "Why must people be unkind? She is such a delightful and gentle woman." She looked intensely at Emily. "Amanda, I mean." Emily stared at her blankly before Georgiana repeated what she had said. "Yes, a really delightful and gentle woman."

Finally, Georgiana kicked her new friend's ankle.

"Owww… oh! Yes. She, I mean Amanda, is a most wonderful person. She volunteered to escort me this evening. I know my aunt, uh, warned her that there would be repercussions against her, you know, being American and having no, um, social station or family to speak of, but being such a lovely person, she did not want me to miss this evening."

Emily saw concern cloud the colonel's face and decided she was doing splendidly. She immediately infused her narrative with a little more drama, a bit more dash, nearly overturning a vase with her emotional hand sweep. "Oh, how thrrrrilled Amanda was to be finally allowed out this evening, the poor,

poor dear. Then to be brutally insulted in a ladies' area! The indignity! The humiliation! The odor! Shocking! And dear Amanda forever thinking of others, you know. Yes, always kind and patient she is, and positively the most beautiful woman alive, don't you think so, too? Even in the morning when her hair sticks out all over and she has that little drool on her lip and her eyes are all crusty..."

Georgiana vigorously shook her head and then cleared her throat, but nothing could dissuade Emily's eloquence now. "It is not I alone who feel this way. No, no, no, I tell you, men fall over themselves into dead, writhing heaps, swept away in *stoopid* admiration wherever she goes, follow her around like *stoopid* little apes. Little hairy apes. Ouch! Georgiana, don't pinch me like that. Where was I?" Her eyes darted from Georgiana's exasperated countenance back to the colonel's. "Oh, she has a little boy, you know, lost custody of him to my old aunt when Cousin Augustus passed. Now she has to beg to be allowed to see her son, you know, her own son! Beg, I tell you! No, that is just so very wrong, unnatural, uh, don't you think? What a magnificent mother she is, too, kind and patient. She is just so very, uh, lovely and beautiful. Did I say that? I did? It must be true then, ha, ha, ha. Yes, yes, yes, lovely and beautiful. And kind. A really good, good mother..."

Fitzwilliam and Georgiana stared at Emily for several moments after her performance faded to a halt.

"Where is she now?" Fitzwilliam's voice was filled with warm compassion. Emily nearly swooned in her amazement. The idiot had believed her.

"She is outside on that farthest back balcony. She thought to hide there until she was able to compose herself a little." Now it was Emily's eyes that threatened moisture. "She's been crying a bit, I have to tell you. She could, um, probably do with some comforting, you know." Fitzwilliam nodded, already headed toward the balcony. The two girls stood in silence.

"Sorry about the pinch, but gad, you were doing it up a bit brown, don't you think?" Georgiana and Emily watched her cousin's retreating form.

"Was I?" She turned a worried look back to Georgiana. "Oh, dear, I so hoped he wouldn't notice my few blunders. I was trying to get in all the bits we wanted. Did I mention kind? Yes I did, didn't I? I liked the 'mother' comment, also. He seemed moved by that, did he not? Huh! It worked much more quickly than I thought it would. Very promising, Georgiana," Emily said with a chuckle. "Yes indeed, very promising."

Chapter 9

The encounter in the ladies' retiring room had humiliated her, and had convinced Amanda more than ever that she would never become accustomed to these people, she would never belong here. She sighed, wishing she had thicker skin, was not so easily hurt, then shuddered from the cold evening. She began to mumble to herself, wondering why Emily had asked her to wait on the balcony. If she had known she'd be going outside, she could have brought her wrap.

"May I join you?" Fitzwilliam hesitated for a moment in the doorway and then approached her, removing his coat to place over her shoulders. "If you notice, I did not provide you with an opportunity to deny me."

She gazed at him, grateful for the warmth of his coat and the kindness of his smile. "Thank you so very much," she said. "My blood was beginning to freeze out here."

They stood silently, each vibrantly aware of the other, looking out over the wintry gardens of this most impressive of mansions. "Miss Emily has told me of your unpleasant encounter just now. That was dreadful, and we weren't much better. I'm so sorry if we hurt you in any way with our teasing." He leaned toward her in confidence. "The trouble with close families is that you fall into a routine of banter and oftentimes forget others may not be aware that it's all meant in fun."

"Oh, do not distress yourself." She smiled sweetly. "I was not upset." Her eyes twinkled with mischief. "Embarrassed and shamed, without a doubt, and extremely mortified, humiliated, in fact, but please don't give it another thought."

They both burst into laughter. He apologized again, much relieved. Then all was quiet. She suddenly felt shy, standing there wearing a jacket still warm from his body, alone with him for the first time when like magnets, their shoulders touched, sending a tremor of excitement through them both. Their gazes met.

He looked longingly from her parted lips up into her eyes. True mirrors of her soul that they were, they showed every emotion within her, every longing, every vulnerability. She would have no resistance to his more worldly experience he realized; she was so sheltered, so trusting and innocent that she could never even imagine the need for such defenses. This woman was all softness, all femininity; his complete opposite in every way.

"You better put your arms into those sleeves before you catch your death." It was the best conversation his keyed-up brain could improvise at the moment with his heart bouncing around in his chest and his lips dry as the desert.

He helped her slip the coat on, and then they both laughed at the overhanging arms and hem. She thanked him, blushing when he briefly rubbed her arms to create some warmth.

"Truly, it is my own fault that I spoke that word and not

another phrase I thought to be… very indelicate; but a phrase which apparently refers to someone who has died. I asked Emily about it as we walked, and she explained it to me."

"You mean 'cock up one's toes'?" Fitzwilliam asked, chuckling already.

Her face was bright pink, and she hesitated, but only a moment before she nodded. Fitzwilliam let out a loud laugh, and she quickly joined in, shyly giggling.

After a while, when their laughter quieted and the stars and moon began to work their magic, they returned their attention to the quiet night. She sighed at the beauty of the stark Mayfair landscape sparkling with its glittering layer of snow and hard rime. Inhaling the crisp air, she whispered her gratitude to God for this magical moment. It had been a struggle all night for her to not to sit gaping at him, and here he was next to her, stirring up emotions that she never even knew existed.

"My son will be impressed when I tell him I have had dinner with a real soldier."

"Indeed?" Fitzwilliam was taking great pleasure in the scent of soap and flowers surrounding her and crossing his arms before him leaned closer, his hip against the balustrade. "And how old is this ne'er-do-well son of yours?"

"Five."

"Ah, the age at which I achieved my emotional peak. I take it he is a fine boy, the very essence of an English gentleman."

"I confess to total prejudice in his favor. He *is* truly the most beautiful child alive, noble and happy, with the sweetest nature. However, spending nearly two years in America may have tarnished his English manners. I believe I have finally managed to convince him that spitting is not a competitive sport."

"He sounds like officer-candidate material to me," Fitzwilliam whispered. She intoxicated him, drew him like a bear to honey as he rested his hands against the wall behind her, trapping her between them. "He is a very lucky young boy to have such a beautiful and devoted mother."

The balcony became very still.

"Amanda, I am certain it has not escaped your notice that I am very enamored of you. Very enamored."

Her heart was pounding viciously. She had been yearning for a declaration of some sort from the colonel, but he had surprised her with his bluntness. He was so straightforward and her reaction was so intense it unsettled her. She smiled briefly then cleared her throat. "Perhaps I should return to the dowagers."

"What is it, Amanda? What do you fear so much? Is it me?"

"No. Not you." She shook her head sadly and sighed. "In truth it would never work, colonel," she said finally, her lashes low enough to hide her eyes, "you and me, together."

"Why ever not?" Taking her hand in his he kissed it then pressed it against his chest with both of his. "You care for me also, you know you do. How can you deny it?"

"You don't understand." She spoke barely above a whisper. "Colonel Fitzwilliam, you and I have no future beyond the moment. I am attracted to you—very attracted, and I am happy to know you have found me interesting. However, you belong to a world I do not understand nor even like. It is a world in which I have already failed miserably." She looked up into eyes that seemed to hold only warmth and love.

"I cannot imagine why you would fail in it, and I refuse to accept that there is no future, only here and now. Give me your reasons, young woman, so that I may bash them away."

"Well, it's all very obvious, there are so many differences. For one thing, you are an earl's son, a British officer, and I am an American citizen, the daughter of a teacher of medicine, a physician." Her eyes wrinkled with self-deprecating humor. "When you become upset, you retire to your country estates. When I become upset, I make applesauce."

He studied her hands, so cool and delicate encased within his large, scarred ones, and they were indeed hands that worked at many tasks, clean and neat but not manicured or fussed over. Bringing them to his lips, he kissed them both. "Is applesauce to be our only impediment, then?" His lips brushed lightly across her forehead, her cheek, her neck. She really did smell wonderful.

Her mind was suddenly very muddled. "No, of course not. That would be childish." She sighed and wondered what that wonderful scent was on his neck. It was very exciting, very masculine. "Well, *ahem*, my heavens, let's see; there's also apple pie and apple butter and apple..." She knew she was making no sense, and her voice trailed off with the heady feel of his warm breath on her closed eyelids.

"Yes, go on. You were speaking about apples, I believe. What other affront am I to battle with regards to apples?"

"Tarts," she rasped. He raised his eyebrows, and his eyes crinkled in amusement. She shook her head in momentary confusion. "Apple tarts, that is. Yes, that's it, apple tarts."

"Ah. Thank you for clarifying that. Well, you may be correct. However, I am only a second son, so my life has long been my own to decide, with my so-called exalted heritage of a level that I can do pretty much whatever I want and still be fawned over outrageously by the peerage." He pressed her fingertips to his heart.

"And, while perhaps you are right and we only have right now, not tomorrow or next week, I cannot help but think that there is more to us than mere physical attraction." All the gentle teasing gone from his eyes, he stared seriously at her. "You have lit up something within me, Amanda, an area that has been dark all my life, an area that I refuse to have go dark again. It is as if I had never lived before."

And suddenly she knew for a fact that nothing would ever be the same; everything he was saying was true. She was feeling the exact emotions as he, also alive for the first time in her life. His feelings mirrored her own so nearly that she shivered, began to entertain a thin ray of hope. It was frightening, allowing herself a moment to stand on the threshold of something wonderful, holding hands with *the* man, the *only* man, who had ever made her heart race and her knees weaken. Amanda pressed her back against the wall and stared mutely up at him and then down at their two hands still tightly interlocked.

The music, the laughter, the three hundred voices had faded into silence. Fitzwilliam tucked a stray lock of hair behind her ear then rested his forearm on the wall next to her head, his smiling lips mere inches away from hers. She opened her mouth to speak, only to close it again while her eyes drifted from his rumpled hair to his shining eyes and down again to his mouth.

She had waited for this moment her whole life. *This is my beloved.*

Resting his hand over her heart, he felt it pounding as hard as his. Her eyes brimmed with joyful tears as both her hands came up to press his more firmly against her breast. The moment had an unreal feel to it, as if two souls destined to journey together throughout eternity had finally been reunited.

They had finally both come home.

⁂

They blended together smoothly, then, their embrace encircling and their mouths slanting each to the other. His arms slipped around her waist and her shoulders, and his hand plunged into her hair. She was eager and pliant and passionate.

How long did they stand there as their kiss deepened, their hands growing more and more bold with passion? Five minutes or five hours—neither of them could later say. They were lost in that kiss, a cessation of time and space wherein she felt she could not hold him close enough, nor did he feel that he could kiss her deeply enough. But they kept trying, nonetheless. With his body, he pressed hers hard against the balcony wall, their tongues caressing. "This is madness," she gasped.

"Insanity," he agreed.

When they finally separated and rested their foreheads together, they smiled, warm and silly and in a besotted shock, breathing raggedly.

Then another even more passionate kiss began, leading into another.

And then one more.

⁂

"Fitzwilliam? Fitz? Where in bloody hell is that old fart?" Darcy muttered. "Richard, you'd better not be taking a piss off the..." He finally saw the couple in the far shadows, recognizing them a second later. The woman had jumped at the sound of his voice and now turned her flushed face away, hiding it in the shoulder of his cousin.

"Pardon, Fitz, oh my, forgive me for intruding." Stunned, Darcy stepped back, attempting to make a hasty retreat from the terrace.

"What is it, Darcy?" Fitzwilliam managed to say finally.

"Nothing, nothing really..." Darcy tried averting his eyes, but they kept flinging themselves back to the embracing couple. "Well, Fitz, I feel quite ridiculous. Georgiana is getting anxious in the crowd, and Aunt Catherine is concerned, wants us to take her home, but it can wait, good Lord, it can wait. Carry on... I mean, please excuse my intrusion." He walked back into the ballroom, cursing his own stupidity.

Amanda pulled back from the embrace to stare deeply into Fitzwilliam's eyes. She was sadly tumbling back down into reality. Even if they could surmount all other obstacles, there was still her son—she would never marry, could never leave her son. He tried to return to that magic, pulling her close in his arms, and she reached up to caress his cheek. "I must go."

"Don't leave, please," he whispered so earnestly. "Stay with me, forever."

She stared long and hard into his eyes. "You could not understand what you ask," she whispered back. "This must end here. Forgive me, Colonel, but there really is no future for us."

"I found the one whom my soul loves." She mourned within at the words. *Was that not the Psalm at last Sunday's mass?* Foolishly, she had believed at the time it an omen of good luck. Her broken heart twisted with the thought. "I am promised to another, Colonel."

His iron jaw clenched, and he took a quick step back, still holding her arms. "I beg your pardon?"

"Yes. I am promised to another. I am afraid that there really is no future for us."

He stared down at her for a few moments. Something was very wrong here. Nothing made sense. "Don't be ridiculous." He chuckled, blithely dismissing her comment with a smile. Hoping to read her thoughts, desiring only to stare again into her eyes, he attempted to lift her resisting chin with his finger. "No. No, I will not believe this. You are teasing me for some reason. Have I offended you, been too forward, is that it? I can assure you, madam, that my intentions are more than honorable. I'm in love with you, Amanda."

Amanda cleared her throat. "Forgive me. It was the romance of the night." She looked away, her eyes misting. "I forgot myself just a little."

What? Fitzwilliam's head shot back. "Forgot yourself '*just a little*'?! You quite amaze me with that immense understatement. Explain yourself."

Amanda began to stammer. "W-w-well, I was s-swayed by the lovely night, by the wine, but I am more lucid now. I couldn't think before, you see. The fact is that I am involved with someone else, and it would be unfair to him, as well as you, to allow this to go on any further." Her voice sounded thin and completely unconvincing, even to herself. "If my emotions have been carried away, I can only explain it by saying I am only human after all."

"Huh!" He threw an amused glance at her, one eyebrow quirking itself to death with its skepticism. "Please do not lie to me, Amanda." His tone became authoritative, firm. It was as if he was reprimanding a recalcitrant child. "I am not an idiot, my dear. There could be no one else, as we both know. What sort of foolishness do you play here?"

What did he mean—could not be anyone else? Was she that

undesirable? Even if she did regret this ridiculous lie, she could not retreat from it now. She yanked her hands free from his grasp and crossed her arms over her chest. "I beg your pardon, Colonel? You cannot honestly be calling me a liar?!" Her tone was icy cold.

"Yes, I can, and a pathetically poor one at that."

"Well, well. Colonel Fitzwilliam, I am not accustomed to having my words doubted in this way, or in any way, for that matter!" She was suddenly livid. "I can assure you that I *am* involved with another! Oh yes! He is a respected physician, and I know him very well from chapel on Sundays. In fact, I go often to his hospital to volunteer my services to the poor. Yes, we are very involved! I am involved unto the brink of receiving and accepting his offer!" Ha! That told him. She pulled and tugged at her dress then ruthlessly yanked locks of falling hair and seemed to pin them directly into her skull. He half expected to see rivulets of blood stream down her forehead and neck.

A disbelieving Fitzwilliam was becoming exceedingly annoyed. "Really? Is that a fact? How very interesting. Come, who is it, then? I insist on knowing his name. You say he is from the hospital. Very well, I am there often to visit my men. I am certain I know him. Well, speak, woman, who is this mysterious man you cannot live without? Tell me—*if you can*! Is it Mr. Cannon? Mr. Braithwaite? Sir Michael Siemons?"

"Sir Michael is nearly eighty-five years old!"

"Madam, after this encounter, I have every confidence in your ability to raise the dead. Now stop bamming me, Amanda! You are hardly the sort of female to be on the brink of betrothal to one man while passionately making love to another! I am not some young buck just come to town."

This was the outside of enough! Even if he *was* absolutely correct in his appraisal, why would he not think another would want her? She believed herself to be attractive in certain lights—true, those lights needed to be very dim and at least twelve feet away. *The nerve of this arrogant turtleback or lobsterfoot or whatever he is*. Her Yankee temper flared red-hot, and she twitched around like a netted fish, unable to stand still in one spot. "Please stand aside. I am returning home."

"Who is it? Anthony Milagros?" *Please don't let it be Milagros*. He had met Milagros and liked the man, but Milagros was tall, dark, and elegantly handsome. Most women he knew adored him. Suddenly he loathed the man. When Amanda's head snapped up at the name, Fitzwilliam's temper detonated. "So it *is* Milagros, is it? I might have known you would be like all the rest, drooling over some goddamn oily Latin type. Well, he is handsome and rich, I'll give you that!"

It was at that moment that Darcy came out onto the balcony, a concerned look on his face. "Is everything all right? You two are making a bit of a racket. People are beginning to become alarmed…"

"Get out!" they shouted in unison. Seeing the furious looks on both their faces, he immediately spun around on his heel and made a hasty retreat inside.

"Well!" She furiously patted her hair down on both sides. "I have never been so insulted nor so abused in my life! Colonel Fitzwilliam, I would appreciate it if you would never attempt to speak with me or contact me again!"

"Believe me, Lady Penrod, that is the farthest thought from my mind! You shall have no cause for further alarm on that front! The joy of the evening to you, madam!" Fitzwilliam released his hold on Amanda's arms so suddenly that she almost fell back against the wall. His fists rested upon his hips as he turned his body angrily away.

She threw down his coat and stormed off.

There was dead silence on the balcony.

Darcy had time only to retreat a few steps into the shadows of the ballroom, coming forward as soon as Amanda ran past, her head lowered. He came to stand just within the balcony doors. "Jesu, Fitz! What in hell happened out here?" Darcy ran his hand through his hair as he walked slowly toward his cousin.

Fitzwilliam looked out over the garden, unable for once in his life to torment his little cousin. "We were passionately in love—for a few minutes, anyway. One of my longer relationships."

Darcy chuckled. "I take it the earth moved?"

Fitzwilliam barked out a laugh. "Well, I've never heard my anatomy called that before, and yes, the South of France did wave." He grunted mirthlessly. "Shit! Give me a moment, Darcy. At present I am in no condition to walk through that room. Is Georgiana all right?"

"She's fine, merely her usual distress at being among such a large crowd. This promises to be a trying come out for us all."

Fitzwilliam saw the bottle of wine and two glasses in Darcy's hand. "I hope that's liquor you have there and that it is intended for me." Reaching over, he brushed aside the glass his cousin proffered, preferring the whole bottle. He took a long, hard draw.

"Did I come out here too early or too late?"

"Damned if I know." Fitzwilliam exhaled loudly and took

another draw from the bottle, finally remembering to pour some into Darcy's glass. They stood in silence for a while.

"She claims to be promised to another. Can you credit that? Promised to another when we were..." He looked quickly away before he continued. "Well, forget the rest of that. I just cannot believe this has happened! Something is very wrong."

"Did she say who the man is?"

"Dr. Anthony Milagros." Fitzwilliam rolled his eyes. Darcy winced, knowing Milagros's attraction to the opposite sex.

"Go after her, man!"

His cousin considered that recourse for only a brief moment then shook his head. "Never, brat! I am a confirmed bachelor, my own man, set in my ways and too old to change."

"You are only two and thirty. My own father was married at four and thirty. You have years left. Do not give up so easily."

"Goddamn it, Darcy, I do have *some* pride."

"Oh, you stupid idiot. When it comes to love, pride always takes second place."

"I have *never* had to chase a woman, *never*, and certainly have no intention to begin now!" With that, Fitzwilliam stormed away. "Beg for *that* harridan! Ha! I have not enough interest in her to even pursue this any further. End of discussion."

Chapter 10

Fitzwilliam leaned against Darcy's carriage, an angry lover assessing his rival's townhouse, the freezing rain fueling his fury. And the townhouse was an awesome sight, more a mansion, one of the largest, grandest homes in London, exceeded by few others, including Darcy's and Catherine's. "Shit. I knew the bastard was rich, but not this rich."

His loyal batman and driver, O'Malley, grunted his opinion. "Ah, well, don' be so hard on yerself, Colonel. Ya have good points—God bless me, even a busted clock is right twice the day. No, truly. Yer a good horseman, the very best I've ever seen, and yer kind to unfortunates… and ya have grand teeth. Oh, the fancy doctor may be filthy rich, an' dark and handsome an' all, and irresistible to the ladies, and…" Fitzwilliam's cold, hard stare stopped the litany of Anthony Milagros's greatness.

Unable to tear his eyes from his colonel's O'Malley took a large swig from his flask and trembled violently from the potent brew. He took out his pipe. "I'll not say another word. Me lips are sealed."

"Bloody hell..." Fitzwilliam cursed as he made his way across the road, and then again as he opened the gate. He began the climb up the granite steps, hissing "shit, shit, shit," on each one. He looked around as he approached the massive and elaborate double-door entryway. "Bloody hell." *Fine, money evidently will not influence him. I cannot possibly kill him. What are my other options?* He pounded on the door knocker.

An ancient butler answered, terror registering on his face within moments of Fitzwilliam demanding entrance. Without saying a word, the trembling servant turned, motioning for Fitzwilliam to follow, slowly leading the bizarre little parade at a snail's pace into a magnificently ornate receiving parlor. Finally facing the colonel he announced, in dreadful tones, that the doctor would be informed of his presence.

The splendid room was lit by the fires within two huge marble fireplaces, one on each end of the room, along with several gilt branches of candles strategically placed, Fitzwilliam sneered, for the sole beatific illumination of the highly expensive furnishings, rare tapestries, and paintings. It worked brilliantly. He walked to the front bank of French windows and turned to get the full effect, sweeping the room with his eyes. He exhaled loudly.

Shit.

Within the elegant mansion somewhere, an unsuspecting gentleman ignored the outdoor gloom and rain. To him, it was a lovely Tuesday evening in winter, crisp, clean and enchanting. Dr. Anthony Milagros had recently returned home after spending a productive but tiring day at his hospital and had put aside the disturbing visions his dearest friend's words had conjured up the day before.

"Bah!" He laughed at his baseless fears, rebuked his own reflection in the dressing-room mirror. He had reacted much too emotionally. Amanda had, of course, been correct, although that would be a first for her. The colonel was a highly decorated, nationally respected military leader, was lionized as a hero, a role model, a modern-day knight in shining armor. He would not act like some rabid dog defending a bone. Would he…?

No! Of course not. Ridiculous.

Anthony laughed softly as he thought back to the Sunday just past when he and Amanda had had their tiny "fracas." It was amusing to think of, really. In fact, as he now remembered it, with two days of hysteria as a cushion, he had been quite understanding during the entire confrontation—tolerant, sophisticated, exceedingly sympathetic.

"Have you lost your mind?!"

"Anthony, let me explain."

"He will call me out, Amanda. I'm a dead man. I will never again see my family, never again see Madrid. Look at these hands… look at them. They are beautiful and perfect, slim, elegant. And to think I will never again play the violin."

"You hate the violin." She dutifully complied with his request and studied his hands. "You play very badly."

"That is beside the point! I will have no time left to practice, will I? I will be dead."

They had stood outside the small chapel both attended for early Sunday mass, the only place in London that allowed

Catholic services. People scurried past, frightened by his extraordinary and spirited outburst, whispering and pointing, crossing themselves. Amanda dragged him by the elbow back into the church and deep into the south transept.

The chief of physicians at St. Theresa's Hospital in London paced back and forth. "I cannot breathe," he announced in amazement, then stopped. "Perhaps this is a heart attack?" He pressed his hand onto his chest. "I think I can hear my mother's voice."

"I do not understand what upsets you so."

"Oh, *dios mio mi vida*, pardon my thoughtlessness," he hissed. "You have told a man who desires you, whose profession it is to *kill people*, I might add, that I am your lover. Is this not correct?"

"Keep your voice down!" Amanda swept her glance around the main room of the church, concerned that they were in danger of being overheard, then returned her attention quickly to her agitated friend. "All right, Anthony, you are partially correct, in a way, yes..."

"In a way?" A ray of hope, that. Perhaps he had misunderstood her. "In what way am I mistaken, *querida*?" His long dark lashes were blinking furiously.

"Well, we had a somewhat intimate moment between us... oh, it was heavenly, Anthony. However, when he expressed a desire to court me, I am afraid I rather panicked, may have led him to believe something of a relationship was occurring between you and me."

He took a few moments to run a bejeweled, elegant hand through his curling locks then perused his cuticles closely. It was a while before he could calmly express himself. He decided he would speak slowly to her in the hope that she could grasp the gravity of what she had done.

"Well, as you know, I am acquainted with this Colonel Fitzwilliam of yours, Amanda. I have been in meetings with him at the War Office concerning his wounded soldiers. He possesses a look and manner not unlike your American grizzly bear. That is, he can be short-tempered, ruthless, aggressive, self-confident due to his rather formidable build. Also, he has fairly coarse hair." He watched her eyes closely for understanding, for a glint of comprehension. "He is vicious, pitiless, and ferocious." She still did not respond. "I like him enormously. But"—his hand went up before him to silence her—"I have no intention of willingly becoming the object of one of his vendettas. He is as unrelenting as he is merciless. He always gets what he wants, Amanda, always, no matter whom he must annihilate."

Anthony searched her face to see if this speech had affected her, penetrated her thick American skull. But no, he saw only hesitation in her sad, blinking brown eyes. She looked like a spaniel. He leaned forward and spoke louder to compensate. "Do you not comprehend me, *querida*??" Perhaps her hearing had gone the way of her brains.

She flapped her hands for him to be quiet. "Anthony, please cease being quite so Spanish. Compose yourself." He spat out an indignant harrumph at that. "Dearest, are you certain we speak of the same man? Richard has been all that is gentle and kind with me. Well, aside from his furious explosion on the balcony. I do not believe that he will pursue me if he believes us betrothed, and I surely had to stop his coming to Penwood, to that house. No, I am confident that, at heart, he is a most honorable man."

"*Betrothed?*" In his burgeoning terror, Anthony heard nothing else. "Tell me, do I have little beads of sweat forming upon my brow? No? I swear that I feel definite moisture about my hairline." He brought his silken handkerchief up to mop his brow then inhaled deeply. "So, my darling—tell me quickly to lessen the sting—*did* you, or did you not, inform him that we were betrothed? Yes or no."

"No, Anthony, of course I said no such thing. I would never lie, not really. Not in so many words. However"—Anthony's breathing stopped—"I may have implied that you were *about* to offer for me.'

Anthony looked horrified, but she continued without noticing. "You see we were… together, in each other's arms. Oh, it was beautiful, Anthony, heavenly. Never before have I experienced such passion, and he was so gentle. Anthony, he told me he loved me." She beamed, her eyes shining. "Do you remember how I would question you about him after your meetings at the War Office? I must confess I have long admired him."

Anthony still looked horrified.

"Anthony, do be calm. He is all kindness. I fear what he truly felt was the need to comfort me, not love me. Emily informed him how a woman who thought I was a servant ridiculed me and tried to have me thrown from the ladies' retiring room. It was very lowering, Anthony. She made me feel very sad." He looked down at her bowed head, his hands rubbing her upper arms soothingly, then leaned forward and softly kissed her forehead.

"All right, now tell me exactly what you said about me to the colonel."

"Is that all that concerns you?!" She was incensed. "Have you heard nothing else?!"

"Amanda! I am *the most* sensitive man alive, as you well know! I am profoundly troubled with how that woman insulted you. I hate that woman. I spit on that woman. Oh no, wait! I cannot spit on that woman because I will be… *dead*! Thank you, Amanda." He grabbed her hands, bending over to look straight into her eyes. "My darling friend, why do you hate me so much?"

"Please try to see this from my viewpoint, Anthony. I am in love with him. There, I have finally spoken the words." She closed her eyes and inhaled deeply before continuing. "It was imperative to say something to him to keep him away. I had to make him believe that I was involved romantically with another. You understand, don't you? You, as my dearest friend in the world, must understand. I have never before asked anything of you, have I?"

"Yes, yes, you have. Many times. Countless times. Constantly." Anthony watched as Father Riley spoke to the few stragglers in the church, after which he glanced quizzically their way. The old priest had an unerring instinct for rooting out trouble. *Like a pig for truffles*, Anthony thought wildly. He grabbed Amanda's elbow and led her deeper into the church.

"May I say something to you, as a close friend who loves you with all his heart and cares deeply about your happiness?

"Of course, Anthony. You know I value your opinion most highly."

"How idiotic can you be?"

She punched him in the shoulder very, very hard.

"No, truly, Amanda. You have a chance for genuine happiness with a man you love and who evidently also cares deeply for you." Reassuring himself that Riley had been diverted once again, he looked down with affection at his friend. "Amanda, *dios mio*, attend me, please. You are a healthy, lovely young woman, and he is a healthy, single man. Grab life and live for a change."

"I have given you my declaration that he will never bother

you, Anthony," Amanda said coolly. "I must discourage this suit somehow, and he truly is an honorable man. As long as he feels that I am spoken for, he will not push me for any deeper sort of a relationship."

"You are mistaken concerning this for two reasons." He sighed and took her hands in his. "First, no one is honorable when it comes to love." His eyebrows rose when she opened her mouth to protest, and he raised his hand to silence her.

"Second, you are throwing away your life. True love is rare. You know I have never been able to replace mine. If you love this man as deeply as you say, well then you are a fool to let it pass. Even if it is experienced only for a moment, true love is rare and precious." He raised her hands to his lips and kissed them tenderly.

"But how can I, Anthony? You know how my life is held in forfeit. I could lose my son if she discovers us."

Anthony turned a compassionate gaze at her. "In the eyes of the law, you have already lost him, *querida*. When will you accept this? Anyway, did I say she would have to know? Liaisons are a national diversion here. In some circles they are even mandated. Are you not aware that one half of the *ton* is always cuckolding the other?"

As her eyes filled with tears, she shook her head.

"It is just not my way, Anthony." She sighed deeply. "I was not raised to carry out the sort of life they lead here. I do not understand these people and I doubt that I could ever be capable of having a relationship outside of marriage vows. I couldn't, could I? No, it is not in my upbringing, but I love him so very much. Oh, I don't know what I should do! You understand this, as a Catholic, don't you? I mean, would it not feel sinful?"

"Only if he is very skillful..."

It had taken only a moment then for Amanda to swat the back of Anthony's head very, very hard.

Remembering, he shook his head and chuckled at his own witticism. "Only if he is very skillful," he repeated to his reflection in the mirror. *Very clever, Antonio,* he complimented himself and smiled, once again at peace and happily looking forward to drinking his very expensive imported French brandy, eating an exquisite meal prepared by his very expensive French chef, and relaxing for hours in the arms of his latest paramour, due at any moment.

Life was, indeed, very good for Dr. Anthony Milagros.

As the valet adjusted the lapels of Anthony's exquisite dinner jacket, his butler scratched discreetly at the dressing-room door. "Enter, Bascome." Swirling a brandy snifter around several times, Anthony took his initial sip, savoring the sweet nectar as he regarded his butler's visage in the mirror.

The ancient gentleman gazed back.

Anthony raised his eyebrows in question and waited. They remained staring silently at each other in the mirror for quite a few moments, the tottering butler apparently unable to vocalize. Anthony finally turned toward him and finished off his drink. "Well?"

"Your lordship…" Bascome appeared distressed.

"Yes, old friend," he said patiently and with mild humor. "I know who I am. What is it you wish to say to me?" Anthony smiled warmly at this most beloved of servants and dear old confidant. "Out with it, please. Be courageous, man. Is there a problem with the salmon? Has the cook overdone some sauce again? What is today's disaster? What?"

As he began to fuss with the cuffs of his shirt, adjusting their length until just the proper amount of lace peeked from the sleeve of his jacket, he suddenly groaned. "If it is the champagne ices, I am afraid you will have to deal with the wine steward yourself this time. He terrifies me."

The butler grimaced, sadly shaking his head. "Your lordship," he intoned again, "it is with great regret that I must inform you… there is a British officer here to see you."

Anthony froze. "Sorry? What did you say?"

"A quite massive British officer, a colonel, I believe, wishes to see you. He is in a somewhat emotional state." Bascome removed a large white handkerchief from his cuff to dab at his brow. "Truth be told, sir, this is the first Englishman I have seen in *any* emotion. It is an unnerving and ugly sight and—*Mother of the Divine Savior, intercede for us*—he has a sword on his side that he keeps touching and—*God have mercy on our souls*—I believe a pistol hidden within his uniform." The elderly butler stuffed his sodden cloth back into his pocket and attempted to stand at full attention, his arthritic five-foot-five-inch aching frame poised for the defense of his master. He dropped his voice several octaves. "Shall I summon the constabulary?"

Anthony blinked for several moments as his extremities became numb. "*Merde*… I will kill her one day. Ah, I have dreams, Bascome, oh yes, wonderful dreams of a world without my dearest Amanda. We will ship her remains to Greece. I have people there you know. No one would suspect." He studied the terrified old man and reined in his rhetoric. "I go down directly. Please pour yourself a glass of brandy. You look as if you are about to have a seizure. Put your feet up, old friend, all will be fine." He pointed to a chair, and when he was certain his butler was settled, he turned to contemplate his own certain death.

Chapter 11

"May I help you?" Fitzwilliam turned to see the familiar and elegant gentleman peering at him from the doorway. "Ah! Colonel Fitzwilliam, how good to see you again. It has been too long." Despite voicing such welcoming pleasantries, however, Milagros did not approach him or extend his hand for greeting. Fitzwilliam was not displeased—it denied him the opportunity to encircle the good doctor's throat with his hands.

"Yes, it has been a while, Doctor. I trust you are well." Without waiting for an answer, Fitzwilliam continued. "I wonder if I could have a moment of your time." Fitzwilliam absently rested his hand on his sword and had the satisfaction of seeing Milagros's eyes nervously follow.

"Of course, Colonel. Please have a seat. My home is your home." The gentleman sauntered into the room and motioned for Fitzwilliam to sit. He himself then sat at some distance away, crossing one leg over the other. "Can I have my butler provide you with anything, Colonel? Port? Brandy? Hostages?" He laughed anxiously, quickly quieting into a subdued cough, and then ended with a penitential throat clearing.

"This is not a pleasure call, Milagros."

Resting his elbow on the chair arm, Anthony cupped his chin while he perused his visitor. "'More's the pity,'" was his mumbled response.

Fitzwilliam had a fleeting impression that he was receiving a sort of sexual scrutiny from the man. He shook off this impression as hysteria or lack of sleep or gas. "I have come to discuss your relationship with Amanda Penrod."

Anthony's eyebrows rose momentarily. "My goodness, we are direct, aren't we?" He cleared his throat. "Yes, well, I *have* been expecting you." A hand went up to smooth his already perfect hair.

"If you have been expecting me, then you must know what I have come to discuss with you, gentleman to gentleman."

"I have a fairly good idea." Milagros settled back into his chair, slouching in an attitude of evidently benign indifference, while in reality, his heart pounded. His fingers pinched at his lower lip while he assessed his opponent. Suddenly he spoke. "Let me make this somewhat easier for you, Colonel."

Fitzwilliam was confused. He had been prepared for mental and mortal combat; however, the man before him did not appear as one whose affections for another were being threatened or challenged. This man seemed totally indifferent to that situation. In fact, as the minutes ticked on, Fitzwilliam began to feel uneasy, anxious, exposed. He shifted uncomfortably, crossing his legs as Anthony's gaze drifted downward, taking in all of his body, from his boyishly disheveled hair, the rumpled colonel's uniform jacket that emphasized the muscled arms and large chest, then down to a perusal of the tree-trunk legs encased in his white uniform trousers, and his well-worn boots.

Milagros sighed and muttered something.

"I told Amanda you would come here." He spoke in a very matter-of-fact manner, drumming his fingers on his chair arm. "I told her it was a ridiculous story, but as you may or may not know, she can often be very stubborn. *Dios mio*, to call her stubborn is an insult to mules."

Fitzwilliam sank slowly onto the settee. "What in blazes are you talking about?" In total bewilderment, he watched as the doctor stood to pour out a brandy from the decanter next to him and then down it in one gulp. Richard waved off one for himself. Anthony shrugged, finished off that second one also and sat down, holding tightly onto his third drink.

"Are you in love with Amanda, Colonel?" Milagros's eyes peered at him from above his brandy glass. That second drink had given him a slightly more courageous tongue.

"Goddamn you to hell! Of all the impertinent, rude questions! Listen to me, Milagros, a man would have to have lost all common sense to get involved with a woman in possession of that sort of temper! She has no conception of restraint, does she?"

"Normally I would defend her with my very last breath. However, no, she does not. But that did not answer my question, did it? Do you love her?"

"Ha!" Fitzwilliam snorted his derision. "You must be insane! She is a good deal too unpredictable for my tastes. No, no, no, that's too kind of an assessment. Actually, I suspect she is mentally unstable. Yes. That's a more accurate description of her true personality. She possesses serious mental impairments."

"But do you *love* her?"

"Well, yes, dammit! Of course I love her, you idiot! Do you think I'd be here making a bloody fool of myself for any other reason? Now, I want to know from you what is going on, because I cannot get a sensible word from her mouth. Are you bedding her? Have you made her an honorable offer?"

"You English aristocrats are so amoral that you are unable to entertain a thought above your waist." Anthony huffed. "It is extremely unromantic."

Fitzwilliam slowly turned his head, and then with a menacing look, he leaned on the table, resting his weight on his fists.

"I always make the mistake of saying exactly what I am thinking at the moment. Very unfortunate..." Anthony's voice shook as it rambled on into silence. He passed a hand over his eyes. "You realize that if you kill me, someone will figure it out. I bleed profusely."

"One last time, Milagros. Are you and she betrothed? I have been making inquiries. Those who know of you believe you *are* secretly involved with someone, although no one seems to know whom. Was Amanda married when you began this affair? Is that it, Milagros? Is she the reason none of the *ton*'s mamas can lure you into an alliance? Is it she who has been your secret lover?" Fitzwilliam's voice was now barely above a whisper.

"*Dios mio.*" Anthony ran his fingers through his hair. "You are going to make me say this out loud, aren't you?" Anthony's voice quivered, and his stomach roiled, but Fitzwilliam continued to glare, his fury barely under control. He finally had enough.

"Answer me, damn you!!"

Anthony leaned forward, all the color drained from his face. "Please understand, Colonel, that what I tell you now could have me imprisoned or worse."

Startled, Fitzwilliam eyed him suspiciously. "What is going on here, Milagros?" He had not anticipated this line of argument.

Anthony angrily began muttering something in Spanish about Amanda, his hands poking wildly at certain emphatic declarations, then mopped at perspiration running down the back of his neck.

Fitzwilliam was listening intently, trying to grasp a word from the too-rapid Spanish, when he suddenly heard a sneeze from the hallway. He stiffened and spun toward the closed door. "Is she here?" He spoke low, but his mouth had set into a cruel, clenched line.

Anthony's head shot up quickly as he too turned toward the hallway. Alarmed and tense, he began to rise.

"Colonel, listen to me! You are under the impression, I believe, that you and I are in some sort of competition for the affections of Amanda, are you not?" Fitzwilliam said nothing but continued to glower. "*That* is your mistake. You see, in actuality, it would be Amanda and I..." Glancing at the door, Anthony swallowed hard and lowered his voice. He coughed and cleared his throat. "It *was* Amanda and I in a competition for *you*."

Fitzwilliam heard a muffled male voice spit out the words "bloody hell" from the corridor, followed by running footsteps, then a door slamming. Anthony groaned and started toward the doorway. "Edmund, wait!" he called just before another door somewhere deep in the house slammed shut. Within moments, a carriage raced from the back of the house and onto the street.

Fitzwilliam and Anthony stared at the closed door for several minutes, then both turned to watch through the French doors as the carriage careened wildly down the driveway. Anthony dropped into the chair, his head falling backward onto the headrest.

"*Merde*!" he whispered miserably.

Fitzwilliam's eyes were huge as saucers as he turned slowly in stunned silence. "Beg pardon?" he managed finally to say.

Chapter 12

Anthony's second nightly delight after his warmed brandy—the superb meal that his chef had prepared with such care—was quickly relegated to the trash. It was now near midnight, and the two men sat silently before the fireplace, each wallowing in his own lovelorn misery. Emptied bottles of wine were scattered amidst the tobacco pouches and cheroot ashes.

"Why doesn't she want me, Milagros?" Fitzwilliam was slumped far down in his chair, his shirt disheveled and his cravat loose around his neck. He tried to rub the burning from his red-rimmed eyes. "Bah! That's an unfair question. I am certain this is as much a mystery to you as it is to me, because, obviously, I'm a perfectly pleasant fellow. The ladies adore me, usually."

"What?" Milagros turned a bleary eye to his companion. The poor doctor did not look like the same fine fellow who had begun the evening with such anticipation. Liquor had dimmed his glamorous eyes, his cravat was now askew, his hair a bit tousled, and he sat loose-limbed, his shirtsleeves unlinked and turned back. Already a heavy, dark beard was beginning to appear on his face. All in all, it was the most slovenly Dr. Milagros had looked in nearly four years. He had been staring intently at the end of his cigarillo, turning the burning cylinder slowly between his fingers. "What are you blathering about now?"

"My God, what a pathetic pair we make." Fitzwilliam shook an empty bottle, then another, finally finding one half full. Anthony automatically held out his glass. "Listen, Jose, I want you to know that your secret is safe with me. I apologize to you for forcing the issue, pushing you to tell me the truth. Shouldn't have pushed, should have minded my own business. But then I would have needed to kill you. However, I imagine I did you a favor, actually. It felt good to admit everything out loud, what? A load off, as they say."

After slanting him an evil look, Milagros flicked his ashes at him. "No, Dickie, it did not feel good. It felt like shit, which is how I now feel. But that is fine. I imagine that I will survive this, no thanks to you."

"No one will learn of your deep, dark secret from my mouth. I swear on my brother's life that I will go to my grave with this knowledge." A slightly inebriated Fitzwilliam poised one finger before his mouth and emitted a soft "sshh."

"Well, if you really feel so badly about this I would appreciate your doing exactly that as soon as possible—go to your grave, that is, Ricardo. It will save me years of anxiety."

"Nonsense, Manuel. My lips are sealed. I have been trusted with worse secrets about many others, much, much worse, ghastly secrets, people you know well, famous people, people of the Empire. Remind me to regale you with them someday, always popular fare at parties. You will be astounded. It will curl your hair."

Anthony groaned, and Fitzwilliam chuckled.

"Seriously, Anthony, I do apologize. Did you care for this person very much? I mean, will you be able to explain to him what happened?"

"That a bloodthirsty, murdering, bastard of a soldier knows our secret? Of course, I am certain he will be thrilled. No, what I will tell him will be some sort of lie, and he'll believe me because he wants to believe me. He really is a good fellow, you know. I am certain that when he stops to logically consider this, he will find it highly unlikely that I would choose you over him, and he will come back to me."

They stared at each other silently for a moment.

"I believe I have just been insulted." Fitzwilliam puffed on his pipe, and they turned to study the fire again, continuing in companionable silence for a time.

Richard was the first to speak. "So, tell me, Carlos, why doesn't Amanda want me? I can almost understand your rejection of me, but why hers?"

"No, no, no, my dear friend, you are not approaching this the right way. It is not you she is rejecting, although now that I know you better, it would be the path I would recommend." Fitzwilliam grunted his protest. "No, no, she is restricted by the custody issue of her child, as I have explained to you at least three times by now." Anthony stubbed out his cheroot and lit another. "Hearing is the second thing lost to old age, or so I am told," he mumbled under his breath. Fitzwilliam scowled.

"Shall I tell you how I met her?"

"I really wish you would not."

"Very well, then, I shall. I met her almost directly after her marriage to Augustus..."

"It's very late. Will this take long?"

"Yes, it will. Be quiet, and maybe you will understand better. Open up that bottle of red substance, whatever it is, and listen. Now you will learn all."

"I knew who Amanda was before even meeting her. As you might suspect, a part of my social life is centered among a rather select and discreet circle of the aristocracy." Anthony held out his glass for Fitzwilliam to refill. "Amanda's husband, Augustus, was a well-known, if not particularly well-regarded, figure at many of our social gatherings."

The room became quiet as a tomb as Anthony allowed that particular revelation to settle. Fitzwilliam's raised eyebrows were the only indication of his shock. Anthony nodded. "And, Richard, that is something which she must never know.

"He had been involved with another for many years, a devoted couple, as if married in every sense of the word; however, there could obviously never be an heir from their union. It was the incessant harassment from his mother that sent him to America in search of a wife, both mother and son feeling it too dangerous to choose from among the upper classes here and thereby risking exposure. Amanda's father was physician to one of Penrod's American relatives, and she would oftentimes accompany him. Augustus requested an introduction, courted her, easily impressing her with his title and manners. She was so very young, unsophisticated by *ton* standards, but all he really required from her was an heir. In his defense, I believe he did care for Amanda at first, but not in the way she deserved, more like one would love an adorable child or pet. Do not become offended at what I am saying, Colonel, please." Richard's eyes had narrowed dangerously. "He also quickly became embarrassed by her.

"I personally grew to know her later, when she came to worship at St. James Chapel on Spanish Place. There are so few places here where Catholics are allowed to worship that we all eventually become acquainted with each other, no matter what status or rank. My own ancestors headed the Spanish Court that founded this same chapel centuries ago, and now I sit beside poor Irish potato farmers and displaced French counts. It is all very odd, but what can one do?

"I found I liked her very much. She was exceedingly spirited, enormously pretty, and quite tenderhearted. We became very close friends, the best of friends. She began to volunteer at the hospital, confiding in me a great deal. She realized she had married in haste without knowing her husband's true character, said he had grown cold and unfeeling. I knew better than she that her marriage was doomed to failure. When she did begin increasing, it was a huge relief to them both. They could now go their separate ways. In the end, sadly, Augustus turned his back on her and the child, hating them both for the rift that had developed between him and Andre. I am afraid he was very vindictive and harsh."

Fitzwilliam rubbed his hand over the back of his neck. "It makes me heartsore to think she has been so mistreated. I am grateful to you, Anthony, for being a friend to her all these years."

Anthony shrugged. "I, too, love Amanda, Colonel. She was there for me when no one else came forward. Four years ago, someone I cared for deeply was killed in Portugal. He was a courier for Wellington when he was captured and... tortured.

Och! Terrible business—war. It destroys so many more lives than is obvious." Anthony cleared his throat and continued. "I received a letter telling me that Mario had been killed, telling me how bravely he died. He is… he was, my life." Tears began to slide down his cheeks, tears which he quickly swiped away.

"I locked myself in this room and cried for hours, the poor servants terrified I would do something rash. My butler, Bascome, sent word to Amanda, and she immediately came.

"I unlocked the door, and she walked in as I threatened to kill myself. I was extremely dramatic in those days." He laughed softly at the memory, rubbing a hand over his eyes. "*Dios mio*, but she was angry with me! By that time, she knew the truth about my life, had lectured me to death about it, and still does, I might add. She was quite forthright with me, saying I was behaving dangerously and that I would soon be exposed by my behavior. She was patient but firm." He sighed deeply and smiled for a moment.

"I believe it was his mother who prodded Augustus into suing for sole custody of the child, considering Amanda an encumbrance. He accused her of kidnapping their child when she returned to America to nurse her father. Eventually he applied to parliament to sever any privileges she might have. He was actually on his way to America to claim his son when his ship went down.

"It was not until her return to England that she was informed she had lost custody of her child. She was told to either leave the child immediately or risk being imprisoned.

"Well, the child became so hysterical that the mother-in-law had to relent, allowing her to remain. That is where she stands today, a sort of tenant at sufferance, a poor relation. If her mother-in-law even suspects that she has interest in another man, she will consider it a final insult to her son and throw Amanda out."

After a long time sitting in silence, both staring into the fireplace, Fitzwilliam relit his pipe, stood, and walked toward the windows. It appeared that in a matter of days his universe had changed focus, centering now upon one exasperating but adorable young woman. He resented the people who had laughed and taunted her, evaluated her unfairly, and found her wanting.

And they would never accept Amanda or any other person without the requisite familial associations, proper ancestry, certainly would never acknowledge someone whose family had physically worked to provide hearth and home, even a physician and teacher as her father had been.

"You know, Anthony, I have begun to yearn for a home and a spouse, children." He puffed on his pipe absently. "I had actually meant to properly court Amanda toward an eventual offer for her hand." He shook his head sadly.

"No, she would never leave her son, Colonel, not even for you, and she would think a liaison the height of sinfulness. What a coil. You would have made a good husband for her."

"Who said I won't marry her?"

Anthony's lips twitched a little. "Ah, you perhaps also have difficulties with the English language? I seem to have just wasted an inordinate amount of time and energy explaining why she will never marry."

"I must have missed that. All I heard is that she won't leave her son, perfectly natural and understandable. I simply won't ask it of her, but we shall marry."

At a loss for words, Anthony began to laugh, shaking his head in mild amazement.

They sat for quarter of an hour listening to a gentle rain outside before Fitzwilliam spoke again. "You know I had a similar conversation to this not long ago. My God, was it only weeks ago I swore that I would *never* marry, that it was something that held no interest for me? What a pompous ass I am."

Anthony grinned devilishly, and Fitzwilliam cocked one eyebrow in mock hauteur. "May I know the reason for your amusement, sir?"

"I hope I do not offend you; however, I cannot but wish you had a brother I could meet."

Fitzwilliam's eyes wrinkled in humor, and he turned to his new friend. "Well, actually, I do have a brother, and we have been wondering why he has no interest in marriage and in producing the requisite heir. I wonder..."

❧

"Is all well, your lordship?" The ancient butler, who had fallen asleep in Anthony's chair, attempted to rise as his master walked into the bedroom's dressing room.

"Sit, Bascome, rest. Why don't you pour us both a drink? I have quite an enjoyable tale to tell you." Anthony allowed his valet to help him shrug out of his jacket.

"I am very sorry that your lordship's friend left in such an agitated state."

"Who? Sir Edmund? Oh, do not concern yourself, old friend. I believe he will return." He leaned down to take the brandy snifter. "I have a good feeling about him."

"What of the colonel, sir? They have told me he showed great promise. Perhaps...?"

Anthony laughed as his valet undid his cravat. "Regretfully, no, Bascome, his interests quite literally lie elsewhere, shall we say?"

"More is the pity. He reminded me so much of our late Master Mario." Anthony nodded and smiled wistfully, lighting up another cigarillo, then sat down to tell his old friend the tale of Amanda and Richard.

❧

On the following morning, Sunday morning, Fitzwilliam felt terribly hung over but remarkably more optimistic, having identified his true enemy. Instead of the dashing Spanish aristocrat he had so feared, he found that the biggest obstacle to his future happiness appeared to be a social-climbing, elderly society matron. The Beast. The mother of Amanda's late husband, Augustus, was tough as steel and bitter from her loss. Upon further reflection, he decided he might have preferred the Spanish aristocrat.

Chapter 13

It was the last Sunday before advent, and the carillon bells announcing early morning mass rang out high above ancient St. James Chapel. The streets were bustling with Spanish Place street vendors, shouting out their raucous greetings to one and all as they loaded their carts, readying themselves for the journey across to Covent Garden. Former soldiers warmed themselves around sputtering campfires, comparing war stories and wounds, exchanging bawdy remarks with the evening ladies who were finally making their exhausted way home.

Fitzwilliam jogged up the uneven stone steps and opened the church's massive wooden doors, music from the men's choir greeting him as he stepped into a musty darkness, taking a few moments for his eyes to adjust. It was a surprisingly large crowd, to his mind, for this early an hour. At the very least, an Anglican service would never interrupt the *ton*'s morning-after recuperation time like this.

He had no trouble spotting Amanda and Anthony. After a squeaky walk up the old center aisle, Richard slipped into the pew behind them. As a rather large British officer, he had caused something of a commotion upon entering the church, but he took this all in stride, excusing himself most graciously for the interruption, even exchanging pleasantries with the people around him. Only one or two of the faithful were brave enough to express their anger with him. Most seemed only sleepy, and others were just plain curious. "Pardon, please pardon..." he kept repeating politely in his rumbling baritone whisper, then he set his hat down on the seat beside him.

Anthony turned almost immediately, amused and nodding in welcoming acknowledgement, but Amanda's reaction was one of stiff-backed bewilderment. On the pew between them sat a sleepy little boy, a beloved cloth toy clutched to his chest. He suckled his thumb as he nodded off to sleep.

Fitzwilliam had composed what he felt was a compelling argument to present to Amanda concerning their joint future. As he would before any battle, he had methodically examined each and every option, attempted to anticipate any unforeseen impediments, and had settled upon a clearly thought-out and logical plan of action. Now that his plan was decided upon, Fitzwilliam was eager to set it in motion. In his experience with battle, delay often meant defeat.

Managing to sit still in his pew for only a few moments, he came forward to kneel on the hard wooden slat. He poked Amanda once in the back, unaware that her face had already passed bright pink and was now approaching crimson. Her hand flew behind to swipe his away. "Amanda," he gruffly whispered, "I need to speak with you."

A chorus of "shhhhs" assailed him from every direction.

"Pardon me... My error... Terribly sorry..." Sufficiently

chastised, he nodded apologetically to all around him and most drifted back into an inattentive daze, unwilling to further antagonize the intruder. After all, he towered over everyone, even kneeling down.

The choir started on their next hymn, the number in large letters on a board in the front of church. Casting about for a hymnal, Fitzwilliam snatched one from the pew behind him, turning to the indicated selection. It was with great relief that he recognized, "O God Our Help in Ages Past."

"How very excellent. This hymn is one of the favorites of my youth," he announced in an ear-deafening aside. Fitzwilliam faced forward and began to sing.

His booming baritone erupted like a bomb in the small chapel, easily drowning out the half-hearted Catholic bleating of the flock. Anthony's shoulders began to shake. Amanda yelped. The child between them jumped as if bitten.

Up on the altar, Father Riley's shoulders flinched, and he turned an annoyed glance in Fitzwilliam's direction, removing his glasses and putting down the outline of the sermon he was reviewing. Many of the faithful in the congregation followed their pastor's lead and strained to look at this most vocal of visitors.

Fitzwilliam, who had always considered singing at the top of your lungs in church the very best reason for attending, appeared blissfully content with the attention and graciously smiled back at one and all.

It was seven-thirty in the morning, and Harry Penrod was bored, bored with the hushed voices and the dim candles, bored with the slow, reverent singing. He was so bored that he was even unwilling to fight, as he always did, the drift into sleep he was feeling. He sucked contentedly on his thumb and moved his tiny hand forward to play with the fringes of his mama's shawl. Even horsey was not of any interest to him at the moment.

It was then that the earth shook, and Harry jumped from the shock, his head spinning around to see what disastrous event had occurred. To his great surprise, behind him stood the largest man he had ever seen, wearing a huge tent of a cloak, which when parted, revealed red material containing shiny brass medals and glimpses of golden braid.

It was a soldier!

Harry stared up at the giant for the longest time, speechless. What to do? What to do? Here was one of those moments his mama had warned him about that could divert him from respectful silence for Baby Jesus. On the one hand, he was only a little boy, but on the other, he *had* promised his mama to remain quiet and out of trouble for the duration of the mass. After all…

Baby Jesus never caused trouble.

Baby Jesus obeyed his nursey and put away his clothes.

Baby Jesus always finished his soup. Privately, Harry had once or twice sacrilegiously thought that Baby Jesus did not seem to be much fun, but still and all, Harry wished he could be like Baby Jesus, if only for a few moments.

Then the giant winked at him!

His little heart pumped wildly. Unable to resist, Harry pulled himself into a standing position to commence reconnaissance. Perhaps beneath that heavy cloak there were gold buttons and braids, more medals, velvet trim—oh, but it could be a hidden treasure trove of delights, this magnificent uniform. He gingerly pulled back the edge of the cloak to peek inside, hoping that the large man would somehow not notice this rather personal intrusion. Never before had he seen so much brass and gold—this must be a very important soldier, he reasoned, and such a huge expanse of red that it made his eyes swim! Pushing the cloak open even wider, he leaned way over and then sighed, disappointed not to see a bloody sword. He closed the cloak and then patted it fondly.

Chapter 14

The child sniffled, vigorously rubbing his nose back and forth across his sleeve, and oh, how Fitzwilliam remembered the days when there was no time for studies or naps or pianoforte lessons, let alone handkerchiefs. He retrieved a clean one from his pocket and held it over the child's mouth and nose. The boy's eyes flashed up to Fitzwilliam's face as he blew his nose loudly into the cloth two or three times. Fitzwilliam then folded it over and dabbed the little nose dry before returning the saturated cloth to his pocket.

Harry stood up on tiptoes so that he could whisper near to Richard's ear, "Thank you, sir."

"You are quite welcome," replied Fitzwilliam, smiling down at the beautiful youngster. With a child's innocence, little Harry disregarded the imposing size of the man, only to see the gentle warmth of his smile, and smiled in return. He continued to regard Fitzwilliam for several more minutes.

"You are a soldier, sir."

"Why, so I am," Fitzwilliam responded, and the child nodded gravely, his eyes filled with respect.

He studied Fitzwilliam thoughtfully. Holding the back of the pew, he rocked back once or twice, his intense curiosity focusing on the many scars of battle he saw, on the soldier's neck and forehead, the faint scar across his jaw, then finally he rested his gaze on a very large and ugly scar on Fitzwilliam's hand. Utterly fascinated, he fingered it tenderly as he sniffled once more. Again he went up on his tiptoes to speak into Fitzwilliam's ear. "From where did you receive this, sir? Was it in a battle?" he asked in his child's little whisper.

Fitzwilliam nodded. "I received that at Waterloo," he whispered back. The boy gravely nodded with all the immense respect due to the significance of that fact, even though he hadn't a clue what a Waterloo was. Then he recollected a wound he himself had received in battle and pulled up his trouser. Twisting his leg around, he pointed to a scar on the back of his calf while he held onto Richard's shoulder for balance. Richard reached his arm about the boy's waist for support.

Richard dutifully studied the little scar and made an appropriately sympathetic noise. He raised an eyebrow inquiry.

"Dorset" was the identification of the battlefield.

Fitzwilliam stifled his chuckle with a discreet cough. "Ah."

They stayed like that for several moments, the companionable silent bonding of two warriors. They were now best of pals, Harry's arm stretched up to Fitzwilliam's shoulder, which he would pat occasionally to comfort his new friend. Fitzwilliam still had his arm supporting the child's waist.

He strained upward to speak into Richard's ear again as he touched the scarred hand. "Did a Frenchie do that to you, sir?" His compassion was deeply serious, and Fitzwilliam nodded, much moved by the child's sincerity.

Harry let that information take root for a moment in his five-year-old brain, and sighing, shook his head.

"Goddamn Frenchies..." he sympathized.

"All right, that is quite enough." Amanda turned, no longer able to pretend ignorance of the conversation behind her.

Harry cast a worried glance up at his mother. "Whatever is wrong, Mama?" he whispered.

"Shush! Harry, please sit down now and pay attention to the mass," she whispered back.

"But, Mama, I wasn't doing anything bad," he explained. "I have to give comfort to my new friend. He is a soldier. Don't look at him. He's been horribly disfigured by war."

Amanda's eyes went briefly up to Richard's in mute apology, but he was grinning back at her, his eyes revealing his deep affection. A defeated Harry sat back down in his seat as his mother began her obligatory reprimand.

Fitzwilliam could not hear what was being said but felt a twinge of guilt seeing as he was equally to blame for the disruption. She was a gentle mother though—kind and firm, loving and sensible. Harry nodded and whispered something back, and then they kissed. Fitzwilliam's heart swelled at the beautiful sight. After a moment, Harry looked back at Richard and smiled contentedly.

It was some time after the service had ended, and Richard now stood at the back of the church, waiting for Amanda, mentally reviewing his prepared comments for her, going over and over in his head the course before them. Absently, he twirled his bicorn hat in his hand as he nodded to the people streaming past him—the street vendors already late for work, the immigrant men who held their poor but proud heads high, the black-dressed, elderly women hurrying home, the street children looking for a few hours' warmth, the Irish housemaids. He especially acknowledged the salutes of several old soldiers and happily spared them as much time and coin as they required.

Anthony reached him finally and accepted his handshake, while behind Anthony, a beaming Harry dragged his mother forward.

"Colonel Fitzwilliam, I am so surprised to see you here." Amanda was breathless as an exuberant Harry bounced up and down on his heels. "Colonel, allow me to introduce you to my son, Harold Augustus Penrod. He is very anxious to make your acquaintance."

"Mama, please let my hand go. I must make my bow. Grandmamma showed me." He took a step forward and bowed deeply, showing a fine leg. "I am honored to make your acquaintance, Colonel." He was for a brief moment the picture of elegance but then ruined the entire effect by sniffling and smiling broadly. "You are ever so tall, sir. I'll bet you can see all the way to India, or Ireland."

Richard beamed down at the boy. "Why don't you see for yourself, lad?" He reached down and lifted Harry up onto his shoulders.

"Oh, Mummy! This is very high up! I should like to be this tall someday! Will I ever be this tall, do you think? How tall are you, sir? I don't think *Tio* Anthony is even this tall!" Harry excitedly pumped his arms and legs as Fitzwilliam turned the twisting little body this way and that to see everything.

Observing the couple stealing glances at each other, Anthony reached up to retrieve Harry. "Let us give your mother and the colonel some privacy, eh? We will await you outside, Lady Penrod, Colonel." As Anthony carried Harry out the door, he could sense the colonel's single-minded intensity and Amanda's apprehensive nerves, and laughed when he turned and saw her gazing anxiously after him.

Fitzwilliam cleared his throat first and adopted his usual formal parade stance. "Amanda, my dear..." he began; however, she spoke simultaneously. "Colonel..."

They both laughed awkwardly.

"Excuse me, madam. I wanted to apologize to you for my behavior the other evening, very unlike me, really. But please, you go first."

"Thank you, Colonel. I was going to comment on the fact that you appear to already know Dr. Milagros. I have only recently learned of this." After one quick glance up at his face, she returned her eyes to a level with his cloak button. "He has also just told me that you and he have recently spoken. Imagine my surprise."

"Yes, and he has told me something of your situation..."

As he spoke, Amanda took a deep breath, her heart strumming. He looked so very masculine and strong and smelled very nice. And very handsome. Yes, he looked very handsome indeed. Amanda's heart was hammering away determinedly and sounded so loud in her head that she heard nothing of what he was saying, only watched his mouth and admired his fine teeth. The knowledge that he had come here to seek her out, that he was truly that attracted to her and that interested made her suddenly bold, feeling desirable and feminine and alive. She trusted him. More importantly, she loved him desperately. Amanda had thought of little else than this man for two weeks and now had at last come to a spontaneous decision.

She was going to live for the moment. She would agree to become his mistress!

Placing her hand on his arm, she interrupted him just as he was beginning the meatier part of his presentation. "Colonel, I have been thinking of what we spoke of at the Winter Ball. Perhaps we should see more of each other, as you said. Much more." Closing her eyes, she inhaled deeply and rushed on. "Perhaps we could meet somewhere? You are an experienced man of the world, and I am sure you know of a place where a man and woman can have some private time together, a place that is discreet and out of the way." Amanda had whispered this in such a rush that she needed to stop and catch her breath. Her face was crimson.

Fitzwilliam stared at her as if she had grown gills. His fine speech went out the window. "I beg your pardon, madam." He appeared to find her words somehow humorous.

Amanda's color brightened even more, and for the first time, she looked directly up into his eyes. "What do you mean, 'I beg your pardon'?" she said, her embarrassment giving her words a harsh clip. "I am suggesting that we should meet. 'In private,' as they say." She raised one eyebrow. "Isn't that what you wanted? We are both adults, and I am a widow, after all. You need not fear that I will be shocked."

Instead, Fitzwilliam was shocked, no longer amused by what he thought had been an embarrassing bit of misspeak on her part regarding 'Private Time Together.' The chit was serious! What was it about this woman that both pulled him so strongly while at the same time could aggravate the hell out of him so easily? He was never out of sorts with anyone else, always smooth and clever and carefree. Why, he was the most bloody charming person he knew, goddamn it.

"I believe you have misconstrued my meaning, madam, perhaps not listening quite as attentively as you should. I said to you that I had *honorable intentions*. That generally would mean calling for you at your home, to take you out riding in my impressive carriage—well, actually in my cousin's impressive carriage—to escort you to the opera, to take tea with you, and to take your son out to the park. In short, madam, I desire assurances that we would suit each other, with an eye toward an offer of marriage." Damn but she was infuriating. He was not just flapping his lips here! How much plainer must he be?

Seeing the anxious look in her eyes, he dropped his voice to the barely audible. "I certainly did not intend to coax you into some sort of sordid secret liaison."

"Well, why ever not?"

"What the hell do you mean, 'Why ever not'?!"

Amanda was distraught. Oh, sweet heaven! All her hopes and dreams were disappearing before her eyes. She was losing this man before ever possessing him. "I believe I made it clear to you that I am not available for courtship, Colonel. However, it is perfectly acceptable here for widows to engage in nonbinding relationships of mutual consent. I am a widow, and therefore I consent."

He took a step back and stared at her in stunned disbelief. He arched his eyebrow in palpable annoyance. Instead of these perfectly clear machinations dissuading her, she continued! "No. To pursue a course toward marriage would be a complete waste of both of our times. I am quite sophisticated, I'll have you know, and very worldly. Yes, I am. And what is more, I am already involved with Dr. Milagros, as I have previously mentioned. However, I have spoken with him, and he has no objections if I meet with you also. So, as you can see, there is nothing to impede our being together." She rocked back on forth on her feet. "It is all very sophisticated."

Fitzwilliam nearly laughed in her face. "Bah and humbug, madam, what a terrible liar you make! You are not involved with Dr. Milagros! I discussed this with him also."

Her eyes narrowed. "My, what chums you both have become! Well, he is the deceitful one, he the liar. I will deal with him later."

His fists balled at his waist. "Amanda, this is beyond enough! I am not going to have you as a mistress, so just put that from your mind. I do not want a mistress! I had a mistress. Actually, I have had several mistresses. I allow myself exactly one mistress per year. Unfortunately, at the present time, I have used up my allotment until the year 1846. And because I have never fully embraced, nor understood, the concept of celibacy, you can understand that it is imperative that I take a wife." As he spoke, he had gradually backed her into a corner and now towered over her, continuing his furious reply. "*I* want a wife and family. I desire that wife to be *you*, and your son to be my family."

Amanda was humiliated beyond belief at his refusal, even insulted. Her eyes darted back and forth while her brain tried desperately to catch up. "But I was led to believe all aristocratic Englishmen want a widow to bed so you did not *need* to marry. Don't you know this, you ill-tempered person?" She shoved his shoulder in her anger. "Oooh, you aggravating man! I cannot believe how pigheaded you are, and here I was expecting you to be happy! I was expecting you to be thrilled! You are spoiling everything!"

Fitzwilliam coming to court her at Penwood was unthinkable. It terrified her. Her mother-in-law would throw her out into the street and bar the door. There was slim chance of a secret liaison succeeding, let alone a marriage! He must be mad, she thought. Marriage?! A marriage would have to be grabbed in snatches. He would have to accept second place to her son. How soon would it be before he grew to hate her, grew tired of the lies, and asserted his lawful rights over her as his possession?

No, she would have to remain single and in control of her own life. But she wanted him so frantically. She loved him so very deeply.

She just wanted to kill him.

"Please control your temper, madam. Remember, we are in a church." Fitzwilliam dragged her by the wrist to a more isolated area of the back of the church. When they had at last reached a secluded alcove, he paced back and forth in frustration, raking his hand through his already tousled hair.

"This must be some new ring of hell of which I was unaware," he muttered, his tone gruff with anger.

In response to this, her arms crossed before her, and her foot rapidly tapped.

"Now, I take it that you doubt the possibility that we can adapt to a marriage that would accommodate your temporary problem with your mother-in-law's custody of your child."

He saw the hesitancy in her eyes as they quickly searched his. *This is splendid,* her heart began to soar. *Perhaps he does understand. That is precisely the problem in a nutshell.* "Well, yes. I am afraid that marriage is just not possible for me at this time."

Grunting, he shook his head. For heaven's sake, he fumed, he could not, in all good conscience, allow her to embark on a relationship with him that would harm her in any way. Her culture was not like his culture, and he realized what she did not, that her preferred course would only lead to tremendous emotional upheaval and guilt for her. He would protect her, even from herself. He loved her beyond all reason, beyond himself.

He just wanted to kill her.

Amanda had spotted the old priest walking toward them and sucked in her breath. She leaned toward Fitzwilliam. "You have possibly forty seconds left to decide. Oh, merciful St. Jude, Father Riley is scowling and is heading toward us. It is mistress or nothing, Colonel. Where do we meet and when?" Amanda's heart stopped. She waited.

Fitzwilliam could hear the voice of the old priest getting nearer and nearer as he greeted the few others that had remained after mass.

"Ye gods! Twenty seconds," she whispered hysterically.

"All right, all right! I cannot believe you are forcing me to do this!" All these months he had been proudly mending his ways, removing ties to the darker sides of his life, and now desired only to take his place as a respectable member of society and set up his nursery with the woman he loved. He was livid. "What days do you attend the hospital?"

"Tuesdays or Thursdays usually, occasionally both."

"Bloody hell! All right, madam, all right. Thursday morning I will send my batman, O'Malley, to meet you at the hospital. Just so that we are clear, I believe you to be seriously deranged. I am agreeing to this fiasco on one condition alone, and that is that we are meeting to discuss our situation! I am in no way sanctioning any sort of liaison."

"Amanda, will you introduce me to this great, huge, hulking English soldier who is inhaling all the breathable air from my church?" Father Riley had arrived.

It had been a trying and busy few days for the colonel. They were to have their "discussion" at the Lions Head Inn, an elegant and discreet place just outside the center of London, a place where Fitzwilliam had brought many ladies of quality over the years. *Too many*, he soon realized as the staff hailed him warmly, and he, in turn, found he was able to inquire by name after family members. He was an important patron, and as such, one of the best rooms was always held in reserve for his use alone, overlooking the exquisite back garden and not the front street with the noise and pollution.

Extremely well-to-do merchants, daring members of the *ton*, and visiting dignitaries mingled, along with anonymous travelers, all scurrying back and forth, assiduously minding their own affairs. There was no permanent housing or residences in the area—an area where there was deliberate inattention to who was doing what to whom. Everyone was anonymous and treated with the utmost discretion.

He had been pacing nervously, wiping sweaty palms, and

trying to calm a pounding heart, but his resolve remained steadfast. A part of him worried that she wouldn't come even as another part worried that she would. He patted once again the packet of papers within his coat.

At last there was a soft knock on the door before it was opened by an older matron in a white ruffled mobcap and black dress with white apron, remnants from a much older, more formal time. Following closely behind came a walking pile of dripping wet veils and hooded cloak. Her boots were squishing water.

"Terrible it is out, Colonel. Quite a rumpus of a storm blowin' out there." The round-faced little woman had escorted Amanda up to the room, and then followed her inside, advancing with bold curiosity to the fireplace to better view the removal of her veil. "Can I get anythin' else for ye, Colonel?" she asked brightly, never taking her eyes from the back of the sodden and discreetly obscured visitor. "For you and yer fine lady both?"

"No, no, thank you, Mrs. Beale." He pressed several coins into her hand and turned her by her elbow to leave. "We will not require anything more from you or your fine staff. All is well."

"I imagine she's a real beauty, Colonel, under all that muck. Poor mite is freezin' and wet, I am sure. I must say she be very polite, very genteel-like." The old woman peeked around his shoulder as he pressed her farther toward the door. "Best to remove all yer clothes, luv, quick as ye can, before you catch yer death." She looked up at Fitzwilliam and winked. "There, dearie, saved ye some time, Colonel. She be the sweetest and the nicest..."

"Yes, yes, she's a real peach. That will be all. Thank you so much, madam. Don't let the door catch your skirt. Please see that we are not disturbed. Thank you..." Even as the matron curtseyed, she pressed her face as far as possible to the side until the door was finally closed on her view.

Fitzwilliam looked over his shoulder, not even certain it was Amanda within, hiding her appearance. "How in hell can you see under all that?" He turned to face her fully after locking the door.

She lifted the heavy black veils and smiled. "It is good to see you also, Richard. This is such a charming inn. I think I recognized several prominent people attempting to keep their faces hidden behind palm fronds. I was quite impressed." Her overly big woolen cloak was dripping wet and so was placed neatly on a chair near the fire to dry, alongside the veils. "No wonder parliament always recesses so early in the winter. They've such a long journey to reach here before dark."

Layers of outer gear had not prevented her clothes from becoming wet, while gusty winds had loosened her hair from her chignon. She was freezing. First rubbing her arms briskly in an attempt to restart her circulation, she then primly smoothed back the dripping tendrils from her face, finally straightening the skirt of her wet, dark grey dress to shyly turn and face him. She looked like a schoolgirl on her first day of class.

Even in such disarray, he found her striking beauty astonishing, and that caused him to renew mentally his vow to spend this time with her only in outlining his "perfect solution" to their problems. "Would you care for a glass of wine?" Fitzwilliam's heart raced as he walked over to the side table where a bottle of claret waited to be opened, along with a pot of steaming coffee and buttered scones. "Or would you prefer coffee or tea?"

She looked up briefly from her intense study of the room. "For myself, it is a little early for wine. However, hot coffee would be very welcome, thank you."

He raked a hand through his unruly hair, wishing to give himself a moment before he reached down for the coffee and cups. He was surprised that his hands shook, and three times he asked if she wanted cream and sugar, to which she always patiently replied, "Just cream, thank you.

"She seemed to know you extremely well," commented Amanda as she turned to face the hearth, warming her hands before the fire.

"Of whom are you speaking? Oh, you refer to Mrs. Beale. No, not really. It is just good business to make patrons feel important and call them by name." Fitzwilliam cleared his throat nervously.

"Really?" she said. "That's odd, since she told me on the way up the stairs that you kept regular rooms here to meet with your 'special friends,' but that this day you had requested a better, larger room. She was quite impressed with me because of that, I believe."

Richard growled, silently mouthing earthy expletives as he poured a second glass of wine for himself, having already gulped down his first. He forced his voice to sound relaxed. "I sometimes have occasion to stay here with out-of-town guests, since my family no longer keeps a home in town. It is not always possible to impose upon Darcy's good nature."

"Ah." Amanda hesitated for a moment in silence. "She also said that your special friends are generally well-titled and wealthy widows and was wondering if I was one of..."

"All right, all right, I get your point, Amanda," he testily interrupted. "No need to bludgeon me to death. Can we forget what the woman said, please?" He was growing increasingly petulant at both himself and at the entirety of London in general. He turned from the table to face her. "We are here to talk about our problem and not about my colorful little past..." He took two steps in her direction, her cup and saucer held out before him, when he saw that she was removing the pins from her hair.

He felt an immediate and earth-shattering slippage in his resolve.

"What the hell are you doing?" he snapped.

At his sharp tone, she looked up quickly, somewhat surprised. "What does it look like I'm doing? My hair is wet, or hadn't you noticed? I need to dry it, so I have removed the pins. Heavens, look at your face! Do we need to alert the press? I have only six of them, pins I mean, to my name and cannot afford to have them flying about." She had picked up a towel from the basin, rubbed her hair briskly, then began running her fingers through, finishing off by tousling it around a bit. "There, that's much better. You will find that I can be a bit frugal... Richard? Are you all right?"

Her hair was much fuller and longer and more astonishingly beautiful than he had anticipated. Damn it. He could not speak. He just stood staring—at all that wet, very long, gloriously thick blonde hair pulled over to the side and cascading down over her shoulder, reaching almost to her waist. It was a dense and shiny mass of tangled curls, a golden halo surrounding her face. It emphasized her very high cheekbones and almond-shaped eyes. He sensed a little tension begin in his chest.

The South of France was beginning to stir, also.

"Richard??" She repeated apprehensively. His eyes had taken on an ominously molten appearance.

"I don't think it is wise for you to leave your wet hair exposed like that, Amanda." He spoke slowly. "You might catch a chill. Perhaps you can wrap the towel around your head or something, perhaps around your face a bit, too." His voice sounded rough-edged as he advanced toward her, and she took the coffee from his hands. He backed away quickly. Clearing his throat and tossing back yet another glass of claret, he again silently vowed to himself to remain on his planned course of action, no matter what.

"Ahem. Ahem. (Cough) While I am certainly grateful that we can have this opportunity to speak, I would not want it to be the cause of your catching a chill, especially since I have planned a sort of surprise. Whether you will feel it is an acceptable surprise will pretty well determine our course of action here today."

Suddenly turning on his heel, he paced a few feet away and began his rehearsed speech, his voice rising to much the same timbre of any general addressing his troops. "Amanda," he intoned, "it is evident that we have a strong attraction for each other; however..." Glancing over his shoulder, he stopped dead in his tracks. "Now what are you doing?" he burst out. A second large crack had appeared in his reserve, and the nerves in his body began to throb.

Sitting on a small stool before the fire, her hair tumbling nearly to the ground, she looked up at him in confusion. Already having placed a boot on the side of the hearth, she stopped, her dainty foot poised a few inches from the floor. "I am taking off my boots and stockings, that is, if it is all right with you, sir. My feet are cold and wet because my boots leak like a sieve. Please go on. Don't let me interrupt."

She reached modestly up under her skirt, her eyes darting in embarrassment to his face, and then she rolled down her stocking. She next removed the boot and stocking of the other foot. "Ahhh!" she exclaimed happily as she wriggled her toes before the fire. "That feels absolutely wonderful, much better. Richard, do go on, please, with your speech, it was very interesting, I am sure."

He bitterly catalogued all the attacks on his resolve unfolding before him: a fine-looking young woman with her long, wet hair flowing around her shoulders and her face glowing with youth and health, the top and bottom of her dress dampened more than enough to cling to her, her arms wrapped around slender legs, trim ankles that peeked out from her skirt and her pretty little pink toes—a sensually explosive cornucopia warming itself innocently before the fire.

"Richard! Are you all right?" She tried to run her fingers through her hair to help dry it but quickly abandoned the attempt because of the snarls. She then pushed it from her face to lean her elbows atop her knees. She demurely placed one row of toes over her others to keep them warm.

"Hmm?" His eyebrows rose with his response, his mind a hopeless mush of confusion.

"You were saying something important, were you not?"

"I was?"

"I'm almost certain you were." She gave him a guilty smile and stood. "Oh, dear, I am not being very attentive again, am I?" Padding over to him, she rested her hands high up on his shoulders. "I am very sorry. Please forgive me for being so rude. Good heavens, barefoot like this, I feel small standing next to you." Smiling contentedly she ran her hands across his shoulders, and then gently stroked down the front of his chest. "It's like I am standing in a hole or something." Her eyes drifted, just for a moment, to his mouth.

Fitzwilliam scowled. "Amanda, go and stand over there, please." He sounded very annoyed.

"Why? What have I done?"

"Just do it, goddamn it."

"If you insist, Colonel." She pursed her lips and walked back to where she had been sitting near the fire. "Fine, shoot."

"I beg your pardon?!"

"Sorry, that was an American phrase. Please proceed with what you wanted to say to me."

He hesitated for a moment and then began again, after further clearing his throat and downing his fourth or fifth glass of claret. He had lost count.

"Amanda."

"Yes, Richard. I have not left. I am listening."

"Right. Yes… where was I?" He began to massage his temple. "Ah… It is evident that we have… strong attraction for each other… damn it to hell, what was I saying? Your fussings, all this to do, have gotten me completely off topic! Oh, yes, I remember—Amanda, I am of an age where I find I desire something more substantial in my life than a meaningless coupling with someone. Forgive my blunt speech, but I do want us to be open with each other." He pinched the bridge of his nose as he strolled to the window, a headache threatening, then rubbed at his chest, feeling as if a ravenous wolf was within clawing to be released. It had been those little pink toes, and he knew it. For no apparent reason, those stupid pink toes had captured his imagination and were now driving him wild.

"Ahem. Ahem." He hesitated for a moment to stare outside. "After years of professing the complete opposite, I find that, since meeting you, I truly do desire a home life and a family. I want to share my thoughts with someone, share my dreams and love and future with one person, and we seem to rub along well together, don't we? Can you understand what I am saying?" He turned to look at her. "As I was saying, I have arranged for something to which I pray you are amenable..." He suddenly exploded. "Bloody hell! Now what are you doing?!"

She froze midway in her process of unbuttoning her bodice, a guilty blush sweeping over her face.

"Now are you going to tell me that your breasts are cold and wet and you need to relieve them of your top?" His voice sounded angrier than he had meant it to be, while his walls of protection continued crashing down around him. The wolf was breaking free.

Brown eyes looked down in shame, and tears began to well. Her hands clasped tightly in front of her. "Please do not yell at me, Richard. I cannot help it if my dress is wet, and I'm cold."

"I don't mean to yell. It's just that I am trying to bare my soul to you here, and you cannot seem to retain possession of your clothes. Now please get yourself dressed again. We are not staying. If you would only let me explain to you my overall strategy..."

He watched in horror as her face crumpled into a blubbery mass of tears. "I am angering you, and you are sending me away." She stomped her bare foot in self-disgust. Throwing back her head, she began to wail and sob with her frustration and anger and disappointment. "Oh, I am such a fool! I wanted to look beautiful! Instead, I look like a sodden pile of rags. But please, Richard, don't force me to leave here. Don't give up on us."

Fitzwilliam reached her in two steps, pulling her roughly into his arms. "Stop it, Amanda. I'm the fool, not you." Immediately their mouths found each other, and they kissed with hunger, licking and biting and ravenous. "Forgive me," he mumbled over and over while her hands grabbed into his hair, pulling him closer. He crushed her to him and lifted her from the floor, those offending pink toes dangling in midair.

"I love you, Richard. You don't know how I dream about you and pretend I talk to you when you're not with me. I love you so much I kiss my pillow each night, and hug it, and wish it was you there with me."

"I am the worst of brutes, bellowing at the only person who matters." He kissed her eyes and nose and feasted kisses on her neck. "Please don't cry, sweetheart. Please. I love you so much. This was entirely my fault. It was a stupid idea to meet here. But you see, I have made some plans. I wanted to explain to you..."

She sniffled and nodded, agreeing with him wholeheartedly. Holding his face in her hands, she stared lovingly into his eyes. "Yes, it is your fault, isn't it?"

He smiled over her head as he set her down on her feet again and reached into his pocket, sacrificing yet another handkerchief to the Penrod family. "Blow," he instructed, and she trumpeted into the cloth. "Well done. Are you finished?" he asked, and she nodded. "Good. Come with me." He lifted her into his arms and carried her to an overstuffed chair, where they settled down, her legs tucked neatly across his lap. She sniffled and snuggled as he nudged her head under his chin, stroking her cheek and hair to soothe her. They sat in easy silence until her sniffles stopped and she finally sighed.

"Are you warmer now?" he asked quietly, and she smiled.

"What is wrong with me, Richard?" she asked after a moment.

"Wrong with you? Now why would you say something silly like that?" He kissed her forehead, gently pressing her head onto his shoulder. "You are perfection."

That was nice, she thought. Nestled in his arms like a child, she began to play with his cravat. "I worried and worried myself sick about today, I swear it. I must have awoken at four in the morning to get dressed and fretted about whether to wear the horrid lavender dress or the dreaded grey dress." She wriggled closer to him, her voice becoming even softer. "Tell me again how I am perfection."

His answer was another deep and thorough kiss. "You are beyond perfection."

"You are just being kind. You are very kind, you know, and brave and decent and honorable. No, I have bungled this whole thing. I'm such an idiot." She sighed once and then once again. "I look pitiful. My nose is running, my hair is drenched, my hands are coarse… feel free to disagree with me at any time," she muttered into his neck.

Fitzwilliam's senses were lost somewhere in her hair, in the fragrance of flowers and soap. He was very glad to hear her humor emerge again. He glided kisses across the top of her head.

"You have brought others here, have you not? What is wrong with me that you don't want me in that way, Richard? Why am I so undesirable to you? I thought I was being alluring by loosening my top a little, but you looked horrified." She hiccoughed then apologized when her head hit his chin.

"We seem to be working at cross-purposes, my love. This has nothing to do with not wanting you. I want you desperately. I hoped you knew that by now." He kissed her waiting lips. "I love you passionately." She wriggled joyfully in his lap and threw her arms around his neck.

"*Merciful heavens*," he moaned with his rampant arousal. "Good God, what in the world was I saying? I can't remember anything at the moment with you bouncing about." He hugged her tightly to him and tried to catch his breath. "Ah, yes. The problem, as I see it, is..." he started quietly, "what I was trying to explain to you is that we *could* meet here, if you truly desire, and begin a relationship with each other, but I know in my heart that you would not be happy, and then neither could I. You would feel used, and worst of all, you would grow ashamed of us, come to blame me and eventually hate me. It is true I've been here with mistresses or one-time lovers, but that is all I wanted from them and all they wanted from me." He kissed her temples and the tip of her nose. "This is very different, though. Don't you sense that we have a greater future than that? I have known that since the very first moment I saw you."

She was very still, her head resting on his shoulder. "I, too, felt from the beginning that we were meant to be together, forever."

He smiled then kissed her mouth softly. "Excellent. I will speak with your mother-in-law tonight, and..." His voice trailed off as she struggled to break free from his arms so that she could look into his face.

"You cannot do that! No! Oh, Richard, you would make my situation so much worse. She will throw me from the house. I will lose any contact with my son. She is only waiting for me to misstep. Please promise that you won't seek her out or speak to her or tell anyone about us."

He raked his hand through his hair. "So what do we do? Do you want us to part ways over this? Does it truly mean nothing to you? You know, Amanda, the culture in this country is quite different from yours. The most sophisticated, wealthy, and titled marriages are oftentimes no more than mergers. After an heir is presented, many of these couples go their own way, and no one thinks ill of them as long as they behave discreetly. An affair with you would not harm me in the least, but for you, Amanda, well I have serious doubts. I truly fear that emotionally it will cause you much distress."

She reflected on what he said. "Though I confess I am very naïve about the mechanics of this, I am also selfish." His eyes and his lips were so close. "I want you, and I want my boy, both. I see no other way for us, no other immediate answer, and I am agreeable if you are. Besides, how could it be a sin to be loved by you? I want to be loved by you. I need to be loved by you."

He saw the truth in her eyes, was moved by the trust he saw there. He was also completely aware that he had lost the fight. His fingers began to stroke her hair. "You are so beautiful to me, and you don't even realize how much. Maybe that's a good thing, because I am at your mercy as it is."

She turned her face to kiss the palm of his hand. "Don't deny us being together, please." Desperate to possess him, she reached her arms around his neck and hugged him tightly.

And that was it, a final attachment to functional thought snapping, the last pitiful reserve breached. His entire world was there before him, lying in his arms. If he were to die tomorrow, he would consider his life as being fulfilled having just known for a moment the love and trust of this one woman.

The hand that had rested so innocently on her hip came to life and began an intimate gentle journey, firmly pulling her closer. Fitzwilliam's speeches and plans, all rational thought, vanished beneath the soft, warm, yielding flesh of a woman, his woman, and the desire in her eyes. He angled his mouth onto hers and crushed her to him, kissing her deeply and passionately—once, twice, and again and again.

When they finally separated, he rested his forehead on hers.

The room was about to burst into flames, and he knew it. He made one more attempt at logic. "Amanda, I am rapidly losing control."

She grunted impatiently, pulling his head down again, pushing his mouth onto hers; his hand came to rest between her silky legs.

"Richard," she said, her voice breathless, "it has been a long time, since before my son was born. Please don't be too disappointed with me."

No longer coherent, he eased her dress down, her breasts bared to his touch.

"I love you," she whispered in awe, her hands touched his hair, his cheek, his mouth. There was no sound in the room other than their breathing.

"I love you," he said simultaneously, a growl beginning deep in his throat as his mouth went down to cover hers. He stood then, with her in his arms, to carry her to bed where, undressing each other wildly, they both went mad.

Fitzwilliam was in the grip of an overpowering insanity, much greater than he had ever known before. On fire, he now possessed no ability for coherent thought. He saw only red from inside his closed eyes and forgot time and place.

It was over much too quickly, the explosive release for both triggered nearly immediately by the anticipation of the deed. He was still inside her as he held her fast and rolled onto his side. Neither one was able to calm their breathing anytime soon.

They lay holding each other for a brief time, and then the madness overcame them again, staying with them much longer and growing even more intense than before.

Chapter 16

A DISHEVELED AMANDA DRAGGED the heavy chair before the hearth and then took up the poker, shoving it repeatedly into an already roaring fire, while the rain and sleet continued to batter the windows. Even though she had noiselessly slipped into her dress, the back of which remained open with its millions of unreachable tiny buttons, the din from her slamming and thumping and grumbling could have raised the dead.

She found she was still in a wicked temper upon the discovery that her shoes remained obstinately damp. Well, heavens, that was apparently a deliberate insult, so she threw them across the room. Beginning to wheeze with her exertions, she now yanked a throw from another chair and tucked it around her lap for extra warmth. It was no use. Nothing seemed capable of warming her this morning.

She snatched a quick glance at the creature she had so recently left reclining upon the bed—the fiend, the sexual deviant. Before her eyes rested a repulsive debaucher—a seasoned rake upon his cot of crime, a seducer of innocents, sated and smug. She colored deeply at the vile sight and cursed herself for being even more drawn to him now that the deed was done, and done so soundly. Her angry stare dragged across his fuzzy barrel chest and his muscular tree-trunk arms and long powerful legs. She trembled with the remembrance of his overblown male…ego. Crazy, mud blond hair was both falling forward onto his forehead and wildly standing straight up around his head at awkward angles. He smiled sweetly at her.

She sighed. He was beautiful.

Fitzwilliam had no idea what to do next, a first for a worldly soldier having just bedded a beautiful woman. Ordinarily, he would kiss her cheek, leave his card, and be off, usually neither requiring nor desiring a second acquaintance. *Au contraire*, to his dismay now he felt possessive and jealous and disgustingly vulnerable. He was the first to admit he was captured, sunk, defeated. *Merde*.

He would make her see reason, *his* reason naturally, because for certain, he would never let her go now, so utterly female as she was—soft and warm. Lord, he remembered the heat of her kisses—kisses on his neck, on his chest and stomach. He remembered the shyness, the tender wondering way she had touched him, stroked him. How she had quivered and moaned with each of his strokes, then her little gasp each time he entered her. He remembered the feel of her silky, warm thigh against his cheek, her trembles when he kneaded and nipped her fanny, her panting when his mouth suckled her breast. Their hands and tongues had branded each other everywhere, their kisses more passionate than any others in his prior and most extensive experience. He abhorred the notion that she could regret any moment of it, any of the magic that they had experienced together.

He cleared his throat loudly. "So tell me, Amanda, what would you be doing right this moment if you were at the hospital?"

At first taken aback, Amanda thought for a moment and then put her head down. "Oh, I suppose I would be with the babies right now." Her head bowed down, she smiled briefly—very briefly. "I spend as much of the mornings as I can with the newborns and young children, holding them and such. I love the babies. The afternoons are generally with the mothers, teaching them how important love and nurturing is to their child. Anthony believes most of these poor women have lived without decent families and cannot understand how to properly care for children, what they should feed them, how important tenderness is, so he has me speak with each mother before she leaves."

The mantel clock ticked loudly. Fitzwilliam was drowning with his memories of loving her and caressing her body. They had fit together perfectly, were custom-made for each other. His hands still were warm from touching her. "You should have more babies of your own." His voice sounded rough with emotion. "You are a good mother, Amanda, an excellent mother. Your son is quite wonderful."

Her eyes began to water, and she turned her face away. "I prefer to not discuss this," she whispered.

It was becoming harder and harder not to dash over and shake her, drag her back into his bed to hold her and comfort her several more times, to love her and worship her. This was not the most advantageous time however.

⁂

They had made love twice. *Twice, and in* broad daylight. *That must be the very definition of a woman of easy virtue. What must*

Richard think of me? She groaned softly and shook her head. Well, goodness. She tried to persuade herself that her behavior in their first coupling was forgivable, since she had been, she now realized, almost as ignorant about passion as the most sheltered innocent. Why, she had no defenses against an experienced man of the world, and not for the first time, she wondered about her marriage.

For one thing, she had never seen a naked man before today, before Fitzwilliam. Her husband, Augustus, never had a naked moment in his life of which she was aware. Why, he never even slept with her. Occasionally he would appear suddenly by her bedside, all quaking and nervous in the darkness, quickly "do the deed," as he called it, and then leave as soon as possible.

No, definitely their first coupling today had been a complete revelation. Her immoral conduct was not her responsibility in any way, was only the consequence of his wicked expertise. He was cunning. He was a devil. He was a man.

All that remained then was the annoying problem of their second coupling, only twenty minutes after the first. *Oh dear God.* She blushed crimson with the memory. Who could have believed such depraved behavior from her? She had succumbed to madness twice within one hour. A second coupling within one hour was just flagrant wickedness, wasn't it? And, frankly, wasn't "it" much slower the second time, more inventive, more intimate, and much more thorough? She shook her head and groaned, her lips moving with her thoughts. *I am vile and sinful and decadent and... loud,* and she blushed even deeper with the memory of just how loud. *Oh, but heaven forgive me, I would run to him again right now, this very second, if he asked.* She opened her clenched eyes and caught sight of the ripped chemise dangling from a curtain rod above the bed, where Fitzwilliam had hastily tossed it.

Anthony was right about one thing. If done correctly, lovemaking certainly did feel like sin.

"Amanda, to whom are you speaking?" Fitzwilliam was rapidly becoming annoyed. Why the little hoyden looked embarrassed to tears by her passion, even as sweet and as innocent as it had been. She had been all warm love and gentleness, completely surprised by the strength of emotions involved in physical love. At the height of her passion, she had gasped his name. Anyway, she had gasped someone's name into his ear. Heaven knows he had been in no condition at that particular moment to comprehend anything.

You could not wait, could you, Fitzwilliam? No, you had to release the beast! What do I say to her now? How can I explain to her what I really had planned for us?

"You think I am an easy woman, don't you?" She was watching his face, thinking how disillusioned with her he appeared. "I do not see how this will ever work out." Her resentful reaction had been exactly what he had predicted it would be, but she loved him so much that she had tried to force herself into behavior that was against her principles. Maybe "forced" was too strong a word, especially since she seemed to recall entreating him for that second time. *Eeeeh!* Everything was ruined. She had shown her true wanton colors, and he was finished with her.

He threw off the covers and boldly stood before her in all his glory, grabbed his smallclothes, and leisurely began to dress. Amanda let out a gasp at his nakedness and turned her back again to him. *You see, the disrespect has begun already.*

"I am afraid you are right, dearest, this is not for us, and I shall attempt to restrain myself from saying I tried to warn you." He smiled at her lovely back with all that soft white skin, and at her delicate sensibilities. She really was adorable. *An easy woman! Ha!* He almost began to laugh out loud at that. He was pulling on his boots within moments. "You know, Amanda, that I love you very much."

He saw the back of her head nod. "No more than I love you, Richard." Her voice was barely audible. She wiped at her nose with the back of her hand.

"All right, then. Let's get you buttoned, and we'll go out, shall we? I have a surprise for you anyway, dear. I was planning to show you earlier, but you kept removing your clothes, if you remember."

"Richard!!"

"Yes, I know, you prefer to not discuss it." He reached into his coat pocket and then handed her the packet of papers he had spent days procuring. She opened them up and began to cry.

❧

Within two hours, the special license Richard had acquired from the offices of his dear cousin, the Archbishop of Canterbury, had been presented at the nearest church. Amanda Sayles Penrod and Colonel Richard Fitzwilliam became husband and wife, yet one more relieved bride clinging to her eager bridegroom within the morally ambiguous London social elite.

In her tearful joy and pride, Amanda struggled to suppress those misgivings and suspicions that nagged her, forced to the background fears regarding acceptance by his family, qualms that he would grow to hate the secrecy this deed would force upon them.

She had married in haste again—true, this time to a man she adored, but as before, a man she did not know. It was her grab for happiness, and so she managed to restrain the sense that her problems were just beginning.

Chapter 17

It was several weeks later, two days before Christmas, and Amanda was smoothing out the counterpane on the bed, her hair again pulled severely back into her braided bun, her dreary dress and worn shoes primly announcing her imminent return to the hospital. She was incredibly happy, her initial fears over the secrecy of their marriage now laughable. Her husband was warm, loving, and attentive, protective in the extreme.

Since their marriage, they had been meeting at the inn secretly, stealing precious moments of happiness. Smiling to himself, he watched her as she tended to this rented room as if it was their home, tidying the bed, dusting and straightening furniture. She sat suddenly on the bed, shaking her head and sighing.

"What is going on, Mrs. Fitzwilliam?" He crouched down before her, resting his arms straight out over her shoulders.

She was quiet for a very long while.

"Amanda, my legs are killing me. Please hurry." Instead of speaking, she bent her head lower, pressing her hands together on her lap. "Tell Papa what is wrong, Amanda."

She sighed. "We may not have the luxury of any more time together."

He felt his chest tightening, and his blood began to boil. He found it hard to speak at first. "I'll find you if you attempt to leave me. I will give you no peace at all."

She looked up, surprised at his intensity, and then patted the bed. "Come and sit next to me." When he sat, she took both his hands and held them tightly, her eyes beginning to tear up. She brought his hands slowly up to her lips.

"You haven't noticed something, I'm afraid, dear," she said.

"What?"

"We've been coming here twice a week for nearly a whole month now or more, and making love like randy little rabbits."

"Did you think I was unconscious of this?" He smiled and hugged her tight, his pain easing a bit.

"Think about it, Richard. Access that wonderful brain above your waist for a moment. We've been meeting together for a whole month, actually, a little more than a month."

He still looked at her questioningly.

"Richard, all women have a certain time when they cannot engage in this..." she leaned in toward him, whispering as if others were listening, "activity. When they..."

"Oh, for goodness sake, Amanda, I am a grown man. I have lived in both Copenhagen and Paris, so I do have a rudimentary knowledge of the female. What does that...?" He stopped suddenly.

She nodded.

"Oh, dear God, you haven't bled, have you?"

"Finally"—she smiled, nodding her head—"give this man a cheroot. No, I have not for seven weeks, and you would not know it, but this is the one area in which I am never late."

He stared at her blankly, and they both exhaled. The future moment they had discussed, the moment God would decide their destiny, had already arrived.

"I wasn't going to say anything yet. In truth, I should wait until another cycle is missed, but I believe I am. The brutal fact is that my breasts are very swollen and sore, and I vomit each morning like a drunken marine."

An amazingly strong emotion surged through him. The enormity of the joy and exaltation filling him, alongside the fear, was a complete surprise. His eyes began to swim with tears, unmanly tears if they were before anyone but her. He pulled her tightly into his arms and kissed her passionately.

"I take it that you would be pleased, then, if this is true?"

"Yes," he answered, trying to compose this rampaging emotion, his voice catching a little. "Forgive me if I find your tale of breast pain and nausea to be absolutely wonderful." He had rarely thought about being a father before and found himself taken aback at the thrill it had brought him.

Amanda pulled from his embrace. "What about Harry, Richard? We still have the problem of my mother-in-law. This is the scandal for which she's waited."

He inhaled sharply, his soldier's brain snapping into position. The war had finally begun, the enemy engaged. Calm settled over him. "Then we leave," he said simply. "We will seize him and leave immediately, head for the Continent. Later we can discuss heading to America, possibly. I will find out about passages and timetables and then purchase a coach to drive us to a safe area. I want you settled in a location with the best of doctors well before your confinement. First and foremost is a secure house for you and Harry."

Amanda patted her stomach. "You make it sound so simple," she whispered anxiously. "What about your inquiries? Have you had any response from your solicitors about our regaining custody?"

Fitzwilliam shook his head. "But never fear, Amanda. I have hired new investigators and have browbeaten my solicitors. We are very close."

"Richard, if we run, it will be too late; we cannot come back. You do realize that, don't you? Are you willing to leave England, leave your family?" Her heart was heavy with the guilt of all that he would be sacrificing for her, all he had already sacrificed—a normal home life, his career, and now his beloved family. It was too much to ask of anyone.

He smoothed the hair from her face. "I have every faith that it will turn out well for us. Better than that, even, because now we have a child of our own on the way. If you've taught me anything, Amanda, it is that God has decided we are ready, He probably had this all planned long before we met. If He believes in us, who am I to argue? Get your cloak now, and I'll call for our coach."

❧

It was nearly seven-thirty that evening when an exhausted Richard returned to the inn. He had sent a message to his father, contacted his solicitors, set into motion the purchase of a sturdy travel coach and horses, but he still had arrangements to make and needed to speak to the War Office, then have a long talk with O'Malley and see what he could set up for his old friend. He nodded his quick hello to the concierge who anxiously motioned him over.

"You've had a visitor, Colonel—*a Grand Gentleman*," he said with feeling and pointed toward the overly crowded public dining room. "And might I say his is the finest Weston superfine with which I have ever had the honor to converse. He has been waiting for you, there at the table to the left of the fireplace, for several hours now." As Richard looked in that general direction, he thought he saw a figure, a man relaxing casually in the corner. He thanked the concierge and cautiously entered the room.

His direct sight line was initially hampered by smoky candles flickering, by waiters running about and diners rising and sitting, by the numerous people milling about between the entranceway and the dining area. The overwhelming racket of chatter, laughing, and dining sounds distracted him while he bobbed his head around one person then the next as he moved forward.

About halfway into the room, the crowd finally parted, and he beheld the tall, dark, and exceptionally handsome English gentleman, his long legs crossed, his champagne-buffed black riding boots brilliantly reflecting the flames from the hearth. The dark green superfine coat (it really was magnificent) and subdued checkered waistcoat set off his brilliantly white shirt and cravat. One elbow was draped casually across the back of his chair while the other hand sensuously stroked the stem of a wine glass resting on the table before him. His eyes never left Fitzwilliam's face.

He was the very essence of stylish nonchalance.

Except for his eyes. His eyes were the very black depths of hell.

"Why, hello, brat, fancy meeting you in this godforsaken place. Are you slumming with friends?" The colonel's greeting for his cousin was accompanied by a cold smile, feeling as he was the wash of displeasure being directed back at him. "You're looking well. Are those new boots?" God how he hated Darcy when he looked so pompous. He had an irrational desire to smack the back of his little cousin's head. As he reached down to finger the magnificent, lapelled satin waistcoat, Richard shook his head. "By God, Darcy, you look nearly as fashionable as your butler. Well, aspire to greatness, boy. Who knows, one day you may equal the man."

Darcy sensed his cousin's belligerence, knew the man as well as he knew himself, and by the position of his jutting chin, realized they were dancing very near the battlefield at the moment. "Nice of you to say I am in good looks this evening. You, on the other hand, look like shit."

Fitzwilliam's gaze narrowed dangerously.

Darcy indicated the chair across from him. "Sit."

His cousin yanked the chair back and settled heavily into it, crossing his ankle over his knee. "How terribly remiss of me to so offend you with my appearance. Apparently, however, my looks improve with frequency of contact, something to do with my famously charismatic personality." Fitzwilliam's counterfeit smile dissolved almost immediately. "Not to mention my heavenly blue eyes."

Darcy never broke his stare.

"Are you drunk?" Fitzwilliam asked pleasantly.

"No, although I have been sitting here for hours, drinking and waiting, watching the time slowly tick on by."

Darcy could outstare a corpse.

Fitzwilliam could not, and his color began to rise. He turned as a waiter passed behind him, unapologetically grabbing a tankard of someone else's ale from the tray, enjoyed at least two large swallows, and then slammed it onto the table. A nearby woman screeched in alarm and threw her napkin over her head.

"Have you been enjoying your little holiday here?" The gentlemanly manner was ice cold.

"Oh, one cannot complain, really. The bathwater can be slightly tepid; however…" He was stopped in midsentence by Darcy's incredulous bellow.

"Damn it, do you realize that the whole family is worried sick about you? Everyone has been frantic—your father, friends, even Wellington was alarmed!" Darcy's fury had nearly pulled him from his chair, and he desperately attempted to regain his composure.

Fitzwilliam managed to control his temper by counting to twenty. Then he exploded. "Forgive me, brat; however, I am a grown man, answerable to no one, and I prefer not to speak of this!" His voice rose with every word until he was shouting. "Where I have been and what I have done is no one's concern but my own!"

Darcy kept watching him, his ire growing more impossible to squelch with every silent moment that passed. Of all the inconsiderate baboons! Of all the self-centered, egomaniacal…! Fitzwilliam's expression remained stoic as he tossed back another swallow.

"Has it something to do with Amanda?"

It was an insightful shot in the dark that showed immediate results. The comment snapped Fitzwilliam's attention back to his cousin. "Tell me what it is in the phrase 'I prefer not to speak about this' that is escaping you?" Fitzwilliam's eyes were dark and furious.

The tension between them was suffocating, intense enough to begin alarming surrounding tables, but Darcy was not going to retreat this time. For all of their lives, it had been the older and livelier Fitzwilliam leading the younger and more reserved

Darcy, guiding him through life's adventures. Darcy had always idolized his cousin, never crossing him or trying to harness his free spirit. However, now he realized Aunt Catherine was correct. Perhaps they had all let his cousin drift unchecked for far too long.

"Who was that veiled woman you left with earlier?" Darcy's question was contemptuous.

Fitzwilliam almost choked on his drink.

"How dare you question me, you half-formed pup!" he shouted. "How long have you been here spying on me?!"

"Long enough to see you leave with your latest conquest. Is this another war widow, or are you back into opera singers? Or was this the wife of some dear friend?"

"Bloody hell!" Fitzwilliam roared, slamming his fist on the table and sending their glasses clattering across the table. "I don't have to answer to you or to anyone!" The waiter, who had been approaching, quickly spun around to retreat back out the door.

"Oh, I understand now. You've been shacked up with some bit of muslin you found, is that it? This place is too expensive for a street whore, or was there more than one? I suppose if you drink enough, any behavior is acceptable." Darcy was pushing his cousin as hard as he could.

"I should call you out for that, damn you to hell!" Fitzwilliam's voice shook with rage as he slowly rose from his seat.

"Again?" Darcy's bark of laughter was rife with scorn. Suddenly standing, he leaned over, his fists on the table. "Well, what is it then?! Who are you holed up with here? I know there's a woman. The concierge said you were here with your wife!"

"Damn you to hell, Darcy, I am!" Fitzwilliam bellowed back.

Oh dear, this could not be a good sign. Darcy's head shot

back in confusion. It appeared Elizabeth's wifely accusations were correct, and his hearing *was* going. His cousin had just said something that could not be, something that made no sense whatsoever. Quite humorous, really. No, no, no. Hell had not as yet frozen over, to his knowledge.

"Sorry?"

Fitzwilliam sank back into his chair, his fury spent. He rested his elbows atop the table; shaking hands raked through his hair. "It's true, absolutely true, man. I am staying here with my wife. Amanda and I were married a little over four weeks ago. No one knows except you now, a half-deaf priest, and my batman. Oh, yes, and the entire office of the Archbishop of Canterbury."

Darcy stared unblinking at his cousin for several moments then smoothed down his waistcoat and straightened his cravat before summoning the trembling concierge over to the table. "Pardon me, my good man. I find that we are going to need a truly remarkable amount of alcohol brought to us, and also perhaps a private room and some food please..." When Darcy looked about, he was surprised at the empty dining room. "Well, damn my eyes—I guess this room will do fine. Where is everyone?"

"Aunt Catherine has her footmen everywhere, looking for you. She is that frantic, imagining you have done some grievous harm to yourself. I had to talk her out of calling in the Bow Street Runners." It was very late evening, and they sat alone in the darkened dining room, the room illumined only by two table candles and the blazing fireplace. Moonlight reflected from snow newly settled on the garden outside the windows.

Fitzwilliam cast his eyes up to heaven. Eloquent as ever, he intoned reverently, "Shit." He turned to Darcy. "How did *you* find me?"

"Natural brilliance, unsurpassed logic, plus I stumbled upon O'Malley. He's a very good man, Fitzwilliam, but it appears he has a weakness for Gunther's ices, as does Elizabeth. This week she has had a craving for lemon ices and figs. I spied him there and followed."

Fitzwilliam leaned back in his chair, a pleased look on his face. "I knew it! They have not said as much, but I do believe his wife, Isabella, has the same craving for ices as Elizabeth, and for the same reason."

"I was not aware that you were allowing O'Malley his marital rights. Conjugal visits are so very egalitarian. Decent of you, old man."

Fitzwilliam threw a chunk of cheese at his cousin's head. "Do you know what is so pathetic about all of this, brat?"

"You mean aside from your breath?"

Richard loosened his collar and then the top of his pants, a heartfelt sigh of relief escaping him as he slouched down into his chair. "As you well know, I have never truly wanted to be married. Anyway, I made the claim often enough."

"And loud enough," Darcy volunteered. Fitzwilliam glowered.

"Well, pardon me, but marriage is necessary only as a means to pass on inheritance. And yet, here I sit, a pathetic love-starved fool, watching the clock for hours on end, counting the days until I see her. Damn me if I can understand how things changed so drastically and so quickly." He reached into his pocket to bring out his beloved pipe. "'Thy glory, O Israel, is slain upon thy high places! How are the mighty fallen.'"

"And now you're quoting the Bible. Dear Lord, we must be near the end of times." Darcy saluted him with his glass of whiskey. "So, how are we enjoying married life?"

Fitzwilliam snorted, grumbling something about Amanda hiding his tobacco pouch. He finally located it in his coat pocket, in the exact spot he had secreted it, and then began to fill the pipe. He used a candle flame to stoke the tobacco, then spread his hands over the immaculate white tablecloth, all the while giving impressive and grave consideration to Darcy's question. His fingers worked out some imperceptible creases in the material. He crossed his legs.

"How are we enjoying married life?" he mused, puffing once, then twice, and then removing his pipe to intently study the bowl. "Well, first and foremost, please allow me to say that I have never quarreled so much in my entire life."

Darcy began to laugh.

"Ah, you laugh. What is truly terrifying is that I include in that statement all of my years of battle against the Corsican." Fitzwilliam puffed. "Well, to continue, may I reasonably assume that yours is the laughter of the well experienced?"

"Oh, yes. It is an unspoken truth that marriage can be a rather intense alliance at first, shall we say, and not always of the romantic bent."

"Intense!" Fitzwilliam began to quickly warm to his subject. "Intense! Darcy, my good man, they are not like us. Not even remotely. Now, I speak not of the obvious—the absence of both logic and reason. No, I refer to certain areas that really should be made plainer to men before they embark upon this life-changing commitment." He puffed on his pipe, suddenly throwing back his head in a bark of laughter.

"First off, I would like to know why they are so bloody sensitive about everything, especially their weight. 'Do I look plumper?' is an almost impossible question to answer. They also, apparently, never forget offenses, even if they do forgive them. The most difficult thing to me is the necessity to trot out innermost feelings and discuss them to *death*." He shook his head, smiling delightedly at some memory then quickly feigned a scowl. "Well, obviously, since a true man has no innermost feelings, I agree with whatever she says."

Darcy shook his head as he settled himself lower in his chair, his long legs stretched out before him. "Elizabeth herself is of the female persuasion. It is her firm belief that over the course of a marriage, women invariably control everything—what we wear, how we raise our children, and ultimately how we behave—and we must willingly go along or die alone. The Benevolent Dictator is how I believe Uncle Bernard referred to Aunt Lucille."

"You're right, I had forgotten that." They both chuckled at the memory.

Richard's eyes wrinkled happily as he puffed on his pipe. "But by God, Darcy, I love every moment. I've never felt more alive in my life. We argue, make love and then have a good meal, laugh and talk. Then we make love again." The light in his eyes could have brightened a small village. "In such a short time, she has become my closest friend, my lover, and my whole life." He puffed thoughtfully on his pipe for a moment. "Sometimes I find I cannot breathe for wanting her.

"And her son, Darcy... I have actually come to love that child as if he were my own. He is so happy, so full of boyish mischief and fun, and so very good-natured. I look at him and wish to God I could again be twenty-five when he is, instead of a doddering old fart in his fifties. He would be a most excellent companion, most excellent." Richard sighed and looked wistfully into the fire. "I miss her so dreadfully sometimes."

"It is overwhelming to love someone more than yourself, isn't it?"

"I believe I would die for her, Darcy, I truly would."

Darcy nodded with complete understanding. "May I be permitted just two questions?"

His cousin nodded.

"Am I wrong to assume that your acquaintance with the lady is of a rather short duration? How long did you know her before your marriage?"

Fitzwilliam shifted uncomfortably in his seat. "Long enough."

"It could not have been more than a few weeks, Fitz."

"As I said, Darcy, long enough. See here, I am accustomed to making crucial decisions quickly, could never have lived through the war if I had not." His eyes glowed with purpose. "And I knew she was mine the moment I met her. Why prolong the inevitable? We both felt strongly about each other almost immediately."

Darcy had no argument for his friend, the deed already done and over at any rate.

"My second question is why are you living like this? Why the secrecy?"

Fitzwilliam put down his pipe to rub the exhaustion from his eyes before he answered. He briefly related Amanda's situation to his cousin and then poured himself another drink.

Darcy whistled softly. "What will you do?"

Fitzwilliam waited a long time to answer. "If we cannot find a solution soon, and by soon, I actually mean immediately, we shall have to seize the boy and leave, secure a coach for

Portsmouth or Dover, go to the Continent, and hide out there for a time."

"Richard, you do realize that you would not be able to come back. You'd be hounded by the authorities. You would both be fugitives."

Fitzwilliam had waited as long as he could for the worst news. "Yes, I know. In truth, I am thinking it will be best if we relocate to America. She still has her family home in Boston and some relations there to help us begin anew. As you know, I have no real means of surviving here without my father's aid, and I could not ask him to support something like this." Fitzwilliam inhaled deeply and raked his hand through his hair again. "We don't even have the luxury now of examining our options. She believes she's with child."

Darcy's eyebrows shot up, and he smiled warmly at his cousin. "By God, Richard, I know it's making it more difficult, but how glad I am for you."

Fitzwilliam could not contain his own smile. "Truth be told, I'm rather pleased myself. I had never hoped to have children of my own."

"America," Darcy said quietly.

Fitzwilliam nodded.

"America!" Darcy repeated, the realization beginning to sink in.

"Will you quit repeating that like we're going to the moon?" Fitzwilliam ground out in irritation.

"Bah! It'll never happen." Darcy tried to rally his drooping spirits. "I cannot possibly credit that Aunt Catherine would allow it!"

They sat in quiet for a long while. "Would you be leaving

soon?" The thought of his cousin's leaving weighed heavily upon Darcy, knowing it unlikely he would be able to return to England once they fled.

"I'd like to wait until the end of January, of course, until Elizabeth has the baby, but that may not be possible."

"Well, how can I help you, Fitz?" Darcy asked.

"If needed, may we stay at your home, Darcy, for one night only? We would be leaving within the next week perhaps. I hate to drag you into this, but I want her to know she has a safe refuge to which she can escape should something go amiss."

Darcy fought off his growing sadness and laughed. "Come on, you great idiot, you know we never need beg favors of each other. Meanwhile, let's get you home. Lizzy is driving me mad with her worry."

When they arrived at the Darcy's house, Elizabeth was at the door to greet them, nearly in tears with her relief. Her hand firmly pressed onto her aching back, she waddled around the two men, staring up at their severe faces, greatly annoyed at not being acknowledged more demonstratively. She kept switching her weight from one foot to the next as they settled farther into the hallway and handed their coats and gloves to the footmen.

Unable to restrain herself a moment longer, she began her outburst. "Richard Fitzwilliam, where have you been? We thought something ghastly had happened to you. You gave us such a fright! Did he not, William? Yes, a terrible fright! Everyone has been out looking for you, did you realize that? Was it something to do with that woman to whom you were attracted? Did you have an argument or something? That is so common, really. You must not take it to heart. Look at William and myself. Remember how horrid he was to me in the beginning? That horrid, demeaning, contemptible proposal he made me at first? But we overcame that, you see. I have forgiven him completely—the insult to my family, the humiliation, the cold disdain for my feelings. We never think of it anymore." Darcy and Fitzwilliam's eyes met briefly over her head, and both valiantly refused to grin. Darcy leaned down and kissed the top of his wife's head.

"Oh! Or was it something else? Did you get ill? Is he ill? *Are you ill?*" she shouted on the off chance that he had suddenly gone deaf.

Fitzwilliam passed by and patted her shoulder then turned to speak in a loud whisper. "Is there any chance she will find a period to this sentence and employ it soon?" He began to ascend the stairs slowly, the fatigue and stress of the past weeks beginning to overwhelm him. "I take it I still have my old rooms upstairs, or have you moved me somewhere else?"

"No, same place as always. Shall we wake you for breakfast?"

"Not if you desire to live." He turned and walked back down the two steps, leaning over to kiss Lizzy on both cheeks. "Good night, beautiful," he muttered, "and thank you for the concern." He then disappeared up the stairs. Elizabeth and Darcy both watched him until he turned the corner of the hallway.

"Well, that is *very* strange, I must say!" Elizabeth whispered, one hand pressed to her lips. She turned to look up at her husband. "Very extraordinary, don't you think? I shall have to go up and speak with him tomorrow."

"Leave him be for a while, please, Elizabeth. And by the way, how did you get down those stairs? Hmmm? Did you call for assistance? I do not seem to see the carrying chair down here, do I?" Sighing, Lizzy rolled her eyes and waddled silently away, shaking her head and holding onto her back.

"Don't you walk away from me, young woman!" Darcy's hands were planted on his hips. "*I am speaking to you, Mrs. Darcy!*"

Chapter 18

December 24, 1817

Dearest Emily,

I hope this letter finds you well and having a merrier Christmas at Penwood than we are experiencing here at Pemberley House. It is with a heavy heart I convey to you that my brother has lost his mind completely and is attempting to take us all down with him. There is to be no Christmas pudding, no mistletoe, no garlands of ivy, no gifts, and no wassail.

"What is left to you, dear friend?" you may ask. We are left with something akin to the Twelve Days of Good Friday rather than Christmas.

We are left with servants hiding below stairs whenever possible, hiding so determinedly that one must drag them from their rooms by their feet.

We are left only with the "Interminable Wait" for the "Blessed Event," although my dear brother grows paler each time he calls it that. He has alienated everyone, including the dogs, and his temper is so tightly coiled at this time that I fear his eyeballs will pop from their sunken crevices.

What concerns me most is that even the doctor has taken umbrage, refusing to return his calls, saying there is "plenty of time yet." He has even refused my brother's requests to install the midwife a month early, and I fear my brother is more persistent than prudent. We will all be glad when this is over.

And dear Elizabeth is sometimes an afterthought in all the horror.

Many thanks to you for allowing me to vent my frustrations like this. You are a true "Friend in Need." I shall look forward to seeing you Boxing Day at Bunny Bridges's holiday gathering, which will probably be the only merry time this year for me.

Yours in friendship,
Georgiana Darcy

Miss Georgiana Darcy did not, in any manner, exaggerate the mood at Pemberley House at Christmastime in the year of our Lord 1817. There were indeed no wishes to stir into the Christmas pudding. There was no mistletoe, no garland, no wassail. A goose life was spared, the fowl in question remaining undressed and happily ignorant of his near-death experience. Perfectly good presents remained unmolested upon shop shelves.

Darcy's fears for Elizabeth's pregnancy had progressed over the past months into an unreasoning hysteria as he envisioned his delicate wife, now much larger horizontally than vertically, in the throes of childbirth. Nightmares disturbed his sleep.

And she had still another month to go. Another four weeks

for that behemoth, that monster, that fiend within her to continue its unchecked growth! Darcy had purposefully removed Elizabeth from the country, from the very bed in which his own mother had died giving birth to Georgiana. He had purposefully brought her to his beloved London, the city with superior physicians and advanced medical practices. He had not, however, counted on the greater crowds, almost twice as large as the prior year, and the noise! London, bursting at this holiday season and still celebrating the allies victory! Was this damned commemoration never to end?

The house remained in expectant quiet and seemed deserted to the innocent outside world, the knocker still packed somewhere within the attic, giving notice that no visitors were welcome. But those who lived within knew better. They who lived there, and all of surrounding St. James, waited.

Volume Three

THE FAMILY
1817

"There is no remedy for love,
But to love more."

—Henry David Thoreau

Chapter 1

DAMN IT TO HELL! Darcy took one last look up the stairs before storming out into the frosty night. *I should not be forced to run like some criminal, driven from my own house, by my own wife.* He paced back and forth on his front stoop, his breath blooming out around him with every heated exclamation, every "harrumph," every "damnation," every "ridiculous" that was spat out. Stomping his feet on the chilly pavement, he slapped his arms to ward off the freezing winter temperatures. *She's lost her mind, that's all there is to it. I shall care for her, of course, for as long as she lives, and if she's not careful, that won't be too much longer.*

He was furious with Elizabeth for her unprovoked behavior, while even angrier with himself for still feeling concern—and to what purpose? It was Boxing Day, the day after Christmas. He had approached their room with the noblest of intents. He would bring supper up for them both, sparing her an arduous trip up and down the staircase. Besides, most of the servants were off for their Yule holiday, and he wanted Mr. and Mrs. Winters to have a well-deserved rest also. He was perfectly willing to pitch in, warm up something or slice something, do whatever culinary magic it would entail to feed his beloved. How hard could it be?

He just required the most minimum of direction, such as just where the kitchen was exactly and how to light the oven, perhaps a recommendation on which pan to use and if he needed some sort of oil, and mayhap she could direct him to where those pans were actually kept, and the silverware—they would need silverware and dishes, too. Lizzy would help him. She liked blancmange. Could that be very difficult? And dressed lamb—that was his favorite.

He was too proud to admit his ignorance to the few remaining servants. Perhaps he should aim a bit lower. By God, wouldn't some nice fruit and cheese be better all around, healthier, less trouble, too? Now, where was the fruit? And the larder? Where was cheese stored anyway?

To his shock, he had been greeted at the door not by his adoring wife but by some hysterical banshee propelling objects at him, great, heavy glass and metal objects, sailing lethally and deliberately through the air, accompanied by screams of "Liar" and shrieks of "How could you?" over and over again.

In his bewilderment, he never noticed the note that lay in shreds at her feet nor the locket she had clutched to her chest. He was too busy with his evasive action, his bobbing and weaving. All he knew for certain was that he was half an hour late in coming to her rooms, and this was his punishment. His ungrateful wife had finally snapped, did not appreciate him, never had. Suddenly anger and resentment could no longer be restrained, and they commenced a series of door slamming and verbal denunciations.

He stomped back into the house and made his noisy way up the stairs and into his own dressing room. *Enough is enough*, he fumed. *I've been far too complacent with her temper tantrums and her stubborn pride. I've spoiled her—just plain spoiled her*. "You are spoiled, young woman, spoiled! I have been far too indulgent with you!" he yelled. He grabbed his greatcoat and gloves and began loudly clomping back down the stairs, challenging her to voice a complaint, casting dire glances toward Elizabeth's dressing-room door. *I will be a doormat for her no longer*. "I will be a doormat for you no longer, madam!!" he bellowed, nodding his head, completely in agreement with himself.

Since her door was wide open, she had to have heard the commotion of this dramatic departure and reentrance, let alone his defiant proclamation, and yet she never appeared. He hesitated at the bottom of the stairs, his breathing labored and his heart pounding. *Damn it! Maybe she's made herself ill*. He could not contain his worries; they had been his constant companion for months. *She's been so quiet lately, and tired. This fit of temper must have been a shock to her system*.

He took a few more hesitant steps toward the front door, slapping his gloves across his palm and then stopping again to gnaw on his lip. *I suppose I could just quietly go up and have a look in at her. She's losing her balance so often—what if she's fallen again?* He continued standing there, unable to leave and unable to go back up.

He could have just as well had "Kick me" painted on his back. Suddenly an object flew down, hitting him sharply on the back of his head. "Don't leave without your stupid hat, Mr. Darcy. It has become chilled outside, and I should not wish to be accused of being the cause of your fever." Elizabeth haughtily spun around and slammed her door shut.

The momentary stillness was followed by the sound of a latch.

Months and months of anxious, heart-stopping apprehension finally broke within him. *Impudent little mongrel!* "Inputil Mingol!" he bellowed absurdly. *I really must get control of myself.* His mind spun like a top, he was so incensed. He was so infuriated. He was angrier and more upset than ever before in his life, let alone in their three-year marriage. *How dare she throw my hat at me!! This is a new hat!* Finally getting his rage controlled enough to form coherent words, he yelled up to her, "Locked doors between us are not permitted in this house, Elizabeth!" He stood at the foot of the stairs and bellowed the clincher, "I forbid them, as you well know!" That told her!

He could contain himself no longer. He charged back up the stairs, two at a time, ending outside her door in a mind-rending and furious temper. "Mrs. Darcy, open this door!" Nothing—not a sound. He tried the handle once and then again. "Mrs. Darcy, this is still my house. You are still, if only momentarily, my wife, and I insist you open this door immediately!" He banged furiously for several moments and then stopped to listen.

Alarm began to take precedence over anger when no sound came back to him. The whole house seemed deadly quiet.

"Elizabeth, are you all right? Elizabeth?! Are you hurt? Damnation, Lizzy, answer me!" He waited a few moments more and then, taking a step back, raised his heel and bashed in the door with his boot. His eyes darted quickly around the room, finding her off to the side by the windows, sitting at her dressing table.

Tears streaming down her face, Elizabeth jumped up before retreating two steps. "How dare you force your way into my rooms, breaking in my door! I was right about you. You are no gentleman!"

Darcy's expression became horribly mottled as his eyes twitched and blinked. He quickly closed the distance to where she stood. "*Are you suddenly deaf, woman?! Haven't you heard me yelling for you to open that damn, bloody door?!*" The rafters shook as he roared.

Elizabeth drew herself up to meet him face to face, figuratively speaking. She was in actuality short of his height by about ten or twelve inches. They stood chin to chest, glaring in each other's general vicinity, breathing hard as if both had just arrived at the finish line of a very long and debilitating race. "*Of course I heard you, you great ape! I simply chose to ignore you!*"

He slammed the exquisite, if slightly dented, beaver hat on his head and bellowed, "*Lis is bast strew…!*" Annoyingly, he was screaming in tongues again and took a moment to compose himself, taking long, deep breaths. Finally calmed, he could continue. "This is the last straw, Mrs. Darcy! I can abide your disrespect, your viper tongue, your bad temper no longer. I am leaving you, and may you have joy of the evening."

"That's the best gift of the season. In actuality, it is the *only* gift of the season!" She hissed directly into his waistcoat buttons, spraying saliva everywhere and sounding much more defiant than she felt. "Just see that you don't return!!"

His eyes narrowed dangerously, and for the first time in their short marriage, Elizabeth thought that perhaps she might have gone a little too far. As he raised his arm, she jumped back, covering her head as if to protect herself from an imminent blow. He was only attempting to wipe his buttons.

"How dare you!" Now he had gone past mere anger into an unknown realm of fury. He turned into a stranger before her very eyes. "How dare you insinuate that I would strike a woman! You really don't know me at all, do you? You never really did."

He turned on his heel and stormed from the room, slamming the door behind him. It banged open again and then closed with a thud. Elizabeth could hear his heavy footsteps going down the stairs and heard him wrench open the foyer door, storming out into the night. She struggled to resist the impulse to run to the window to call him back, so she sat down at her dressing table very quietly, holding onto the edge of the seat cushion. Her heart was pounding furiously. *Maybe he'll turn around and come back. All couples have their little ups and downs, don't they? If he would come up here and take me in his arms, why, that is all I really want, some assurance that he still loves me.*

But what if he meant it? What if he never does come back?

Her blood ran cold. Although not normally one to give in to tears, they ran freely down her cheeks now. *When will this nightmare ever end?* She tenderly patted her huge stomach and shifted restlessly on the dresser chair, thinking nothing of the tremendous pressure increasing on her bottom and her back. She rose awkwardly and waddled to the window in hopes of seeing him turning in the street, to see him walking back to her, but all was deathly quiet. He was gone already.

⁂

It had been a brief hour before this unpleasant encounter with her husband that Lizzy had received the note along with the return of her long-lost locket. Up until then, it had been an idyllic day with all the concern over Fitzwilliam's whereabouts behind them and then the joy of his happy news. She had actually even forgotten about the locket.

Darcy had made his annual appearance at the Boxing Day breakfast for the staff, passing out their Christmas bonuses—hefty bonuses to compensate for his increasingly irrational behavior. Then the couple exchanged their own special gifts in private and spent the afternoon quietly and happily alone, laughing and talking together.

She was confused at first but overjoyed that the precious item, the only thing she had ever received from her mother, was returned. *Wherever did this come from?* It had taken her several minutes to understand what was being implied. At first she thought the note was from Jane, but that made little sense. *How did Jane get my locket?* Her brows beetled in confusion. No, it wasn't Jane's stationery, but it *was* on Bingley stationery.

"*Miss Bennet,*" the note began.

Miss Bennet? There is only one person so ignorant and pig-headed enough to still call me Miss Bennet. She began to read again,

Miss Bennet,

It appears our darling Darcy misplaced your trinket several months ago when he stayed with me at Netherfield for our private visit, a visit we thoroughly enjoyed alone at my home. It must have fallen from his coat when he removed it, the locket being discovered upstairs in my bedroom. I had intended to return this during my visit with you at Lady Catherine de Bourgh's home, but I was mysteriously misrepresented to her and had to leave before I could accomplish my mission.

I hope this hasn't caused you any alarm. I had thought to discard it, but then realized it may have sentimental attachments for you. It obviously has no other value.

Please give Darcy my love and relate to him, for me, how I dearly I look forward to his next visit.

Regards,

Caroline Bingley

Lizzy sat very still, her mind so paralyzed that it was unable to wrap itself around this tidbit of news. Darcy was at her house? No. Fitzwilliam Darcy? Her Fitzwilliam Darcy? When could he have visited? She and Darcy had been in each other's pockets for months now. The only time he was away from her was when he assisted her father in returning home, and when he went away to assist Charles at Netherfield...

Elizabeth was still clutching one bit of the shredded letter when Darcy entered her dressing room, arrogantly proclaiming that since there remained no footmen at home to carry her downstairs, he would, like his mud hut–dwelling forbearers, provide primitivelike sustenance for his woman—peach tarts, plover's eggs with mint jelly, fresh fruit, cheese, and toast tips. All that she needed to tell him was how.

He stopped when he saw her furious stare. "Lizzy, whatever is wrong? You look like you've fought a ghost!"

It was a terrible argument. Tensions that had been repressed but building were exploding everywhere with horrible accusations and threats, most of which, thankfully, were shrieked in words that were unintelligible. When he finally stormed out, she sat at her dressing table, staring at a gaping hole where there had once been a door handle and lock. Now, like her marriage, the lock and handle lay in shattered pieces upon the floor. She was numb. She clutched her poor little locket to her heart and felt physically ill. She never thought for a moment that he would become so angry that he would actually kick in her door.

Oh my God Oh my God Oh my God! Could he really be having an affair with Caroline? No, this I cannot believe. I will not believe—he is the best of men. I'll kill him. Oh dear Jesu, maybe he has the right of it, though, the way I treat him, and I look like a sea cow anyway. Who can blame him for finding comfort with another? I wish the baby would come, that it was all finally over. Caressing her stomach, she began to sob, not really noticing that the persistent back pain and occasional kicking, her daily companions for so many months, had finally ceased.

❧

It was a half hour after Darcy's dramatic exit that those horrible pains returned with a vengeance, the pain her doctor had been dismissing out of hand for the past week, worse now by far. There was also a queer pressure on her bottom, distracting her from her wallowing in abject misery. Moaning, she wiped away tears with a knuckle and quickly sat down, loudly blowing her nose with her delicate Belgian lace handkerchief. It never occurred to her to call for the doctor or even to have mentioned those earlier discomforts to her husband. *Of course, now there is no husband to tell.* It was the sort of whiney type of reflection that caused her to abruptly renew her wails.

At that moment, the only room in her thoughts were for Darcy and Caroline Bingley. Could they have deceived her for so long? If so, how long had the two of them been communicating with each other? Laughing at her? Caroline was beautiful, the little weasel, as well as an extremely skilled flirt and always desperately grasping for a husband, any husband. *But why my husband? Let her get her own life and husband and leave mine to me!* Elizabeth trembled with anger and humiliation. *How could he walk out on me now, like this? How could he leave me for that hussy?* When she then looked at herself in the mirror, she gasped—blotchy face, red-rimmed eyes, hair jutting out at bizarrely odd angles, a belly that looked like she had swallowed a hedge. Reinvigorated by her inventory of personal faults, she began again to yowl, her tears increasing in volume and running down her cheeks in miserable rivers.

Eventually, though, even a cast-off blob of a wife needed food, and so she clumsily stood, bracing herself against her dressing table then waddled the few steps to her now-cold afternoon tea tray. The pressure on her bottom intensified, followed by an odd sensation of water running down her legs. She was aghast at seeing the liquid stain begin to spread on her beloved Turkish carpet. "Oh no!" she cried in distress. "Why must everything happen to me?" She was furious. She stomped her tiny bare foot in her rage and did what all devoted wives do—she blamed her husband. "Well, thank you very much, Mr. Darcy! This is just typical, isn't it? This rug is one of a kind and very expensive, William, brand new, not even four months old!"

That was the exact moment the enormity of what was happening finally struck her… and just seconds before the first real labor pain hit. She gripped her belly and felt her knees begin to vibrate.

"Uh-oh."

She snatched wildly at the back of a chair. "No, this cannot be." After a moment, she calmed her breathing then attempted the trip from the chair back to the table, thinking to make her way slowly toward the door.

Another, stronger pain in her back knocked her to her knees.

"Cara," she gasped out to her maid. "Cara!" She tried to call louder, but she had no volume, no strength, and the house remained so quiet. All Elizabeth could hear was the clock on the mantel.

Where in heaven's name is Cara? Why is it so quiet? Now on her hands and knees and utterly helpless, she pulled open her broken door and peered to the left, down the long, empty corridor and then to the right. *Sweet Jesus, this cannot be labor*, she tried to reassure herself. *It must be something that I ate, perhaps merely indigestion. I have four weeks left—they owe me four weeks! I am not ready for this, besides which the doctor said first babies are always late... always. That dim-witted, bloody imbecile promised me! Yes, and then Jane will be here, my father will be here, Kitty and Mary will be here. No, this just cannot happen now. I forbid it.*

She grabbed onto the leg of a hall chair and, dragging it toward herself, managed somehow to sit. She looked like Buddha with her legs spread to accommodate her low-hanging belly and her hands resting on her knees. Sweat had begun pooling up under her arms and between her breasts. Moisture thickened at the roots of her fringe of bangs. "Mrs. Winter!" It was no use. Her voice sounded like a frog croak.

Not a sound returned to her.

"Could they all be down at supper?" she asked upon hearing her mantel clock strike seven-thirty. "Oh, no! Elizabeth, did you forget it is Boxing Day? The staff is off enjoying their holiday."

She spoke aloud in this manner with the belief that the sound of a voice would calm her.

It did not.

Oh dear. She gulped and pressed her hand across her forehead. *I must remain calm, must remember to breathe. I am in the middle of London, at Yuletide, surely someone is about—somewhere. Where is Georgiana? Georgiana will help me. Dear sweet, gentle, little Georgiana. What a truly wonderful sister she has been to me. She'll make such a good aunt. I do so adore her*. She began to call out her beloved sister-in-law's name but remembered that sweet, gentle, little Georgiana had run from the house that morning, unable to stand the tension any longer. She had fled to some holiday party with Emily and two other young girls. *Scrawny little ingrate, leaving me to wallow here like a beached whale, alone and helpless*.

Another pain caused Elizabeth to double over and scream.

~

Amanda Fitzwilliam was making her first steps into her new life, and to liberty, the American Revolution's motto of *Don't Tread On Me* her silent mantra—very silent. It was early evening, and her mother-in-law, finally recuperated enough to enjoy the holidays, had taken Emily and Georgiana to another one of the interminable holiday house parties that the upper classes apparently thrived upon. She would be gone for three glorious days. The timing for their escape could not have been more perfect.

When Amanda was certain that the old woman had departed and that the servants had left or were distracted with celebrations for the evening, she bundled up Harry and waited for her husband's arrival. She waited as long as she could before her nerves just snapped. Grabbing a small bag that she had prepared with a few clothes for them both, she quietly slipped down the stairs.

Without her husband to accompany her through the streets, necessity developed a new plan. She spoke with one of the maids that had befriended her, telling her to get together a bag, that they would be going away visiting for a few days for the holidays. That girl was now sitting on the back stairs, nervously waiting and chewing away at her bottom lip. "Come along, Mary. Have you packed a bag for yourself? Good. This will be great fun, you'll see."

Setting her bag down for a moment, Amanda picked up the sleepy Harry, reclaimed her small valise, and then began leading the way down the stairs, out the back door, and across the avenue, racing against the quickly fading daylight. "Hurry though, Mary. We must hurry. Night is falling. It is only a few blocks."

Since the elder Lady Penrod's instruction to Mary had been to feign friendship with the American while secretly reporting back regarding Amanda's activities, Mary reluctantly agreed to accompany her. "I don't know, ma'am," she squeaked out. "Won't 'er ladyship be that mad at me for this?"

"Nonsense, Mary, it is but for a few days at most, a little holiday just for ourselves with some friends." Amanda craved sweets at the moment and thought that would be a certain allurement. "There will be lots of chocolate and cake." She stopped then for a moment to resettle her child more comfortably on her hip. She hadn't realized how much Harry had grown and how heavy he had become, but it was much quicker to carry him than to coax the tired child along.

Lord, but the boy was heavy.

❧

It was a strange little procession that scurried through fashionable Mayfair and on toward St. James Street, attracting not a slight amount of attention from the few souls brave enough to face the frigid evening temperatures. Amanda forced herself to slow her pace, trying to avoid the curious glances of passersby, plus, she was quickly tiring with the added weight of Harry in her arms. "Only a few blocks more," she called out loudly to reassure Mary. Darkness had already settled in among the tree boughs heavy with white sparkling powder.

A pair of gentlemen rushing past doffed their hats. A curious dog followed them for a block or more and then lost interest. Sleigh bells rang in the far distance. They heard intermittent laughter from unseen dwellings, and then a harp begin to play "God Rest Ye Merry Gentlemen" in a home gaily lit with candles. They slowed for a moment to rest and listen as faraway voices sang, "*Good tidings of comfort and joy, comfort and joy...*" But too soon, the song ended, and there was silence surrounding them.

The truculent maid kept lagging behind, mumbling angrily and struggling with her nearly empty suitcase. "Mary, please keep your eyes forward. I don't know why you are so concerned with what is behind us. Please walk faster."

Amanda tried to remain calm. Although they were to have waited for Richard's arrival to help spirit them from the house, he was late, and she had panicked. He would know to find her at the Darcys' house. He had told her she would be safe there.

❧

It was then she noticed that the Darcy's ornate wrought iron gate was unlatched and creaking, swinging freely. Apprehension grew within her. Following her gaze up the drive to the vast portico, she found it odder still that one of the double front doors was also open, illuminated from within by a dimming fireplace at the rear of the two-story, white-marble foyer. The front lamps were cold and unlit.

She walked hesitantly forward, drawing closer and closer to the forbidding black rail that surrounded the property, her heart pounding with unknown fear, unrealized danger. The night was so very quiet, eerie and still. *Try to think logically now, 'manda, even if you are a woman.* Her husband's oft quoted and lovingly meant jibe caused her to grow bolder. After pushing back the imposing gate, she made her way up the circular drive to the front, setting Harry down finally before she attempted climbing the brick stairs. She instructed Mary to wait for her at their base and to hold her son's hand then cautiously made her way to the door, calling out a "Hello!" as she pushed the front door fully open. "Mrs. Darcy, are you here?"

She heard a woman scream.

Chapter 2

Lizzy was struggling to rise when she heard the voice calling out to her from the entrance below. "Help me, God." Her plea was nearer a whisper. With her legs trembling, her palms scraped and bleeding, her heart pounding, she managed to pull herself into a crouching position then lost her balance once more and screamed as she fell sideways, hitting her stomach against the chair. The pain was excruciating, whether from the fall or from within unknown. Terrified for her unborn child, she wrapped her arms around the little one and began to weep. Within moments, a presence knelt before her, and she blindly reached out to it, feeling a rush of relief when she clutched onto the warm, soft hand of another human being.

"Thank heaven you're here." She gasped for air then slowly opened her eyes to tiny slits. "By the way, who are you?" She was staring into the face of a stranger.

"Mrs. Darcy, please forgive me for barging into your home. The door was open downstairs, and I became alarmed when I heard your cry. Here, allow me help you."

Elizabeth took a few more moments to catch her breath, resting back on her heels to look curiously about. Before her was a woman around her age, blonde and very attractive, dressed in an old-fashioned cloak and bonnet. Behind the woman stood a terrified-looking maid holding the hand of a frightened little child. Elizabeth inhaled deeply, a modicum of calm slowly returning. She shook her head. *These histrionics will not do*, she reasoned. *I must get a grip on her emotions*. Elizabeth gazed intently into the strange woman's eyes.

"Forgive my present state. I am not usually so blunt when speaking or lax in my hospitality." Suppressing all of her instincts toward hysteria, she forced herself to smile. "It appears that you have me at a slight disadvantage, however, madam, since you seem acquainted with me, although I do not recall the pleasure of meeting you before."

"I am Amanda Fitzwilliam."

"I am exceedingly grateful to meet you." Lizzy's eyelashes began to flutter furiously. "What did you say your name was?"

Amanda was too distracted to hear the question as she helped support Lizzy in her struggle to stand. They lurched first one way then the other, amidst the associated grunts and "oofs" and "oh mys." There were one or two very polite apologies regarding unexpected toe injuries, but by and by, they achieved an upright position in relatively short time.

In thanks, Lizzy squeezed Amanda's hand and then rested her weight momentarily against the other woman's supportive body. Having regained some of her composure, Lizzy pulled back slightly to search her face.

"Are you Fitzwilliam's Amanda?"

Diverted with clearing a path through the debris for them to walk, kicking away a small footstool and then shoving the table away slightly with her hip, Amanda answered without thinking. "No, you have it backward. I am Amanda Fitzwilliam." Amanda quickly looked up and laughed in her embarrassment. "Oh! Yes, I am Colonel Fitzwilliam's wife, Amanda, and you know that is the very first time I have been able to say that to anyone." She was beaming.

"I am Lizzy Darcy." Elizabeth's eyes began to tear up with her joy. "You're American, did you know that? What am I saying? Of course you know that. I sound like an idiot. We've been expecting you"—Lizzy hugged Amanda warmly—"just not today." Then, just as suddenly, Lizzy doubled over in pain.

"Forgive me for stating the obvious, but I do believe your labor has begun, Mrs. Darcy."

Elizabeth swallowed hard and shook her head, her body beginning to quake. "I cannot be in labor, because, you see, I have it on good authority from my physician that I am not due to deliver for another four weeks. These back pains I have been experiencing all week are false. Evidently they are the product of my overly educated female brain."

She stopped to press a hand against her mouth. "But truth be told, I am a bit apprehensive, Mrs. Fitzwilliam, a bit overwhelmed. I am beginning to think he has been wrong all along." A sudden sob escaped her before she regained her poise. "You see he never listened to me nor examined me, never even acknowledged how large I had become when I questioned him. My only solace was that he had engaged a noted midwife."

"Well, there seems to be distinct evidence that your doctor has miscalculated, Mrs. Darcy. May I ask where everyone is? You say a midwife is to be here? If she is not already in residence, someone should be collecting her immediately." The quiet in the house was fast becoming oppressive. Amanda hadn't seen any servants, and there had been no candles lit in the foyer and no footman at the door.

"Many of the servants have gone home to their families, celebrating Boxing Day. The midwife is terrified of Mr. Darcy's ranting and will not come until she is assured that the doctor is also here. The doctor refuses to be in the same room with my husband a moment before it is necessary. My sister-in-law has run off and abandoned me, and last but certainly not least, Mr. Darcy and I have had a disagreement, and he left in great anger."

Elizabeth halted her rant for a moment to wipe tears away with the back of her hand. She pointed at the doorway. "You see, he broke my door there, barged in like a drunken madman." Lizzy choked on her sob. "God, I love him so."

Amanda looked in amazement at the door frame. "My stars, Mr. Darcy did that? It's hard for me to imagine him losing his temper at all. He is such an elegant gentleman." Another pain caused Lizzy to unexpectedly bend over, nearly toppling Amanda with her sudden shift in weight. After a moment, she relaxed, and they continued their slow progress.

Upon reaching the bedroom, Lizzy sat down heavily on the edge of the Darcy family's massive heirloom bed and resumed her attempts to tamp down her unbridled fear, watching as Amanda pulled off the counterpane and top sheets. Her voice, when she next spoke, was shaky. "Well, Mrs. Fitzwilliam, it is indeed a pleasure to meet you. Please tell me something of yourself. Do you have family here? You should have used our home for the ceremony, you know. The more I think on it, the more disappointed I am becoming. Richard and William are closer than brothers. You would think…" Elizabeth gasped and doubled over with pain, almost falling to the floor. Spasm after spasm of throbbing agony was washing over her, covering her, overwhelming her senses.

Amanda stooped down before Elizabeth and gathered up her hands. "Mrs. Darcy, have you at all begun to time your contractions?" she asked gently. Lizzy shook her head no, clinging tightly to Amanda's hands. The fear she had so desperately been trying to hold at bay was finally beginning to overtake her.

Chapter 3

Little Harry stood at the doorway, transfixed, fascinated by the scene unfolding before him. Clearly this was one of those moments that Colonel Fitz had told him about, those moments in a gentleman's life where he must care for the welfare of his ladies. He slipped his hand from the distracted maid's and walked purposefully up to his mother. He crouched down, holding his knees tight, and stared intently, first into his mother's face and then into Lizzy's. "Is Mrs. Darling unwell, Mama?" He squinted, examining Lizzy's face closely, deciding what he saw there could not be good. He was greatly concerned, worried about her weakened appearance. Suddenly he shouted into her ear, "*Did the Frenchies do this to you, madam?!*" Lizzy turned a surprised look at him and then at Amanda.

"We are having a bit of a problem with the concept of the French," Amanda explained to her quietly. She turned to her son. "Dearest, despite what the colonel says, French people are not responsible for all the pain in the world."

Harry's eyes rounded as he stared back at her, clearly registering his doubt as to that statement. He then looked behind them on the carpet. He tugged on her sleeve. "Mummy...?" he whispered.

"Dearest, why don't you wait for Mummy in the other room. Mary, could you please take him out to the sitting room?"

"But, Mummy," he whispered again, anxiously.

"Mummy is very busy at the moment, sweetheart. Go with Mary now."

"But, Mummy, look. Mrs. Darling has wet the carpet. Will she be in trouble? Oh, I hope not. She's not well. Will Mr. Darling make her sleep outside like Grandmama makes Ruffles?" His eyes were wide with concern, and he placed a protective hand on Elizabeth's shoulder. Again, he shouted into Elizabeth's ear, "*I say, will you be in trouble? Please do not be afraid. I shall protect you.*" He lowered his voice and turned back to Amanda to plead for leniency. "I don't think she meant to do it, Mummy. You see, she is not feeling at all well. I think she must be very old, poor dear."

"Oh fiddles." Amanda had not heard Harry's rather rude comment about Lizzy's advanced age. Amanda had been staring where her son was pointing, at the large water stain on the carpet. She looked back at Elizabeth.

"Mary," she called over to the maid. "Go downstairs and get someone from the household up here immediately. Look everywhere. Please take Harry into the next room. Harry, you will remain in the sitting room, and you will behave like the wonderful boy you are, all right, my angel?" The maid grabbed Harry's hand but remained motionless, staring wide-eyed as Lizzy struggled with her growing fright.

"Mrs. Darcy, I am afraid that, early or not, your baby is coming quite quickly." Amanda helped Lizzy off with her wet underclothes then to lie back on the bed, placing pillows beneath her head. She ran to a cupboard and grabbed sheets from within.

"After you bring someone up here, I want you go back downstairs and wait for Colonel Fitzwilliam. Mary, do you understand? Are you listening to me?"

The maid began backing out of the room. "I'll just take Sir Harry with me now, mum."

"No!" Amanda felt a sudden apprehension. "Please just settle Sir Harry into the adjoining sitting room and leave him there, where I can see him." At her maid's raised eyebrows, Amanda almost succumbed to the urge to shout. "Give him that Mother Goose book from my valise to read and then go and wait for the colonel downstairs. Harry, you will wait in the next room and read aloud to Mrs. Darcy and me. That will help Mrs. Darcy very much. Do not stop reading—read very loudly, Harry, until the colonel comes for you!"

When she looked back down into Elizabeth's eyes, they were bright with terror. "Mrs. Darcy, please listen to me. There can be only one of two things happening here. Either your physician has made an error in your delivery date, or"—she hesitated with the second, knowing it was the most dangerous of the two for the child—"or the baby is coming early. If it is the former, I will be perfectly able to assist you. I have assisted in many births at my father's hospital in Boston."

Elizabeth fought off her panic. "What if it is the latter?"

Amanda swallowed. "I don't really think it is."

Elizabeth looked straight up at the ceiling and nodded.

After waiting patiently through a few minutes of quiet

counting, Elizabeth squeezed Amanda's hand. "Mrs. Fitzwilliam, I have heard that extreme stress or shock can bring on labor. Is that true?" Amanda dampened a cloth in cool water and gently wiped Elizabeth's forehead then used her fingers to tenderly comb her hair back from her face.

"I have heard that also, and it may be possible, although my father never mentioned that. Why do you ask?"

Elizabeth stared intently back at her. "I received a letter that upset me to such an extent that I initiated the fight with Mr. Darcy and drove him to walk out." Another pain shot through Elizabeth, and she gripped Amanda's hand convulsively. "He is really such a good man. He looks so calm on the surface but is in actuality more like a duck. All the turmoil is going on beneath the surface."

Amanda smiled, holding Elizabeth's hand. "You must love him a great deal."

"I love him more than my life."

It was nearly twenty minutes later, and the contractions appeared to have abated. As Lizzy relaxed, her curiosity returned. "So I am now wondering whether my husband was aware of your coming here this evening. He never informed me."

Amanda sat beside Lizzy, holding her hand and dabbing a cool cloth across her forehead. "You know how men are. I mean besides the general lack of imagination or patience on their part, they are really quite unable to deal with more than one situation." She wrinkled her nose. "It is best when they are presented with one problem at a time, you know. Anything more than that seems to muddle their thinking."

"I agree with you completely. The bigger picture is all they see, and they never concern themselves with small details like packing or servants or food. The most terrifying words I ever hear William utter are"—Lizzy dropped her voice several registers and sounded very aristocratic—"All that is required, Elizabeth, is...' After he makes that pronouncement, I know it will probably be up to me to get the impossible accomplished."

"And have you noticed that they never listen? I swear to it," continued Amanda. "I tell Richard times, and he arbitrarily adds or subtracts a half hour...always. When I speak, he nods and nods, but he never remembers what I say. But then of course, he cannot remember what I said because he did not listen in the first place. Now, this evening he was to be at the door at seven in the evening. I waited another half hour but could not wait a moment longer, and we took off on our own. He never listens."

"Do you love him very much?" Elizabeth smiled up at Amanda.

"With all my heart."

❧

"Can Mrs. Darling hear me, Mummy?" Harry called out from the adjoining room. "Am I helping her?"

"Yes, dearest. You are helping Mrs. Darling very much."

Harry was into his fifth rendition of Mother Hubbard, none of them the same, the many words he could not read replaced by his vivid imagination. He had a gift for creating fanciful tales from the kernels of his children's stories, embellishing details and adding his own characters and animal sounds. For this reading, Mother Hubbard was a woman named Mrs. Darling, deathly ill with a stomach ache from eating green apples and currently having a baby in France. She and her baby were then going to eat chocolate cake. Amanda and Lizzy both smiled in amusement as they listened.

Then the pains began again, growing closer in time and much greater in intensity. "I believe you are now two minutes apart. Things should be moving more quickly now." Amanda leaned over Lizzy and gently smoothed back the sweat-dampened hair that had matted on her forehead. "Mrs. Darcy, I will try to feel for the child, if I have your permission?"

Elizabeth nodded and then smiled, her eyes crinkling in amusement. "I think that we are embarking onto a level of acquaintance where we may begin calling each other by our Christian names, do you not agree, Cousin Amanda?"

Amanda laughed as she sat on a stool between Lizzy's legs. "Yes, I believe you are right, Cousin Elizabeth."

Another contraction hit Elizabeth like a thunderbolt, and she grabbed at the sheets, her body constricted in pain. Amanda waited a moment until the pain subsided, and then, while she pressed her hand on Lizzy's abdomen, she felt for the baby's head, finding it very near the opening. She was telling Lizzy to be prepared soon to push when a familiar voice was heard from the downstairs' landing. It was Fitzwilliam, calling out first Amanda's name and then Elizabeth's.

Chapter 4

Fitzwilliam walked into the empty foyer and looked about, frightened by the unusual quiet. His first impression was that someone had broken into the house and, beginning to panic, he called out his wife's name, then Darcy's and Elizabeth's. The stillness in the house was suddenly broken by a scream from the upstairs and Amanda's voice calling to him.

"Amanda!" he shouted, terrified, then was relieved when she called out calmly to him again, "I'm fine, Richard… fifty-one, fifty-two… up in the bedrooms… fifty-five…"

"I was by Penwood House at eight exactly. Why did you not wait for me?" Richard protested as he climbed the steps, up to the living quarters. "That is completely unacceptable, Amanda. Whatever were you thinking, walking around the streets alone?"

At the sight of the colonel entering the dressing-room doorway, Harry whooped happily and threw down his book. He ran toward him, leaping into his outstretched arms. "Hello, son. Whatever is going on in here?" The colonel stopped cold at the sight of the broken sitting-room door, overturned tables, and debris littering the floor of the hallway.

Harry took a deep breath. "Well, it is all very exciting. Mrs. Darling has been hurt by the Frenchies and is crying, but Mummy said she won't be made to sleep outside for wetting the carpet." Harry scratched his earlobe and nodded his head seriously while he relayed his version of the night's events. He took another deep breath. "Mrs. Darling is crying really very loudly sometimes because her tummy hurts, and she is anxious that when someone named William comes home and sees the wet carpet, he will be angry and spank her. She keeps calling his name out and says she loves him, though. She feels really, really sick, and we must protect her. Mama thinks she may throw up a baby."

Just then another contraction brought yet another, even louder scream from Elizabeth. Putting Harry down, Fitzwilliam ran into the room.

"What's going on in here?" he demanded. "Amanda, are you all right?"

At first he saw only his wife, and then his eyes found Lizzy on the bed. He spun around, uttering a startled, "Oh my God!" Lizzy's bare feet and part of her legs were peeking out from under the sheet that Amanda had placed for privacy over her open and bent knees.

"Richard, thank heavens you're here. Please find someone to fetch the doctor immediately, and the midwife. I sent Mary down ages ago, but I don't understand what's taking so long, and where is everyone?"

"Hello, Richard." Lizzy's voice was very faint.

"I saw no one when I entered, not even Darcy. For God's sake, where is he? He's been a hovering pain in the ass for eight months!"

"They had a disagreement, and he walked out, left the poor thing alone and unguarded."

"If I could just say something in his defense." Lizzy lifted her finger to gain attention.

"The fool is nearing a breakdown. He probably just needed to get out of the house and walk it off. He'll return."

"Well, I hope you're right. Anyway, can you please take Harry somewhere safe? I was so frightened before; it appeared as if Mary was going to walk off with him."

"I told you to wait for me, did I not? Then you would not have needed to bring that maid with you. You never listen to reason. You're always in such a rush..."

"Pardon me...hellloooo. Remember me?" Lizzy's exasperation with them both was unexpectedly cut short. Her face contorting into a dumb show of horror, she clutched at the sheet, her knuckles turning so white it looked as if bare bones were grabbing the covers. Writhing with mind-numbing pain, she abandoned any thought of humiliation that Richard was witnessing her terror, witnessing her body being torn in two. Her eyes clenched tightly shut, and her shoulders came up off the bed with her grinding yowl. The contractions were coming in constant waves, increasing in their intensity as she felt the alien body within her begin to shift. After several excruciating moments, she gasped, the endless internal tightening finally easing, her cries dying off with a muffled sob. After a moment, she took a deep breath of relief, pushing her sweat-soaked hair back from her forehead.

"Elizabeth, how very nice to see you. I am sorry, however, that you seem to be in some discomfort." Fitzwilliam had no idea what would constitute proper conversation in such a situation.

He chose poorly.

"Discomfort?" Lizzy stared at him in stunned disbelief. "*Discomfort!* Why you… Sir, try pulling a ten-pound capon through your left nostril, and then we shall speak of *discomfort*!"

Fitzwilliam wanted to dissolve into the floor. "Well, forgive me, Elizabeth. I certainly did not mean to offend. Are you well, then?"

Lizzy was panting and furious. "*No! I am in agony, you lackwit*! And let me tell you, someone had better get this thing out of me and be quick about it!" Then Lizzy gave another howl of pain. "*And find my husband—now*!"

"Right. I'll be off then." Swiftly turning on his heel, Fitzwilliam ran from the room and snatched up little Harry on his way. He continued running across the hall and down the grand staircase. "Harry, let's make ourselves scarce, shall we?" When he reached the foyer, he came upon some returning servants hesitantly peeking around the corner, turning and looking curiously around at the empty room, frightened by the disembodied screams. Mr. and Mrs. Winters appeared in the doorway, coming up from the servants' floor below.

"Colonel Fitzwilliam! What are you doing here? Where is the night butler?"

"Winters, get the doctor here at once. Mrs. Darcy has begun her labor." Mr. Winters immediately signaled a footman as Fitzwilliam turned to speak with Mrs. Winters. "You are needed upstairs without delay, I am afraid. Tell me, do any of you know the whereabouts of Mr. Darcy?"

They all looked at one another sheepishly. Lizzy's maid, Cara, hurried forward and began relating to Fitzwilliam the horrible fight that had taken place between the Darcys—apparently a brawl with enough slamming doors to send the few remaining staff scurrying downstairs.

"There was a letter from that horrible Miss Bingley, and then they both just went mad." Cara's eyes were huge with worry and terror. "I must go up to my mistress!"

Good Lord, he'll kill himself if he's run out just when she needs him! "All right, everyone, we must find Mr. Darcy immediately. Winters, please organize runners. Send out every available servant across the city. Search him out first in his usual destinations. I will provide you with alternate locations if that fails. Go! I don't care whom they inconvenience or embarrass, just find him! Has anyone gone for the doctor yet?"

"Yes, Colonel Fitzwilliam. I have just sent Chippers out. It should not be long now, sir."

"Where's Mrs. Fitzwilliam's maid?"

Winters stared at him. "Whose maid, sir?"

"Mrs. Fitzwilliam, Winters. Oh, I forgot you don't know. I have recently married. My wife arrived here this evening with one of the maids from Penwood House. She should be here somewhere."

"I haven't seen any maid, sir, but I shall go down directly and ask." Fitzwilliam nodded and shifted Harry to his other arm.

"Congratulations, if I may say so, Colonel."

"Thank you, Winters. Now let's get this place humming!"

"Yes, Colonel!"

Fitzwilliam returned upstairs and stood helplessly outside Lizzy's door, wanting to help but ridiculously terrified of venturing inside. He was still holding Harry in his arms. "Is Mrs.

Darling going to die, Colonel Fitz?" Harry's face was hidden in Fitzwilliam's neck, his little fists clutching the colonel whenever he heard Lizzy cry out.

"No, Harry. Mrs. Darcy is not going to die." The poor little boy should not have to worry about such adult things, but Richard felt it important to be close at hand if Amanda needed him. After all, he reasoned to himself, he had endured the horrors of his own army gone mad at Badajoz, had fought the Frogs in hand-to-hand combat at Salamanca, was a hero of Waterloo—no, he would not retreat.

"You see, Harry," he began, "childbirth is a mystical and spiritual experience for a woman, son, and though it may be somewhat painful, a woman doesn't mind the pain. In fact, she welcomes it, greets it with open arms, because she will have a child like you to love when it is over."

Just then they heard Lizzy viciously scream, "Never again... *never* again... If he ever attempts to touch me, I shall kill him, I shall cleave his tongue..."

Ignoring this, a rapidly pacing Richard continued, his voice louder to cover her words. "As I was saying, Harry, although women are typically timid and not physically strong as men are, they are by nature gentle and soft spoken, compassionate and selfless. That is why the good Lord gave this responsibility to them. Childbirth is a joy which completes a woman. It is what gives her life meaning and purpose..."

Elizabeth then let out another, louder scream which included a string of obscenities that had not had its equal since his dear friend Major Patrick Harrison had been shot in the fanny during a duel of honor outside of Copenhagen.

"...or maybe not. Time to call retreat, Harry."

He went downstairs and took a chair in the smaller front parlor, near a window within view of the doorway so that he could look both outside and into the long hallway should someone come. He settled the exhausted Harry onto his lap, cuddling the child's head and kissing his soft cool hair. He then set about removing the child's shoes and coat.

"Are you and Mummy really married?" *An important lesson learned, Fitzwilliam—little children have big ears*. Harry was struggling to keep his eyes open while still managing to clutch his tattered cloth horsey tightly in alternating arms as his coat sleeves were being tugged off.

"Yes, Harry. Your mother and I married, but we had to keep it a secret, even from you."

"Then you're my poppa now?" Harry lifted his face up to the colonel and smiled with such a sincere look of love and adoration that it gave Richard's heart a wrenching tug.

"Yes, Harry. I am your poppa now. And you are my son."

Harry stretched his arms around Richard's neck for a hug. He sighed in his contentment. "Good." Then he yawned.

Tears welled in Richard's eyes, his hold tightening on the child. "Well, why don't you snuggle in and try to get some rest? You look very tired, and I've heard these things can take a while. If you like, I can tell you some more of my stories about that horrible little Frenchman."

Chapter 5

After two miserable hours, Darcy had walked off his anger and was turning onto St. James Street, although still several blocks from his house. His hands were thrust deep into his pockets while his thoughts were miles away from where they had started, the anger that had propelled him into madness now completely dissipated to be replaced by a mental assessment of Elizabeth's upcoming final month. He shook his head in wonder. How in hell would they survive? His glance drifted far ahead, down the street to where their house stood, spying in the distance what appeared to be the bright light from the front foyer of their townhome. He stopped dead in his tracks. *I must have left the door open. Oh, what an idiot!* He quickened his pace.

As he came closer, he could hear panic in the raised voices coming from the vicinity of his house, the shouted commands in the still night. Apprehension began to grip at him. The figure of his butler, Winters, was recognizable on the top stair, pointing to the left as a footman went running in that direction. Then he saw another one of his footmen change direction as soon as he spotted him, and was fast approaching, waving his arms frantically.

"Mr. Darcy, come quick. It's the baby!"

"What about the baby?" Darcy bolted past the gasping footman. "Is Mrs. Darcy all right?"

"The baby is coming now, sir."

Darcy was startled at first then greatly confused, his panic intensifying. "But we have four weeks left..." By this time, another figure was out the door, off running to the right, when Winters spotted Darcy and waved to him from the threshold.

"Mr. Darcy, thank heavens you've returned, sir!" The poor old retainer was gasping for breath. Darcy had reached the gate and could see curtains from neighboring homes being pulled back and people gazing out. He pushed his way past several gentlemen who had crossed the street, curious as to what was wrong.

"We have several footmen out trying to find a doctor, sir. Please do not be alarmed."

Darcy charged up the front steps two at a time and grabbed his butler by the shoulders. "What in bloody hell do you mean? Where is Doctor Baire? Where are the other doctors? Where is the midwife? Have you not tried to find the midwife? Who is with Mrs. Darcy?"

Darcy had just walked, actually run, into his worst nightmare.

"We have at least five footmen out searching, sir." Winters's voice shook. "I am certain it won't be long." Although he was attempting to look confident, Darcy could see the fear in the old man's eyes.

"Darcy!" He heard Fitzwilliam's voice from inside and ran instinctively toward it, quickly seeing him at the doorway of the smaller ladies' parlor. He held a sleeping child in his arms.

"Who's with her?" Darcy's breathing was uneven.

"Amanda and Mrs. Winters, and her maid, I think."

Darcy was at the top of the stairs before he could finish.

"Stop pushing now, Elizabeth. I am going to feel your stomach again."

Darcy looked uneasily at the figure lying on the bed, nearly hidden by Mrs. Winters and the maid as they crisscrossed his view. Cara ran around to the other side of the bed, and he then saw his Lizzy being held in a half-sitting position against another maid, his wife's fingers clutching desperately at the covers beneath her. Amanda turned toward him slightly as she sat down on a stool placed between Lizzy's legs.

It was the sight of blood smeared across Amanda's apron that finally shocked Darcy back to his senses, roused him from his frozen stance in the doorway, and propelled him swiftly into the room.

"What the devil is going on here, Elizabeth?" An anxious-looking Darcy walked quickly to the side of the bed. "You are not due to deliver for another four weeks." With that futile objection voiced, he pulled the maid from behind his wife to take her place, supporting Lizzy's back. Kissing her neck and cheek, he tightened his arms around her.

"Are you all right?" he whispered into her hair. "Please be all right." He pressed his eyes closed to compose his escalating emotions and prayed that the good Lord would spare him from having a heart attack until he knew his wife was safe.

Amanda gave him a sympathetic look. "Evidently someone failed to inform the baby of the delivery date. I assure you, Mr. Darcy, your child is coming now."

"William, please calm yourself." Elizabeth could feel his pounding heart beneath her cheek. She looked up at him, tears streaming down her face. "I only thank God you are finally here. I love you, William, remember that, *whatever happens*. Please forgive me."

He did not like her words. Frightened by what they implied, he roughly kissed her mouth then pulled her firmly back against himself and closed his eyes to fight off his own stinging tears. "Nothing to forgive," he finally managed to say, his voice thick with emotion. "Love you so much, Lizzy."

"Did you know that Fitzwilliam and Amanda were coming here this evening?" When he did not respond immediately, she shook her finger at him. "You must tell me things like this, William. I haven't even prepared a room for them."

"I could not, Elizabeth." In his concern for her, he actually had forgotten about Fitzwilliam's escape, but that was something he would never admit. "Fitz swore me to secrecy. Besides, I..." He looked on in terror as her face began to contort, a sudden scream erupting from her as she stared straight at him. Her hands were clutching and tearing at the sheets. It was a mind-numbing scream. It was ear-deafening. He shook his head at the ringing in his brain.

"Elizabeth, please be sensible. He made me swear." He realized she was not angry with him, only in the midst of a labor pain, when she squeezed his hands until his fingers nearly popped like little balloons. He tried not to flinch until she relaxed her hold.

"Is everything all right?" he asked Amanda, dreading the response. "Is this normal?"

"Everything appears to be fine, Mr. Darcy. Although she has had a rather rough time of it, she is a strong and brave young woman. I am very proud to call her Cousin. All right, now push again, Elizabeth; we shall soon see the crown hopefully."

Lizzy began crying and laughing, eager that the end might be within sight. She weakly pressed her head against Darcy's chest. "Amanda and I have progressed to using our Christian names. We feel we are quite well acquainted by now." She inhaled raggedly. "Well, here we go again." She began once more to push and cry and grunt and swear with pain.

❧

"Are the pains always so tremendous? I thought they would build up gradually. Perhaps there is something more happening here since the child is coming so early." It was less than a quarter hour later, and Darcy was shocked by Lizzy's grueling labor.

"Actually, the child appears to be full term, so do not be concerned with that. Unfortunately, I think your wife has been having pains for longer than you know. Since they were in her back, she failed to identify them as her labor." Amanda turned to the side table for a towel, certain the birth was only moments away.

Elizabeth suddenly screamed in pain and clutched at his arms, gripped with panic. Something was wrong, very wrong, the pressure on her back excruciating. She began writhing in agony, these contractions far stronger than any before. "My baby, my baby," she gasped. "Oh my God, William… my baby."

"Do not push, Lizzy!" Amanda immediately felt around Elizabeth's stomach as her mind spun through all her experiences years before at her father's hospital. "The baby has stopped somehow."

"*Do something… anything… Save my baby.*" Lizzy was hysterical. "*William, whatever happens to me, save our baby.*"

"What is it?!" Darcy demanded. "Please tell me what is going on!" Lizzy's cries were ripping open his heart. "Where is that damned doctor?!"

Amanda gently felt inside and realized the child was presenting face forward, the back aligned to Lizzy's back. Her father had spoken of this sometimes occurring, but she had never seen it before. During his lessons, he had explained the grave danger it presented to both mother and child. The need was to open her wider, and there was only one way Amanda knew of to do that.

"Oh, I am so stupid. All the signs have been there! Lizzy, I am sorry, but I believe we must get you into a different position." Amanda reached out her hand to grab Lizzy's arm. "Since we have no birthing chair, I think you'll have to squat or kneel."

A shocked Darcy had already motioned for the maid to take his place. He was instantly at Amanda's side and pulled her hand from Elizabeth. "Excuse me," he said in a harsh whisper, "perhaps we should wait for the doctor to arrive."

Amanda struggled to pull back her hand from his grasp. "Mr. Darcy," she whispered, "She is in agony. The child is facing forward, a very difficult and dangerous delivery, especially for a woman so small." She then spoke in a lower voice, hoping Elizabeth would not hear. "We really have few alternatives. Elizabeth is weak and may not have the strength or the will to take much more."

The anger on Darcy's face quickly dissolved into fear, the full impact of what she was saying hitting him brutally hard. Not waiting for his answer, she pulled her hand away and pushed the sheets farther back. "No! Wait! This is barbaric!" he shouted as Lizzy grabbed his arm.

"Please, William, do as she says." She was growing weaker

by the moment. "Remember, if you must choose, choose the child. Please, please, promise me this." He could see the agony in her eyes.

"What do you want me to do?" he asked Amanda, his voice hoarse.

"Help me get her out of bed. Get behind her—you must support her weight as she kneels over this pillow." Not really certain of what she was doing, she grabbed one from the bed and threw it to the floor. "If that doesn't show quick results, you will have to help her walk about. Hurry, please. This should open her more—I will try what I can to turn the child."

Darcy and Mrs. Winter struggled to bring Elizabeth to the side of the bed, and then he grasped her under her arms, supporting her as she began to stoop. Amanda pulled up Lizzy's nightdress to massage her belly.

His heart was near breaking. How could she feel so light and look so huge, and still be so small? How could any of this end without disaster? Would she disappear in his arms like a fog, insubstantial, fragile? She had begged him to choose the child if it came to it, but how could he? She was his whole life. He would surely go insane without her, would never want to live, and it would be this damn child's fault. No, he would choose Lizzy over *it* if it came to that, without a moment's hesitation, would never allow Lizzy to die if it was within his power, even if she never spoke to him again. No. His only desire was to stop her pain by whatever means possible. He watched as Amanda knelt before his wife, her hand probing inside, and willed himself not to pass out from the tension.

"I believe it's moved a bit..." The next few minutes were an eternity as Amanda alternately rubbed and massaged Lizzy's stomach with one hand while the other felt within for any change. "It *is* moving! The baby is turning," Amanda held her breath as she made small, twisting motions with her hand.

"One more push, Lizzy," Amanda ordered.

"Push, darling, push," called Darcy simultaneously.

"It's coming—the head is clear." Amanda continued her probing and gentle pulling. Within another moment, the baby swished through, slimy and wet, cradled in her waiting hands.

Darcy gasped out in a choking sob, "Thank God."

An exhausted Lizzy collapsed back into his arms, and he clutched her tightly to his chest, unknowing and unseeing of the activity happening around them. She was pale, she was weak, but she was alive. Alive and, incredibly, smiling.

After cutting the cord, Amanda brought the child to a table. She ran her finger around the child's mouth, after which she began to pat its bottom, softly at first and then a good little slap. The wail that emitted from the baby was heard throughout the household. They heard it in the hallways, in every bedroom, parlor, and convenience, and it continued, down into the servant's hall. It was heard even by people walking outside. There were a full two seconds of quiet before the cheers started from below, from the basement on up throughout the house.

"Mr. Darcy, you may help Elizabeth back into the bed." Amanda's voice seemed to come from miles away as he lifted Lizzy up into his arms and placed her gently down. Her eyes blinked and then finally opened to his.

"God, I love you, Lizzy," was all he could say before he kissed her forehead. "I love you."

"Have we a son or a daughter?" she asked weakly, but Darcy did not hear nor care. She was alive.

"Mr. Darcy, would you like to meet your son?" Amanda had wiped the worst of the moisture from the child and had wrapped him in a soft towel.

It was a moment before her words penetrated. He was only just beginning to breathe again. *Did* he want to meet this child, this little interloper who had caused so much trouble and upheaval? Who may have nearly caused his Lizzy her life? He felt oddly indifferent about the prospect, caring only that his beloved wife lived, but there she was laughing and nodding. That is a good sign, he thought vaguely. Suddenly, memories flooded over him of his father's rage and grief being replaced by an equally ferocious love at the sight of his newborn daughter, even though Georgiana survived but not his wife.

Yes, he thought, *perhaps I should meet this son of mine.*

Darcy's first breathless impression of the wriggly, warm bundle in his arms came as a complete surprise. "Oh, my God, he's beautiful. Lizzy. He's absolutely perfect." A groundswell of instantaneous love washed over him, shocking him with its force; protective adoration for the child nearly overwhelmed him. And then the boy opened his eyes. When Darcy saw his Elizabeth in those eyes, and then himself and then his mother and father, a laughing sob escaped his lips, and he brought the infuriated little face to his, kissing it tenderly, his heart overflowing with love. How could he have sacrificed this precious life, this angel? How could he ever have chosen between them? It was inconceivable to him now. "Lizzy, he's so… huge!"

The baby, looking baffled at all this intense scrutiny, gave a tiny sneeze, and Darcy began to laugh all over again. He took the child toward the window for better light.

"Mr. Darcy," Amanda called out. "Excuse me, but I suggest you bring that child to his mother before she leaps off the bed. We are not quite finished cleaning the afterbirth yet."

"Oh, Lizzy, forgive me." She had already squirmed to the edge, about to launch herself across the floor and claim her son in another moment. He swiftly brought the child over to her eager arms, and she reached out, bringing the tiny bundle into her embrace. Darcy sat behind her and held them both, the new parents gazing lovingly together at their child.

Darcy took off his neck scarf, wiping the perspiration from Elizabeth's face, kissing her over and over, hugging her head to his chest. "I love you, William," she whispered. "Thank you for my son."

⁂

It was over.

With the new family huddled together on their bed, the very proud and proper Mr. Darcy finally gave in to his own tears as his arms wrapped around his world.

His wife and his child were alive.

Chapter 6

AFTER ALLOWING THEM THEIR first few moments as a family, Amanda took the baby to the side table where a basin of sudsy warm water was waiting. She washed the child gently, checking that his cord was securely protected, carefully cleaning between each finger and toe, then wrapped him in a soft blanket and placed the bundle back into the couple's waiting arms.

Darcy took her hand and squeezed it tightly. "Forgive my actions, Amanda. How can we ever thank you enough?" Amanda wiped away a few tears of her own as she laughed at the disheveled man before her, his hair flying every way, his neck cloth gone, his shirt half pulled out and hanging at the sides.

"You have a beautiful child and a wonderful wife, William. Be good to them both, and that will be payment enough." Darcy surprised her then by suddenly cupping her neck and pulling her face down for a proper kiss firmly on the mouth, and she giggled as he instructed her never to tell Fitzwilliam that he had done that.

A timid knock on the door by a maid brought the information that the doctor had arrived. He entered the room much like an avenging angel, striding over to a chair, flipping off his heavy cape, furious over his disturbed evening at the opera, and unmoved regarding the seemingly early arrival of the infant. "This was most inconvenient, most ill-timed," he announced to no one in particular as he gave the tiny child a cursory examination. That it was not a tiny, premature infant, but a healthy seven pounds plus, put him further out of sorts, and he placed the blame for any incorrect calculations solely on Darcy and Elizabeth, who had thoughtlessly misled him.

After this pronouncement, he ordered everyone from the room so that he could examine Elizabeth. The last thing Amanda heard as the door closed behind her was Darcy's furious voice saying it would be over the doctor's cold, dead body that he would ever leave his wife or his son again.

At that moment, Amanda realized she was exhausted, wanting nothing more than to see and hold her own little boy and to see and hold her own husband. She washed off her hands, removed her stained apron, and made her way downstairs.

The staff was milling about the ground floor, accepting glasses of the champagne Fitzwilliam had ordered opened. Some were emerging from their safe haven below, while others had just arrived back from their Boxing Day holiday with their families. They were thanking her and congratulating each other as she passed by, relief evident throughout the house. "Where are my son and the colonel?" she asked Mr. Winters at the foot of the stairs.

"We're in here, Amanda," Fitzwilliam called out softly.

She entered to find little Harry sound asleep in Fitzwilliam's embrace and her heart was touched deeply by the sight; this was her whole world. Her only reason to exist was there before her—a child looking so small and safe in a gentle husband's arms. Crouching down next to the settee, she rested her cheek on Richard's shoulder and thanked God silently for his goodness.

"Has he been asleep long?" she whispered, softly stroking her son's hair.

"Yes, well, a good bit of the time." Fitzwilliam tenderly laid his arm across Amanda's shoulders, concerned at how weary she looked. "Before he grew bored and fell asleep, he *was* curious enough to ask me where babies come from."

"And what did you tell him?"

"Cornwall."

As tired as she was, he still could manage to make her laugh.

"Well, what did we have?" He spoke softly, loving the tender look in her eyes whenever babies were involved. "It is over, I take it? I heard an infant's wail. I figured it was either the babe, or Darcy discovered I spilled brandy on his better night robe."

Amanda nodded. "A little boy… quite large… very loud."

"In other words, a typical Darcy. Excellent! How is Elizabeth?"

"Blissfully happy and relieved that it is over. We had a spot of trouble at the end, but God was with her."

Fitzwilliam tucked a few stray hairs behind her ear, then he wiped a tear from her cheek. She brought his palm to her lips to kiss.

"You look tired," he whispered, and she nodded.

"And how did the imperturbable Darcy manage?" His eyes had taken on a dreamy, emotional quality as he watched her.

"Wonderfully. They should force all fathers to be present at their children's births."

His hand moved lovingly across her back, caressing her body. "I suppose that now you will want me to do that for our child?"

"Would you?"

"I imagine it would depend on when I felt I was up to the task."

"And you would be up to the task... when?"

"When pigs throw pies..."

She laughed softly. "Well, it would be only fair, wouldn't it?" She whispered. "After all, you were there for the ecstasy of the conception. You should be there for the agony of the birth." Her sudden smile was filled with such tenderness and wonder that his heart nearly burst.

He was overwhelmed as always by the depth of love that he felt for this woman and with his concern for her own pregnancy. His fear for her upcoming labor and delivery had been churning up within him from the moment she told him. Hearing Lizzy's screams this night had merely given that fear a terrifying substance. Never again, he vowed, would he allow her to get with child—never would he place her life in jeopardy.

His hand came up to caress her cheek. "You know, I think I've loved you for years, from the moment I first saw you in the distance, walking across the park in St. James Square. But I never loved you more than I do this very minute."

Her manner turned very serious. "It appears our carefully laid plans for escape tonight have been ruined. What do we do now?"

"I would say sleep. I'm exhausted. I don't know about you."

She nodded and allowed some of her tension to disperse. "Good. I don't know that I'd be up to traveling right now. It's been quite a day."

"I went to the house, and they said you had already left. Why didn't you wait for me? Did your mother-in-law return unexpectedly?"

She picked lazily at strands of Harry's hair and grunted. "We evidently had another miscommunication concerning time."

Knowing his protest of innocence would be futile, he let it go. "I dismissed the coach I had hired to take us to Portsmouth in the morning. I told him I would send a message when to return. I think it best if we cross over to Copenhagen as soon as possible, though. I have several friends still living there. And then, when you are safely delivered, on to America, perhaps."

Her returning smile could not disguise growing apprehension, and she sighed. He was giving up so much for them—his career, his family, his friends… his very country.

"Here, come up and sit by me and let me take care of you now. You look like you're about done in."

She stood slowly and settled into the seat next to him, snuggling under his arm and resting her head on his shoulder. Pulling her closer, he leaned down for a kiss, first lightly on her forehead and then deeply upon her mouth, their tongues stroking slowly and gently, thoroughly caressing each other.

Chapter 7

It was two hours later, and Darcy was strolling around their bedroom, unwilling to return his son to the family cradle. He was enraptured with the small, sleeping bundle in his arms, so warm and soft and defenseless. This was his heir, the man who would carry the Darcy name and heritage and fortune into the future, the comfort and pride of his parent's old age. It was heavy baggage for such tiny shoulders, but Darcy would be there to help his son every step of the way, every moment he was needed, until his last breath. He kissed the little head, enjoying the innocent scent unique to babies, his life already in forfeit, never to be the same.

Lizzy kept drifting off to sleep, however, unable or unwilling to concentrate on her husband's excited chatter, so he made his way soundlessly down the stairs to the front parlor, where he found his cousin sleeping. Both Richard and Amanda were snoring disgracefully, and the colonel did not immediately respond to Darcy's initial gentle requests to awaken. Finally, an exasperated Darcy gave the bottom of his cousin's boot a very hard and swift kick. "Fitz, you pathetic sloth, wake up and meet your new cousin."

"What!" Fitzwilliam awoke with a start, snorted and then gasped. He shook his head to clear it from sleep. "What time is it?!"

"Half past three in the morning."

"You bloody bastard! You're lucky I didn't have a… a pistol in my hand or… a sword… sharp object… lightning-fast reflexes… lethal…" His snores resumed before his head fell back onto the settee.

"Wake up!" Darcy hauled off and kicked his boot again, much harder. "Get up, you imbecile. Meet my son."

Fitzwilliam's eyes finally blinked open and focused on the bundle in Darcy's arms. Yawning broadly, he slowly stood, hoisting the still-sleeping Harry higher onto his shoulder. "Never tell me this is the brute that woke up the entire of Mayfair with his bellowing?"

"Hellacious, wasn't he?" Darcy beamed as he pulled back the blanket.

"Well, I'll be damned. What's he calling himself these days?"

"Bennet George Darcy."

"Benny Darcy?"

"Good God, no! Sounds like a public-house proprietor. We'll call him George."

Fitzwilliam was very impressed, already feeling the bonds of family for the tiny fellow. "He's rather immense to have come out of our little Lizzy, isn't he?" he whispered. "Ooh! Look at that head! Fitzwilliam proportion head—very promising. He'll be a brilliant scholar."

Darcy nodded proudly. "Yes, and Lizzy assured me that this is our last child and that I can never touch her again." By the smile on Darcy's face, Fitzwilliam knew she would soon be required to revisit that declaration.

"God, but he looks a great deal like your father, doesn't he?"

"That's because he's bald."

"No, don't be absurd. Look at his nose and the drool on his chin. Uncle George is stamped all over this face. I think I'll get him a little powdered wig for his christening."

"You would be godfather, you know."

"The immense good fortune of this child just keeps accumulating."

Darcy laughed. "The doctor examined him and Elizabeth and said they are both splendid." He tenderly kissed his son's head. "Although, I could have said as much."

"I'm surprised you allowed that glorified barber anywhere near them after this evening."

Darcy cooed at his child. "The fucking bastard is lucky he left with his manhood still attached, isn't he, little one? No, he'll not come anywhere near this house or my family again, I can guarantee that." Darcy rubbed his nose against his boy's tiny mittened fist. "Not if he wants to retain possession of his spleen." He then continued relating to the child all manner of bloody things he would visit upon the good doctor. "Amanda's friend, Anthony Milagros, will be called for tomorrow. I've heard very good things about him."

Nodding, Fitzwilliam leaned down and kissed the child's forehead, then discharged another loud, lusty yawn in the baby's face. The baby wrinkled his nose and shook his head in disgust, making the two men laugh uproariously.

"Go on upstairs and get some proper rest. Should I send a note over in the morning to Lady Penrod about Amanda?"

"No. I believe we have burned that bridge this night. Evidently, Amanda's maid ran off with one of your footmen, probably back to the old woman to report. In fact, we may have no place to go after tonight, Fitz. Is it still all right if we stay here on a temporary basis?"

"Do you even need to ask?" He shook his head. "She saved Elizabeth's life tonight, Fitz, as well as my son's. I'm sure of it. You both can live here as long as you desire."

As Fitzwilliam was stretching his arms and long legs, he barked his laughter. "Thank you, Cousin, but I'm certain you'll wake to regret that offer. The fact is, though, that the marriage cannot be hidden anymore. We're well in the soup now, and in a way, I am glad of it."

"I don't know how we can ever thank you, and especially Amanda. When I think what might have happened here last night..." Darcy's voice began to break when suddenly he laughed. "He is so big, Richard! You have to see his skinny feet. I can't believe he came from my little Lizzy. He'll tower over you and me one day."

"He is here and healthy, and that's all the counts, brat. Thank God this ordeal is over." When Fitzwilliam turned to wake Amanda, he found her sleeping soundly. She had fallen facedown and was snoring on the spot where he had been sitting. He shook her shoulder to wake her. "The entire household was vying for the happy task of blowing your brains out if this had gone on any longer."

Chapter 8

Wearing a borrowed nightgown from Elizabeth that was both too short and too tight, Amanda fussed about Harry's bed for a final "tuck in and hug tight," although the recipient of all her motherly attentions was already dead to the world.

The little boy had not awakened when Fitzwilliam carried him up the stairs—so exhausted that he did not wake when he was laid down on his little bed or when his mother undressed him and slipped a nightshirt on him. Amanda watched her son as he slept, an angel still new and innocent and sweet. If only they had been able to slip away tonight. If only she could be free, even for a moment, of the terror of losing him, a terror so overwhelming that she was sorry her husband had even awakened her.

She was both emotionally and physically exhausted from the day's events, her mind a jumbled mush with nightmarish visions of her boy being ripped from her arms, her boy screaming for her, her boy suffering because of her weakness of loving another.

The reality was that any hope for escape was probably finished. She had long suspected that servants had been watching her, waiting for her to cross the mistress. Someone would be rewarded handsomely this night. They would not wait until the mistress returned from her holiday party, she would be told immediately. The authorities would come in the morning to take away her son, and she would be forced to beg permission to return with him to Penwood House.

Once more her existence would be solitary, alone for years in that wretched house. In fact, the loneliness would be even worse now. Richard had opened a door for her to a life unimagined, a life with a passionate, caring partner. It was a life she could not openly live, if at all, for years to come, and then only if Richard was willing to wait for her.

Who was she trying to fool? After this night, they would be lucky to meet at all, let alone like thieves, sneaking around to steal forbidden moments. How long could he wait for her? Why would he wait for her? She ached only for what every other woman seemed to have and she could not: a home and a family. With growing melancholy, she steeled herself to the obvious. There could only be this night as a family, as a normal couple together.

Fitzwilliam looked distracted and tired after having spoken at length with Darcy. He was wearing Darcy's borrowed night robe, brandy stains and all. He reached his hand out to Amanda. "Come on to bed now, love." After kissing Harry's cheek, she nodded kindly to the nursemaid who would keep watch over her son during the night, and then they walked silently into Richard's usual room.

He closed the door and went immediately to the desk to take up a large stack of letters waiting for him, turning up the lamp light to read them. There was correspondence from the War Department, from Wellington, from his father. All demanded his immediate attention, all were questioning his whereabouts for the past month, all had their own anxieties, their own requests of him.

"Are you coming to bed soon, Richard?" Amanda sat on the edge of the bed, watching him, seeing the concern in his eyes, or the humor, or the aggravation, depending upon whose letter he was reading. Her heart calmed suddenly when she realized there was one good thing to come of all this tragedy. At least he would be safe. At least now he would not be made to sacrifice so much.

"In a moment, dear." He pulled his chair out and sat, taking up his pen to give his response to the more urgent of the letters.

Amanda retrieved his clothes still lying where he had dropped them. She folded them and placed them neatly onto the chair. She waited and watched for her husband to come to bed, refusing to sleep this last night.

There were only a few hours until dawn when he finally pulled the covers back. Although a fire blazed, the room felt damp and cold. Amanda's gentle fingers touched his mouth.

"I thought you were asleep already, Amanda. You were so tired. Why don't you try to rest?"

Instead she reached for him, pulled him down, began to kiss his neck, his ear, and then began to nip at his shoulder, her hand moving slowly down his chest and stomach.

His breathing stopped. Concern fought with lust as he gathered her tightly into his embrace. "Amanda, you're trembling." His voice sounded rough. She had been through so much, and this boldness was very unlike her. He smoothed the hair from her face, sighing and confused. She had so many different moods, this new wife of his, with so many mercurial emotions concerning sex that they baffled him. Sometimes, when she seemed the most amorous, it was actually just a plea for comforting. Sometimes it was simply from insecurity, sometimes lust. There were preferences for how and where, preferring curtains pulled tightly and total darkness, clean sheets, a tidy room. Certain positions took a little coaxing, but with enough prior notice could be accommodated.

On the other hand, he knew that men needed absolutely no excuse for sex nor did they care a whit where or when or how. It was all to the good and very basic.

Her hand continued its achingly slow descent.

The South of France saluted.

Responding immediately, Fitzwilliam moved her body beneath his, gently drawing her long, silky legs about his waist. He grasped her bottom, and his breathing quickly turned to panting. She whispered his name over and over, reverently, like a prayer between kisses that rapidly became fierce and savage and hungry.

He rose up on his elbows to take some of his weight from her, but she urgently shook her head. "Come back," she whispered.

"Amanda," he said hoarsely, "I'm too big… the baby. I'll smother you both. Let me at least support myself a little."

She grabbed at him, clutching and pulling until his beautiful mouth was again on hers, and then he was inside her again and carefully pressing her deeply, rhythmically into the bed, but she wanted to feel covered, protected, possessed. She grabbed at him desperately, moving her hips until it rendered him helpless and unthinking, and he soon forgot his much larger size and weight, forgot her delicate condition, forgot the boy and nurse in the next room, forgot that he was a guest in his cousin's home or that there were innocent people living in respectable homes outside their window. He growled and yelled, and his body soon trembled its release. Finally, they lay there, breathing as one.

It was several moments before he raised himself onto an elbow to gaze down in the moonlight at her, a look of stunned appreciation on his face. "Good God, woman," he whispered. "You'll have me burst into flames one of these days." He smoothed some hair from her face and kissed her nose then laughed softly. "I don't know why I am bothering to whisper, I'm certain shutters are being slammed all over Mayfair from the racket we just made."

Her fingers caressed his face, fingers tracing each line, each crevice, while she skimmed her hand across the scar on his jaw and she smiled briefly at the memory of their lovemaking.

"Amanda, stop," he said gently, capturing her hand. "You're touching me like I'm going to disappear. I am not, you know." He tried to laugh it off and kissed her forehead, beginning to remove himself from her. "I wish you would have faith in me, trust that all will be well. I won't let anything happen to you or the boy."

"Don't leave me yet," she pleaded. It would be hard for him in the shadows to see the panic in her eyes or know how fiercely it rose in her chest. *This could be our last night together, my darling, for many years to come*. She forced her voice to sound cheery. "It feels much better to make love properly, I mean in the dark like this, doesn't it? Making love in the afternoon light felt rather badly behaved. I was always embarrassed to know that you could see me when I called out your name."

He enveloped her again with his body and arms and whispered into her ear, "I believe shrieked would be more accurate." She cuffed him affectionately on his shoulder, and they both laughed softly.

They remained in each other's arms, talking in whispers, laughing and touching intimately. It was a while before he slowly began to feel the stirring again and once more began to kiss her mouth, her eyes, her throat… feeling the madness in them both returning.

❧

Darcy still could not sleep and restlessly paced, his gaze falling across the broken door handle to Lizzy's dressing room. Whenever he passed, he felt a tremendous stab of guilt strike at his stomach. Tragedy had ventured so easily into his home and had nearly taken all that was dear to him. His thoughts punished him, endlessly replaying the fight they had had and how this evening could have turned out so differently if not for Amanda.

His eye caught torn pieces of paper surrounding the dressing-table chair. Reaching down, he picked them up and patiently assembled them upon the table, finally reading Caroline's note to Elizabeth, finally understanding what had happened.

"So this is what started the whole thing," he sighed raggedly. "A nasty bit of revenge from a rejected woman." He sat down heavily on the chair and reread the letter again.

I have to accept my own part in this. I kept the truth from Lizzy when I might have avoided this whole trouble by only being honest with her. I certainly was no gentleman; she was right about that. His disappointment with himself was tremendous, even greater than his anger at Caroline, but he would not lose his control again. Never. Least of all over that vain and silly trollop.

"William?" Lizzy raised her head upon hearing him enter their bedroom.

"Why are you awake? You are supposed to be resting."

"I heard you sighing in there and grew concerned."

"How are you feeling?" He took her hand in his and kissed her forehead.

"As if I'd been hit by a runaway carriage. Is everything all right? Good, then I need to see my son again."

"He is beautiful, Lizzy." Darcy picked the child up from the large cradle and brought him to her. "Have I mentioned that before?"

As she smiled, he lay down beside her, the baby nestled between them in her arms. "I am so sorry, Lizzy, for this whole evening," he finally said. "What a mess I created with my temper. I will never forgive myself."

"Oh, of course you will, at least you should, and probably sooner than I will consider appropriate." She patted his arm lovingly. "Remove your boots, please, dear."

She is feeling better. He laughed to himself as he pulled them off.

"William, you must stop whipping yourself. We will have many more fights before we are finally too old and infirmed even to recognize each other. When that time comes, we shall, hopefully, be polite acquaintances."

He snuggled back into bed beside her. "I am normally such a sane, dignified gentleman of the world. Why is it that around you I completely lose my wits?"

"Your wits are merely the first of many sacrifices to come."

The quiet warmth of the room and the strong bonds of love and family kept them quiet and content for a long while. Then, suddenly unwilling to delay a moment longer, he hugged her tight and said a silent prayer before delivering his long-overdue confession. "I found the letter from Caroline," he whispered. "I never realized before how evil and cruel she could be. I must confess to you, Elizabeth, that I did see her at Netherfield, but only because she had tricked me into going there. She forged a message to me from Charles, saying he needed help with a problem. I thought it concerned Jane and didn't want to stress you if it was something I could handle alone." He scrubbed his face roughly. "So much for my consideration. Anyway, I left immediately upon learning of her deceit."

Stunned for a moment, she said nothing. "But you could have told me, William. I would have understood." She then remembered her sporadic pregnancy ravings and sighed. "... Or not. Well, perhaps it *was* best that you said nothing. But that trip was months ago. Why send the note now, when we are so vulnerable? Could she have deliberately timed the letter's arrival?"

He could not speak for a long while. "If I thought that, I don't know what I would do to her, can't even let myself think. But I tell you we won't ever again see or hear from her. I will have to tell Bingley the whole story, and you will need to confide in your sister Jane so that we can arrange our visits with them without coming into contact with Caroline. Is that all right with you, Elizabeth?"

She nodded. "I would never lose Jane through this. I think they will both understand. I hope so, at any rate."

"Now, go to sleep. I'll put the angel back into his cradle."

Chapter 9

All around him, as far as he could see, Fitzwilliam saw babies, cooing babies crawling where there should have been the mutilated dead bodies of grown men. This was unacceptable. It was going to take him all night to collect these children and bring them somewhere that would be safe, and then who would feed them? He turned to his sergeant major, sorry to observe that the entire side of the poor man's head was still blown away. He tried to help the soldier reattach the jawbone of his shattered face then pointed to the babies crawling between them, around them. The man nodded in silent understanding, and they both began to walk to the glacis surrounding the burning fortress.

Fitzwilliam was standing once again at the siege of Badajoz, and the constant pounding of the cannonade in his dreams gradually altered itself into ordinary knocking on their bedroom door, easily dismissed at first, but soon the unrelenting persistence grew closer and louder, and Richard awoke.

Amanda's eyes, however, had blinked wide open immediately with the certain knowledge of what was happening. "Don't say a word," she whispered into his ear. "Ignore her. Please." They heard someone call his name. It was the morning of their third day at Pemberley House, their departure delayed for many reasons—contentment at being together finally, complacency over their success at escaping, minor difficulties in obtaining just the right coach, passage to the Continent becoming intermittent, ruled by the weather. Besides, no one had bothered them. The sense of urgency had diminished.

"Colonel Fitzwilliam. It's the nursemaid, sir. Mr. Darcy is at the dressing-room door and says he must speak with you immediately. There are some people outside, sir." She sounded anxious.

Fitzwilliam scrubbed his eyes with his hand to force the sleep from them. He heard Darcy in the distance bark an order down to someone on the first floor, sounding angrier and more urgent now. "I must see to him, Amanda. Darcy would never be pounding on our door like this if it wasn't important." She attempted to stop him, but he patted off her hand and was pulling on his smallclothes, breeches, and shirt before she could say anything more.

He walked quickly across their bedroom, pulling open their door.

"Excuse me, please, Colonel, for disturbing you like this, but Mr. Darcy is that insistent."

"Yes, that's quite all right. I understand. If you would, bring the child in here to his mother." He turned toward Amanda to give her some instruction, but his breath caught at the sight of her. She stood in the corner of the room, looking small and petrified. He smiled faintly at her and then whispered to the nurse as he passed, "Please close the door to the bedroom after I leave." She nodded in understanding.

"What has happened?" Richard watched as Darcy stormed past him into the sitting room. Plainly about to explode with anger, he turned around at the table before the fireplace, his hands on his hips. Richard raised his hand to stay him, giving a quick glance at the closed bedroom door. "And please keep your voice down. I don't want Amanda unnecessarily alarmed." It was a moment before Darcy could calm himself enough to speak.

"I'll tell you what has happened." Darcy moved closer. "The world has gone mad. That's what has happened. There are at least a dozen hideous-looking Bow Street thugs out there—poor old Winters was nearly struck by one of them. They tried to force their way into the house, the bastards! Luckily, *my* hideous-looking thugs are bigger and so managed to keep the scoundrels out. But here's the thing—I believe they are demanding the boy be brought out immediately. I overheard someone exclaiming loudly that the child had been kidnapped, if you can imagine a mother being accused of that! And a crowd is quickly gathering. Evidently, the entire area has suddenly decided to use a good woman's personal tragedy as diverting entertainment."

"Damn it! I am so sorry to have brought this to your doorstep. I should have known. Blast, we should have left yesterday."

"The point is that we must shield Amanda and the boy. I cannot permit a child to be taken from his mother, most especially a member of my own family, and they are both part of this family now." Darcy was storming back and forth before the fireplace, pounding his fist into his hand.

"You know you're beautiful when you're angry."

"Oh shut up. Now, how do you want to handle this?" He sat down on the edge of the desk, his arms folded before him.

"I was informed that there is a clerk of the court present with some sort of legal document to deliver, probably a court order. I say we present a type of combined front of bullshit, intimidate the man enough to buy some time, perhaps even turn the crowd against him until we locate someone who can return to override any immediate custody order he may have."

"Well, we outfoxed footballers four years our senior at Harrow, we should be able to bluff our way through this." Fitzwilliam began rubbing the back of his neck with his hand. "Bloody hell, this is entirely my fault! Amanda tried to warn me about the woman's vindictiveness, but I thought she was overreacting. Never imagined the old witch would take this to the courts! I've been expecting her footmen to come first with her demands. Damn, I suppose I should have listened, taken this more seriously. If only we had more time!"

"Have you heard anything from the lawyers? Surely, now that you are her husband, she'll have more standing in the courts."

"As a matter of fact, I have Drake and Poole working on something very promising." He placed a bare foot on the seat of one of the chairs, resting his forearm across his knee. "But they must request a review by parliament. You know how it is, with all the lawyers involved and then the mind-boggling slowness of the House of Lords—this could drag on for some time. Shit! Well, if he does have a court order, we have little choice in the matter. The boy shall have to be returned. Oh God, this will break Amanda's heart. She obsesses over that child, is terrified of being separated from him for even the smallest moment."

"How could someone be heartless enough to separate a mother and small child permanently? Do you think the old woman is only bluffing?"

"I have no idea. Bah! The whole thing is out of our hands, for the moment anyway. I know the child would not be in any physical danger left alone with his grandmother. From what Amanda has said, the woman adores the boy, dotes on him. I have no doubt he would be well cared for. We *will* eventually obtain custody, of that I am certain."

Darcy studied his cousin intently. "Frankly, I don't foresee Amanda taking a separation from her son that lightly, Richard. She seems a most devoted mother." Darcy's memory went back to his own exhausted and half-dead wife begging him to take her life to spare her child's, and then further astonishing him by clawing her way across her bed to reach her baby. He felt the unease of impending disaster. "I don't believe mothers are easy in their minds over any separation from their children, no matter how slight a duration."

"Well, naturally I understand that. I am not totally insensitive. I'll explain my reasoning to her. She's a good, loving wife, Darcy, as well as a good mother. She understands that in a proper marriage the husband must sometimes make hard decisions and the woman must follow. She's a truly wonderful person."

Darcy shifted nervously, alarm bells clanging away loudly in his head. After all, he had been married longer than his cousin. He gave an involuntary shudder.

"What is it now, Darcy?" An exasperated Fitzwilliam was getting heartily tired of being contradicted.

"Well, a wonderful wife she may be, Fitzwilliam, *but*... she *is* a woman, too, and an *American* woman at that. She may not be as *obedient* as you wish."

Chapter 10

By the time Fitzwilliam threw on his coat and boots and he and Darcy had descended to the foyer, the small group of curious onlookers had grown, scattered now both up and down the street and beginning to drift across the square. Carriages on the avenue occasionally needed to maneuver around the milling crowd, and two had even stopped to fight over right of way. The sight that had attracted everyone's interest was the gang of rough-looking Bow Street Runners assembled before Pemberley House, the undisputed jewel of the avenue. All of those said runners were large, hideously ugly, and disgraceful-looking.

It was great fun.

To further pique the crowd's delight, the runners were facing equally distasteful-looking footmen, coachmen, and gardeners, brutes all, attired in the exquisite Pemberley livery of scarlet and grey. They stood guard on either side of the doorway where poor old Winters was under intense verbal attack.

"What is the meaning of this?" Darcy's sudden appearance

at the door hushed the crowd—the show had begun. He scanned the onlookers, measuring their mood, then confronted the official-looking gentleman who was apparently the occasion's spokesperson.

"Might I come in, sir?"

"No, you may not." The crowd shuffled uneasily.

Dramatically, a document was withdrawn from the gentleman's inside pocket. He nervously cleared his throat. *Ahem.* "Charges have been filed with the local magistrate demanding immediate resumption of custody of the child of the late Sir Augustus Penrod to Lady Marguerite Penrod, his mother. We have reason to believe that the child in question was kidnapped"—the crowd gasped—"two evenings past and was brought here." Smatterings of appreciation emboldened the man. He turned a dignified and self-righteous face to the crowd.

"How dare you toss about such inciting accusations!" Darcy barked. "I should have you thrown into the street, you and your pack of apes!" The crowd grew unhappy with this response, judging it to be possibly undignified and still being unsure of their collective position. A few disparaging remarks were thrown into the air.

Meanwhile, Fitzwilliam had stepped up and snatched the court order from the clerk's hands. He read it through thoroughly.

"Take this gang of thugs and leave my property immediately," Darcy commanded.

"No, sir, I can assure you that with the safety of a child involved, we will not." There was a smattering of applause. "I have the law on my side, and you, sir, should have a care for what you say." He was a truly proud man at that moment. He smiled smugly.

Fitzwilliam folded up the order and stuffed it into his coat pocket. Casting a murderous look at the clerk, he elbowed his way before Darcy. The clerk's smug smile quickly evaporated; he was suddenly intimidated, tongue tied in the presence of a minor celebrity. "How dare you speak to this fine gentleman in such a manner!" Fitzwilliam barked. "Have you no shame? Do you have any idea who this man is? Do you? Well, sir, I shall tell you. Why his great, great, great, well, many greats I can assure you of that, grandfather was executed as a traitor by none other than the magnificent Henry VIII himself!"

That brought a confused murmur from the crowd—impressed but confused.

"Not helping… not helping…" whispered Darcy in a loud aside.

"No child has been kidnapped," Fitzwilliam continued contemptuously—unfazed—loud. "The little boy is here with his *mother*, my wife, sir, *my* wife, I say, who was detained to help with the birth of this very man's son!"—Oooohs and aaaahs and several "How very nices"—"An act of pure Christian charity, if ever I heard of one!"—"Yessssss," it sounded as if a snake was loose among the masses—"There was no intent to kidnap, no nefarious plan, only the concerned love of one mother for another and for that woman's unborn child. My God, you should hang your head, sir, for making such a slanderous indictment! *And in England*." Fitzwilliam's explanation was repeated throughout the crowd for the benefit of those in the back who were straining to hear. At that point. the general mood began to solidify.

Not to be outdone, Darcy then elbowed his way forward—handsome, elegant, and superior, an Adonis. The women sighed. "And do you know who this man thinks he is… pardon me…

do you know who this man is?" he pronounced loudly. People in the back began to bob and weave for a better look. Several then began to recognize the out-of-uniform Fitzwilliam, word spread, and the excitement grew.

"Yes, that's right. None other than The Waterloo Colonel himself!"—"Nooooo!!!"— "Yesssss! The man who risked life and limb, in point of fact, was very nearly mortally wounded in the horror that was Waterloo. A lone soldier fighting for King and country, for the very freedoms we all take for granted as our birthright, willingly sacrificing everything, well, nearly, anyway, in the name of His Royal Highness King George and our beloved and sacred kingdom—our blessed land—*our England.*" The crowd began to nod vigorously and applaud. Many wiped away a tear or two.

A vendor on the street merrily commenced selling hot chestnuts from his cart, tuppence a bag.

While this altercation was taking place, a tall, white feather could be seen bobbing its way through the crowd, accompanied by people yelping, shrieking, and jumping to the side when it passed. It was Fitzwilliam who first heard the traditional verbal tirade that always preceded this particular visitor. "Grab your codpiece," he groaned, tunneling his hair into tall peaks. "We're doomed."

"Out of my way, you common ruffian! Who are your people, you jackanapes?! Are you all escapees from some type of penal colony? Am I to be jostled and set upon by a confluence of desperadoes who have not as yet grasped even the merest concept of hygiene?"

Anxious for her first visit to her newborn grandnephew, Lady Catherine had planned to arrive in fine style. She was dressed in an outlandishly expensive Lady Collette outfit, including a brand-new tricorn hat purchased specifically for Tuesdays. The hat, which had been originally tilted rakishly upon her head, was now beginning to migrate forward, listing precariously over one eyebrow. She had fortunately decided against her new wig but did succumb to a light hair-powdering and one patch. The patch was also on the move.

Becoming more aggravated with each step, she stopped at the side of a portly gentleman who had been loudly laughing, rudely gesturing with his fingers. She banged her reticule across his head. "Who are you, sir, and who are your people?!" She vigorously shoved her hat back up from over her eye.

She had never been so furious, had never been so indignant. Her hair powder flew every which way as she shrieked about how this rabble should beg the forgiveness of God for exhibiting such impertinence in the presence of their betters, then loudly expressed England was doomed if this was to be its future!

"Stand aside, I say! Stand aside and let my aunt through!" Darcy reached for her arm and pulled her into the foyer doorway.

"Darcy, who are these hooligans?! I demand to know all their names, do you hear me? Jamison, get quill and paper. I want lists made and addresses taken." Her umbrella banged down on the hand of one of the nearby officers.

"Take your filthy hand from my nephew's door. How dare you, sir! Are you mad?! Do you know who I am?!" The awestruck crowd began applauding, even though they had no idea as yet who she was.

"Aunt Catherine, please calm yourself. I am perfectly able to handle this!" Even as he mouthed the words, Darcy knew that he had lost all control of the situation, becoming a supporting player in the drama unfolding upon his own doorstep.

"Madam." The clerk's voice broke. He began again. "Madam, we are representatives of the crown and have been granted the *authority* by the magistrate to regain custody of Harold Augustus Penrod by name, this very day or up to twenty-four hours hence. If Lady Amanda Penrod will return the child *immediately* to her ladyship, any and all charges will be dropped. If not, then we *unfortunately* will be forced to return with the selfsame magistrate to arrest Lady Amanda Penrod for"—he turned toward the crowd for support as his voice now crackled with uncertainty—"kidnapping?"

The crowd gasped politely, for good form only now, not so vehemently as before.

When the clerk turned back, he was suddenly confronted with the depth of fury being released from Lady Catherine's eyes. He leapt a step in fear.

"*How dare you*! I shall contact Liverpool himself about this insult to our family!" The runners who had positioned themselves alongside the man grew visibly ill at ease.

Recognizing now that Lady Catherine was easily the greater power of the two, the crowd began calling out rude remarks at the clerk and his retreating men.

"Jamison!" Catherine bellowed to her ever-present butler. "Go straight to Lord Liverpool's house and bring my cousin here to me at once!" A great cheer rang out in the street at the prospect of the popular prime minister appearing. Several of the huge Bow Street Runners turned and fled, braving a gauntlet of taunts and whistles and kicks. The clerk repeatedly bobbed and weaved to avoid Catherine's umbrella, his white knuckles still clinging to the doorframe. She suddenly pointed a bony finger in his face.

"*Marvel not at this, for the hour is coming in which all that are in graves shall hear this voice. And they shall come forth, they that have done good, unto the resurrection of life; and they that have done evil, unto the resurrection of damnation!*'" Catherine's arms were stretched out before her as she bellowed to the sky.

The crowd went mad. "Brava! Brava!" they screamed.

Several people lost very fine hats as they sailed through the air.

The runners began to flee the crowd in earnest for their lives. Only one person, the clerk, had remained for the entire, terrifying soliloquy of Lady Catherine. "Your ladyship," he begged, he whined. "Please! There is no need to bother our dear prime minister, no need to get into such a fever. Nothing can be done this day, I am sure. Can't help but think this is just some sort of misunderstanding." After bowing nearly to the floor, the man turned and fled as if chased by the devil himself but called over his shoulder as he ran, "You still have only twenty-four hours to return the child."

He was chased down the block by a rain of snowballs and hats.

Chapter 11

"FROM WHERE IN BLOODY hell did that come?" A bewildered Darcy turned toward his aunt after closing the foyer doors, still reeling from the vision of her bowing to the cheering masses.

"I have no idea." Inhaling deeply, she stared dreamily up into the heavens, her lips pursed dramatically. "It's something from the Bible, I believe. I would have been a remarkably proficient actress, you know." She smoothed the sides of her coiffure, tucking any stray hairs back beneath her now properly positioned tricorn hat with feather. She then dusted the hair powder from her shoulders and smartly snapped her nomadic patch back onto her left cheek. "Of course, so would Anne, if her health had permitted her." They all turned to stare at Anne, who had snuck in behind her mother. She narrowed her eyes to squint back at them all and weakly coughed.

"All right, young man." When they reached the center of the room and stood before the fireplace, she turned to confront

Fitzwilliam. "Where is this female with whom you have been ensconced?" She held up her hand when he attempted to form his angry rebuke. "Save your breath. I know all about that disgusting inn and your scandalous behavior. It is her son of whom they speak, I imagine. By God, I think you have finally crossed the line this time, young man. This has all the potential of becoming a greater *ton* scandal than even you could imagine!"

As a fuming Fitzwilliam again attempted to open his mouth to respond, Amanda called out from the bottom of the stairs, "Richard?"

She looked small and pale and drab standing alone in the doorway, dressed once again in her detested dark grey jumper and high-necked black blouse. Her hair was pulled back into a severe knot.

"Aha! So there you are!" Catherine turned. Her whole body seemed to twitch into place as her hands folded primly before her. "Madam, how dare you cause my family this humiliation, this mortification, this..."

"Silence, Catherine!" shouted Fitzwilliam. "I warn you to think very carefully before you say anything."

Uncaring of all else, Amanda walked past Catherine and up to her husband. "Have they finally come for him?" Her voice was barely audible.

Fitzwilliam nodded, his eyes shining with his heartbreak for her; she looked frightened and so vulnerable. He wanted badly to hold her and kiss away the sadness. Placing his hands upon her shoulders, he gave them a gentle squeeze. "We had a visit from a representative of the magistrate. He came with a court order for Harry." A premonition of disaster made him pause before continuing. "I am afraid Harry must return to your mother-in-law within twenty-four hours. I am so sorry, my love."

Amanda closed her eyes and pressed her fingers to her mouth, giving herself time enough to tamp down her emotions. "It is no more nor less than I expected. Well, there's nothing more to be done, I suppose."

Fitzwilliam cupped her face with his hands, and she smiled back bravely, blinking away her tears. "That's my good girl."

"If you would help me find Harry's shoes, I will return with him immediately. We don't want her to be any more upset than necessary."

Fitzwilliam nodded and began to tuck in his shirt. "We can then go directly to our solicitors and see what will be our next action."

"Let me know what they tell you as soon as you are able, Richard, if you would. Perhaps you can send a message over with Georgiana when she visits Emily, only please ask her to be as discreet as possible. I will warn Emily." Amanda looked composed as she searched the room for her child's things. No one could tell her heart felt as if it were shattering.

"Fitzwilliam, I demand a word with you!" Catherine could barely speak; she was absolutely furious at being so ignored. "What is going on here?"

"Not now, Aunt!" His movements had stopped, and he glared down at Amanda's bent head.

"Oh, William, I have left my new cloak in the colonel's suite. I trust that is acceptable." Seeing her son's shoes on the side of the settee, she bent to retrieve them, her movements heavy and slow. With growing sadness, she felt each step, each decision, each action that was taking her farther away from her beloved husband. She scratched her forehead, trying to remember all the little things she wanted to tell him. "Richard, I put the wedding ring in your top drawer. It will be safer here."

"My home is completely at your disposal, Amanda." Darcy watched in sadness as his cousin's face drained of color. An ominous silence had filled the room.

"Fitzwilliam!"

He ignored his aunt's repeated call and grabbed Amanda's wrist, pulling her before the fireplace to speak in relative privacy. "What do you mean, Amanda, 'Send a message with Emily'?" His eyes narrowed to slits. "Why would I have need to send a message to you with Emily when you will be accompanying me, at my side at all times?"

Amanda stared, blinking at her husband for several moments before speaking. "Whatever do you mean, Richard?"

"You heard me well enough, I think. Harry may be returning to Penwood, but you certainly cannot. I would never allow you to return to that life." The forbidding scowl on his face disguised his growing alarm. "No. You will remain here with me in Darcy's home. Harry will be returned to his grandmother, and he will be fine there. You said yourself that she adores the boy. He will be very well looked after."

Her heart began to pound. "Excuse me, but we have discussed this, Richard. You cannot have forgotten so soon." She saw no enlightenment dawn on his features, no hint of understanding, his face unyielding. She grabbed his arm when he dismissively turned away. "Richard, stop and remember, please. I told you that my son would come first, always. I will be returning with Harry. My place is with my little boy until this problem is settled. Oh, please do not look at me so indignantly. Just send me a note with Georgiana, or it will have to wait. In the future, when her anger cools, we can again arrange to meet somewhere. Darcy will be much more helpful to you with the solicitor than I could ever hope to be." The room was twirling about her, and she pressed her eyes closed. Perhaps this was only another nightmare, and she would wake up soon to snuggle back into her husband's embrace.

He pulled from her grasp and began to pace.

"Richard, I insist upon knowing…!"

"Stay out of this, Catherine! This does not concern you." He stormed back to Amanda's side. "I am afraid I did not make myself clear to you before. Our circumstances have obviously changed. Your return to Penwood is *not* in the best interest of our situation, Amanda, not in the best interest of our family. No, madam, not by half. Your place is with me as *my wife*, and you will not be leaving, I can assure you of that. Not today nor on any day in the future." His voice sounded unyielding, his appearance more distant than ever before; the look of disdain in his eyes alarming. The fact was that he hated himself at that moment, hated his betrayal of her trust in him, but he appeared unwilling or unable to stop himself. He could not lose her now, or ever. He would die first. She turned her back on him and tried to walk away. He grabbed her arm. "You belong to me, Amanda. *I own you.*"

Amanda stared up into a stranger's face, her nightmare coming to life. "*Own me?* What are you saying?" she whispered. "Oh, don't be ridiculous!" Her voice shook. "Richard, we discussed this before we were married. My place is with Harry; he is just a child. My place is with my son." Her first bout of daily morning sickness picked this moment to hit with a vengeance, and she tried to fight back her growing nausea. For a few horrible moments, she feared she would cast up her prior evening's dinner directly into his face.

"Ridiculous, am I?" he roared, mistaking her discomfort for disgust. "Listen to me, woman! You are my wife! You carry my unborn child! No, madam, you can put all thoughts of leaving from your mind. If I have to lock you in your room, you will remain with me!" He reached for her.

"No!" Stepping back, she screamed, "Do not do this, please!"

Darcy went again to his cousin's side, trying to pull him back. "Richard, stop." Fitzwilliam shrugged him off then appeared to calm for a moment.

Suddenly grabbing a porcelain vase, Fitzwilliam violently smashed it against the wall. "So be it, Amanda, so be it. But the child in your belly is mine, and by God, I swear it will never be raised by you!"

She slapped him then with all her strength, stopped by him as she tried for another. In the stunned silence that followed, Harry's wails of terror could be heard coming from the top of the staircase where he stood naked, water dripping from his shaking body. He had heard his mother's screams and immediately darted from his bath, terrified for her. Quickly reaching him, the nursemaid lifted him into her arms and ran with him back to the safety of his room.

"*Enough!*" yelled Catherine, slamming her cane onto the floor. The shocked room became suddenly quiet. "Stop this instant! You are saying things in anger, dangerous, hurtful things, words that can never be taken back nor forgotten!"

Darcy rushed forward to grab onto Fitzwilliam's arm as his cousin and Amanda stood toe-to-toe, glaring hatefully at each other. Fitzwilliam violently pulled his arm away and stormed from the house, Darcy following in his wake.

"What a bloody mess," Catherine murmured after a few moments.

Chapter 12

Lady Catherine Julietta Fitzwilliam de Bourgh, countess, socialite, wife, mother, sister, and aunt, sat alone with the sobbing American girl, reflecting on her own long and full life. A woman of experience, age, and status, she had lived through nearly everything the world could throw at her. Little had surprised her through the years.

Oh, there had been the premature birth of her daughter, Anne, and then her daughter's subsequent lifelong illness.

There had been the sudden marriage of her only sister to the man Catherine had truly loved above all others.

There had been two separate women at court making sexual advances toward her for some unfathomable reason.

There was that unfortunate discovery of an inebriated Prince of Wales naked atop an underage chambermaid on the floor of her favorite coach. They were playing "Hide His Majesty's Scepter and Orbs." That had been a real stunner, with the coach subsequently sold as quickly as possible.

And, of course, there was always the fact that gowns she had worn only two years prior could mysteriously shrink, accompanied by an oddly proportionate increase in her shoe size. This, too, never ceased to astound.

But nothing had prepared her for the events of this morning.

When she initially discovered from her favorite informant that her nephew had been brazenly living at Darcy's for two days with the woman from the Winter Ball, she had come prepared to do battle royal. She arrived with the determination to put a stop to the scandalous affair immediately.

That was before she discovered they were already married.

That was before she discovered they were already expecting a child.

Merde.

And there he was, pacing back and forth, the pain and desperation in his eyes tearing at her heart. He was her problem child, the one she had worried herself sick over for more than thirty-two years now—had been troublesome since the day he was born, sickly and frail. And now look at him, the big ox. His chaotic personality so mirrored her own sometimes that it brought a lump to her throat.

To see him now and witness his world disintegrating around him was more than she could bear. Whether the woman was suitable for an earl's son or not, they were married and bedded and with child, the deed done.

Another unsuitable wife for yet another of her nephews, she grumbled as the battle raged on before her. *Whatever is wrong with these young people today*? She crushed her fan in her exasperation. *Have they no sense of form or propriety? Do they imagine they can marry anyone they fancy, in some havey-cavey manner, whenever the whim takes them? What was all this modern nonsense about love, love, love? It was enough to make one ill. Why, if tender feelings were a reason for marriage, most of the* ton *would die single. Generations of bloodlines would disappear. Heritages would be lost.*

She grunted. *Oh bother!* If that was what her beloved rascal wanted, she would move heaven, earth, and hell to fix this for him. She would not risk alienating another nephew. She had worked too hard reestablishing herself with the other fool.

She had learned her lesson with Darcy.

Harry's jacket and stockings lay in a heap by the settee, and Amanda crossed over to pick them up. Suddenly overcome with grief, she sat and began to weep, her handkerchief pressed tightly to her eyes. So many dreams had been crushed this morning, so many cruel words, all her illusions now in pieces.

A hesitant Catherine came to stand before her, waiting for the girl to get a grip on her feelings. She looked about the room and frowned. Good Lord, how she despised public displays of emotion like this.

She rolled her eyes. "Please stop crying, madam." Catherine tried to sound sympathetic as she poked her finger hard into Amanda's shoulder, but the muffled sobs only increased. When no other verbal response came forth, she began to tap her foot impatiently. She bent far over at the waist to scrutinize the bawling figure, much as if she were studying a flopping fish on the bottom of a boat, then she straightened herself once again. She cleared her throat. "There, there," she muttered in a flat, uninterested voice, her attention and gaze wandering aimlessly toward a particularly fine tapestry against the far wall. It was lovely in cream and blue. She must find out something about its design from Elizabeth…

Amanda looked up, her tears subsiding. "Oh my, I should go up and see to my son." She wiped the backs of her hands across her tears and sighed. "Excuse me, Lady Catherine."

"One moment of your time first, if you please, madam. I have a few questions. It will not take long."

Amanda nodded, apprehensive in the presence of this formidable little powerhouse.

Catherine smiled amiably. "How long ago did you trick my nephew into this marriage?" Catherine's previous heartwarming display of empathy was evidently now officially over.

"I beg your pardon!" Amanda felt her back stiffen. "If you must know, the colonel and I were married four weeks ago." She sniffled and loudly blew her nose.

"Four weeks ago! Unheard of! You knew each other, what, two or three weeks at the most, and you are already married and with child? I don't believe you! But I imagine that is how you were able to force my nephew's hand in marriage." Catherine's cold smile grew wide, but her eyes narrowed to slits. "He is a man of great personal honor from a distinguished family. It would be simple for you to contrive a marriage to improve both your class and breeding."

This was beyond enough. Amanda blew her nose again, even louder. "Excuse me, but I have no need to give you any explanation regarding either my marriage or my expectancy. It is absolutely none of your business!" Amanda sat up straighter and stared directly back, her chin a little higher. "Indeed, the very fact that you feel you can insult me with impunity makes me question your own class and breeding!"

Catherine's eyes flashed with anger. "Upon my word, you are an impudent little baggage, aren't you? Of all the ungracious… A common American such as yourself will never be accepted by the ten thousand. I imagine with your experience, you realize that by now!"

Amanda's eyes blinked rapidly. "The ten thousand what?" She always seemed to have a problem when following these English conversations.

"The upper ten thousand, madam—*the Haute Ton*! Good heavens, but you are an ignorant chit!"

Amanda placed her arms across her belly and looked angrily back at the countess. "Ah, yes, now I understand you. Well, I have never once harbored any aspirations to be accepted by that vicious and amoral group of inbred ninnies."

"And what a good thing that was, madam, since you never were! You see, unlike the Americans, we English prefer to embrace our traditions and ensure our bloodstock. As an earl's son, Richard is far above you in class, my dear. Far above! You have benefited from his unfortunately long-standing rebellious nature. That is all. Even as a second son, he should have been made to choose a bride only from within the select few acceptable families of his rank. It is known as the upper classes and something of which you would never understand." Catherine's expression was one of superior condescension.

Amanda's eyes flashed wide with anger. "I know of which you speak, and indeed we have heard of it happening in America also; however, it is frowned upon and referred to by another word."

Sneering, Catherine gave a mirthless laugh. "Oh, really, and what word is that?"

"Incest."

The countess's head snapped up to glare at the brazen package before her. *Well, well, well.* The little Colonial had surprised her with her rude effrontery and tactless style. She was beginning to like the woman. Evidently not easy to intimidate, she would certainly need to be a strong wife to stand up to Fitzwilliam.

"Well, it is all well and good for you, my dear, to dismiss the ruling class of England, but what of Richard, madam? What of your husband? These are the very people from whom he comes. Can you dismiss his heritage so completely? And whether or not you approve, not only is your son a baronet and therefore a member of that class, but you now carry the next generation within you as we speak."

By the time Lady Catherine had finished her speech, morning sickness was again turning Amanda's face pale, and she swallowed back the bile that had flooded her mouth. His aunt was right. Whether or not Amanda approved of this culture or their mores, her husband and son, and now her unborn babe, were lifelong charter members.

"Are you ill, madam?" Jesu, the little watering pot was looking bad enough to stick her spoon in the wall! The last thing Catherine needed now was for Fitzwilliam to return to a dead wife.

"The morning sickness..." Amanda emitted a soft belch. "Macaroons seem to help."

"Ah." Catherine nodded and tried desperately not to enjoy the young woman's sudden discomfort. Somewhere far upstairs in the Darcy house, the baby began to cry, and they looked at each other, involuntarily smiling. Instinctively, Amanda rubbed her hand across her stomach.

The quiet truce between them continued for several moments until the child's cries could no longer be heard.

"Forgive me, Lady Catherine, if I have spoken rudely to you. Oftentimes I speak before I think. You are right that I owe it to Richard to be more understanding of your culture and ways. I have tried, but as you say, my heritage always locks me out. It has been a bitter experience for me at times."

Catherine studied her carefully. "Do you love my nephew, madam? I am afraid on this score I will have to take your word for it, since there is no Bow Street Runner who could possibly confirm it for me." Catherine's question was so unexpected that Amanda hiccoughed and then sneezed, her tears forgotten.

Amanda smiled briefly. "Yes, madam. I love him more than my life."

Catherine watched her for a while and then nodded her head. "Bold words for some, but I believe you. You certainly love your son a great deal. Anyone with that much devotion for one person usually exhibits the capacity for the same amount of devotion to others whom she loves."

"I only wish Richard could understand my situation better." Amanda spoke so softly that Catherine had to strain to hear her. The girl was staring blindly out the window, again drying her tears with the back of her hand.

"I don't think a man could ever understand what a mother would do for her child, though I was pleased to see that Richard feels paternal attachment already. But men could never feel the bond that a mother feels, could they? To have life grow beneath your heart for so long. I may regret admitting this, but I do empathize with you, Amanda. Perhaps he will also, in time."

"I hope so, Lady Catherine." Amanda felt the tears welling again in her eyes and rested her head back on the settee.

"When did you lose custody of your child?"

Amanda inhaled deeply before she answered. "It was while I was in America, two years ago. I had gone home to nurse my father, who had developed consumption. Regardless of what my late husband later said, he did know I was going and why, and that I planned to return. My father subsequently died."

"My Anne was also felled by a weakness in her lungs. But this was from birth, a premature birth. She has been fighting for her health all her days, as have I for her." Lady Catherine's voice was calm and quiet.

"Have you visited any of the lung clinics?"

"Of course I have, young woman," Lady Catherine snapped. "What a ridiculous question! We have tried everything. Initially, my husband resisted treatment for her, preferring to deny any imperfection in his child. By the time we investigated, it was too late, wasn't it? Men always believe they know best." They both shared a womanly nod and an understanding eye roll at the follies of husbands before they looked away from each other.

"I was unaware that I had lost custody until we returned and my mother-in-law took Harry from me. Apparently, Augustus was on his way to America to claim his son when his ship went down." She lowered her head. "He, too, betrayed my trust."

Catherine was very quiet. "It seems we have both had some unfortunate experiences with husbands. Well, Amanda, we have never had a marriage fail in this family, and I certainly could not allow one to do so on my watch."

"Richard can be rather bullheaded, Lady Catherine." Amanda hiccoughed.

Even as she contemplated what her new niece said, Catherine's mind had begun to wander. She smoothed out her dress and patted down her flyaway hair. *I must have my seamstress let out this gown. It has grown considerably smaller with cleaning. I imagine she is using much cheaper material. Thankfully, I haven't paid her in quite a while.* "Tell me, madam, were your parents long in the colonies? Did they reside in England before they emigrated?"

"No, Lady Catherine, they were both at least third-generation Americans."

A clearly disappointed Catherine shrugged. "Ah, well. Pity, that." Catherine's gaze drifted up and down Amanda's face and figure. She certainly was a beautiful young woman with graceful manners, straight white teeth, nice skin. Quite surprising, really, considering her disgusting origins. With proper training and decent clothing, she could be almost presentable.

If only she wouldn't speak.

"Your parents were both of English descent, however, were they not?" *Have pity on me, please, dear merciful Savior in heaven.*

Amanda eyed the old dragon, barely suppressing her grin. "Well, actually, Lady Catherine, my father was half Scottish as well as half English; however, he was a staunch Royalist until his death."

"As well he should be, and even beyond." Catherine was beginning to warm to this family. "Well, that is very commendable and, may I say, surprisingly welcome news. Now what of your mother, madam? I trust that she was fully English."

Amanda forced herself to look away and not to laugh outright. "My mother was lamentably only partly English, your ladyship."

Catherine frowned. She truly hated flies in her family ointment. "I see, I see. Might one enquire what her other 'part,' as it were, was?"

Amanda locked her gaze onto Catherine's. She felt, rather than heard, Catherine's breathing stop with anticipation.

"My mother was half Abenaki."

Catherine blinked for a few moments.

"I beg your pardon?" she questioned her politely. "Is that somewhere in Wales?"

Amanda steeled herself. "No, your ladyship. Actually, that is not a city. It is an Indian nation. American Indian. The Abenaki people are located mostly in Maine—northern Maine to be precise. My grandmother was of the Passamaquoddi tribe."

The countess paled, emitting a small moan. In fact, Amanda noted the exact time when her ladyship retreated to her own little happy place, shutting the door tightly to her conscious mind. Her eyes glazed over, and she began to hum tunelessly.

"Lady Catherine?" Amanda prompted. "Excuse me... Lady Catherine?"

"Hmm?"

"Are you all right?"

"Good heavens." She pinched the bridge of her nose. "Are you still here?" She looked absolutely bleak. "Well, well, well. I would suppose there is nothing we can do about that now." Catherine sighed and bravely smiled. "I am sure there is no need to be quite so detailed in our explanations." She narrowed her eyes and took a better look at her new niece, determined that whatever could be salvaged from this wreckage would be found and utilized. "Yes, well, I can present you most favorably when the time comes, with ample instruction and a good hair stylist. Perhaps a good diction coach can be applied for." Catherine nodded to herself, in full agreement with her own assessment.

"As long as you're not a papist!" Catherine burst out with laughter. She snorted. *La, what a disaster that would be.* "Good Lord in heaven, I can deal with anything but that!"

She chuckled delightedly and licked her lips at her own witticism. She chuckled until she caught Amanda's eyes shift guiltily away, taking with them a look of absolute horror and total remorse.

Catherine's chuckle degenerated into a pathetic whimper.

"Oh, *merde*," she finally groaned.

Amanda, who would normally have taken offense at these remarks, suddenly began to laugh. To her surprise, she found she was beginning to like this insane old woman who was daffy and vain and outrageous. Lady Catherine actually reminded Amanda of her own mother, though she would never dare to tell her. Gracie Sayles had been a beautiful, outspoken, and passionately funny woman who had adored life, her husband, and her beautiful little daughter, and had died much too soon.

"Richard was angrier than I have ever seen him. What if he truly sues for a formal separation?"

Catherine shook her head, her eyes softening as the woman before her struggled on so bravely to neither cry nor vomit. She handed Amanda a clean handkerchief and a glass of water. "I have seen you both together, and I am positive he loves you at least as much as you love him. I believe he just needs time to cool that horrible Scots temper that goes off periodically—a gift from his mother's heritage, by the way, not in any way to be confused with the Fitzwilliam side's more elegant manner of dealing with crisis." Catherine mused for a long moment.

"Amanda, we have at least twenty-four hours to bring the child to Penwood. I want to speak with you further, but I want you and the boy to leave here before Richard returns. It would be best if you two had some space between you at the moment. I suggest you and the boy come home with me and rest."

Still somewhat suspicious, Amanda looked at the regal dragon. "Why are you being so kind to me? You dislike me, or have you forgotten?"

Catherine's eyes twinkled. "Do not flatter yourself, dear. My feelings for *you* are not nearly that engaged. However, I do love both of my nephews as if I had borne them myself. Darcy has married and is happy, blissfully, so it appears, in spite of all of my dire predictions. He was a good man before marrying Elizabeth and, as hard as this is to admit, he has emerged an even better one because of that union.

"I would like to see that happen to Richard. Will you come with me to my home? We can talk there about what needs to be done."

Amanda sat back on the sofa for a long time, looking first confused, then tired, then resigned. "Yes. Let me get our things." She suddenly held her hand over her mouth and groaned. "Might I hope that you have macaroons at your home?"

Chapter 13

Fitzwilliam paced nervously in the huge visitor's parlor of Rosings House, twirling his badly battered military hat around and studying every knickknack and picture, none of it registering in his conscious mind. He wondered if he would see Amanda today. It had been two days. Over two days, actually—fifty-three hours and twenty-five minutes. He wondered what he would say to her if he did see her. A very small part of him was still furious at her words and vowed never to speak with her again. However, the entire remainder of him missed her so greatly that he had to fight the impulse to run bellowing through the house in search of her.

He hadn't eaten or slept in their time apart, and the previous night had been the worst night of his life.

"Hello, Richard." He heard her gentle voice, and his heart constricted in pain. He turned quickly around.

"Hello, 'manda."

They stood in an awkward silence, not wanting to look at each other but too weak to look away.

"You look tired, Richard," she said softly, and he nodded.

"I haven't slept very well." Not sterling conversation, but it was a beginning. "You also look tired…" His sentence ended on a somewhat hopeful note, then he berated himself for being so shallow. Seeing the dark circles under her eyes and her pale lips, he decided to speak with Catherine about ensuring that she ate enough and rested.

"Lady Catherine says she has developed a plan to regain custody of Harry. She seems very convinced this will work."

"Well, she averages five delusional days a week, so I wouldn't put much stock in it." He was attempting to add a comical tone to his voice but made sure to remain distant and polite. "Is he is still with you, then? They haven't taken him?"

"Yes, praise God. Lady Catherine has been calling in all of her favors for us. Evidently, she really is related to Lord Liverpool. Your family never ceases to amaze. It has given us more time to fight this."

"Capital, excellent." He handled his hat nervously. "If anyone can command favors, it is certainly Catherine." Part of the hat braiding came off in his hand. "By the way, 'manda, about the other day," he looked around and then stuffed the braiding into his pocket. "I don't want you to think I would actually take our child from you. I was angry and lost control of my emotions, very unlike me, really. I know you have little reason to trust me now, but I vow I will support you and whatever decision you make about the baby."

"I, too, am sorry for what I said, Richard." She seemed to struggle with the right words to say. "It seems I deliberately went out of my way to say what would hurt you. Forgive me. I would never, ever consider our time together to have been a mistake. Our child is precious to me. And you *will* make a most wonderful father."

The grim lines by his mouth softened, but they had said so many things to each other. It perhaps was too soon to forget, even if they could forgive.

"We do seem to have some pretty powerful arguments, do we not?"

Unable to answer, she stared intently at her clutched hands as if fascinated by them. He watched as her emotions effected changes across her beautiful face. "Yes. We both seem to possess rather overly passionate natures."

My God, *look at her. A man would swim an ocean for a just moment with her*. And he knew instinctively that he would never leave her, would never love another. He would willingly wait a lifetime for her.

"Darcy believes our problems stem chiefly from the simple fact we are both legally insane and that we will most likely blow each other's brains out within the year." His heart was pumping wildly, and all he could think of was the smell of her hair and her soft skin and her tenderness when she made love to him.

She agreed sadly and shrugged, then looked down again to her hands.

"He also declares that there are no two people in the world better suited for each other."

Quickly, she looked up, joy flooding her face with color. "Did he? Did he really?" She sounded so reassured. "Oh, well, I must say that was very sweet of him."

"I am not quite sure he meant that as a compliment, Amanda."

At that moment, Catherine glided into the room. "Ah, the lovebirds! How wonderful to see you both speaking so civilly to each other. So much better than all that screeching incoherently at the top of your lungs, don't you think?" She smiled beatifically at the stiff, awkward, and miserably unhappy duo.

"Well, that's enough of that. I hate to break up this heartwarming scene, but I believe our carriage is arriving outside, Richard. Amanda, you will wait for us here. If we are successful, which I believe we will be, we may finally settle this custody issue in your favor. Are you ready, Nephew?"

"Yes, I am ready, Aunt Catherine." He placed a hand on his hip and stood facing her. "But for what exactly am I ready? What is this plan you have devised? And believe me, I await in stark terror for your reply. You have no idea how it chills me to the very marrow of my bones to go along with one of your schemes, unknowing of what to expect."

I shall call the decorator and have this entire hallway redone in a Persian motif. Yes, that would be very good, since I do look so very well in blue silk. I draw the line, however, at wearing turbans. Too fanatical a fashion statement, if anyone was to ask me... Catherine was walking serenely past him when his words finally took root in her brain. Aghast and insulted, she snatched first her reticule and then her gloves from Jamison, after which he was forced to follow her at a respectable distance, holding up her cloak as she angrily paced back and forth. "Whenever have I ever done anything to cause you or anyone else any concern?!"

Fitzwilliam whimpered, and his hand went immediately to his flip-flopping stomach. For unknown reasons, Catherine took this motion as some sort of an apology and an admission of his gross unfairness toward her. "And see that you don't!" No one understood what that meant either.

❧

An outside footman opened the door and nodded to the butler. At last donning her cloak Catherine motioned for Jamison to open the great doors, aunt and nephew emerging into the brilliant winter morning. Almost immediately, the most magnificent coach Fitzwilliam had ever beheld approached the front portico of Rosings House, pulled by four immense, matching black Arabians.

Emitting an impressed whistle, he turned toward his aunt, a suspicious gleam in his eye. "Who in the world owns this, then?" He searched for a crest or some indication of the owner, but there was nothing, only the black mirrored reflection of themselves standing there. A coach this magnificent was reserved for royalty; not even a duke or an earl would dare be this ostentatious. It was large enough for the entire royal family.

Four liveried guards riding abreast of the carriage confirmed his impression. A wigged footman in black and gold jumped down from the rear of the carriage and ran to open the door as another came from nowhere to offer his hand in assistance. Catherine motioned for Fitzwilliam to follow as she was handed into the coach. The footmen bowed to him.

"Richard, you know Mrs. Fitzherbert, do you not? I believe the last time you saw her you were ten years old and setting fire to a chamber pot." Catherine spoke cheerfully, nearly bubbling over with good humor and pride. "Maria, as you know, was my dearest friend during my single days at court. We had such good fun." The lady smiled warmly at Lady Catherine while taking her hand and giving it a loving pat, then turned to Fitzwilliam.

Chapter 14

Mrs. Maria Fitzherbert was rightful wife of George, Prince of Wales, the future George IV, King of England, or so she was regarded by certain members of the upper ten thousand. The prince had married the twice-widowed Mrs. Fitzherbert in a Catholic ceremony, and they had lived secretly together until, sadly, the King dissolved the marriage and forced his union with another. Now in their older years, it was Mrs. Fitzherbert in whom the prince confided, regarded as his soul's true life partner. Although he still kept many mistresses, she was his dearest friend.

"It's an honor to see you again, madam." Fitzwilliam took her hand and kissed it. Long accustomed to royal circles, he was polite but not in awe. He was confused by her presence.

"The honor is mine, Colonel Fitzwilliam. I don't believe my husband and I have properly commended your valor at Waterloo." She smiled warmly at him, her eyes crinkling with warmth. "We followed the campaigns very closely over the years. You are very highly regarded as a true hero in our home, sir."

Teatime at Penwood saw the dowager Lady Marguerite Penrod hard at work at her desk, penning instructions to her solicitors, menus for the week ahead with treats that she knew her grandson favored, rejection letters to the many applicants for position of governess. Beneath these neat stacks were more important letters—letters from and to boarding schools. The farther she could send the child, the less influence the American would have. The less influence the American would have, the better chance her grandson would be brought up properly—as an English gentleman befitting his rank and title.

Her butler scratched lightly at the door, entering discreetly the moment he was instructed. He walked solemnly to her side, the beautifully understated calling card lying face up in the center of the silver salver. When she did not immediately acknowledge him, he coughed softly to draw her attention. She slammed her hand down onto the desk.

"Did I not tell you I was to be left alone this afternoon? Why must every instruction I issue be compromised?" She sighed angrily. "Whoever is out there, send them away."

"Forgive me, madam. I thought perhaps you would make an exception in this case." His eyes drifted anxiously to the card. He appeared very nervous.

Curiosity getting the better of her, she gave him a calculated, hard glare then snatched the card from the tray. Within moments, her expression swept from annoyance to ecstasy. It was then felled by a look of apprehension. Ordinarily she would have been overjoyed at the tremendous honor of a visit by none other than Lady Catherine de Bourgh herself. However, she had been made recently aware that her appalling daughter-in-law was somehow involved with both the countess's nephews, meeting scandalously for a liaison with one and hiding her son at another's home. Alarm spoiled what would have been her immense pride at this unprecedented visit.

Surely Lady Catherine de Bourgh would not assign any responsibility to her for the whole unseemly affair. Why the woman wasn't even English—was a savage American, in fact, and certainly never again to be welcomed into this home. Yes, that's what she would assure her. Possibly together they could even force Amanda to return to America, demand to have her deported. Or shot. Lady Catherine de Bourgh had connections, tremendously powerful connections.

Lady Catherine assuredly is as very much opposed to this match as I am, perhaps even more so... Yes, indeed, this could be my entrée into the higher circles of the aristocracy. Very likely, Lady Catherine de Bourgh will be extremely happy to see the back of that American and is seeking my assistance. She may even recommend me for vouchers to Almack's, even perhaps an invitation to Carlton House!

In fact, the more she thought about it, the more Lady Penrod believed that to be the most probable reason for the visit. After all, they were sort of kindred spirits in this whole fiasco. Lady Catherine would have no doubts as to her assistance in this. No, Lady Catherine de Bourgh would see that she had a most loyal ally in Lady Marguerite Penrod.

"Please show her in immediately," she commanded in a most exasperated manner. "Why ever are you just standing there? Move!" *Imagine leaving Lady Catherine in the foyer, cooling her heels!* She smoothed down the imperceptible wrinkles in her dress. *How's my hair?* She quickly rose from the desk to check her appearance in the mirror, when in the reflection, she saw Lady Catherine enter.

She stepped forward, grandly extending her hands to her illustrious guest, a huge, welcoming smile on her lips. The smile evaporated quickly and turned into stunned and frozen shock at the personage who entered after Lady Catherine.

"The Woman" was being led into the room by an army colonel, her hand resting companionably upon his arm.

"Lady Marguerite Penrod, may I introduce Mrs. Maria Anne Fitzherbert, and I believe you already know of my nephew, Colonel Richard Fitzwilliam." Lady Penrod curtseyed so low that she had trouble arising. Her heart was pounding.

"I am incredibly honored that you are in my home… that either of you are in my home… incredibly honored…" Words were tumbling out at a frightening pace. A genuine Royal worshiper, Lady Penrod continued to bow before Mrs. Fitzherbert. "I never thought I would ever… I mean I have seen you, naturally…"

Mrs. Fitzherbert turned her body toward Catherine, snapping open her fan. "Please ask her to keep her comments brief. Our head is beginning to ache." Mrs. Fitzherbert sat, unasked, on the settee, with Lady Catherine beside her. Richard humbly retreated into the background, witnessing female deception and cunning at its best.

~

Mrs. Fitzherbert fanned herself languidly, opening her mouth once or twice but ultimately said nothing. She turned toward Lady Catherine. "Countess?"

"Mrs. Fitzherbert has come to speak to you about a very delicate matter that is causing her, as well as myself, great concern."

As she spoke, her eyes swept across the expanse of threadbare carpet. Lady Penrod swallowed hard and suddenly noticed how very threadbare that ancient Turkish carpet actually was.

"Of course, of course. To what do I owe this...?" Lady Penrod's voice trailed off when she saw that Mrs. Fitzherbert had become quite pale. She spoke behind the privacy of her fan. "Have you brought the vinaigrette?" she whispered to Catherine. "We may have need of it. Our head is beginning to pound. There is something about these surroundings... perhaps an odor...?"

A suitable amount of time was passed in humiliating silence before the quiet was shattered by the high-pitched screech of Mrs. Fitzherbert. "I shall begin. Lady Penrod!" The woman in question jumped several inches at a sound that could just possibly slice through glass. "My husband and I have been informed of a most unnatural situation in this household regarding custody of a child."

The little color there was in Lady Penrod's cheeks now turned bright pink. "I beg your pardon?"

"The child in question is the son of Colonel Fitzwilliam's wife." Mrs. Fitzherbert turned her gaze directly at Lady Penrod. "Both my husband and I have taken a great interest in this situation, as we are both quite fond of the colonel."

Lady Penrod's heart stopped beating as she tried to comprehend what was being said. For several minutes, the only noise in the room was the mantel clock, her attention drifting as she considered the dual thrill and horror that the regent was even remotely aware of her existence. "I was unaware that they had married."

Mrs. Fitzherbert's shrill screech rang out again. "Both my husband and I would look most kindly upon a rethinking of the custody situation. Lady Catherine has assured us that her solicitors would be most willing to meet with yours to discuss a rearrangement that would be advantageous to all parties concerned."

Lady Penrod gripped her chair arms during the ear-shattering experience. Once or twice, she opened her mouth to speak but then retreated in fear. Finally she whispered to Lady Catherine, "May I speak?"

Catherine nodded coldly.

"Please forgive my forwardness, but what possible interest would you have in this matter?" Her voice was barely audible.

Mrs. Fitzherbert raised her quizzing glass and stared, dumbstruck, for several moments. "Colonel Richard Fitzwilliam is a decorated war hero and a dear friend to our family. The colonel has honorably received your daughter-in-law in marriage and will be able to provide a most satisfactory home for the child, a child, I might add, who is only five years old and needs his mother. We would strongly recommend your immediate reassessment."

Lady Penrod's ears were ringing. That tone could not be natural, surely. She looked at Lady Catherine and then at the colonel, neither of whom looked as affected as she was by the pitch and tenor of that hideous voice. Her hands were shaking, and she longed to stick a finger in her ear and vigorously shake things around. "Forgive me, truly; until this moment I was unaware they had married. I thought…" The two old dragons returning her gaze stared at her blankly. "Well, I am certain that you know what I thought." She whispered in confidence, not wishing to offend the colonel. Finally, she made a furtive little motion to stand.

Mrs. Fitzherbert gave her a look that could stop a clock. "You would not stand in our presence, would you?" Her voice clearly registered her astonishment.

"No, no. Of course not." She sat again at the edge of her seat. "You see, my grandson *is* a baronet. He should be raised in this house, by people of his class and rank. Amanda is... is... an *American*. Would they be up to the task, do you think?" There, she could not make the problem plainer. Lady Penrod stared at them both as if this was all the explanation that was needed. The chit could not possibly be up to the task of raising an English gentleman.

Lady Catherine struggled to stand, a faint burgundy color rising up her chest into her neck and slowly spreading across her cheeks. She was furious—no, she was beyond furious. She was enraged. Mrs. Fitzherbert placed a steadying hand on her back, while she herself hid her twitching grin behind her fan. Knowing her friend's immense pride, she wondered briefly if Catherine would soon explode.

"Are you insinuating that my nephew, I repeat, *my* nephew... the son of an earl, the nephew of an earl, the grandnephew of a duke, would be unequal to the task of raising a... a... *baronet*?!" Fitzwilliam's chin dropped down to his chest, and he attempted to disguise a short bark of laughter which he could no longer suppress, while Mrs. Fitzherbert's fan rose to completely cover her face, as she too struggled for composure.

Catherine began to choke and cough. She reached back to clutch the armrest of the settee from which she had just risen, her little feet alternately slipping out from beneath her. Mrs. Fitzherbert grabbed one of her arms while the colonel quickly came forward to grab the other. He slapped her on her back once or twice, causing Catherine to turn an angry glare momentarily toward him. She finally plopped back down into her seat, her face flushed and blotched.

"But she is a papist!" Lady Penrod flinched, immediately realizing her mistake.

Mrs. Fitzherbert turned slowly to their hostess. "How dare you. We are stunned at your ignorance, madam, at your bigotry. Are you even remotely aware of the families involved here? We hope you realize, madam, that although titles cannot be refused—*Lady* Penrod—they can be revoked!" Mrs. Fitzherbert was shrieking in fury. Dogs blocks away began to take notice. The chandelier quivered.

"Whereas our dear colonel may very well inherit the earldom if his brother does not marry and produce an heir, your grandson may be considered too young, or your family too unworthy, of his current title. There are many scenarios that could take place with very little effort on our part. But mark me, madam, we will make that effort."

Lady Penrod gasped, and her face went completely white.

"We also were considered unworthy, if you remember, perhaps not due to our heritage but because of our religion." Mrs. Fitzherbert's voice rang out clear as a bell. "We do not intend to see another good woman be tortured by small minds if we are able to assist her!"

Lady Penrod was destroyed.

Their mission clearly accomplished, Lady Catherine and Mrs. Fitzherbert rose as one, Catherine smoothing both her skirt and her bodice, returning her little feathered hat to an upright position from its resting place over her ear.

Mrs. Fitzherbert continued. "It is suggested that you contact your solicitors and discuss this situation with them. We will await your decision, say, within forty-eight hours. If you decide to be more reasonable, we shall leave you our solicitor's card so that yours may be in contact immediately. Think hard on this, madam."

She had saved the best for last. Looking down her long nose at the shaking woman before her, she cast a cold stare up and down the woman's body. "Mark my words, madam. *We have the power to turn society against you.*" Her voice was clear, hard, and deliberate.

"*Never doubt for a moment that we will not,*" added the now inexplicably alert Lady Catherine.

Turning to Lady Catherine, Mrs. Fitzherbert nodded, then they both turned to Richard. "Colonel, will you assist us back to the carriage? We are feeling quite distressed. Quite dissatisfied. When we next speak with our husband, he will be quite displeased!"

He leaned into the carriage and stared, dumbstruck, at the two old tabbies, both of whom were now laughing like schoolgirls. "Well, that was a bit of fun, I must say." His aunt shook out the folds of her gown as she gasped for breath. "Heavens but that woman is a horrible snob. Imagine objecting to the girl because of her religion! La, what a small mind."

"I do not believe what I just witnessed!" Standing in the open carriage door, he studied each woman carefully, a stunned look on his face. "I am appalled, shocked to my bones, in fact, by that blatant display of treachery and blackmail." He shook his head. "It was absolutely magnificent, and I bow to the masters. I could kiss you both. Thank you, Mrs. Fitzherbert. I can never repay you for this."

Lady Catherine and Mrs. Fitzherbert both beamed back at him, proud as peahens. "Nonsense, Colonel. We shall still have to wait and see. It is not a *fait accompli* by any means, you realize. Have no illusions that my husband would truly revoke the child's title, please, but we can ensure that the woman's life *will* become a social nightmare, as she now knows. No one in the *ton*, *no one*, would willingly move backward in status. One would rather face the black plague.

"And I truly do empathize with what your wife has gone through. Whatever I can do to help her, believe me, I will." The look in her eyes softened, grew gentle as she spoke, remembering her heartbreak at having her marriage invalidated, her husband forced to marry another.

Fitzwilliam tucked the lap robe around his aunt and kissed her hand. "Richard, come, get into the carriage. Are you not returning with us?" Catherine looked at her nephew, her voice sounding disappointed.

The events he had just witnessed were the first real ray of hope he had experienced in over a month, and he looked away, trying to hide the emotions that threatened. "I will definitely come, but not now. I have some ends to tie up first and a bit of groveling to do with Wellington for my family's future."

"I know you will not fail me, Richard. You, more than so many others, understand honor and where your heart lies."

He leaned into the carriage and took her hands. "Aunt Catherine…" He hesitated, not knowing how to say what was in his heart. With that, he took her into his great arms to hug her close. "Aunt Catherine," he repeated hoarsely, "I can never thank you enough for what you have done today. How can I ever repay you both?"

This was her boy returning to her finally, the man she knew he could be, the man unafraid to show his love, gratitude, and devotion. Her hand patted his cheek, and she resumed her usual haughty demeanor. "Name two of your children after us, the girls, preferably. This will ensure that they will be greatly proficient in anything they undertake and that they will be considered diamonds of the first water for their beauty."

He let out a bark of laughter and kissed her forehead. "Consider it done."

She cupped his chin and smiled at him. "I will remind you of all this love and devotion at our next *bataille, mon fils.*"

Laughing, he kissed both of her hands.

He took Mrs. Fitzherbert's hand and kissed it gently, thanking her once again, then backed down from the carriage door and smiled up at them both. "Please tell my wife I will come to her as soon as I can. I *will* be there sometime tonight, though, I promise." He stepped away, and the footman closed the door, the four horsemen who would ride on either side of the carriage bringing their mounts into position. Through the back window, he could see the two old friends as the carriage drove off, giggling and laughing over their great triumph.

Chapter 15

It was much later that evening by the time he finished speaking with Wellington, his aunt's house already closed and in darkness, everyone abed. Fitzwilliam was waiting anxiously for Jamison to bring Amanda down into Catherine's overly ornate family parlor. The night and the whiskey had gotten away from him while he and his general discussed old battles, the Ordnance Board, the future, and a hundred other topics. He kept delaying his leave-taking until the peer finally threw him out, muttering about how much more courage it seemed to take the soldier to face his little bride than it had taken him to face the army of Napoleon. A slightly inebriated colonel finally climbed into his borrowed carriage and called up to the driver to take him to Catherine's.

As he waited, he looked about himself at the ostentation—the flamboyant, imported furnishings, the crystal and gilt, the priceless statues and artwork—all the incredible opulence that constantly surrounded his family and, especially, his aunt. He would never admit it to a soul, but he loved this gaudy old room.

For eleven years, he had experienced a life that the aristocracy could never imagine, and it had changed him. Commanding both viscounts and pig farmers, fighting alongside butchers and thieves, dining with emperors, sleeping with whores and countesses, he had come to realize that the Americans were right about one thing—there really *was* little difference between people.

He remembered the laughter and love between the soldiers and their women in camp—poor people who had nothing in life but each other. He certainly could not settle for less in his own life. He wanted the same tender love that any lowly cottager would. He needed the same sense of family and security taken for granted by any tavern keeper. There was only one woman for him, and if he had to wait a lifetime for her, he would do so. She was his heart and soul, his partner and closest friend, the first true love of his life, and the last.

He stopped before a portrait of his father and his father's two sisters, Catherine and Anne. Catherine, as the eldest, was seated in the forefront, a countess already at twenty with the hauteur and superior look that had made her famous—fair-haired, porcelain-skinned, and incredibly beautiful. Behind her on her right was Anne Fitzwilliam, Darcy's mother. Anne would have been nearly eighteen years old, with the dark hair and aristocratic beauty that Darcy inherited. He remembered her as a sweet and happy woman, gentle with the children and always deferring to her husband, often laughing as she hugged her son to her. Her warm eyes were softer and kinder than Catherine's.

To the left of Catherine stood his father, also with dark hair and piercing blue eyes, an incredibly good-looking young Corinthian, just eleven months Catherine's junior. Fitzwilliam swelled with pride at the sight, wished he could have known him in his wild youth. He was ridiculously proud of this father, who looked high-spirited and eager to take on the world. The three had been close in age but vastly different in temperaments.

This trio before him were links in a chain that reached as far back as the Conqueror, links in a chain of which he was a part, taking it into the future through his children and their children.

Of a sudden, he felt very proud and very humbled.

Amanda entered quietly, relief at the sight of him flooding through her—his size, his broad chest and shoulders always making her pulse quicken. The thought struck the moment she saw him, and her heart and her path were clear as glass before her. "'Whither thou goest, I shall go, where thou lodgest, I shall lodge, thy people shall be my people, thy God my God,'" she whispered, causing him to turn.

"Hello," she said simply.

He nodded, the sudden boulder in his throat impeding his speech.

"I was expecting you to come earlier." He was pale and looked slightly ill. "Are you all right, Richard?"

"Yes." His voice cracked, and he cleared his throat. His first sight of her had robbed him of breath. His second had almost robbed him of speech. She looked gloriously disheveled. In fact, she had hurried downstairs without her robe, not even taking time for slippers. It was only moments before that she had finally fallen asleep, exhausted and depressed, giving up on his ever coming over that evening even as Lady Catherine had assured her of his continued love for her.

"I am sorry to have come so late," he finally said, and then inhaled deeply. "I've been visiting with the peer, obviously drinking a bit, also. He possesses some extraordinarily powerful whiskey." She looked gorgeous as she pushed back the cascade of blonde hair from over her face, a face which was still flushed from sleep. He could see the imprint of the pillow wrinkles on her cheeks. "Of course, what I call whiskey, he calls Irish holy water."

Amanda laughed rather over brightly and nodded, crossing her arms over her chest to fend off the cold. She wished she had her slippers nearby.

"Oh, for heaven's sake." The faintly exasperated voice seemed to come from nowhere.

Incredibly, Fitzwilliam could hear his aunt muttering behind the closed door to the hallway. He turned his head to listen.

"Catherine, is that you?" The muttering stopped. There was silence.

He could hear the shuffling of feet behind the door.

"Did I say that out loud, Jamison?"

"Yes, madam."

"*Merde*."

Fitzwilliam exhaled in exasperation. "Aunt Catherine, is that you?" he called again, louder.

After several seconds, the voice from nowhere spoke. "No."

He walked over to the door and snatched it open. Amanda watched as he leaned his body into the doorway. "Could you please afford us some slight privacy?" he asked in a respectful but strained voice.

"Whatever do you mean? I am merely standing here. It's nothing to do with you. Please stand back. I need my rest.

Close the door. I am very old and tired. I have a bad heart. For heaven's sake, Richard, move your hand! You are letting out the heat. I am not made of money, you know! Watch your feet." With that, the door was snapped shut in his face.

He turned toward Amanda and shook his head. "Now, where was I?" he asked absently.

"You weren't anywhere that I could tell," said the mysterious voice that was not behind the door.

"Aunt Catherine!!"

Amanda's hand pressed over her mouth as they both grinned. Trying hard not to laugh, Fitzwilliam grumbled with his amusement.

"Aunt Catherine!" he commanded. "Stop your eavesdropping and go to bed! You are old and tired, remember?"

"I am not eavesdropping, young man." The muffled voice managed to sound very insulted. "I am merely standing here, in my own home, by my table, which..." There was a loud crash and thud, followed by a muffled scream.

Fitzwilliam put up one finger and walked to the door, opening it.

"Are you all right?" he asked.

"Yes, of course I am, but I fail to understand from where that table came. Jamison?"

"France, madam," he replied.

"Merciful heavens, I am perfectly aware of that! I mean now, Jamison. When was it placed here?!" Her voice was very agitated.

"I believe that would be thirty-four years ago, madam."

Fitzwilliam looked back at Amanda and rolled his eyes, after which his head disappeared again into the open doorway.

"Will you please go away?" he asked. "I am begging

you, Aunt. If I pay you something, some unbelievably large amount, will you leave us? Please? Allow me some small privacy for this, please."

When he began closing the door, it was pushed open again. A white, blue-veined hand was the only thing visible as it reached up to his hair and patted it down.

"Did you just spit on your hand before you patted down my hair?" he asked indignantly.

"Oh, I did no such thing. Now be still. Of all the rude, impertinent accusations to make! Bend down lower. I will have you know that members of the aristocracy do not have 'spit' as you crudely refer to it, young man. We do not acknowledge saliva in any form. Straighten your collar. There, you look nearly presentable." She grumbled in aggravation, "Do you even *own* a brush?" Grabbing his chin, she brusquely turned his face from side to side. "For heaven's sake, Richard, what did you use to shave—a shovel?"

"Leave now, Catherine, and I may spare your life." There was a moment of quiet from behind the door. "Go, woman! I intend to begin ravishing my wife shortly; however, I will not even consider it before I see that little dwarflike body of yours waddling down this corridor! Away with you! Shoo!"

"Oh, all right!" she finally capitulated. "By the way, *mon chou*, I should tell you that when you two finally get around to reconciling and retire upstairs, Amanda is occupying the large blue suite down the east corridor, not your usual bachelor room at the end of the west corridor." She reached up to kiss his offered cheek then turned on her heels to leave. "You have finally earned an upgrade in accommodations, Richard. Well done, you."

Watching his aunt leave, Fitzwilliam exhaled a long, relieved breath then turned back into the room to face Amanda. He was alone finally with his wife, and his heart was beating wildly with so much yet to tell her and so many plans for their future.

"My God, but you look striking," he murmured gruffly. His mind was momentary mush. His initial impulse was to toss her backward atop a table. *I am in full control.* In his finest "addressing of the troops" voice, he began.

"Amanda, I want to speak with you about our situation. I know we are waiting for an important decision to be made, but I do not want that decision to come between us. I want you to know where I stand with or without that decision, especially after that slight setback we experienced at Darcy's home. We are married for life, for better or worse. If you feel you must return to your mother-in-law's house, I will wait for you, for however long this custody procedure takes."

She opened her mouth to speak, but he raised his hand to stay her, taking a few tentative steps in her direction, nervously clasping and unclasping his hands behind his back. "I was a fool, Amanda, an ass. I betrayed your trust. I broke a sacred promise to you, and that is indefensible. I have no excuse to offer you for my actions. I can only say how much I love you and hope that you can forgive me. As I have said, I spoke with Wellington today. It has not been announced yet, but Arthur is to be made Master General of the Ordnance soon, and he is recommending me for appointment on the Board. He was quite enthusiastic that I had finally made my decision and assures me that the position comes with a very generous compensation, enough for me to take a house here in town, a small house but large enough for the three of us, if and when needed. Or should I say four of us? Nevertheless, I will be here for you and Harry and our baby."

"Richard, please let me speak. I have something to say to you." She shook her head forcefully as tears began to stream down her cheeks.

"Amanda, do not say something now we will both regret. I need you desperately, and I am convinced you need me also. We were meant to be together."

Sobbing, she tried to speak, but he rushed in once again. "Give me another chance, for heaven's sake!" He cupped her face with his hands. "You must have some small feeling left for me, some affection. I refuse to believe I've destroyed us completely. Can't you find some way to forgive me?"

She placed her hands over his and closed her eyes. "Richard, you listen to me now before you say another word. We have received a note from my mother-in-law." Trembling, she looked up into his eyes. "She has already made her decision."

"Amanda... say it quickly. It will hurt less. I swear to you I will not abandon you. I am yours forever."

Finally calming a bit, she kissed his palms. "Oh, my darling, darling husband..." Her voice caught on a sob. "Richard, it is over. My mother-in-law has agreed to allow us to keep Harry. She has agreed to work together with us to reverse the custody through the courts and parliament. She only asks that she not be separated completely from him." It was a few moments before either could speak.

"Did you hear me? It is over, Richard. It is over, and I love you. I love you now and forever, more than my life." He stared at her in stunned silence.

It was over? Surely she must be mistaken. In her terror, she probably misunderstood the note.

It was over? She nodded happily at his befuddled expression. "Yes. That is why Lady Catherine was eavesdropping so blatantly. We have both been waiting anxiously for your return."

It was over? His arms slowly surrounded her, crushing her to his chest, tears coming unashamedly to his eyes.

It was over. His whoop of happiness shook the rafters.

He could not at first comprehend what that meant, his mind first rejecting this thin beacon of light then eventually becoming blinded with its sunburst. It was finally over. He kissed her eyes and nose and throat and lips, the shock rapidly turning into relief, an overwhelming relief that exploded within them both, and they began to laugh and shout their joy. He twirled her around in his arms. They kissed hungrily and with all the energy that God can provide two people wildly in love. Over and over again, kissing each other senseless, kissing each other until they both wanted more—much, much more.

He tumbled backward onto the sofa and pulled her down onto his lap, laughing and moaning happily with each intimate touch, each caress. "I cannot believe this," he muttered into her hair. "You realize we must name our first daughter Catherine and the second, Marie. Good Lord, how else can we ever repay them? They did it! Those sly old foxes actually did it."

She nodded merrily, laughing and nibbling his jaw. "I think we should just go ahead and name all of our children after them, boys and girls." Her head rested on his shoulder, and she noticed a few nicks on his cheek, touched that he had drunkenly shaved, especially before coming to see her, then alarmed that it looked something more akin to attempted suicide by razor. He must have been so very nervous, she thought, and her heart squeezed with love. He ran his thumb across her lips and inhaled her sweet Amanda scent, the scent of soap.

"God, how dearly I love you," he whispered.

And so the dance began that very next day at noon, when the elder Lady Penrod's people contacted Lady Catherine de Bourgh's people, who in turn contacted the colonel's people... Runners, carriages, and paper began their fluttering ballet, shuffling around Mayfair and St. James at an alarming speed until the final "i" was dotted and the final "t" was crossed and every lawyer involved was as rich as Croesus.

Chapter 16

On a beautiful, crisp Saturday morning several weeks later, March 12th to be exact, in the year of our Lord 1818, a certain young Mr. Darcy, a Mr. Bennet George Darcy to be precise, was officially welcomed into the Anglican Church community by none other than the Archbishop of Canterbury himself, Charles Manners-Sutton, or Cousin Chum, as Aunt Catherine had often referred to him during their childhood.

Before the magnificent baptismal font at St. George's Cathedral, his doting uncle, Colonel Richard Fitzwilliam, stood proudly, his pregnant wife, Amanda, at his side. Cradled within his strong arms, B. George Darcy screamed bloody hell, furious at the dribble of holy water running down his forehead, affronted by the laughing comments and oohs and aahs, aggravated by the ribbons and ruffles on his gown and the lace on his cap. They'd pay one day, they'd all pay, just as soon as he figured out who they all were.

Intoning aloud for his tiny cousin the promises of lifelong devotion to God and church, the rejection of Satan and all his wicked ways, his "uncle" Fitz chuckled at the impressive display of impatience, the seven pounds of hubris encased in satin. And while family and friends gathered round to wish the newest addition into their privileged world a holy and happy life, the realization came to the boy's adoring father that this would probably be the first in a lifetime of family gatherings, both happy and sad, to be shared between the Darcy and Fitzwilliam households.

As he listened to the head of the Church of England explain the spiritual as well as physical role of parents in a child's life, the importance of godparents, the love of family and ritual, Darcy's thoughts drifted back to a little country assembly hall where he had condescended to dance only with Caroline Bingley and her sister, Mrs. Hurst. His friend, their brother, Charles, had indicated a sweet-looking young thing, the sister of the beautiful girl with whom he had danced, sitting out the current set due to scarcity of partners, egging him on to dance with her.

Elizabeth. His beloved, beautiful, Elizabeth.

"*She is tolerable*," he had brayed like a donkey within her hearing, "*but not handsome enough to tempt me. And I am in no humor at present to give consequence to young ladies who are slighted by other men.*"

Smiling down on her lovely face now, he squeezed her hand tenderly as it rested snugly within his elbow. She had brought him love and joy and family. His world was richer because of her. "I love you, Miss Bennet," he whispered in her ear, moved by the tears of happiness shining in her eyes.

"*I had not known you a month before I felt that you were the last man in the world whom I could ever be prevailed upon to marry.*" She laughed softly as her insulting rejection of his first marriage proposal flashed through her memory. Then she sighed. He was magnificent and handsome and noble. Her world was richer because of him.

"No more than I love you, Mr. Darcy."

Shortly before Easter, 1850

Darcy joined his cousin as he rested outside on the grand terraced veranda. He carried hidden within his coat a bottle of whiskey, two glasses, and a carafe of water, proudly brandishing them as he approached. Fitzwilliam had already been alerted by the clinking and clanking of the glassware and was now waiting patiently on one of two large lawn chairs they had placed for optimal viewing of the vast driveway into Pemberley.

"I say, Buccleuch?" Darcy loudly called out, greatly enjoying his cousin's annoyance.

"Damn it to hell, brat, you know how I detest being called that. Why do you persist?"

"Well, if you're going to answer your own questions, I wonder that you even waste your breath."

Fitzwilliam emitted a derogatory sound through his clenched lips.

"No mouth farts, please." Darcy glowed with pleasure. "Has Amanda reconciled herself to becoming a duchess yet?" He carefully placed his purloined goodies onto the table and then settled himself in his own chair.

Fitzwilliam harrumphed. "She was only recently coming to terms with being an earl's wife after... how many decades has it been? Now it appears it was my fault all my old cousins died childless within a year of each other." Richard took the glass that Darcy offered and watched eagerly as the whiskey was poured. "She hates the name, you know, says it sounds as if someone is coughing up phlegm. She cannot stop laughing whenever we are addressed." His mood brightened considerably, relishing their rare treat. "How did you get this past the old gargoyles?" He smacked his lips at the forbidden taste.

"Really, Richard, I am the master of my home, the king of my domain." With an indignant huff, Darcy lowered himself deeper into the chair, elegantly repositioning his cuffs and collar.

"I imagine that is why you hid the bottle as you walked by the windows."

Darcy gazed with haughty condescension at his cousin. One eyebrow arched. "I hid the bottle for the same reason you've got those two pipes stashed beneath the table." Fitzwilliam grunted happily at being reminded of their presence and reached below to bring them up.

Their doctors would be disapproving of these liberties with their health—their wives would be livid. It made it somehow all the more enjoyable.

As he lit his own pipe, Darcy became aware of the trouble his cousin was having when he noticed for the first time the glasses perched upon his nose. "Since when do you wear spectacles?" He watched as Fitzwilliam swiveled his head around like a bird eying a worm. It began to be a nearly comical attempt to bring a flame even remotely near the bowl of his pipe. Darcy leaned over to guide the light.

"Thank you, brat, I don't." Fitzwilliam puffed vigorously once or twice in triumph. "Wear glasses, that is. They're not mine. Since you feel the need to snoop, these are Amanda's. I stole them from her dresser when I rifled through it this morning." He stifled a chuckle. Looking very proud of himself, he leaned his head back and blew the pipe smoke into the air. "Aaahhhhh," he sighed. He was in heaven. "The woman's blind as a bat for reading, you know."

"Good God, why were you going through her dresser?"

"Well, nosy bits, I was looking for the tobacco pouch she stole from *my* dresser, of course." He shook his head as if Darcy had mortar for brains and clucked his tongue in annoyance. "You know perfectly well she won't allow me to have tobacco since that episode with my heart." The spectacles were quickly slipped into his pocket. "She'll go mad looking for these." He beamed.

"Fitzwilliam, as wealthy as you are, you could provide your wife with more than one pair of spectacles, could you not?"

"Well, a lot you know. Amanda has at least six pairs of these things." Fitzwilliam glared indignantly at his cousin. "And it took me a devil of a time to find and hide them all."

Darcy shook his head sadly, "Have you no shame?"

Fitzwilliam gave this a fleeting moment of thought. "No, why do you ask?" He puffed on his pipe and grinned wickedly. "Heavens, man, how else can I obtain the vital information with which to torment my beloved if I do not go through her private things? My God, Darcy, what kind of marriage do you have?"

It was one month after the passing of the indomitable Lady Catherine de Bourgh, having lived to be an exquisitely lively eighty-nine years, her wits about her until nearly three weeks before the end. And it was one week until Easter. Easter for the two men had always been with Catherine and her daughter at Rosings Park for as long as they remembered. They had decided the tradition would continue on at the Darcy's magnificent home, Pemberley.

Darcy and Fitzwilliam were now resting on its grand veranda, awaiting the arrival of their children and a large number of grandchildren, who would be joining them for the holidays.

"Elizabeth only this morning informed me *all* the children will be in attendance this year. Tell me it isn't so, I beg of you."

"Yes, Cousin, as horrible as that thought is, it is true. From what I've been told, all of ours will be here with assorted spouses and children, as well as your three and their families." Fitzwilliam grinned, his pipe securely clenched in his teeth. He removed it as they clinked their glasses and downed their drinks in one swallow.

"Well, that settles it." Darcy placed his empty glass down on the table between them. "I'll have to sell immediately and go into hiding. God help Derbyshire." He puffed on his pipe, unable to suppress his grin.

Glancing furtively over his shoulder to ensure they weren't being watched by the wives, Fitzwilliam poured them both another drink. Their children, the next generation of cousins from the Darcy and Fitzwilliam families, were very close and famously rowdy when together.

"From what I hear, most of them were to meet in Matlock to stay overnight before setting out, in which case, poor Matlock has very likely raised a white flag by now, and they will all descend at the same time." Fitzwilliam slouched down into his own chair, his head resting on the back cushion in order to better enjoy the sun's warmth on his face. His pipe dangled from his mouth.

"Have they said why they all accepted the invitation this time? Not that I begrudge them coming, bloodcurdling thought that it is, but I believe it's been many a year since the whole family was together for a holiday. In fact, I don't think it's ever occurred before. Usually in-laws or business or school claim a few casualties. This may very well violate some sort of municipal health regulation."

"I believe they felt badly about Catherine's passing, thought perhaps we all needed the support." Fitzwilliam took a puff on his pipe and grew serious for just a moment, staring absently down the long road. "They have all turned out to be truly splendid people, really—proud of each and every one. I mean, if you can ignore the shootings and screaming."

"Elizabeth tells me that Anthony, however, will be absent, that he is traveling to Egypt"—Darcy turned his piercing gaze toward Richard—"along with the very elegant Sir Edmund Percy. That's rather a surprise, don't you think? He's rarely missed a holiday before in my memory. And as a matter of fact, how does he even know Sir Edmund?"

Richard became very still.

"Is there anything you wish to finally share with me, Richard?" It was highly diverting to watch his cousin squirm as he did. "You know how futile it is to try and keep anything from me—I shall drag the truth from you one day."

"Well, their acquaintance is of long standing—only natural,

really—they are both members of the Royal Academy Board, both interested in antiquities." He was withering under Darcy's relentless stare. "I know nothing," he finally blurted out. Fitzwilliam's eyes went everywhere but to his cousin. "Good God, it's like having two wives," he mumbled.

They sat in silence then, their minds going over the past years and the loved ones who would not be joining them this Easter.

Lady Catherine, the Grande Dame, passed shortly after her beloved daughter, Anne. Losing Anne had taken the desire to live from the old girl, and in the last few weeks of her life, her mind began wandering to prior days. She was once again aghast at that impudent Elizabeth Bennet, fought her battles with that horrible American Amanda Penrod, and chased her "horrid little nephews" after they disrupted one of her parties. She also redecorated constantly, now only in her mind, but always of the highest quality. The entire family missed the daffy old woman dreadfully.

For many, many years, between the Darcys and the Fitzwilliams, there had been a constant flurry of children, carriages, nannies, and dogs throughout elegant Mayfair, and then all those children had also descended merrily upon Aunt Catherine's for tarts, biscuits, and cakes. Mayfair would never look the same again.

Mr. Bennet had passed away over twenty years before, followed the next year by Charlotte Collins in childbirth. Mr. Collins was inconsolable for many months until he finally found his comfort with Mary Bennet, who had been secretly yearning for him the whole while.

Caroline Bingley had finally married a very wealthy

tradesman and had settled in Edinburgh. She never had children and quickly regretted her removal from London society. London society, it can be reported, did not return the sentiment.

Lady Penrod died a short four years after Amanda and Richard's marriage, and Harry immediately became one of the wealthiest nine-year-olds in London, inheriting both her London townhome, where he now lived with his own family, and another home in the Lake District.

Fitzwilliam and Amanda had eight children besides their wonderful Harry. His brother, Regis, passed two years after their marriage, and his beloved father passed five years after that, thereby making Richard the seventh Earl of Summerton. Happily, the sixth earl had lived long enough to meet the eighth earl, along with several spares.

Darcy and Elizabeth had three children altogether. He was now Sir Fitzwilliam Darcy, knighted for his outstanding leadership in his beloved Derbyshire and for his innovations in drainage.

Georgiana had married a naval lieutenant and had two lovely children, a boy and a girl. Her husband was now an admiral. Incredibly wealthy, he had traveled several times around the world for the crown, often with his beautiful family in tow.

Wickham was killed by the drunken husband of some woman with whom he was having an affair, and Lydia quickly married another "bad hat," as Lizzy would say. No one heard from her very often anymore.

Kitty remained unmarried and divided her time living happily in the country with either Elizabeth and Darcy, or as now with her sister Jane and brother-in-law Charles, proud grandparents to adorable twin girls over whom they doted in excess. They were spending their Easter holidays in Ireland.

Darcy lifted his head at a distant sound. "What was that?" The four hounds lying beside them on the veranda immediately stood and leaned forward in anticipation.

"Evidently it was a minor brain seizure," Fitzwilliam mumbled absently after scanning the empty horizon.

Darcy slumped back down into his chair and turned his face up toward the sun. "Just out of curiosity, how many grandchildren *do* you have now? What is the latest estimate?"

Fitzwilliam's eyes fluttered, and his head came up momentarily. "I haven't the foggiest notion. I'm not sure they've all even been named and categorized yet." He rested his head again against the chair back.

Darcy laughed. He knew his cousin better than that, knew the man was aware of them all, whether his own or Darcy's or Georgiana's. Each child, each name, and each birthday was precious to him. Family parties at his home were constants over the years, for any reason, and they were legendary.

"I don't understand how you had eight children and I only three. It makes no sense." Darcy strummed his fingers on the arm of his chair, his narrowed gaze fixed on his cousin. He absolutely hated to lose any competition to this man. "You're no more virile than I. Quite the contrary, in fact."

Fitzwilliam gave a snort of derision. "Bah! I am virility personified. It oozes from my every pore."

"Oh, is that what that is?"

"My seed practically leapt into her womb, for heaven's sake."

"Rather like a virus."

Fitzwilliam chuckled and began to fuss with the spectacles he had again taken out and was wearing.

"Come to think of it, you suddenly stopped having children after Edward was born. Certainly Amanda was still young enough. Maybe you weren't, but she certainly was. Did she finally come to her senses and boot you out of the marital bed, you randy old goat?"

"No, Darcy, as usual, you have everything backward and wrong."

"Then how did you manage to finally stem the procreational tide?"

"Well, Cousin"—Fitzwilliam began lifting and lowering the spectacles rapidly, trying to ascertain just how myopic his wife really was—"I simply took the matter into my own hands, shall we say..."

"God in heaven, I am always so regretful after I ask you a question." His head turned at a distant sound. The dogs also stood again, alerted to activity in the distance. They began barking and shot off the veranda.

"You know, Darcy, whenever I feel out of sorts or dreadfully depressed or nauseous, I think of you, and..."

Darcy turned his attention back to Fitzwilliam, briefly touched by this remark. He kept listening, but the sentence was never finished. His one eyebrow shot up in inquiry. "And...?" he encouraged.

"What? Oh, nothing." Fitzwilliam flapped his hand. "There is nothing to add. I just think of you whenever I get nauseous or depressed. Brat, is that them turning into the drive?" Fitzwilliam was squinting into the lowering sun.

Darcy turned his gaze toward the far road. His face lit up with an immense smile. "Yes, you old baboon, I believe it is."

Fitzwilliam was up like a shot, slapping his aching knee. A huge smile spread across his face as one hand came up to shield out the setting sun and the other rested on his hip, his eyes trying to make some sense of the dust in the distance.

"*Amanda!*" bellowed her husband. "*Front and center!*"

"For heaven's sake! Fitzwilliam!" Darcy winced and covered his ear nearest to his cousin. "Inside voice, please, child." He thought for a moment perhaps he was spending too much time with his grandchildren. "What I mean to say is, please exercise a little self-restraint and decorum."

Then he himself turned to face the house. "*Elizabeth!*" he bellowed. "*Your babies are here!*"

It was an amazing sight, far in the distance, one after another, the beautiful family carriages turning onto the two-mile-long entrance to the main drive. Beyond the river, they could make out Harry and Alice's carriage in the lead, as always; he was the undisputed leader among the cousins. After his carriage usually came his dearest friend Bennet George Darcy and his family. Following them both was a parade of the remainder of the cousins, or the Fitzwilliam Mob, as they had been christened by London society.

Following after the families' vehicles were the carriages carrying nurses and nannies and maids and valets, then carriages of luggage, gifts, and toys.

It was a most impressive parade descending upon beautiful old Pemberley.

As they watched the carriages maneuver in the far distance, Fitzwilliam turned to Darcy.

"Cousin, before the Mob arrives and while we are blessedly still in quiet, shall we drink a toast to the 'old girl'?"

Darcy smiled and nodded. "I had the same idea." He poured another drink into their glasses.

"To Aunt Catherine," Fitzwilliam began.

"Beloved matriarch of our family," Darcy continued.

"Grande Old Dame," said Fitzwilliam.

With one clink, they tossed back their whiskeys. Both smacked their lips and smiled, enjoying in silence their personal memories of her.

Darcy stretched his arms and legs, stiff from waiting. "By the way, did you receive a copy of Alice's play for this year's family theatrical? I believe there was a rather unnecessarily large part in it for you." Darcy was incredibly proud of his youngest daughter's gift for writing.

"You mean *Meticulous and Libidinous—A Tale of a Tribune and a Centurion*? Yes I did, and I can tell you I don't care much for my part. The centurion, Libidinous, is bullheaded and loud, randy as a rabbit, and incredibly sloppy."

"Well, what of my part? That tribune fellow, Meticulous, is just a finicky, overconfident snob. Proud as a peacock; thinks he knows everything. However does she come up with these characters of hers?"

After a brief silence, the two old friends burst into raucous laughter.

Closer than brothers still, they went forward to greet their families.

Karen V. Wasylowski is a retired accountant living in Bradenton, Florida, with her husband, Richard, and their many pets. Karen and Richard spend much of their free time volunteering with the St. Vincent DePaul Society and Stillpoint House of Prayer, both charitable organizations that assist the poor living in the Bradenton community.

They are also actively involved with Project Light of Manatee, an all-volunteer organization that provides literacy instruction to poor immigrants and to members of the community who cannot read.

In the Arms of Mr. Darcy

Sharon Lathan

If only everyone could be as happy as they are...

Darcy and Elizabeth are as much in love as ever—even more so as their relationship matures. Their passion inspires everyone around them, and as winter turns to spring, romance blossoms around them.

Confirmed bachelor Richard Fitzwilliam sets his sights on a seemingly unattainable, beautiful widow; Georgiana Darcy learns to flirt outrageously; the very flighty Kitty Bennet develops her first crush, and Caroline Bingley meets her match.

But the path of true love never does run smooth, and Elizabeth and Darcy are kept busy navigating their friends and loved ones through the inevitable separations, misunderstandings, misgivings, and lovers' quarrels to reach their own happily ever afters...

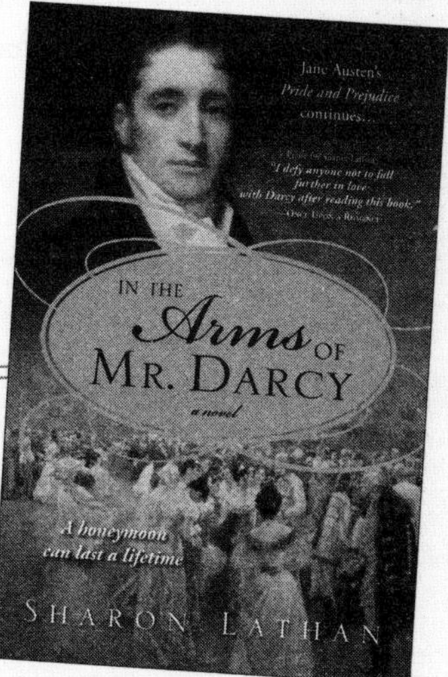

"If you love *Pride and Prejudice* sequels then this series should be on the top of your list!"
—*Royal Reviews*

"Sharon really knows how to make Regency come alive." —*Love Romance Passion*

978-1-4022-3699-0
$14.99 US/$17.99 CAN/£9.99 UK

WICKHAM'S DIARY

AMANDA GRANGE

Jane Austen's quintessential bad boy has his say...

Enter the clandestine world of the cold-hearted Wickham...

...in the pages of his private diary. Always aware of the inferiority of his social status compared to his friend Fitzwilliam Darcy, Wickham chases wealth and women in an attempt to attain the power he lusts for. But as Wickham gambles and cavorts his way through his funds, Darcy still comes out on top.

But now Wickham has found his chance to seduce the young Georgiana Darcy, which will finally secure the fortune—and the revenge—he's always dreamed of...

Available April 2011
978-1-4022-5186-3
$12.99 US

Praise for Amanda Grange:

"Amanda Grange has taken on the challenge of reworking a much loved romance and succeeds brilliantly." —*Historical Novels Review*

"Amanda Grange is a writer who tells an engaging, thoroughly enjoyable story!" —*Romance Reader at Heart*

Mr. Fitzwilliam Darcy:

THE LAST MAN IN THE WORLD

A *Pride and Prejudice* Variation

ABIGAIL REYNOLDS

What if Elizabeth had accepted Mr. Darcy the first time he asked?

In Jane Austen's *Pride and Prejudice*, Elizabeth Bennet tells the proud Mr. Fitzwilliam Darcy that she wouldn't marry him if he were the last man in the world. But what if circumstances conspired to make her accept Darcy the first time he proposes? In this installment of Abigail Reynolds' acclaimed *Pride and Prejudice* Variations, Elizabeth agrees to marry Darcy against her better judgment, setting off a chain of events that nearly brings disaster to them both. Ultimately, Darcy and Elizabeth will have to work together on their tumultuous and passionate journey to make a success of their ill-timed marriage.

978-1-4022-2947-3
$14.99 US/$18.99 CAN/£7.99 UK

What readers are saying:

"A highly original story, immensely satisfying."

"Anyone who loves the story of Darcy and Elizabeth will love this variation."

"I was hooked from page one."

"A refreshing new look at what might have happened if..."

"Another good book to curl up with… I never wanted to put it down..."

THE OTHER MR. DARCY

PRIDE AND PREJUDICE CONTINUES...

MONICA FAIRVIEW

"A lovely story... a joy to read."
—*Bookishly Attentive*

Unpredictable courtships appear to run in the Darcy family...

When Caroline Bingley collapses to the floor and sobs at Mr. Darcy's wedding, imagine her humiliation when she discovers that a stranger has witnessed her emotional display. Miss Bingley, understandably, resents this gentleman very much, even if he is Mr. Darcy's American cousin. Mr. Robert Darcy is as charming as Mr. Fitzwilliam Darcy is proud, and he is stunned to find a beautiful young woman weeping broken-heartedly at his cousin's wedding. Such depth of love, he thinks, is rare and precious. For him, it's love at first sight...

"An intriguing concept...
a delightful ride in the park."
—*AustenProse*

978-1-4022-2513-0
$14.99 US/$18.99 CAN/£7.99 UK

Darcy and Anne

Pride and Prejudice continues...

Judith Brocklehurst

"A beautiful tale." —*A Bibliophile's Bookshelf*

Without his help, she'll never be free...

Anne de Bourgh has never had a chance to figure out what she wants for herself, until a fortuitous accident on the way to Pemberley separates Anne from her formidable mother. With her stalwart cousin Fitzwilliam Darcy and his lively wife Elizabeth on her side, she begins to feel she might be able to spread her wings. But Lady Catherine's pride and determination to find Anne a suitable husband threaten to overwhelm Anne's newfound freedom and budding sense of self. And without Darcy's help, Anne will never have a chance to find true love...

"Brocklehurst transports you to another place and time." —*A Journey of Books*

"A charming book... It is lovely to see Anne's character blossom and fall in love." —*Once Upon a Romance*

"The twists and turns, as Anne tries to weave a path of happiness for herself, are subtle and enjoyable, and the much-loved characters of Pemberley remain true to form."
—*A Bibliophile's Bookshelf*

"A fun, truly fresh take on many of Austen's beloved characters."
—*Write Meg*

978-1-4022-2438-6
$12.99 US/$15.99 CAN/£6.99 UK